"Would you mind coming down to the department for a few minutes?" Detective Mankiewicz said.

Something was wrong. My stomach churned with sudden fear. I couldn't let Ty see it. I put a hand on his shoulder.

"I'm not sure." I hesitated. "I'd hate to leave my son here by himself."

"This won't take long," the detective said.

I looked at Ty. "Will you be all right here by yourself, big guy?"

"Dad," he said, flushing, "I'll be fine."

I turned to Mankiewicz. "Okay if I follow you in my car so I can pick up my daughter from church on the way home?" He nodded.

I followed Mankiewicz out onto the stoop, then turned to close the door. "Remember to lock it," I told Ty as I pulled it shut. "Love you."

I joined the detective on the driveway. "So what's going on?" I dreaded the answer.

"I'm afraid I have some bad news," he said. "I didn't want to say anything in front of your son."

The words stunned me. "Is it Mary? Has she been in an accident?"

"Not exactly. Let's talk about it at the station."

For a moment I was speechless, unable to move. *Oh, God, she's left me. She wants a divorce.* I didn't want to consider it might be something worse.

MICHAEL W. SHERER

has been a bartender, commercial photography assistant, magazine editor and public relations executive. He finally decided to take a chance and go out on his own in 1988—the year his first novel was published. Since then Michael has worked as a freelance writer and marketing communications consultant. Formerly on the board of directors of Mystery Writers of America, Midwest chapter, Michael has published six novels in the Emerson Ward series and is currently hard at work on his next book. He currently resides with his family outside Seattle. Please be sure to visit Michael's website at www.emersonwardmysteries.com.

MICHAEL W. SHERER

ISLAND LIFE

WORLDWIDE®

TORONTO • NEW YORK • LONDON
AMSTERDAM • PARIS • SYDNEY • HAMBURG
STOCKHOLM • ATHENS • TOKYO • MILAN
MADRID • WARSAW • BUDAPEST • AUCKLAND

To Valerie,
my muse and loving wife.

Recycling programs
for this product may
not exist in your area.

ISBN-13: 978-0-373-06262-1

ISLAND LIFE

Copyright © 2008 by Michael W. Sherer

A Worldwide Library Suspense/March 2012

First published by Five Star Publishing

www.Harlequin.com

Printed in U.S.A.

ISLAND LIFE

ACKNOWLEDGMENT

As always, I am indebted to all the people who helped along the way with encouragement, inspiration and vital information. Special thanks to Gary Goldfogel, M.D., Whatcom County Medical Examiner, Bellingham, Washington, for explaining what can and can't be done in a forensic examination, answering innumerable "what-ifs" and reminding me that what happens in an M.E.'s office is not even close to what's portrayed on television crime shows. Thanks, too, to Al Noriega, lead investigator, King County Medical Examiner's office, for patiently answering my questions. Evy Shively at the Department of Children and Family Services and Paul Evans at Child Protective Services helped explain what happens to kids who go into the foster care system. Michael Iaria, attorney, helped with legal questions. Last, but not least, Detective Pete Erickson, Mercer Island P.D., walked me through investigative procedure.

Any mistakes are mine alone. The rest is fiction.

Finally, thanks to Patti Murphy for her generous donation to the Senior Foundation of Mercer Island by "buying" a character in this book, and to her husband, Tom, for being a good sport and agreeing to be immortalized in print.

ONE

"How do you live without someone who's been part of your life for twenty years?"

"Depends," Sarah said, enigmatic as usual.

The irony of therapy—basically paying to talk to someone—is that you end up talking to yourself a lot, a characteristic most of us associate with crazies on the street. I wondered how dissimilar I was, really, from them. What separated me from them other than a shower, shave and clean clothes?

"Where's my hoodie?" Kelsey yelled from the second floor, but I could already hear her bounding heavily down the stairs. She came into the kitchen with a look of annoyance on her normally pretty face. I winced involuntarily when I saw the black circles around her eyes—not from lack of sleep, but from too much mascara—and my reaction only deepened her vexation.

"What hoodie?" I asked, trying to smile pleasantly.

"My Juicy." She could barely keep the exasperation out of her voice. "The pink one," she added, just in case I was a complete moron and severely fashion-impaired.

"Probably in the laundry, sweetie."

"The laundry? Da-a-d! I wanted those things washed last night!"

I sighed. "Sorry. I forgot." She folded her slender arms, shifted her weight onto one foot, pouting.

"Now what am I supposed to do?"

"You know, you could have put a load in all by your-self if you needed clean clothes." The logic was lost on her. My smart, funny, attractive and utterly spoiled, almost fifteen-year-old daughter stabbed me with one more blood-letting look, tossed her head and flounced out of the room. I shook my head. I had never under-stood why a girl that pretty would want to cover it up with so much face paint. I didn't mind her wear-ing makeup. It was the quantity that bothered me. She'd never admit to being pretty, of course. Letty, my mother-in-law, never wasted an opportunity to remind her that "Pretty is as pretty does." Kelsey would likely have to wait until adulthood to objectively recognize that her grandmother had all the warmth of a January day in Juneau.

Kelsey was smart, too—way smarter than either of her parents—which made me sometimes wonder whose child she really was. She wouldn't admit that, either, since intelligence was pretty low on the list of quali-ties required to run in Kelsey's circle of friends, or even belong to her peer group. Looks, fashion sense and the ability to lip synch all the misogynistic, foul and mean-spirited lyrics from the latest gangsta rapper hit were far more important. It was just a phase, I kept reminding myself. And when it was over there would be another phase in its place to deal with.

The ring of the phone saved me from her laser beam stare of death. She leapt for it and snatched up the re-ceiver.

"Hello? Hello?" She frowned, held the phone away for an instant, then pressed it to her ear again. "Hello?" She appeared to listen, and handed it to me. "For you, I think." I took the receiver and said hello. There was no response. I heard a soft click and the line went dead. "That was strange. Did they say who it was?"

Kelsey shook her head. "Maybe it was a wrong number. Sounded like gibberish to me, like some foreign language."

I pressed a button on the phone and checked caller ID. The number was blocked. "Then why did you think it was for me, sweetie?" She shrugged.

"Um, Dad?" A soft voice piped up behind me.

I turned. "Yeah, Bud?" Tyler had his nose in a paper bag on the kitchen counter. His hair, dark as a glass of stout, was whorled with cowlicks, making him look as if he'd just woken up. He had, but he always looked that way. He was shy, quiet. A serious child. Small for his age, he always seemed to be swimming in his clothes. It made him look younger than ten.

"Is this my lunch?"

"Sure is. Something wrong?"

"Um, no." He turned his big blue eyes my direction. As usual, they hid his thoughts, but not the fact that his adolescent brain was churning them out at a rate of hundreds per second.

"It's just that…" He paused. "Well, Mom always puts applesauce in there."

"Right, kiddo. Sorry." I almost left it at that. I had a million things to do, and it wasn't important. At least not to me, not right then. Ordinarily, I would have let my children's small criticisms bounce off unnoticed. With a full schedule, though, the morning already felt rushed, and my own impatience had somehow left me more vulnerable to their small slights.

Then again, it could have been because nothing was ordinary anymore.

I took a step toward the refrigerator, but the shadow

that crossed Tyler's face for a split second stopped me. In that instant there was something in his eyes—hurt? guilt?—that shifted my self-centered focus outward to a slightly bigger picture. There, I saw my kids' accusatory looks, heard their unasked question—where's Mom? Mom would have remembered laundry and applesauce.

"Tell you what," I said. "I'll give you a ride to school. If we leave a little early, we can swing by the store and get whatever kind you want. Okay?" He shrugged, then nodded, but didn't meet my gaze. I put two frozen waffles in the toaster and finished washing and cutting up some strawberries while the waffles heated. The sound of the water running in the sink was strangely soothing. The repetitive motion of rinsing, stemming and cutting each berry under the rush of cold water from the faucet stilled the anxious thoughts in my head, leaving it blissfully empty for a brief moment. The toaster's metallic twang jarred me back to reality. I plated the waffles and joined Tyler at the table. We gave each other a quick half-smile of acknowledgement and started eating in silence.

No doubt there was even more going on in Tyler's head than mine, but none of it needed discussing even if it was ready for the light of day, so our silence wasn't strained. Sitting there together, in fact, provided its own form of contentment. It's a guy thing. Men aren't programmed for conversation, particularly idle chit-chat. It's not in our genes. We can do it when prompted, but it's sort of like getting a dog to walk on its hind legs. It's mildly amusing, but there's not much point to it.

Kelsey bounded back into the kitchen wearing an entirely different outfit. She stopped in front of the table and looked from Tyler's plate to my bowl and back.

"Where's my breakfast?"

"I didn't know what you wanted. I'll make you something if you'd like."

"No time." She reached over Tyler's shoulder, snatched the uneaten waffle off his plate and skipped away.

"Hey!" He whirled, arm outstretched. Kelsey was already out of reach, mouth full of waffle. "Dad! Kelsey took my waffle!"

"I saw it, Bud. I'll get you another." I pushed back from the table and walked to the freezer. On the way, I threw my daughter a disapproving look, hoping she'd take the hint and apologize to her brother, maybe even offer to get him another. She was already shrugging into her backpack.

"Dad, don't forget that I've got practice after school, then I'm going to Jennie's house to do homework before we do our community service project. I probably won't be home for dinner. 'Bye. I gotta go or I'll be late." A mouthful of waffle made the tumble of words barely intelligible.

"Wait! What? When will I see you, then? When will you be home? Need a ride? Do you have your phone?" I shot the questions at her almost as fast as she'd rattled off her schedule for the day, but not fast enough to get a definitive answer before she was out the door.

"I'll call you," she said over her shoulder as she dashed out. When had I completely lost control? The two separate occasions on which I'd stood in a hospital delivery room garbed in green like a B-movie Martian and cut their umbilical cords, I decided. Then again, maybe I'd never been in control. My life felt as if it was lived on a runaway train, just waiting for enough speed or a curve sharp enough to send it off the tracks into the mother of all wrecks. But the breakfast table was still, my son's face calm. No one here seemed panicked except me. I reached out and tousled Tyler's hair. A little messier couldn't hurt.

"Come on, Bud. Go brush your teeth and get your coat. Time to go." I'd already long forgotten the phone call.

"RIGHT, IT DEPENDS." I conceded Sarah's point. "If it's a casual acquaintance, I suppose it's not much of a loss. Sort of like getting a wisdom tooth pulled before it ever comes in. You know it's there, but you never really notice. When it comes out, you sort of poke at the space with your tongue for a while until you forget you ever had one.

"If it's one of your kids, you probably can't wait until they leave home. I'm already looking forward to an empty nest, and I still have years to go." Sarah smiled.

"This is different," I went on. "It's like my life was taken away from me. I don't know, like suddenly discovering after all these years that you're adopted, or were raised by wolves. You wonder what's real and what's a lie. You wonder who you are, where you really belong. You live by a certain set of rules, then all of a sudden, the game changes and there are no rules. How do you go on if you don't know what the game is? How do you live if you don't even know what the rules are?"

"How do you want to live?" Ah, the therapist's principal artifice—answer a question with a question.

"Any way but this. I hate living like this."

"Like what?"

"I don't know what to do. I don't know what to think."

"Rather than focus on what you believe you're supposed to do or think, let's talk about what you feel.

What is it you hate about living like this?" She was determined to get it out of me.

"I feel guilty, and I don't know why. I feel relieved, and that just makes me feel more guilty."

"Relieved?"

TYLER AND I STOPPED AT the grocery store and bought a box of cinnamon-flavored applesauce. I remembered picking apples when I was a kid and helping my mother cut and cook them and press them, still steaming, through a Foley food mill. The kitchen smelled wonderful for days afterward. We packed it in plastic containers and froze it. Throughout the year, the containers would come out on occasion to accompany a pork chop dinner or Sunday pancakes or gingerbread for dessert. Now applesauce comes in little single-serve plastic tubes. Kids squeeze it into their mouths like toothpaste.

I wondered why I'd never taken my children to an apple orchard, never given them the chance to experience an autumn day in the crisp outdoor air and then in a warm kitchen redolent of cooked apples and cinnamon. Was life so much busier now that we had no time to make applesauce? We couldn't sacrifice one day of our normal routine for a family activity that the kids would remember all their lives? My father had never taken part in making gloriously sweet and spicy pink soup out of crunchy, freshly picked apples. That didn't mean I couldn't. I looked ruefully at the box Tyler held. I was shortchanging my kids, depriving myself.

I stopped at the bakery on the way out and bought a tall double latte and an almond biscotti. I couldn't afford it, but it was a habit that would be hard to break. I had become addicted to lattes—the Northwest's version of a plain cup of Joe—almost from the first one

I ever tasted. It had reminded me of *café au lait* in
Paris—dark, roasty, aromatic, bitter coffee sweetened
with steamed milk and lumps of sugar. The taste alone
was enough to wake you, never mind the jolt of caf-
feine. Tyler fidgeted impatiently while I dreamed of
fresh croissants laden with butter and strawberry jam
in a Paris café.

"Want a donut, kiddo?"

"No, thanks." I couldn't even distract him with a
bribe. Didn't he know how short childhood really is?
We drove to school, still early enough that there wasn't
yet a long line winding into the parking lot. Near the
end of the drive we finally ran into a string of half a
dozen cars. Slowly, we inched our way, a car-length
at a time, to the bus shelter where each car stopped
to disgorge its contents of kids, coats, knapsacks and
lunch boxes. The car in front of us pulled up to the
drop-off. Tyler slung his backpack over one shoulder,
picked up his lunch in one hand and grabbed the door
handle in the other. When our turn came, he bailed out
like a paratrooper and hit the ground running before I'd
stopped.

"'Bye, Dad." He swung the door shut.

"See you after school," I called through the open
window. "Love you, Bud." He was already gone. I rolled
away to make room for the car behind me.

I took the floating bridge into downtown Seattle.
Traffic was light since it was after nine, but you never
knew in this town. A little rain—something we get frequently at certain times of the year—and the freeway
might have been jammed. As long as I've lived here
I've never understood the native population's lack of
common sense. Granted, rain doesn't fall all the time
in Seattle. That's a myth. Summers here are quite beau-

tiful, in fact—sunny and dry as tinder, turning lawns brown and putting forests at high risk for fire. But it's as if people are in denial. It rains, they forget how to drive. It rains, they forget how to build roofs that don't leak (the old Key Arena), crumble (King Dome, since imploded) or collapse (Husky Stadium). Water is everywhere, but Seattleites still have trouble figuring out how to get over it, or out from under it.

The bridge I crossed—a mile-and-a-half expanse of steel and concrete across the surface of Lake Washington—is a good example. Actually two bridges built side by side, both essentially resemble a series of barges tied together and anchored to the bottom of the lake with cables. The original bridge was built before the start of World War II. Fifty years later, a new one was constructed to add more lanes. When it was finished, work refurbishing the old one began. Rumor has it that someone forgot to close a seacock one day. Overnight, a big storm filled a section with water. The weight dragged the next section underwater so it filled up, too, and so on, like dominoes, until the bridge resembled the *Titanic*. Half a mile of bridge went to the bottom.

The region has had more than its share of catastrophic bridge failures. I wondered if I was having one of my own, or if I could shore up the damage before the accumulated weight of too many things gone wrong pulled us all into the silent darkness beneath the surface.

The bridge was floating just fine at present. Rush-hour stragglers, often as discombobulated by sunshine as rain, were behaving themselves. At least I didn't have to depend on a ferry to get off the island. The glossy surface of the lake made me wonder which ocean Mary was flying over this time. I wondered if there was a bridge in the world long enough to traverse the ocean that had opened up between us.

The trip into town was quick. I followed Interstate 90 to its very end—or beginning if you're traveling east to Boston. A left on 4th Avenue, and another left on Jackson took me down toward Pioneer Square. I circled a few blocks looking for street parking, unwilling to shell out twelve bucks to park in a lot for the short time I planned on being there. Finally fed up, I wedged into a loading zone, turned on the emergency flashers, locked up and left. I drive a white minivan, plain enough to be mistaken for a delivery van instead of a passenger car. Instead of crossing my fingers, I thumbed my nose at the gods and dared them to send a meter maid—excuse me, "traffic control officer"—rolling by in one of those scooters.

The receptionist didn't look up when I stepped off the elevator. I walked past her desk, feeling as inconsequential as a wisp of fog. Back past several offices and cubicles sat the space I had called mine for the past three years. A desk, two-drawer file cabinet and two chairs all covered in matching wood-grained plastic laminate furnished the small ten-by-twelve office. The window overlooked the century-old iron-and-glass pergola on the square below. The pergola had been reconstructed a few years before after a truck had cornered a little too closely, clipped a post and brought it crashing down.

The office had never really felt like mine, and now it wasn't. Devoid of personal items, it had reverted to its former anonymity, waiting to be transformed by the next occupant. For now, it gave no indication of the sort of work done in this place. It could have been an office in almost any corporation in America.

Easing into the chair behind the desk, I turned on the computer. While it booted up, I picked up the handset on the phone and checked voicemail—no messages. I turned my attention to the computer. None of the forty-seven e-mail messages in my in-box were personal or important. I erased them all and shut down the computer. I went through the desk drawers one more time to reassure myself I'd taken everything. A guy from research named Dave stuck his head through the open door-frame. I don't think I ever knew his last name.

"Last day, huh?"

"Yeah, this is it."

"Well, good luck."

"Thanks." I gave him a half-smile.

He hung awkwardly in the doorway for a moment, hands braced on either side of the frame. With a flush of embarrassment, he gave a short wave and disappeared from view.

I took a last look around, then got up and walked out. No one in the surrounding offices said a word to me as I left. After I picked up my paycheck, my e-mail and voicemail boxes would be cancelled and wiped clean, my name purged from address lists, and I would disappear from corporate consciousness like a wave receding on the sand.

"¡Hola!" TYLER'S SMALL VOICE sounded distant, followed by the slam of the front door.

I looked at my watch. The day had disappeared on me. Where had it gone? What had I done to fritter away the hours since breakfast?

There was a muffled thud from the kitchen that reverberated through the floorboards. Tyler's backpack, no doubt, let go from some height. It wouldn't take

much. The weight schools required kids to lug back
and forth would cause Governor Schwarzenegger to
break a sweat. Judging from the sounds that followed,
a small but ravenous boy foraged for food.

"Hello?" Tyler's voice called again, closer now.
"Anybody home?"

"In here, kiddo," I responded loudly.

The door to the den burst open and banged against
the rubber-tipped door stop. Tyler stood in the doorway
wide-eyed, dribbling crumbs from a toaster pastry on
the floor as he took a bite. His quiet demeanor and small
size belied the dynamo that hummed inside him.

"Whatcha doin'?"

"Working. How was school?"

"'Kay. Whatcha workin' on?"

"Making sure we won't starve for another couple of
months."

"You got a job?"

"No, I got a new client today." A small company
that needed help with a trade show. The first, I hoped,
of many, since I was now unemployed.

"Oh, yeah? Cool." Tyler took another bite, filling his
cheeks like a chipmunk, and chewed thoughtfully. My
attention drifted back to the work on my desk. Tyler interrupted my thoughts. "So, you ready?"

"Oh, jeez, you have soccer practice today?"

"Hello? Earth to Dad. Yes, I have practice today."
Fist on one hip, he threw me a look.

"You don't look like you're ready."

"I'll change in the car. I've got all my stuff. Come
on! Let's go!"

"Okay, okay. Let me get my shoes and a jacket." I
followed him out into the hall.

"Dad! We're gonna be late!"

"I'm coming!" I slipped into a pair of deck shoes at the front door. "Keep your shirt on. Wait, I take that back—take your shirt off and get your jersey on."

"Very funny."

"WELL, YES, relieved. I just hate the fighting. It's not even that. We don't even fight that much. It just seems like we're walking on egg shells around each other. I'm always on pins and needles waiting for the next crisis to unfold. I dread it."

"What makes you uncomfortable?"

"The tension. I hate confrontation, but we never seem to be able to resolve anything when we talk. So we let it fester, and it feels as if one of us is going to explode at any moment. So I feel relieved when she's not there."

"It sounds as if you would rather live this way." I thought about it for a moment. Sarah delicately put the end of her pen in the corner of her mouth. The unconscious habit made her seem more human. More fallible. Less judgmental. I still squirmed uncomfortably. "Maybe. But whenever I even think about it, I start to feel guilty."

"Why?"

"I'm not supposed to feel this way. I made a commitment. We're supposed to work things out. And I can't imagine the alternative. It would be hard on the kids—terrible, in fact. And financially, it would be a disaster, I think. We're living on the edge as it is. I don't know how we could swing it financially. It just doesn't seem feasible. I can't even afford coming here. And I just can't imagine life without someone who's been there for twenty years." I shook my head. "I don't see any viable options."

"But you're not happy now, are you?" The brutal truth of her words landed like a blow, leaving me breathless and queasy. The room started to go dark as a bleak future yawned blackly in front of me, inescapable and immutable. Tears welled up in my eyes. A feeling of helplessness threatened to pull me under and drown me in a sea of depression. I swallowed hard, determined not to let her see me dissolve into a puddle of emotions.

"I guess that's the point." My chest felt so constricted that the words were barely audible. I cleared my throat and swallowed hard again. *"I hate living like this."*

A KNOT OF CHATTY soccer moms stood a few yards away from the midfield sideline, fairly reeking of estrogen. I wandered over with the notion of being sociable and joining in the conversation. One or two glanced my way, silently acknowledging me as I approached.

"Hi," I murmured to those who looked up, politely trying not to interrupt. "How are you?" No one made a move to open the circle, and a couple of them unconsciously closed ranks, turning inward as I got closer. It was like walking into an invisible and impervious wall. I bounced off, changed direction and circled at a distance. I moved well past them, and stood on the sidelines farther down-field.

One other man stood at the edge of the parking lot on top of the embankment on the far side of the field. He had dark hair and chiseled Asian features. Another dad probably, avoiding the soccer moms even more studiously. He watched the boys on the field intently. Dressed in a dark suit, he looked out of place. A sweater over a dress shirt with khakis constituted formal dress in Seattle, I'd discovered. While still worn, suits and even ties were rarely seen outside a downtown office high-rise. For a moment he appeared to stare at me. I couldn't be sure from this distance. An odd chill ran through me. I shook it off and turned back to the practice.

Tyler hustled up and down the field, his short legs churning to keep up with some of the larger kids on the team as they drilled. A tall, lanky kid named Alex loped toward Tyler as the ball came his way. Ty started dribbling upfield. Instead of stealing the ball, Alex just bowled into Ty, knocking him over. Laughing, he dribbled the ball the other way. Tyler got up slowly, but he didn't look hurt. I looked over at the coaches, but they either hadn't seen it, or didn't consider it serious enough to warrant a whistle.

"Hey, you're both on the same team," I called. "Take it easy out there." The kids were oblivious and the coaches didn't seem to care. I'd seen Alex get away with dirty play like that at several practices, even during games against other teams. Ty hadn't been hurt. He didn't need me to step in and fight his battles for him. Not yet, anyway. But I tired of kids like Alex who thought they could do anything they wanted. I looked over at the women still gabbing at midfield. Alex's mother exuded the same air of superiority. *Let it go.*

Tyler was up and running, an earnest look on his face as he focused his efforts on chasing after the ball. I knew I should shrug it off as my son had, but I couldn't. It festered like the remains of a splinter you thought you'd tweezed out.

Three more times Alex physically moved players off the ball with plays that a sharp-eyed ref would have red-carded him for. Sure, one could chalk it up to youthful exuberance and inexperience. The kid was too good, though. He appeared reckless, but there was awareness, purpose, in his actions. Almost as if he disguised his true intent.

When the coaches ended practice, the kids ran whooping and hollering to the sidelines to get juice and snacks that one of the moms had brought. It reminded me I would have to check with Ty to see when our turn was. While the boys descended on the refreshments like flies at a picnic, the moms drifted apart, picking up the shirts and shoes, bags and water bottles that littered the grass. I slowly made my way over to Alex's mother, putting myself between her and the crowd. She bent over a sport bag, but looked up when she felt my presence.

"Hi, I'm Jack Holm," I said, making an effort to keep my voice pleasant. "Tyler's dad." I waited a beat, but forged ahead when she didn't reply. "Just a suggestion, but you might want to have a conversation with Alex about good sportsmanship."

"Excuse me?" She stood upright, a frown on her face. Her loud response attracted the attention of a few of the moms scattered behind me.

"Alex played a little rough out there today."

"Are you a coach?"

"No. I just think your son ought to recognize that all those other kids are his teammates, not tackling dummies."

"Who do you think you are?" she said, her voice rising. "I didn't hear any whistles out there. I didn't hear the coach tell Alex not to do his best. I don't see why my son should apologize for being a better player than the other boys. And if you're not a coach, maybe you ought to mind your own business."

"This was obviously a mistake."

"A big mistake," she spat. "Sounds to me like your

son is the poor sport. It's a rough game. If your kid can't take it, maybe he shouldn't play." I could feel my ears burn and my face flush. My stomach knotted and a black acorn of pain planted itself behind my left eye. Exactly the feeling I had when I tried to talk to Mary. A small gathering behind me had heard at least a portion of her tirade. I clamped my jaw shut before saying something I really regretted.

"You might be right." I nearly choked on the conciliatory words. "Sorry to have bothered you." Before she got in any more last digs, I turned and quickly walked past a group of moms. They averted their eyes, pretending they hadn't been listening. I scanned the crowd of boys. Tyler stood off to one side, head down, intently sucking on a juice box and examining the grass in front of him.

"Hey, kiddo," I said lightly. "Great practice. You really hustled out there. Ready to go?"

"Yeah, sure." He grabbed his sport duffel and shuffled after me as I headed for the car.

I looked up the embankment to get my bearings. The man standing there earlier had disappeared, along with the car that had been parked behind him. I glanced over my shoulder at the field, curious. Tyler and I had been the first to leave.

"You really took a tumble out there today," I said when Ty caught up with me. "You okay?"

"Yeah." He shrugged. We finished the walk in silence. As we drove out of the lot, Ty piped up again. "Um, Dad? What were you talking with Alex's mom about?"

"I told her I thought she ought to talk to Alex about being a poor sport. She looked really ticked." I sighed.

"She didn't take it well. I'm not sure what her problem is." Ty was quiet for a moment. I glanced over. He fidgeted and turned his head away to look out the window. I returned my attention to the road, waiting him out.

"I wish you hadn't done that," he said finally. "It'll just make things worse."

"What things?" I kept my tone light, hoping I sounded merely curious. He didn't respond. I tried again. "Has Alex been bothering you at school?"

"He bothers all the kids. Alex is a real A-hole."

"Watch yourself, buster."

"Well, he is."

"If it's a problem, tell someone. Let your teacher know."

"He's sneaky, Dad. He knows how to keep from getting caught. It's better to just try to stay out of his way."

"Good strategy, kiddo."

"Doesn't always work, though."

"What happens? Does he pick fights?"

"Nah, nothing like that." Ty waved a hand, a look of disdain on his face. "It's more like—whaddya call it?—a hit-and-run. He'll just do something mean and then he's out of there. Like, the other day we were in music class? And Mrs. Burke is showing us different musical instruments? So, like, we're on percussion, so she hands out all kinds of things to the class—triangles and cymbals, drumsticks and gourds and stuff.

"So we're trying this stuff out, and Mrs. Burke says she has to leave for a minute. Like, the second she's gone, Alex takes his drumsticks and starts drumming on Trina's head. Real hard. I mean, she was even crying. But by the time Mrs. Burke came back in, Alex was back in his seat like nothing happened. She didn't even see that Trina was hurt."

"And no one said anything?"

"What's the point? Mrs. B didn't see it, so she wouldn't do anything about it. And whoever told would just get grief for snitching." Welcome to the cold, cruel world. It's dog-eat-dog out there, and no one ever said life was fair. I sighed again. The problem was, Tyler was right. Kids like Alex grew up to be rude, obnoxious adults like his mother.

My cell phone chirped, and I struggled to fish it out of my pocket without driving off the road. I managed to flip it open after the third ring.

"Dad, we need a ride," Kelsey's breathless voice came over the phone. "Can you pick us up?"

"Sure. Where are you?"

"Jennie's house. Her mom was going to take us down to do community service, but now she can't, so we need a ride."

"I got it. You said that. Jennie's house is the one down near the middle school, right?"

"No, that's Amanda, Dad. Jennie's is, like, near the south end center. You know, you go past it and down the hill a little and then take a right?"

"What's the address, Kelsey?" I said impatiently.

There were muffled sounds and then she was back on the phone with the street number. "When will you be here?"

"Give me five minutes." I shoved the phone back in my pocket with a flustered sigh and looked at Tyler. His normally serious face was split by a wide grin of amusement.

TY WALKED INTO HIS ROOM in an oversized T-shirt and a pair of boxer shorts with Homer Simpson's face imprinted on the back side. I couldn't remember if I'd noticed the switch before, from pajamas to these. The shock sent momentary panic through me. Where had the little boy gone? Who was this person inhabiting my son's body?

"Teeth brushed?"

"All done."

"And you're sure you finished your homework?"

"Yes, I'm sure."

"Story?" I asked. "Pick a book."

"I can read, you know." He took a book off the nightstand, opened it to a bookmarked page and handed it to me. I sat on the floor next to his bed and settled in to read. Nine-thirty already, and I was beat. It felt good to sit. I read a few pages out loud, making up voices for the different characters. Completely absorbed, Ty looked up accusingly when I stopped in the middle of an action-packed paragraph.

I handed him the book. "Your turn."

"Just a few more pages. Please?"

"Nope. You did say you know how to read."

"Oh, all right." Reluctantly, he took the book from me.

I slowly got to my feet, working the stiffness out of my joints, then gave him a quick peck on his forehead. "'Night, kiddo. Love you." His nose was already buried in the book. "Don't stay up too late. Lights out in half an hour." I turned to go, but he stopped me.

"Dad?" I looked at him over my shoulder. "Yes?"

"Where's Mom?"

TWO

CREATURES of habit, Ty and I sat at the breakfast table—waffles for him, yogurt and berries for me—contentedly chewing in silence. Ty stared into space, off in another world.

"I like breakfast," he said, suddenly coming back to earth.

"Oh, yeah? How come?" He took another bite, chewed, then tried to talk with his mouth full.

"Becauf it'f like eating deffert wifout having to eat yucky thtuff firft." I smiled. Breakfast had become one of my favorite times of the day, too, when it wasn't rushed. It was the calm before the storm, a moment of peaceful reflection in which to gird for the battles of the day. When the children were younger, mornings had been hectic, frantic even. Getting them dressed, fed and organized for childcare or school before rushing to work had always been an exercise in stress. What should have been a pleasant way to start the day was usually marred by hurt feelings, power struggles over what to wear, what to eat or a dozen other insignificant issues, and sheer frustration caused by the lack of time. Forget calm, rational order. I called it "barely controlled chaos." Now that they were more independent and self-sufficient, mornings went well as long as they were up early enough.

Kelsey stepped lightly into the kitchen—no bounding today—a thoughtful look on her face. I glanced at the clock on the wall. She was dressed and primped for school earlier than usual.

"Where's Mom?" she asked quietly.

The question hung there for an instant like a breath on a cold morning.

"I think she's on a trip," Ty said with confidence. The look he gave me suggested he harbored a couple dozen other notions in his busy brain.

"Dad?" Kelsey ignored her brother.

I gave a short sigh. "I don't know. She *might* be on a trip." As usual, Mary hadn't left a note, just me holding the bag. Two days now, and no word.

"A trip? She said she'd take me and Amanda to the mall this afternoon."

"And it has to be this afternoon or the world as we know it will cease to exist?"

"Well, yeah." Her expression said I must be an idiot to think otherwise.

"Why don't I take you? As long as your homework's done, that is. I can drop you at the back if you're worried about someone seeing you." She flushed and thought about it.

"I suppose." She didn't sound convinced.

"Want me to pick you up at school?"

"Uh, no," she said quickly. "That's okay. I'll walk home. We can leave from here." She walked to the cupboard and pulled down a bowl for cereal. "I'm hungry." I breathed an inward sigh of relief. With the logistical problem solved, the missing mom was forgotten for the moment.

"SOMETIMES I WISH she was dead. I have these fantasies that she's died some tragic death. I don't know, like in a car crash or something. Or one of the health problems

she constantly complains about actually turns out to be real and not just a figment of her imagination. Cancer, maybe. Or some rare disease with no cure. Isn't that sick?" I couldn't believe I admitted it. As if the dark reveries that more and more frequently scuttled like roaches in and out of my consciousness grew brazen enough to brave the light of day.

"Do you think so?"

"Well, I'm not sure it's normal. I mean, my God, this is someone I love. Why would I want her dead? I can't imagine ever hurting her. How could I be so vindictive I'd want her dead?"

"Have you ever hurt her?"

"You mean, like, hit her?" A wave of revulsion swept through me. "God, no. I have a hard enough time getting rid of spiders. I would never hit her. I've never even spanked my kids. I don't think I could stand how they'd look at me after doing something like that.

"No, I wouldn't want her to suffer. I don't want to hurt her. When I have these fantasies, I just imagine her dead."

"What do you think that's about?"

"I want her gone. I don't want to deal with her problems anymore."

"Her problems? Or your problems?"

"Her problems. The constant illnesses, the drinking, all of it. It's like she's checked out anyway. It's like she doesn't care anymore. She embarrasses herself in front of friends, in front of the kids even. They're not dumb. They know what's going on. I just can't deal with it anymore."

"Aren't her problems your problems, though?" I had to stop and think about what she meant.

"JACK HOLM."

There was silence on the line, and I wondered if it was another computer-dialed call from a solicitor. I was about to hang up in frustration when a voice finally responded. "Oh. Sorry. Is Mary there?"

"No, she's not. May I take a message?"

"You're her husband?" The voice sounded confused.

"Yes, I am. And you are?"

"I'm sorry. Would you just tell her that Jane Adams called? I'm the room mother in Tyler's class. Mary signed the volunteer sheet at the beginning of the year, and I was just checking to see if she was still interested."

"I'll be sure to tell her. Does she have your number?"

"Oh, no, probably not. Let me give it to you." I grabbed a pencil and jotted down the number she rattled off. "If you'd just let her know I called?"

"I'll do that." I started to hang up, but her voice stopped me.

"Um, Jack, is it? You wouldn't be interested in driving some kids on a field trip, would you? The kids love it when a few dads come along." I sighed. I'd done my share of driving and chaperoning when the kids were little. But a pang of guilt reminded me it had been a long time since I'd pitched in. "Depends on when it is. If you can't find anyone else, I'll try to fit it into my schedule."

"Wonderful," the woman gushed. "I'll get back to you and let you know, if that's all right." I cradled the phone, wishing I had a second line. I'd been hoping we could make do without it. We didn't need the added expense. But if this kept up I'd have to bite the bullet. I couldn't spend the day fielding calls from the PTA, volunteers, solicitors, Mary's friends and moms arranging play dates and then turn the phone over to my children after school. I'd never get any work done. *Damn her. Where is she?*

The phone rang again, startling me. I picked up.

"Jack, it's Terry McAuley. I'm not sure if you remember me." I tried to place him, but didn't have it by the time he finished. He didn't let the silence get uncomfortable. "We met at that food conference last year?" It came back to me slowly. McAuley had moderated a panel on food safety in Chicago. He'd posed smart questions and kept the discussion lively. I'd been impressed enough to go up to the dais afterwards and toss him a compliment. I was surprised he remembered me and told him so. After some chit-chat, he offered me an assignment to write an article for the magazine he edited. He said a mutual acquaintance recommended me, and easily convinced me to write the piece.

I reached over to hang up. The phone nearly slipped out of my grasp. My palms were sweaty. I noticed a damp stain spreading under the arms of my shirt. Only days earlier, I'd lain awake nights soaked with perspiration, wondering how I would keep up with the bills. Now I sweated whether I'd be able to handle the work I was taking on. *Take that, Ellis & Mower.*

A month had passed since the agency told me I was being let go. I should have seen it coming. The situation had been strained ever since I'd arrived three years before. I'd been comfortably ensconced in middle management at a large ad agency in Chicago, helping a half-dozen blue-chip brands with their marketing communications programs. A small Seattle firm, Ellis & Mower, had come calling out of the blue and recruited me for a higher level position. The thought of being a bigger fish in a smaller pond tempted me.

Mary and I had talked about it, weighing the pros and cons of pulling up Midwestern roots and transplanting them in the soggy Northwest. It had been a gut-wrenching decision, fraught with emotional landmines, not least of which was what we'd do if it didn't work out. In the end, I convinced Mary, the kids and myself that everything we'd heard about the quality of life in the Northwest would make the move worth anything we gave up. The kids would benefit the most, I suggested. Safer neighborhoods and better schools meant greater freedom for them, cheaper cost of living for us, or so we thought.

But it had gone sour from the beginning. We experienced no problems with Seattle itself. Visually stunning, the area stays green year-round. Though winters can be gray and dreary, I liked to tell people that the best part about them is that you don't have to shovel rain. At least winters usually don't offer howling winds that take the temperature below zero.

No, the problem was at Ellis & Mower. The people who had hired me left to form their own firm before I got there. The president of the company had reassured me that the agency was still committed to bringing me on board, and that my position was more important now than ever. But the folks I ended up working with weren't sold. The defectors had taken some clients with them. The team I joined protected the clients they still had and weren't inclined to go after the kind of business I'd been hired to work on. I was an outsider, and the natives weren't about to make it easy for me to join the in-crowd.

That it took so long for them to give me notice surprised me more than that it happened at all. I'd almost gotten used to the vague limbo in which I'd been placed.

That purgatory had been uncomfortable; getting canned put me into a nearly full-blown panic. I couldn't bring myself to tell Mary the bad news for two days, two days to bring my heart rate back to something close to normal and take a full breath.

When I told her, Mary said with a conviction I didn't feel, "You'll get another job."

"There are no jobs out there." I'd looked. I'd been keeping my eye out for some time, just in case, but the economy had been in shambles for years after the dot-com bust. And while Wall Street and economists all said we were in the midst of a recovery, no one was hiring.

"You'll find something," she said firmly.

"I'm not going to get another job. I'm going out on my own." I saw her eyes fill with the panic I'd been feeling. "How can you…? We can't afford…" The questions swirled through her mind until she finally latched on to one. "Where will you get the money to pay for office space? Aren't things pretty tight right now?"

I nodded. "There probably couldn't be a worse time, but I'm done working for other people. I might find a job, but it probably wouldn't be what I want to do or even what I'm good at. It would most likely mean taking a pay cut. And there's no such thing as job security anymore. Doing my own thing may be the best thing I could do, and if I don't try it now, I may never be able to."

"You're not going to take out a loan, are you?"

"No. I'll work out of the house."

"Here?" She paled. "You're going to work at home?"

"Sure. Why not? You're gone half the time, anyway." The life of a flight attendant.

"No reason, I guess." But the unhappiness on her

face had left her looking even more dour than usual, if that was possible.

My damp palm still rested on the phone. I picked it up and called Mary's friend Diane. No one answered. Maybe the two of them had picked up an extra trip together. I didn't leave a message. I looked up the number for the airline S-O-D— supervisor-on-duty—and started to dial. *If she wasn't on a trip, did that mean she'd left me?* I disconnected before the call went through.

The phone jangled the moment I set it down, making me jump. When I answered, though, there was no one on the line. I held on a moment to be sure, and thought I heard breathing.

"Is anyone there?"

I heard silence then an accented voice. "You have something of mine."

"Excuse me? Who is this?"

"I want it back."

"I'm sorry. I think you have the wrong number." I spoke to a dead line.

"My problems? My problem is that I'm picking up more and more of the slack at home—taking care of the kids, doing housework. At the same time I'm trying to get a new business off the ground. My problem is that I'm starved for affection and intimacy. My problem is that instead of a partner I now have dead weight dragging me under. It's like having another child to take care of. No, worse. Yeah, I guess you could say that her problems are my problems."

"And if she was gone? Would your problems be gone?" My brows knitted as I contemplated the question. Sarah endured the silence patiently. The small

office was cluttered, but comfortable. Papers and books littered the desk and credenza against the opposite wall. A flurry of notes of all sizes and colors covered a cork board on the wall above the desk. A maroon Oriental rug hid the nondescript industrial carpet. I took up a third of the twill-covered couch. My fingers idly toyed with the knitted afghan draped over the backrest. Sarah occupied a mismatched easy chair, a brass floor lamp next to it casting a bright pool of light over her shoulder onto the notes in her lap. The casual, almost careless, feel stood in stark contrast to the light maple modern groupings in the anteroom. Split personality? The office, I decided, more closely reflected her personality. But it made me wonder if she saw a therapist of her own from time to time.

"No," I said finally. "I guess not. I'd have total responsibility for the kids and the house. I still wouldn't be getting any. And I'd be even more hard-pressed to get the business going to provide for the kids." Sarah said nothing, waiting expectantly.

"But I wouldn't have her problems to deal with anymore," I went on. "I wouldn't feel all this horrible stuff that makes me so uncomfortable I want to climb right out of my skin."

"If her problems are causing yours, instead of hoping that she suddenly vanishes from your life, what happens if her problems go away?" A way out? It was as if someone had turned on a light somewhere in a dark cavern. Impossible to tell the source, but there was definitely light.

"You mean fix her problems?" Just as quickly as hope had arisen, the light started to flicker and fade like a candle sputtering in a breeze. "I can't fix her problems. She's the only one who can do that."

"True."

"And she'll never agree to counseling. I've tried. I begged her to get help. She won't."

"You're sure?"

I nodded."Positive. She doesn't believe in it."

"Then you can't fix her problems," Sarah agreed. The light went out. "Unless they're yours," she went on.

"I don't get it." I frowned. "You mean, I'm her problem? I don't think so. I don't think wanting to be close is a problem. I don't think wanting to be intimate, to have sex more than once every month or so is a problem. Do you? I don't think wanting her to be involved in the kids' lives instead of spending days at a time in bed is asking too much."

"She wasn't always like this, though. Would you want things to be the way they used to be? How would you feel if things were back to normal?" Sarah hooked her fingers in the air like quotation marks around her last word. "What if her problems were gone?" I had trouble imagining it. I wondered why my response hadn't been an immediate yes. We'd had a lot of good times. It had been a good marriage. Hadn't it?

Sarah saw my indecision. "Humor me here. Let's go down this road for a bit and see what we see. Is that all right with you?"

I shrugged. "Sure, I guess."

She nodded. "Good." She shifted in her chair and pulled the clipboard that held her notes onto her lap. "Tell me a little about her. How did you meet?"

KELSEY RUSHED INTO my office—formerly the den— without knocking, and started talking before the door was half open. "Dad, can you take me to town? I have to pick up some things for a chem-phys project." The day had been full of such interruptions, usually breaking into the middle of a thought or a phone call. In fact, I hadn't been home for more than twenty minutes since picking up Kelsey and Amanda at the mall. Irritated, I looked up from some notes that needed deciphering.

"Puh-lease?" Her concession to manners was delivered with just a little too much attitude.

"Where the hell is your mother?" I snapped. As soon as the words came out of my mouth I regretted them. Kelsey took a half-step backwards with a startled look, as if physically struck. Worse was the fleeting mistrust in her eyes.

"I'm sorry, Kels," I said, trying to sound consoling despite a lingering resentment. "That was a rhetorical question. I'd be happy to drive you into town. I didn't mean to be short with you. I just wish you'd thought of it when we were already out." She looked leery for an instant longer, then softened a bit.

"Sorry," she said, sounding chastened. She shrugged. "Bad day?"

"Just hectic. Doing everything myself is going to take a little getting used to, and there've been a million interruptions." I would have to remind myself to have a sit-down with the kids and spell out some rules to follow when I was "at work." I had a feeling, though, that my work day had been permanently shortened to the hours in which the kids were at school.

She looked around the den, noting the changes I'd made to turn it into a workspace, and shoved her fingers into the pockets of her low-cut jeans. A band of bare midriff showed between the jeans and her top. Like watching an object change in the shifting light of a passing cloud, I suddenly became aware of the aura of sexuality she innocently projected. She was quickly blossoming into a woman. She had her mother's heart-shaped face and generous mouth, but her willowy frame already was nearly a head taller.

She shifted from one foot to the other. "Um, so how's it going?" Her interest, whether real or feigned, surprised me. Coming from someone convinced she was the center of the universe, I saw it as another sign of her growing maturity. Or an attempt to make up for angering me with her intrusion.

"It's going okay. Thanks for asking. I got another small job today, which is encouraging."

She nodded. "Cool."

She said little on the way to town, a far cry from the days when she would cheerily babble on about everything in her world. I realized I missed that little girl. I tried to initiate conversation a couple of times—asking her how her day at school had been, what her friends were up to—but gave up after eliciting less than intelligible responses. Maintaining a meaningful dialogue with a teenager takes the skills of a career diplomat, or a hostage negotiator. The typical adult male, hobbled with that gender-based incapacity for small talk, has pretty poor odds of conversing with a teenage daughter in more than infrequent monosyllables. So, managing to exchange a sentence or two with her consistently surprised me.

"I have dance class tonight," she said, interrupting one of our silences.

I glanced at her. She looked out the windshield and didn't offer anything further. "Do you need a ride?"

"I guess." I saw her shrug out of the corner of my eye. It was a yes-or-no question, and I wondered why she seemed so noncommittal. I often picked her up from dance because Mary didn't like driving at night, but I couldn't think of an occasion on which I'd dropped her off. Until the past month, I got home from work too late to take her.

"Do you usually get a ride with Amanda?" I wondered aloud.

"Yeah, I guess. Normally, I just take the bus to Amanda's after school, and her mom gives us a ride when it's time for dance."

"But you didn't go to Amanda's today."

"Nah, she had a dentist appointment."

"I can take you." I saw her shrug again. Some things I couldn't leave alone despite my discomfort. "What else is on your mind?" I thought she was ignoring me. "Kels?"

She looked uncomfortable. "It's no big deal. It's just there was this creepy-looking guy hanging out at school today."

"A student?" I didn't like the sound of it.

"No, some man. Out in the parking lot. Outside the commons, actually. Just standing there, staring at us through the window."

"Creepy, how?"

"I dunno. He was dressed real nice. It was just the way he looked at us."

"When was this?"

"During lunch." She went quiet for a moment, then blurted out, "Aren't you worried?"

"Of course, I'm worried. Did you tell someone at school?"

"Not that. About *Mom*." She seemed incredulous that I could be so dense.

My brow furrowed in momentary confusion. "Well, sure. A little, I guess."

"You act like you don't care at all."

"Of course I do. Look, sweetie, I'm sure she's fine. Yes, I'm a little concerned that she hasn't called to let us know where she is. But you know your mom. If she ended up someplace like Tokyo, she probably hasn't called because of the time difference." Kelsey didn't look very reassured. "Really, you shouldn't worry, Kels. It's not like she hasn't done this before."

THERE WAS A framed watercolor on the wall, a pretty picture of tulips in a ceramic pitcher done in soft, pastel shades of blue, pink and purple. It was soft around the edges as if a little out of focus, which lent it a calming influence. I got lost in it while my thoughts followed a trail of breadcrumbs back in time.

"She said she loved me, and I allowed myself to believe her." Sarah waited for me to elaborate. I tried to pick my words more carefully. "I don't mean I think she was insincere or untruthful. What I mean is that I was so ready for love, so ready to be in love, that I accepted the fact that she loved me. It was exciting and wonderful.

"We were walking through the park holding hands the first time she said that. We couldn't have been dating for more than a few weeks at that point. We'd just been to a movie. It was summer, and it was still light when the movie let out, so we decided to walk back to her apartment.

"I know for a lot of guys those are the three most frightening words in the English language. I remember at the time being struck by the fact that I didn't get scared when I heard them. They sounded so natural coming from her. Sort of like saying, 'That was a good movie.'"

"So, when did you tell her?"

"That I loved her?" Sarah nodded. *I let my thoughts drift back in time again. "Not long afterward. A couple of weeks, maybe. In bed, after making love." I smiled self-consciously. "Typical male, huh?"*

"Oh, I don't know. I think a lot of men hope their lovemaking does the talking for them. Sometimes it takes a lot of courage to say it out loud, especially for the first time."

"I suppose. It wasn't as hard as I thought it would be. Like I said, I think I was ready."

"And now?"

I was silent for a few moments. "Now, I wonder."

"What about?"

"My feelings. Whether or not they were real." I paused. "This is hard to explain. They were real. I just wonder whether they were my true feelings." I shook my head and paused again. "Mary told me she knew after our first date that she wanted to marry me. I was so tired of being alone and so ready to have a relationship, to experience true love, that I sometimes wonder if I adopted her feelings as my own. I mean, we had a blast together. We had fun. We enjoyed each other's company. We did things together. And she loved me. Why wouldn't I love her, too? We seemed to complement each other so well. We used to say that she made me feel and I made her think. It was the kind of relationship I'd been looking for. But I wonder if that's what I felt because that's what she—and I—expected me to feel. That's what I was supposed to feel because she felt that way."

"What do you think?"

It was a long time before I answered. "I'm not sure."

AFTER I MADE DINNER, took Kelsey to dance practice, cleaned up the kitchen, helped Ty finish his homework, picked Kelsey up from dance, made sure Ty took a shower, did a load of laundry so Ty had clean soccer clothes, got Ty into bed and read him a story, pried Kelsey loose from the computer long enough to finish her homework and straightened up the family room, I fell into an easy chair and turned on the television. It had the narcotic effect I'd hoped for. Within five minutes, my brain switched off, and I sat mesmerized, unmoving, while images flickered across the blue screen.

Kelsey stood ten feet away, a little to one side, hands on her hips. The television put me into such a stupor that her presence didn't even register at first. It took another moment before I realized she wanted my attention. I finally tore my gaze away from the screen to look at her. The consternation on her face aged her somehow. The effect startled me, rousing me from the fatigue that had washed over me.

"Dad, I don't think Mom went on a trip." Her voice was solemn, her face dead serious.

"How come?" I sat up straight.

"Her suitcase and stuff are still in the garage. I looked."

I thought a moment. "Maybe she just took a carry-all—you know, that big handbag she has?" Mary had a habit of leaving her airline suitcase in the garage by the back door when she came home from a trip. Her clothes absorbed the smell of stale cabin air on the airplane. She hated being reminded of it when she was home, so she left her clothes in the garage until she was ready to do laundry. The washer and dryer sat in the mud room right inside the back door. The first thing she always did when she got home was strip down to her bra and panties inside the back door, throw her uniform in a hamper and put on a robe.

Kelsey shook her head slowly. "She always takes her suitcase if it's a two- or three-day trip. She only takes the carryall if it's a turn-around. Where is she, Dad? Where's Mom?"

I sighed. "I don't know, sweetie. I just assumed she was on a trip. I figured she must have picked one up from crew scheduling at the last minute and didn't have time to tell us." I hadn't wanted to think Mary's curious absence was anything other than an unscheduled trip to pick up extra money or do a favor for a friend. I hadn't wanted to consider what her departure might mean if she wasn't working. That hadn't stopped my imagination from taking unplanned trips into dark territory. I couldn't admit those apprehensions to myself, let alone my children.

"Wouldn't you know it? This is so like her!" Kelsey's voice rose into a whine. "Just when I need her, she isn't here." The sudden shift in her demeanor took me by surprise.

"Hey, it'll be all right," I said consolingly. "Is there anything I can help you with?"

"No, Dad, I need Mom," she said, distraught. Her eyes teared. There was more to her distress than a hissy-fit over being inconvenienced, I sensed. Both her voice and her face held a note of fear. The same fear I felt.

THE INCESSANT TAPPING WORKED its way into my dreams, first as the cane of an old man walking down a cobblestone street, then a flicker clinging to the trunk of a dead tree, rhythmically poking its beak into the bark. The dreams shifted yet again, as dreams do, and I found myself in a bunk aboard a sailboat rocking in the ocean swells. Someone on deck called my name, the voice distant and thinned by the stiff breeze.

"Dad! Dad!" The voice was an urgent whisper. "Wake up! There's someone downstairs!" The rocking boat transformed into a hand shaking my shoulder. I sat up slowly and groggily rubbed sleep from my eyes.

"Kelsey? What? What is it?"

"There's someone in the house! I heard noises!"

THREE

I HELD my breath and listened intently while my eyes
searched Kelsey's face in the faint light coming through
the window. The fright and alarm limned there sent my
pulse racing.

"I don't hear anything," I whispered.

"I heard it! I'm not kidding, Dad. There's someone
in the house!" I nodded and swung my legs out of bed.
On the way to the door I grabbed the cordless phone off
the bedside table and handed it to Kelsey. "Stay here. If
you hear me yell, dial nine-one-one." I padded down the
stairs in boxers and T-shirt still shaking the sleep from
my head, and strained to hear any unfamiliar noises. I
wondered what the hell I'd do if I surprised a burglar,
and looked for anything that would serve as a weapon. I
moved as silently as I could into the living room and
paused, heart pounding, to check all the shadows in the
corners, mentally picturing where each piece of furniture belonged. Seeing nothing out of the ordinary, I
quickly strode to the fireplace and quietly picked up a
poker.

Now armed, I made my way from room to room,
switching on bright overhead recessed lights as I went.
Nothing. Not in the front hall, the den, the dining room,
or the family room. I poked my head into the laundry
room, then walked through to see if the garage door was
secure. I found nothing out of place, no fallen pictures
or tipped-over vases that could have wakened Kelsey.

In the kitchen, Kelsey's cat sat by the back door and watched me indifferently while I flipped on the porch light and peered out into the yard. Again, nothing.

I switched off the light and looked down at the cat. Its food and water bowls stood empty. Shaking my head, I filled them both. Without so much as a meow of thanks, the cat hunched its shoulders and stuck its nose into the food. I turned to go and nearly ran into Kelsey, kick-starting my heart again. I jerked back in surprise, frightening her.

"It's okay," I said, putting a hand on her arm. "You startled me, sweetie." I pointed at the cat. "I think that's your culprit. There's no one here."

"Are you sure?" She clutched the phone like a club. "It sounded like someone was moving around down here."

"Just your imagination, Kels. Honest, I checked everywhere. No one's here. Go on up to bed and try to get some sleep." She gave me a skeptical look, but turned and shuffled off. I put the cat food away and started to turn off the lights, then thought to check the back door just to be sure I'd secured it as I always did before going to bed. It was unlocked.

PROMPTED BY THE BEEP, I left a message. "Um, Greg? Jack Holm. Hey, I wondered, um, if…have you talked to Mary recently? Uh, give me a call when you get in, would you? Thanks." It was the third such message I'd left on people's answering machines or voice-mail, the fourth counting the S-O-D's. If I knew the numbers of more of the people Mary worked with, I would have called them, too. Most recently, though, she'd been flying with Greg and Diane. I called Carmen, even though she still lived in Chicago. She and Mary had been close. None of them had been home—no surprise. Most flight attendants don't have normal nine-to-five schedules, but I found myself irritated at the lack of results after four tries. Time to try another avenue of investigation.

I picked up the phone again and called our friends the Whitmans, hoping to talk to Bill. Cathy answered.

"He's at work, Jack," she said with a touch of surprise when I asked for him.

"Oh. Of course. I thought I might catch him…" I let it hang.

"No, as a matter of fact he's been gone a while, so you would have had to call pretty early. I'm sure he's in the office, though."

"I'll try him there, then. Thanks. Say, has Mary talked to you recently?"

"No." She hesitated. "Not that I can think of."

"She said something about getting together with you guys, and I wondered if she'd mentioned it to you."

"No, but that sounds like a great idea. Do you know what day she was thinking about?"

"I'm not sure, to tell the truth. Maybe next weekend. Why don't I check with her and have her give you a call?"

"That would be terrific. We haven't done anything in ages."

"Good. I'll have her get in touch." I hung up wondering if she would tell Bill about my call when he got home. I wondered if they would think it strange that I hadn't called him at all. Coming up with pretexts for these calls was getting harder. How many more people would I have to lie to? How long could I keep up this pretense that everything was just fine?

"SHE'S REALLY GONE."

"Gone?" *Sarah looked puzzled. I shrugged and looked away.* "Gone where?"

"I don't know." *I met her gaze.*

"She's just gone." *Her statement begged an answer.*

"Yep. Gone, as in, I don't know when she's coming back. As in, I don't know if she's coming back." *It occurred to me that I had been holding all the questions—where, why, when, with whom, how, how long—at bay, not wanting to contemplate the possibilities.* "I don't know what to think."

"Has she done this before?"

"Not like this." *I shook my head.* "Party too much and end up spending the night at a friend's, sure. I've almost stopped worrying when she does that. Almost."

"Not this time?"

"I don't know. I've called everyone I can think of—friends, the people she flies with—but no one's seen her."

"How long has it been?"

"Too long." *Sarah looked at me expectantly.* "Several days," *I amended.*

"And you have no idea why she left?"

I shook my head. "None. At first, I thought maybe she'd just picked up an extra trip without telling me or the kids. I thought maybe she realized with me starting up this consulting business that we could use the extra money." *I thought for a moment.* "To tell you the truth, I was so relieved she wasn't around, I just figured maybe she finally decided to pull her weight and contribute for once."

"You can't think of any other reason she might have left?"

"A family emergency, maybe?" *I hadn't considered*

it. Like all the other questions, I hadn't wanted to. It meant I'd have to put in calls to Mary's family, too.

"There's that." The way she said it suggested she had something else in mind.

"What, you mean like a fight or something?" She held her gaze, but said nothing.

"You think maybe she ran away?" I shook my head. "Honestly, I can't think of anything I've done to make her just up and leave. Things haven't been great. I told you that. But I can't believe she'd walk out on the kids. That's one of the reasons I don't think either one of us has ever really considered the 'd' word. It wouldn't be fair to the kids."

"Maybe she was unhappy, too."

"Well, she hasn't exactly been Little Miss Sunshine. But I don't think she's been any more miserable than I have, and you don't see me walking out."

"But you've thought about it."

"No, I've thought about what it would be like without her," I clarified.

"Ah." It sounded more like an accusation than an acknowledgement. "From what you've told me, her behavior has become more erratic. And she's been drinking more?"

"Well, she's always liked to party. It affects her differently now. Its effect is more pronounced. But, yes, I guess so." She nodded absentmindedly while I talked, as if impatient.

"That could be a symptom of her unhappiness, don't you think?"

"I suppose."

"You don't think one of her friends is covering for her?" Another surprising thought. I mulled it over.

"I guess it's possible, but I don't think so. Besides, if

*she was walking out on me, wouldn't she have packed
some things? Left a note? Something?"*

*"I don't know. Hard to say what went through her
mind." The room was quiet enough for a moment that
the ticking of my watch registered loudly in my consciousness. She nibbled the end of her pen.*

*"No use guessing," she said finally, her tone busi-
nesslike. "You'll just have to wait until you find out
where she is and why she left. In the meantime, you're
getting a taste of what it's like living without her. Let's
talk about how you feel about that."*

I REMEMBERED, BARELY, to pick Tyler up from school at
three-thirty. I arrived late, but not so late that he faced
the ignominy of sitting in the office until I showed up.
They reserved that for kids in the lower grades. Instead,
he'd walked up the street to the parking lot overlooking
the soccer field where he usually practiced.

I almost missed him. I passed the first entrance to
the lot before the sight of his familiar figure and dark
tousled hair registered. Bushes obscured the lot, ren-
dering my double-take useless. Trusting my instincts,
I slowed at the next entrance and turned in. Ty stood to
the side at the far end, backpack slung over one shoulder, headphones draped around his neck, CD player in
hand. He'd been bugging me to get him an iPod or MP3
player, but it wasn't in my budget.

A car had pulled up beside him, the driver obviously
engaging him in conversation. Ty kept his distance,
but appeared interested and unconcerned. I saw little
through the car's tinted rear window except a vague
profile. A hand gestured out the driver's window, the
arm sheathed in dress shirt and suit coat—a man. I gave
the horn a tap as I pulled up, startling Ty. The driver's

profile turned, as if checking his rearview mirror, and he drove off quickly with a chirp of tires on pavement. I turned into a parking space to let Ty climb in.

"Who was that?" I said. "Somebody's dad?"

He buckled himself in. "I dunno. Some guy."

"Some guy? Didn't we have a conversation about stranger danger?"

"He wasn't gonna grab me or anything. Anyway, I was too far away."

"What did he want?"

"Nothing. We were just talking. He asked me what CDs I listen to. Wanted me to show him the ones in my backpack."

"That's strange."

"Not really. He told me he wanted to get something cool for his daughter for her birthday, but didn't know what she might like." I considered him, uncertain how concerned I should be.

"Okay, but next time be a little more careful about talking to someone you don't know." I kept my tone light. Despite the explanation, I didn't like the way the man pulled away so quickly once aware of my presence. A queasy feeling made me wish I'd taken down the man's license plate.

WE PASSED YET another hole in the ground where a house once stood. They dotted the island as if Clifford, the big red dog, had been burying bones. The last ice age thrust the island hundreds of feet up out of the water. From the air, the clay-covered rock looks like a footprint with no toes. Receding glaciers scraped the top flat and scoured steep ravines down the sides. By the 1970s, most of the flat parts had been developed.

Now, enormous, multi-million-dollar waterfront

ringed the shoreline, standing shoulder-to-shoul-
ke a stockade against invasion. Large view homes
clung precariously to the walls of ravines. The rest of
the island consisted of mostly small, suburban neighborhoods of single-story ramblers and ranch homes.
With no place left to build, real estate prices kept going
up with demand for the island's safe streets and good
schools. Almost the only way on the island was through
attrition. As the elderly died off or moved into retirement communities, incoming families bought the outdated homes, with no view let alone waterfront, for
figures far in excess of a half-million dollars. Then they
knocked them down and built McMansions on the lots.

We'd been lucky. We'd gotten a good enough price
when we sold our house in Chicago that we'd been
able to buy here. But it had been a stretch. Even in our
short time here, the house had appreciated so much we
wouldn't have been able to afford it if we moved in
now. It took both our incomes, and losing my job wasn't
going to help. Seeing another new house going up made
me wonder if we'd be able to afford the property tax re-
assessment that would likely go with it.

"Dad, come on! Can't you go any faster? We're going
to be late."

"No, I can't go any faster. And it won't kill you
to be a few minutes late." I barely kept the exasperation out of my voice. Something about my children's
whining sets me off, especially when my mind is elsewhere. Instead of countering with calm logic, I always
get sucked in, ensnared in their emotional manipula-
tion. *Deep breath.* "Besides, it can't be helped. It's not
my fault your coach scheduled practice on Wednesday
when you have CCD." I pulled into the lot that we'd left
less than two hours earlier, and Tyler threw the door

open and ran down to the practice field before I shut off the engine. I locked up and slowly followed. Alex's mother had already staked her turf on the sideline, surrounded by what looked like the same group of women that had paid fealty a few days before. Determined to avoid a repeat encounter, I skirted the edge of the field to the far sideline and watched practice from there.

Sometime later, I felt a presence and turned. A woman approached from behind, her eyes following the action on the field. Attractive in a healthy sort of way, she had girl-next-door features. Her lack of makeup gave her a youthful appearance. Her straight sandy hair was pulled back into a short ponytail, and she wore khakis, a light cotton turtleneck and a tan bush jacket. She stopped on the sidelines a few yards away and silently gazed out at the running boys. I did the same, but in a minute or two, the woman drifted to a spot a few feet to my left.

"It's Jack, right?" She watched the boys as they attacked the goal in groups of three, dribbling and passing until they drew close enough to shoot.

"Right." I turned and looked at her, curious.

"Way to go, Rory!" she called.

I turned my gaze back to the field just in time to see one of the boys on the field race away from the goal with both arms in the air.

She took a step toward me, putting out her hand. "Sue Thorvahl," she said.

I matched her firm grip and searched my memory banks. "Oh, you're Amanda's mom." Kelsey's friend Amanda, the girl she practically lived with when she wasn't home.

Sue nodded. "I saw what happened the other day

ngela," she said. I looked at her quizzically.
ex's mom?" she prompted.

"Oh, right. Guess I went a little overboard."

"Not at all," she said hurriedly. "I wanted to tell you I
thought it was great. About time someone told her off. I
see way too much of that kind of behavior around here.
One of the tradeoffs of living here, I think. Too many
people used to getting their own way." I raised an eyebrow. She mistook my surprise at her candor for disbelief. "I swear, some of the adults here are more spoiled
than their kids."

"Money will do that to some people."

"Maybe. I never thought money was an excuse for
bad manners, though."

"Well, I guess I can be thankful I don't have that
problem," I said.

She laughed. Whooping and hollering from across
the field made both of us look up. The boys dashed
madly for the far sideline. Practice, apparently, had
ended. I shoved my hands in my pockets. In unison,
we shuffled slowly across the field toward the knot of
activity as if somehow hoping to postpone the inevita-
ble. Tyler and another boy ran toward us, cutting and
weaving on the way, like two exuberant puppies.

"Dad, can I have an overnight at Rory's on Friday?"
Tyler called breathlessly, still twenty feet away.
"Please?"

"Can he, Mom? Can he?" the other boy chimed in.
Nearly a head taller than Ty, his sandy hair, pale blue
eyes and fine features suggested a male version of the
woman next to me. At this age, the likeness made him
almost too pretty, effeminate even. But in a few years,
when his features hardened and matured, he'd be strikingly handsome.

Sue and I exchanged looks. I sensed her embarrassment matched mine. I nodded. "It's okay with me, kiddo, if it's okay with Rory's mom. But it isn't polite to invite yourself, you know."

"Of course he can." Sue tousled Rory's hair.

"Are you sure?" I asked. "After all, my other child will probably already be there."

"The more, the merrier." She laughed.

Tyler caught my nod of approval. "Great! Thanks! Thanks, Dad!" He and Rory ran off, heading back to the far sideline to pick up their duffel bags and water bottles.

"Sorry," I said when they were gone. "I hope they didn't put you on the spot."

"No problem." She waved away my concern. "The kids have friends over all the time. Want me to call— Mary, is it?—and arrange a time after school on Friday?"

I shrugged, suddenly uncomfortable. "Either one of us, doesn't matter," I lied.

THE NIGHT PASSED slowly. I tossed and turned in the big, empty double bed as if tugging and pulling on ill-fitting clothes to make them more comfortable. Most of the time I spent in that strange state between dreams and wakefulness, starting at sounds to full consciousness and looking blearily at the clock. Then I drifted uneasily back into a swirling torrent of disjointed thoughts and emotions that dragged me along like a riptide in a kaleidoscopic sea or a car in an amusement park funhouse ride.

My eyes snapped open one last time with a certainty that sleep would elude me. The red digits on the clock read 4:37, twelve minutes fast. I lay quietly and stared at the dark ceiling, and wondered how many mistakes I'd made. How many times had I mulishly stuck to a point of view simply out of pride? How often had I seemed dismissive of others' feelings because mine were more important? I wondered if regret served any purpose in life. If so, of all the mistakes, which were significant enough to regret, and which should I just let go? Would any of it be different now, even if I'd acted differently then?

Street lamps and the blue glow of the clocks on the microwave and oven provided enough light in the kitchen to fumble for coffee. I started a pot, and while it was brewing chased down some vitamins with juice and filled the cat's bowls with food and water. The brewer gave a final hiss and burble, signaling the coffee was ready. I poured a cup and took it with me to the office. I closed myself in the den, sat at the desk and turned on the desk lamp. The bright light was harsh in the early morning gloom, making me squint and blink. I looked up the number in my address book just to be sure, checked my watch, and placed the call.

When my mother-in-law answered, I said, "Letty, it's Jack." She probably sat in her kitchen having coffee and reading the paper.

"Jack, how's the weather there, dear?" Discussing the weather was a ritual with Letitia Beaumont. Weather was her metaphor for life, always changing, sometimes bringing gloom and sorrow, while giving warmth and light and joy to others. It was both pretense for and subject of her news, the events in her life. I let her ramble and guide the conversation. We'd get around to why I'd called soon enough.

"How are the kids?" she asked when she'd filled me in on all the travails of her life.

I went through the litany of their latest accomplishments, then answered her questions until she was satisfied she'd gleaned all the important details she could.

"Is there anything I can do for you, Jack?" she finally asked, her voice airy. She knew I hadn't called just to chat, especially since it's one of my lesser skills.

"Have you talked to Mary recently?" I tried to keep my tone nonchalant.

"Why, no. I haven't heard from her in several days. That's not like her."

"No, it isn't," I agreed genially. "She's been awfully busy lately between work and the kids." Actually, it was just like Mary. Before her father died, she called him almost daily to talk about nothing at all. Relations with her mother, though cordial in recent years, had always been more strained. She dutifully called Letty every week or two, but Letty liked to think herself more important than that.

"Is anything wrong?"

"No, nothing." I'd rehearsed my answer. "I just wondered if she'd talked to you about the holidays this year."

"No, she hasn't. My, that seems so far away."

"Not too early to be thinking about it. We hoped you might come out here for Thanksgiving this year." I couldn't speak for Mary. For my part, it was a lie.

"Why, thank you. That's so sweet of you. I'll have to give it some thought. Of course, I'd love to see the kids." We exchanged some more pleasantries, and I finally extricated myself without getting grilled about Mary's whereabouts.

I'd run out of recourse. There was only one thing left I could think of to do.

FOUR

The small reception area was furnished with three steel chairs upholstered in vinyl the color of pumpkin pie. Between two of them stood a steel-legged pressboard table covered with similarly shaded plastic laminate made to look like wood grain. A plastic rack of brochures and flyers on topics ranging from drug abuse to domestic violence was bolted to the painted cinder block wall. Inside a display case on another wall hung a poster of a recent D.A.R.E. fundraiser with a photo collage of smiling volunteers serving spaghetti and smiling people eating it.

A pane of inch-thick clear acrylic was set in the opposite wall. On the other side of it sat a uniformed dispatcher in front of a bank of electronic equipment. She was on the phone. I could see her mouth moving, but no sound penetrated the glass. Mounted on the wall next to the window was a phone handset. It had no dial, just a single button. I waited patiently, and when she put down the phone, I picked up the handset. It felt slippery in my hand. I wiped my palm on my pant leg, raised the handset to my ear and pushed the button. The dispatcher turned to look at me through the glass when the buzzer sounded.

She picked up an identical handset. "Can I help you?"

"I'd like to report a missing person."

"And you are?" I told her. She wrote down my name on a pad of paper. "All right. If you'll wait a moment,

I'll see if I can find an officer who's free. You can have a seat if you like." She pushed back her chair, stood up and took the note pad back into the office space behind her command center, disappearing around a corner. I sat down in one of the vinyl chairs and scanned the brochures. I pulled one out, but when I caught myself reading the first paragraph over again for the fourth time, I put it back.

In addition to the glass entry door, four doors led off the little anteroom, all steel, all painted the same light gray-green as the walls. On the right, just inside the entry, stood a set of double doors with a keyed lock in one of the door handles. On the left, a single door had a black pad about six inches square mounted on the wall next to it. A red light glowed in the center of the pad. Next to it was the first of the two windows looking into the dispatch area. No one sat behind it. *Is she really missing? Am I doing the right thing here? She's just upset about something. She's staying with a friend I haven't thought of. What should I make the kids for dinner? Oh, damn, Ty's got soccer practice—no, that was yesterday. Kelsey has dance class tonight, that's it.*

Two more single doors were framed in the wall opposite the outside entrance. One had a black pad on the wall next to it like the door into the dispatch area. Security doors, opened by placing a magnetically encoded badge against the pad. *Why is it taking so long? Why is my heart hammering like I've just been pulled over for speeding? Where the hell is she?* The last door had a square pane of glass criss-crossed with wire mesh set at most people's eye level. I stood up, then stooped and peered through it. I ambled over and bent forward for a better look. A corridor on the other side led toward the main entrance to city hall and the city offices beyond.

Maybe chicken for dinner. Why the hell did she do this to me? To us?

Halfway back to the chair the sound of a door opening startled me. I turned nervously to see a man size me up as he approached. He was short—maybe five-seven or -eight—and solidly built. A gut flared south of broad shoulders then curved suddenly inward where a black leather belt cinched gray silk slacks around his narrow hips. His shaven head reflected a pink sheen of health under the bright overhead lights. A wide, neatly trimmed Fu Manchu mustache separated a sharply hooked nose from a craggy chin. In leathers, he would have looked right at home in a biker bar. He was only modestly less scary in dressy clothes. They looked too expensive to afford on a cop's salary.

"You're Mr. Holm?" The voice, a rich baritone, intimidated me less than I expected. I nodded, confused. "Detective Ed Mankiewicz." He didn't offer his hand.

"Oh, sorry. I expected…someone else," I said lamely.

"A uniform? Normally, one of our patrol officers would take your statement. You're lucky; you get me." He flashed a grin so quickly I almost missed it. "I understand you want to report your wife missing?"

"That's right. I'm starting to get really worried."

"Here, let's sit down." He gestured toward the chairs. When I sat down, he perched on the edge of a chair on the other side of the table, putting space between us. "She's been missing since when?" he went on.

"Sunday is the last time I saw her."

"And you live together?"

"Yes, of course." The question surprised me, maybe because I felt guilty about sometimes wishing we didn't.

"Kids?"

I nodded. "Two. A girl, fifteen—sophomore this year. And a ten-year-old boy—fifth grade."

"I've got a couple about the same age." His smile— a real one this time—was incongruous on a face that appeared as if it could chill blood. It gave him a completely different look, one that small children probably found quite lovable. "Does your wife work, Mr. Holm?"

"She's a flight attendant." I told him which airline she worked for. He watched me without speaking. "Actually," I went on, "that's why it took me so long to decide whether to come down here or not. At first, I thought she'd gone on an unscheduled trip without telling me or the kids."

"Is that something she'd be likely to do?"

"Well, yes and no. She would pick up trips occasionally as a favor for friends or to earn more money. But I can't think of a time when she hasn't told us about it."

"Okay. Why don't you start at the beginning. Tell me about the last time you saw her. When did you know she was gone?"

"Sunday morning. I got up around seven, I guess. Later than I usually do. Mary was still asleep, so I went for a run. I got back around seven forty-five, had something to eat, checked e-mail. The house was pretty quiet. I figured Mary was still asleep, so I took a shower in the downstairs bathroom, got dressed and went out for coffee and a Sunday paper. I got back around ten-thirty, I think." I stopped for a moment to form a mental picture of that morning. "I read the paper for about an hour, and I began to wonder why the house was still so quiet. I went to check on Mary to see if she was still asleep, but she wasn't there. I looked around the house, called her name a few times, then remembered that she'd said something the night before about doing some shopping on Sunday. I checked the garage, and her car was gone. So, I figured she'd gone to the mall."

"What about your kids?"

"They both spent the night at friends' houses. Tyler came home around noon on Sunday. Kelsey showed up around two, I think."

"And when your wife didn't come home?"

"I was a little worried at first, but then I thought she must have picked up a trip."

"How would she do that? Go about picking up a trip."

"Call crew scheduling and see if they needed someone. Flight attendants bid for certain schedules each month. My wife usually bids schedules that have about four three-day trips a month, then drops two or three of them because she doesn't want to work that much. Lately, though, we've been a little strapped—I lost my job a month ago—so she's been flying more, either her full schedule or picking up a trip here and there."

"But you don't think she did that."

"The longest trip she could pick up is three days. Which means she would have been home Tuesday. And she didn't take her suitcase. I hadn't even noticed, but my daughter did."

"So, if she'd taken a trip, she should have been back by Tuesday." He paused. "Today's Thursday." Logic said I'd been remarkably calm all week under the circumstances. I hadn't panicked and gone running to the police because I was sure she would come back with some rational explanation, and I would have ended up with egg on my face looking like the boy who cried "Wolf!" But it sure sounded fishy when he said it. He waited expectantly.

"When she didn't come home, I called all her friends, at least all the ones I could think of. I thought maybe she was upset about something and was at a friend's while she worked it out."

"Were you and your wife having problems?"

I felt a flush creep up my neck and into my face. "I don't know. I wouldn't say problems, exactly." Judging from his expression, my waffling wasn't convincing. I searched for the right words. "Look, we've been married for twenty years. We've been through rough patches—everybody does—but nothing we couldn't work out. So, no, I wouldn't say we had problems. No more than most couples, I wouldn't think."

"But you thought she might be staying with a friend to work something out?" Why did everything sound more incriminating somehow when he repeated it back to me?

"I didn't know what else to do. She hadn't called. She couldn't be on a trip. I was really starting to worry."

"What else did you do?"

"Called her mother. First thing this morning. She hasn't heard from Mary. I thought maybe there'd been a family emergency. But even then, you'd think she would have called."

"You'd think so," he said slowly. He looked at me for a moment as if trying to make up his mind about something. Then he took a deep breath, blew it out and looked down at the clipboard balanced on one wide thigh.

"Okay, Mr. Holm, let's get some basic information and go from there." He picked up a pen in his right hand and held it poised over the form on the clipboard. "Your wife's full name?" I answered a litany of questions, giving him a physical description and a promise to bring in a recent photo, our address, the make and license number of Mary's car, what she'd most likely taken with

her. All I could think of was her purse, which I did my
best to describe. I watched him write it all down, seeing
only the top of his bald head as he bent over the form.
When he finished, he straightened, thumbed open the
clip, slid the pen under it and gently released it, pinning
the pen to the report. He gazed at the display case over
my right shoulder and stroked the mustache on either
side of his mouth with a thumb and forefinger.

"All right, here's what we're going to do," he said
finally, turning to look at me. "We'll get an APB with
a description of your wife's car out to the King County
Sheriff's office and the state police right away, so they
can keep an eye out for it. Then we'll check with area
hospitals to see if anyone matching your wife's description has been admitted in the past four days. Once I've
gotten the ball rolling here, I'll stop by your house, if
that's all right, and get that photo. I want to get an in-
teragency e-mail out with that and your wife's description as soon as possible."

I nodded. "Of course."

"While I'm there, maybe you can give me a list of
the friends and family members you've already called,
as well as anyone else you can think of she might have
talked to or gone to see."

"Why people I've already called?" I was confused.

He gave me an impassive look before answering. "If
your wife doesn't want to talk to you for some reason,
Mr. Holm, then she could have convinced friends to
cover for her. They'll be less likely to do that if they
know we're involved."

"Oh. That makes sense." I paused. "So, what should
I do?"

"Go home. Put that list together for me, and try not

to worry." He gave me a reassuring look that didn't do much to ease my fears.

"Okay. Well, thanks. How soon should I expect you?"

"Give me about an hour. Oh, and if you could, try to find the name and number of your wife's supervisor at work. We'll want to follow up there, too, just in case."

"All right." I hesitated, but he didn't say anything more. "I guess I'll see you in an hour or so, then." I turned to go.

"Hang in there, Mr. Holm," he called after me. "She'll turn up."

THE SILENCE ASSAILED me as soon as I set foot in the house, making me pull up short in the laundry room. I cocked my head to listen, and gradually the house's background noises registered one by one—the whirr of the furnace fan, the low hum of the refrigerator, the creak of hinges on the fireplace screen as gusts of wind found their way down the chimney. I moved slowly and quietly into the kitchen, then into the front hall. Everything felt familiar yet strangely out of place. The house had never felt so empty, as if the rooms had been stripped bare of furnishings. I looked around, seeing prints and paintings on the wall, knickknacks on the tables, furniture as if for the first time. Maybe I was the one thing out of place, or maybe the house just missed Mary's presence. I shook off the feeling and went to the den to work.

The sound of the doorbell sometime later interrupted me, and I looked at my watch, surprised to see that an hour had passed. The bell rang again. I hurried to the door. On the other side of the panel of leaded glass framing the door, a man on the stoop angled a look at the front yard. I swung open the door and he turned toward the sound.

"Is this a good time?" he said.

"Detective. Right on schedule. Sure. Come in." He wiped his feet on the mat and stepped past me into the front hall, eyes quickly taking everything in, including pairs of boots and shoes lined up on a mat inside the door. He picked up one foot and bent over, reaching for the heel of one of his expensive-looking loafers.

"You don't have to take your shoes off," I said quickly. We noticed soon after moving that a lot of people in the Northwest remove their shoes at the door. It had more to do with the wet weather than copying Japanese custom. I discovered I liked walking around the house in socks, rather than shoes, but it wasn't a rule we enforced.

"Nice place." He swiveled, took another look around, then turned to me and smiled. "Would you mind if I took a tour?" It seemed an odd request, but his interest seemed genuine.

"Sure. Be happy to show you around." I couldn't think of a reason not to. I pointed out the living room next to us, and he poked his head in. I led the way upstairs, first to the kids' rooms, where he stopped just inside the door and looked around, hands clasped behind his back. I mumbled an apology about the mess. He waved it off with some comment about kids being kids. In the master bedroom, he followed me inside and turned a small circle. He let out a low whistle when he saw the jetted tub through the bathroom door, and walked in to take a closer look. I followed. He rotated once, then stepped into the walk-in closet. Raising a hand, he trailed sausage-shaped fingers across the clothing hung along one side—Mary's clothes.

"Must be nice having this kind of space." He turned and walked past me. There was no note of envy in his voice. "Seems to be the one thing you can't have too much of." He grinned.

"I guess we're lucky we get any closet space at all."

He chuckled. "Don't I know it." I was willing to bet, judging from his taste in clothes, that closet space was split more evenly between the sexes in his house than in mine. I led the way back downstairs and walked him through the rest of house—dining room, kitchen, laundry room, family room, another bathroom. He paused in the family room to look at a collection of framed family photos in a bookshelf, examining them slowly without comment. We ended up in the den.

He looked around appraisingly. "So, you work out of the house now?"

"Since I got laid off, yes." I motioned toward a chair and sat at the desk. "The job market is so tough, I figured my chances were better if I just did my own thing. Can I get you anything? Something to drink?"

"No, thanks, I'm fine." He held up a hand, palm out, then put it on his knee. "What kind of work are you in?"

"Marketing communications."

"Advertising? That sort of thing?"

"Just about everything except advertising. Promotion, public relations, sales literature, trade shows, sales training…" I let my voice trail off, hoping he didn't want more explanation.

He nodded, apparently satisfied. "Business good?"

"Considering I'm just getting started, not bad."

"Well, I don't want to keep you. We've both got work to do, I'm sure. Did you have a chance to find a photo and put that list together?" I faced the desk, picked up both of the things he asked for and swiveled back. He slid a palm under my outstretched hand and waited. I placed them on his hand. He pulled his arm back and studied the photo on top. It was a snapshot of Mary I'd taken a couple of years before. We'd taken Kelsey, Tyler and three of Kelsey's close friends to Ocean Shores for the weekend to celebrate Kelsey's thirteenth birthday. I reserved two suites in a hotel on the beach, one for the girls and one for Mary, Ty and me. On our second afternoon, I caught Mary unaware while we walked the beach. She stood at the water's edge where the waves dissipated to little more than a line of froth that rolled up and down the sand. She was looking out to sea, the afternoon sun lighting her face. Her long auburn hair waved in the strong breeze like tongues of flame against the clear blue sky. Her features were relaxed save for the hint of a smile. I hadn't seen her look that happy, or beautiful, for a long time.

"Good-looking woman," Mankiewicz said. "Do you have an envelope I can put these in? Don't want them to get messed up."

"Sure. Sorry." I turned back to the desk and dug a big manila envelope out of a drawer.

He lifted the flap with one hand and slid the paper and photo off his open hand into the envelope. Then he stood. "We'll get this out right away, and I'll start looking into this list." He turned for the door, and I followed him out. On his way down the front steps he said he'd be in touch. I had the fleeting feeling of being dismissed from a doctor's office after a thorough exam and then being told to wait until test results were back before getting a prognosis.

"FAMILY MEETING," I said at dinner that night.

The three of us sat at the kitchen table. I'd put a piece

of salmon on the grill, tossed a salad, steamed some broccoli and made a small pot of rice. Tyler had said "yuck" to the salmon and broccoli, but said he'd have some salad. Kelsey had turned up her nose at the salad and vegetable, but said she'd have a bite of salmon and some rice. Instead of telling them to eat or go hungry, I ended up making a grilled cheese for Tyler and nuking some frozen peas for Kelsey.

"How long is this gonna take?" Kelsey asked anxiously. "We have to leave for dance in, like, ten minutes."

"I know. It won't take long."

"So, what's up, Dad?" Tyler said brightly. The uneasiness in his eyes belied his tone. Family meetings were usually called to talk about something serious.

"I didn't want you guys to worry, but I don't know where Mom is."

"She should be back by now, huh?" Tyler said.

Kelsey was silent.

"Yes, she should be back by now. At least she should have called. I've been checking with all her friends, but nobody's seen her."

"How about Gamma?" Tyler asked. "Maybe she went to Gamma's house."

I shook my head. "I thought of that, too. I spoke with Gamma this morning, and she says she hasn't talked to Mom in a while. So, today I went to the police to see if they can help."

"The cops are going to be out looking for Mom?" Tyler's eyes widened. "Cool!"

"What did you do to her?" Kelsey finally said. The accusation in her voice and her eyes stunned me.

"What do you mean? I didn't do anything to her."

"She wouldn't just leave us. You must have made

her mad, or something." Her voice rose, and I could see tears in her eyes.

"Kelsey." I made an effort to keep my voice calm and low. "Honestly, I don't know where Mom went or why. She said she was going shopping on Sunday. That's all I know. Now, I'm worried."

"You sure haven't been acting like it." She was still on the verge of tears, but her eyes flashed with anger, too.

"Of course I'm worried. I have been all week. I've been doing everything I can to find her. I just didn't want you guys to get scared." But now they were. I could see it in their faces. Tyler's brave front was crumbling, and Kelsey's anger evaporated as quickly as it had formed.

"You think something's happened to her." Kelsey looked as if she didn't want to know.

"I'm sure she's fine, wherever she is." I tried to sound reassuring. "If she'd been in an accident, someone would have called us."

"If she's okay, then why do you want the police looking for her?" Ty asked in a small voice.

"Because they might be able to help find her faster. There are lots of policemen, and they can look all over the place. It would take me forever to look everywhere they can."

"Oh." He thought about it for a minute. "You're not gonna have her arrested?"

"No, kiddo," I said gently. "Of course not. Why would they arrest her?"

"Well, if I ran away, I bet I'd get grounded. I thought maybe when grown-ups run away they get arrested."

"She didn't run away, stupid," Kelsey said vehemently. "She wouldn't do that to us." She looked warily at me for confirmation.

I managed a half-smile. "She's probably taking a little vacation. Sitting on a beach somewhere thinking how nice it is not to have to cook and do laundry for ungrateful children." I reached over and tickled Ty in the ribs. I knew better than to initiate physical contact with Kelsey. She was still at an awkward age when even hugs for anyone but girlfriends were rare. Instead, I gave her a smile while Ty tried to wrestle my arm away so she would feel included. She still didn't look altogether convinced things would turn out all right, but her eyes were dry.

"Come on, Dad. I'm gonna be late." She got up from the table and took her plate to the sink.

CONCENTRATION WAS NEXT to impossible. Friday had rolled around already, nearly a week since everything had changed. Thoughts of Mary kept popping into my head. *Where is she?* Had she been harboring the same dark fantasies I had? Had she imagined a life without me and found it attractive enough to try on, like a designer outfit she really didn't need? Could she be that bold? I'd admitted to myself, even to Sarah, that thoughts of a life without her had crossed my mind. But maybe a passing phase, a rut, a rough patch was at the root of that sort of reverie. I was certain, however, that I didn't have the stones to just walk away. Did she? *Stop it!* I forced myself to focus on work. Every time Mary's face swam into view or I found myself staring out the window, I shook it off and redirected my attention to the tasks at hand. I wrote copy, had a phone conference with a graphic designer, discussed a cocktail reception menu with a caterer, and called for competitive prices from several suppliers of promotional products.

It seemed like only moments later that Tyler came bounding in the house with his usual bellow of greeting, followed by a thud of the front door solid enough to rattle the windows. That someone so small could have such boundless energy never ceased to amaze me. I tidied up my desk and went to meet him in the kitchen where he helped himself to a snack. When he finished, we organized his things for his sleepover at Rory's. He picked out jeans and T-shirt for the next day. I made sure he had clean underwear and socks, a toothbrush, an oversized T-shirt to sleep in and his soccer gear. We stuffed it all in a duffel, and headed for the garage.

"Hey, don't forget to call me tonight," I told Ty when we pulled up in front of the Thorvahls' house.

"How come?" He looked surprised.

"'Cause I'll miss you too much without a goodnight call." I smiled and tousled his hair.

"Yeah, right." He grinned and hopped out, dragging the duffel behind him.

"I'll see you at the game tomorrow," I called after him as he ran up to the door.

My cell phone rang on the way home—Kelsey, looking for a ride. I detoured to the high school. She waited for me outside the gym, purse and book bag in one hand, nylon duffel in team colors in the other. She got in, a little breathless, and told me she had to get home to change into her cheer squad uniform for a game later.

When we pulled into the garage, Kelsey hauled her bags out of the van after her and raced into the house. By the time I got into the kitchen, I heard dull thumps through the ceiling as she banged around upstairs. I opened the refrigerator and a couple of cupboards,

checking their contents, weighing the choices. I glanced
at my watch. Plenty of time. I pulled leftovers from the
refrigerator. Fifteen minutes later, a batch of fried rice
warmed in the electric wok. I cored and sliced an apple
and put it on a plate, then set a place at the counter.

Kelsey flounced into the kitchen another twenty minutes after that dressed in a short pleated maroon-and-
white skirt and matching top, a bulky hooded white
sweatshirt over one arm. The sweatshirt had the school
insignia over the left breast and the name "HOLM"
stenciled on the back. She slid onto a stool.

"You look great," I said, dishing up a plate and set-
ting it on the counter in front of her.

She gave a little toss of her head, and one corner of
her mouth turned up at the compliment. Her hair was
the same deep auburn as her mother's, but she used an
iron to take all of the waviness out of it. She'd pulled
it straight back into a ponytail, but long tendrils with
reddish highlights fell on either side of her face. She'd
obviously spent time putting on her face, too. I still
thought she went too heavy on the eyeliner, but the rest
of it looked as if applied by a pro.

"So, are you spending the night at Amanda's?"

She stopped chewing long enough to reply through
a mouthful of food. "I don't know yet."

"You'll let me know?" She nodded and kept chewing.

After I dropped Kelsey off, I returned home for the
fourth time that day. The house was quiet, and I was all
too aware that I avoided thinking of anything to do with
Mary. My head hurt from all the unanswered questions.
I plopped into a chair in front of the television and let
the electronic images work their narcotic effect.

At ten-thirty, the phone rang. I roused myself from

my TV-induced stupor and hopped into the kitchen, one leg half-asleep, to grab it on the third ring. It was Ty. I asked him if he was having fun, what he'd been doing and what he'd had for dinner. After a few minutes of digging for teeth, I said goodnight and asked him to put his sister on the phone.

"She's not here," he said.

"Are you sure? Is Amanda home?"

"I dunno. Hang on." There was a bang in my ear as he dropped the receiver on a hard surface, the muffled sound of his voice calling Amanda's name growing more distant. It was a minute or two before someone picked up the phone again.

"Yeah, she's here," Ty said. "You wanna talk to her?"

"No, Ty. Put Rory's mom on the phone, would you?" I waited another minute until she got on. "Hey, Sue, Ty tells me that Amanda's there, but Kelsey's not with her. Didn't she come over to spend the night?"

"Gosh, I don't think so. Let me check." Again, muffled sounds, this time as if Sue had put her hand over the mouthpiece. Then she was back. "Amanda says Kelsey's not staying over."

"Well, she isn't here. If Amanda's home, the game's over, I take it. Could you ask Amanda if she knows anything else? Maybe who Kelsey was with?"

"Of course." She sounded concerned.

A different voice got on the phone. "Mr. Holm, I saw Kelsey at the end of the game to see if she was going to come over. She said she wanted to stay home tonight. So I asked if she wanted a ride, but she said she already had one."

"Do you know who with, Amanda?"

"No, but I saw her leaving the game with a couple

of guys we know. They might have stopped in town for something to eat first."

"I suppose. Who were they? These guys aren't in your class, are they? They can't be, if they're driving."

"Well, yeah. It was Roy and Bobby."

"Roy and Bobby who?"

"Roy Jensen and Bobby Givens. They're both juniors."

"And completely honorable, no doubt."

She didn't miss the sarcasm. "They're good guys, Mr. Holm. Kelsey's fine."

I sighed. "I'm sure you're right, Amanda. Thanks for letting me know."

"Jack?" Sue came back on the line. "Sounds like Kelsey went out with a couple of kids. She'll probably be home any minute."

"Probably. Hey, thanks for the help." I hung up, rationalizing my fears. I was overreacting. But Kelsey didn't come home in a few minutes, or a few minutes after that. Curfew came and found me pacing the floor, willing the phone to ring. Determined not to panic, I forced myself to sit and watch the news. When the sports segment wrapped up, though, it reminded me that another half hour had passed without any word. I paced some more, took deep breaths and made myself sit down again and be numbed by bad jokes and celebrity patter on a late-night talk show.

When the phone's ring jarred me, I didn't know whether to feel relieved or angry. I snatched it up and barked, "Where are you?" Silence answered me. Then a man's voice said, "You have something I want. Have you found it?"

"Who is this?" A chill ran through me. The Asian accent—I'd heard the voice before. "What do you want?"

For a moment he didn't reply, and I thought he'd hung up, a wrong number again. But what he said next made my blood run even colder.

"When you find what is mine tell no one, if you value your children."

"Who are you?" I demanded. "You've got the wrong number, whoever you are. I don't know what you're talking about. If you don't stop calling, I'll have the police trace your calls." I heard a soft click, and the line went dead. I checked caller ID—a blocked number again. Frantic, I dialed Kelsey's cell phone. No answer. I forced myself to take a deep breath. The caller had dialed the wrong number, surely. Whatever the man wanted, I certainly didn't have it. His barely veiled threat concerned someone else's children, had been intended to motivate—or panic—someone else, not me. What could he have lost that would make him use that sort of coercion? I shivered. And worried some more.

The clock read close to midnight when I heard the back door open. Kelsey came into the family room, face flushed, eyes round and bright, smiling with excitement.

"You are so grounded," I said in a low voice.

She stopped dead in her tracks, saw the storm clouds in my face. Her smile disappeared. "Why?" Her head swiveled as she looked around the room, searching for something unseen. "It's not that late, is it?"

"It's an hour past curfew. Nearly midnight, young lady. I've been worried to death."

"But my curfew is eleven-thirty." All wide-eyed innocence.

"Since when?" Her deflective maneuver almost worked, but I shook my head and went on before she could answer.

"Doesn't matter. You're still late. You didn't call to

let me know where you were. You didn't answer your phone. You didn't ask permission to go out in the first place." I ticked off her transgressions on my fingers. "Where the hell were you?"

"But we didn't do anything." Her voice and posture took on a defensive tone. "Honest! All we did was go to town and get a drink at McDonald's."

I shook my head. "I don't care. You should have called. You blew it."

"Da-ad!" Whiny this time, and her eyes filled with tears.

I held up a hand. "I don't want to hear it. I can't believe you did that after what's happened this week. Your mother disappears without a word, and you think I'm not going to worry when you don't show up by curfew?" I said nothing about the strange phone call, about how it had amplified my fears. "What on earth were you thinking?" My voice rose as the words tumbled out until I nearly shouted.

Kelsey shrank under the onslaught, and tears trickled silently down her cheeks. "I'm sorry! Dad, please, I'm sorry." The plaintiveness in her voice brought me back to my senses and instantly filled me with shame. I had good cause to be stern. But the fear on her face reflected pent-up anger and frustration and concern that had festered inside me for far longer than the past week. I let out my breath, and the rage slowly drained away, leaving me feeling hollow and slack.

"I'm sorry, too," I mumbled. "You should have called. Now go to bed." She sobbed and turned away, glancing at me tearfully over her shoulder as she left.

FIVE

KELSEY lay on her side, a knee drawn up, one hand tucked under her cheek, the other curled around a small plush Snoopy doll, the last of her stuffed animal collection. The sheet and blanket were tangled up between her legs—one was under the covers, the drawn-up leg on top. Long-legged blue plaid flannel pajama bottoms and a white cotton tank top apparently kept her warm enough. Her face was slack in sleep and devoid of makeup. *There's the little girl I've been missing.* I reached down and gently nudged her bare shoulder.

"Come on, Kels," I said softly. "Time to get up." I nudged some more.

She yawned and stretched, then slowly opened her eyes, squinting against the bright light of day. "What time is it?"

"It's eight." I'd already been up for two hours, having spent another mostly sleepless night unable to stop the random firing of synapses in my brain. As if infected with some computer virus, tens of thousands of half-formed thoughts streaked through the neural pathways until they fizzled and faded scant seconds later, doing nothing but hogging processing power and memory. Once up, I shuffled three miles at a slow jog through the early morning air, noting its crispness, the changing colors of the leaves. The long days of summer had somehow slipped past without notice. Where had I been?

"But it's Saturday," she protested sleepily.

"Come on, get up," I said more firmly. "Let's go. We're going to meet your brother at his soccer game this morning." She came fully awake and now looked at me askance. "No arguments," I said. "Get dressed, get your bed made and your room cleaned up, then come down for breakfast." She rolled out of bed without saying anything, but I had a feeling that she mentally conjured exotic ways to do me in. Thirty minutes later, she stepped charily into the kitchen, glancing at me from under her eyebrows with head bowed. She shuffled to the cupboard. I kept my head down, my eyes on a magazine, and listened to the sounds of a cereal bowl and box being pulled from the cupboards, the sliding of a drawer and clank of a spoon, the soft sucking pop of the refrigerator door opening, and then the tinkle of dry cereal being poured into the bowl followed by the splash of milk. Out of the corner of my eye I saw her carry the bowl to the kitchen table and sit down. We pretended to ignore each other, but stole covert glances—cold war tactics—each acutely aware of the other's presence. She still nursed hurt feelings, I imagined, and I still tended embers of slow-burning anger because she had compounded the worry Mary already put me through.

I excused myself and went up to brush my teeth and take away the bitter taste of too much coffee. On my way downstairs, I poked my head into Kelsey's room. She'd made the bed neatly, picked her clothes up off the floor. Pleasantly surprised, my disposition suddenly softened. *She's a good kid. Give her a break.*

I walked to the bed and straightened a pillow. My fingers bumped the edge of something hard beneath it. Curious, I lifted a corner, revealing a small framed picture of Mary, a good one taken at a picnic the summer before. She laughed at something unseen or an unheard joke. I smiled at the memory and touched a finger to her cheek. The feel of cool glass under my finger dispelled the reverie like someone brushing aside a cobweb. I glanced over my shoulder, then quickly put the pillow in place.

In the kitchen, Kelsey had finished her cereal and put her dishes in the dishwasher. The table and counters were clean. I paused to admire her efforts.

"Thank you," I said. She shrugged, the first sign of détente. "You just about ready to go?" She shrugged again. So, okay, it also took some time before the Berlin Wall came down.

WE RETURNED HOME from soccer triumphant. Ty's team, the "Red Demons," had come out on top 3–2 against the opposing "Jaguars." On the way, Ty couldn't stop reliving the game, excitedly giving us a play-by-play, drawing us in with his infectious enthusiasm. I'd never seen him so talkative. High on adrenaline, he rolled from one story to the next almost seamlessly, like a well-edited highlights reel. Just when I thought he was winding down, he'd say, "Oh, oh, remember when…?" and off he went again. Even Kelsey got caught up in his high spirits, encouraging him, prompting his recollections with color commentary of her own. I didn't tell him that the most exciting part of the game wasn't his play, which was brilliant of course, but the moment the referee tossed Alex's mom from the game for arguing a call. After two warnings, the ref had given Alex a red card. When Angela got in his face about it, he sent her packing.

We pulled into the garage singing an impromptu fight

song, and tromped into the house like a college march-ing band. Once inside, we broke ranks. Ty raced up-stairs to change out of his soccer gear. I called after him and reminded him to bring his dirty uniform back down to the laundry. Kelsey wandered off to the family room to boot up the computer and check e-mail. I gravitated toward the kitchen, thinking I should probably put to-gether a grocery list.

Ty stormed into the family room a few minutes later and stomped up to Kelsey. "Stop messing with my stuff," he said.

"You've been in my room again." He glared.

"What are you talking about, squirt?" She didn't bother looking at him. "I wouldn't be caught dead in your room. I might get fleas, or lice or something."

I threw a warning shot across her bow. "Kels."

"If it wasn't you, then who was it, huh?" Tyler went on doggedly. "Dad wouldn't mess with my stuff."

"I didn't go in your room, Ty, honest." Kelsey's tone now sounded mollifying, and her face lost its belliger-ence. "Show me what happened. Maybe we can figure out what's going on." Her change in attitude almost to-tally defused him. It certainly surprised me. I wondered when my daughter had suddenly become so skilled at conflict resolution. Kelsey followed Ty out of the room. I shook my head and decided not to question good for-tune. A few moments later, though, I heard Ty's voice call me from upstairs. "Dad?"

"What's up?" I responded loudly. I didn't move, still holding out hope that they wouldn't suck me in.

"Dad?" Kelsey's voice this time. "I think you better come up here." So much for diplomacy. It sounded like they needed mediation. I sighed. I hated being the ar-biter of whose feelings had been hurt worse or who had committed the bigger transgression. I walked heavily up the stairs. Kelsey stood in the hall outside Ty's door with her arms crossed, watching me approach. Ty stood behind her in the middle of his room looking around.

"What seems to be the problem?"

"I tried to explain that it wasn't me," Kelsey said with exaggerated patience.

"Ty?" I called through the doorway.

"I don't know, Dad." He looked perplexed. "My stuff's all messed up."

"Is anything missing?"

"I don't think so."

"Then it's probably just your imagination."

"I'm not so sure," Kelsey said, coming up behind me. "Come look." I followed her to her room, curious. She walked into the center of the room. I stopped in the doorway.

"See?" She moved her arm in a sweeping motion. "Same thing as Ty. Everything's been messed up."

"Sweetie, it looks the same as it did before we left for soccer. I know because I looked to see if you'd made your bed like I asked you to."

"No, Dad. It *looks* the same, but everything is just a little different."

"Different how?"

"Well, like things have been moved. Well, not moved, exactly, but like picked up and put down again, but not quite in the exact same position. I don't know how to explain it." A shadow flitted through my head like a fast-flying bird, too quick to identify. Reflexively, I turned my head, then chided myself for being paranoid. "Pretty good, you guys," I said, smiling. "That's a good goof. You had me going."

"I'm serious, Dad." Kelsey's solemn expression didn't crack.

"No joke, Dad," Ty called from his room.

"Same thing, then, Kels—is anything missing?"

"Well, no," she admitted.

"Then I think you guys are dreaming. Nobody was here, or they would have taken stuff."

"Maybe it was a ghost," Ty said, coming up the hall.

"Maybe," I conceded. "In that case, I hope you sleep okay tonight." He shivered. "Well, that's the only explanation. As long as nothing's missing, I wouldn't worry about it. Okay?" I waited until they both acknowledged me. They seemed all right. I turned and went back downstairs. For the heck of it, I toured the downstairs rooms slowly, taking inventory. Nothing appeared missing. Everything seemed to be in its place. My kids had imagined it. But when I got to the den I had the strangest feeling that someone had been in there. It was hard to tell. The den wasn't messy so much as it was cluttered. With so many things going on at once, I tended not to put things away but organized projects in piles— on the desk, the bookshelves, the filing cabinet, even the floor. Like Kelsey, I felt rather than saw differences in the placement of things—a stack of computer discs on the desk that seemed to be turned at a slight angle, a file folder just a hair away from where it had been, the desk lamp a tad off center. But maybe the strange phone call the night before had given me the notion that someone had searched the house.

I shook my head, conjuring up a mental image of the last time I'd been in the office, then blinked a few times and looked again. All my stuff was there. I couldn't think of anything that wasn't where I'd left it. My gaze fell on a framed photo of Mary and me celebrating our fifteenth anniversary on a beach in the Caribbean. It sat in its usual spot on a shelf over the desk.

"You're nuts," I said aloud, to convince myself. Without thinking, I reached over and repositioned the photo a fraction to the left.

THE REST OF the weekend was a blur of grocery shopping, housecleaning, yard work, cooking, spending time with the kids, and even trying to put some time in on the article I owed Terry McAuley. By Sunday evening, I was bushed, but content, satisfied with all I'd accomplished. *Superdad strikes again. Take that, Gloria Steinem.* I finally took a moment to sit and read the Sunday paper in the family room where Ty watched TV.

Ty jumped to his feet at the bong of the doorbell, and raced for the door. "I got it," he called as he disappeared.

I followed slowly, uncomfortable with the idea of him opening the door to a stranger, but I arrived too late. By the time I made it to the front hall, the door stood open wide. Ty stared open-mouthed at whoever stood across the threshold.

"Is your dad home?" a deep voice asked. Ed Mankiewicz stuck his shiny pate through the doorway and looked toward me.

"Come in," I offered. He took a step inside. Ty hadn't moved or changed expression. "This is my son, Tyler," I told him. "Ty, this is Detective Mankiewicz." Ty swallowed hard and blinked, seeming to remember himself.

"How d'you do?" he said politely, putting out his hand.

Mankiewicz smiled and bent forward, engulfing Ty's hand with one that looked the size of a catcher's mitt in comparison. "Nice to meet you." He straightened and turned to me with an apologetic look. "I'm sorry to bother you, especially at this time of night on a Sunday. Would you mind coming down to the department for a few minutes?" Something was wrong. My stomach churned with sudden fear. I couldn't let Ty see it. I put a hand on his shoulder. The warm feel of his small bones under my big hand calmed me, giving me the strength to keep my expression relaxed, pleasant.

"I'm not sure." I hesitated. "I'd hate to leave Ty here by himself."

"This won't take long." I looked at Ty, torn between concern for him and a desire to placate authority.

"Will you be all right here by yourself, big guy?"

"Dad," he said, flushing, "I'll be fine."

"Lock the doors behind me, okay? And if Kelsey calls, tell her I'm on my way." I turned to Mankiewicz. "Okay if I follow you in my car so I can pick up my daughter from church on the way home?" He nodded.

I grabbed a jacket from the front hall closet and followed Mankiewicz out onto the stoop, then turned to close the door. "Remember to lock it," I told Ty as I pulled it shut. "Love you." I joined Mankiewicz on the driveway. "So, what's going on?" I dreaded his answer.

"Just a few things I wanted to clear up." My brow furrowed. I didn't feel right about leaving Ty alone at night just to go clear some things up. Mankiewicz must have sensed my reluctance.

"I'm afraid I have some bad news," he said. "I didn't want to say anything in front of your son. Best we talk about it at the department."

The words stunned me. "Is it Mary? Has she been in an accident?"

"Not exactly." He hesitated. "Let's talk about it at the station." For a moment I was speechless, unable to move. *Oh, God, she's left me. She wants a divorce.* I didn't want to consider it might be something worse.

"I DON'T UNDERSTAND." I sat at a metal table in an interview room. Mankiewicz and I had arrived almost simultaneously at the city hall parking lot. He'd led me inside the public safety department and swiped his ID badge on one of the security pads to gain access to the inner sanctum. Instead of taking me to his office, however, he'd brought me here, and I didn't know why. The room was devoid of furniture save the table and two other chairs besides mine. The shiny beige tile floor reflected the white glare of the fluorescent lights in the dropped ceiling. On TV a rectangular two-way mirror would be set into one wall. These walls were solid.

"This is a better place to talk," he said. "It sometimes gets a little noisy out there. Can I get you something to drink? Coffee, or a soda?"

"No, thanks." I shook my head, still confused. I swallowed hard and realized that my mouth was dry as a bone. "On second thought, a glass of water would be great if you have it."

"Sure. Be right back." He stepped out into the hall, leaving me alone with a head full of half-formed thoughts and images swimming in and out of view like fish darting through coral. Before I could hook one long enough to get a sense of it he came back with a plastic cup of water from a cooler in the hall. A tall, solidly built man who looked to be in his thirties joined him. He wore the uniform of a King County Sheriff's deputy. He took a seat without a word, opened a spiral-bound notebook and set it on the table. I eyed him, curious.

"This is Officer Talbot," Mankiewicz said with a gesture toward the deputy. "He's been helping out in the investigation." He handed me the plastic cup.

I gave Mankiewicz a nod of thanks and took a sip of the water. "You said you had bad news?" I said when the water unglued my tongue.

"I'll get to that," he said gently. "I want to run through some things first, if you don't mind." Apparently, I didn't have a choice. He would have told me right away if she'd been in an accident. This had to be something else. I nodded.

"You said the last time you saw your wife was Sunday?" I looked from Mankiewicz to the sheriff's deputy. They watched me without expression. Somehow it suddenly seemed very important to be sure. I gazed at the table, focusing inward.

"As far as I know, she was sleeping when I went out for a paper Sunday morning." I locked eyes with Mankiewicz. "She wasn't there when I got back."

"What time was that again?"

"Around ten-thirty."

"And you said you got up around seven?" He consulted a note pad on the table.

I nodded. "About. Kitchen clock said seven-sixteen, I think, when I went out for my run."

"What about Saturday night?"

I thought for a moment. "Well, like I told you, the kids were gone, staying with friends. I made some dinner and took a plate up to Mary." His brows knitted, and he put up a hand.

"Where?"

"Our bedroom."

"Why? Was she sick?"

I flushed. "No. Sorry. It's where Mary hangs out. She calls it her 'office.' She likes to sit in bed and read or watch television. She even does all her paperwork there—you know, pay bills, fill out flight reports for work, study for emergency drills, whatever. She's comfortable there."

"So you served her dinner in bed?" He got it, but his face still held disbelief.

"Well, yes." I felt embarrassed under his gaze. I glanced at the silent deputy, but his expression gave nothing away, making me even more uncomfortable.

"Was that a pretty normal occurrence?"

"A few days a week," I admitted. "More often since I've been working at home, but even when I worked downtown, I made dinner when I got home. Even if Mary didn't have to work, she was usually pretty tired from running the kids around, so I'd bring her dinner upstairs." I shrugged, as if it wasn't anything unusual for a doting husband. Most seem to have trouble serving their wives breakfast in bed once a year.

"What did you have?"

"For dinner?" I had to stop and think. "I just kept it simple. I remember I didn't feel much like cooking. Let's see…grilled chicken, some plain pasta and a vegetable. Green beans."

"Anything else?" He raised an eyebrow.

What was this, a cooking show? I bit back my irritation. "I had a beer. Mary had wine." Maybe a little too much wine, but I tried not to count anymore.

"When was this?"

"I don't know. Late. We didn't eat until after nine. Might have been closer to ten."

"Okay, so what did you do then?"

"Read a magazine. Watched some television."

"Did you see your wife again that evening?"

I looked at him, puzzled. "Well, sure. I went up a

while later to get her plate and see if she wanted anything else. And she was there when I went up to bed, around eleven-thirty. She'd already fallen asleep, but she was there."

"Nothing was out of the ordinary? You didn't argue or get into a fight? Anything like that?"

"No. Why?" I felt my heart starting to race, and the room seemed warmer. "What's going on, anyway? Is she leaving me? Is that what this is about?"

"Leaving you?" he echoed. "Why would you think that?"

"I don't know." I squirmed in my seat. "You said it was bad news, and she's gone, for one. Like I said, things haven't been as good as they could be between us. But I figured it was just a rough spot we'd get over. Maybe she was more unhappy than I thought." My voice trailed off.

He held his gaze a moment longer, then seemed to make up his mind about something. "A King County Sheriff's deputy found your wife's car earlier today. It was abandoned in the woods off the road, out past North Bend."

"Mary… Was she…?" He held up a hand, cutting off my questions. I looked to the uniformed officer, but he said nothing, apparently deferring to Mankiewicz.

"The Sheriff's department called in the state patrol and got a pretty big team out there to conduct a search," he went on. "Your wife was found in a shallow grave nearby. I'm sorry, Mr. Holm, but she's dead." He spoke calmly, quietly, as if having a normal conversation. I heard the words, but part of me wasn't sure I heard them correctly. Another part of me found the news strangely unsurprising, as if I'd been steeling myself for something like this ever since she'd disappeared. But nothing prepared me for words like that, and nothing describes what it felt like to hear them. The concept was so over-whelming, so unimaginable, so horrific, that it was like receiving a massive wound, like having my legs blown off by a landmine. The shock simply numbed me. I saw everything around me with crystal clarity, heard the rasp of my breathing, smelled the sharpness of my own sweat and a lingering trace of the deputy's citrusy-sweet cologne wafting across the table. I tasted an acrid bitterness in the back of my throat. But I couldn't feel anything. As if I was cocooned in layers of cotton.

I worked my mouth until words finally came out. "Dead? How…?" Mankiewicz kept his face impassive, but his eyes flicked across my features.

"We're not sure yet what happened. Your wife was assaulted. That much is obvious. Do you know anyone who would want to hurt her?"

"Hurt her?" I repeated. "She was killed? No, I don't know anyone who would want to hurt her, let alone kill her. My God!" I heard my voice turn shrill. I slumped in my seat and took a breath to stop my heart from pound-ing. "I can't believe this," I muttered.

"Believe it," he said. "We found her purse still in the car, but no cash, no driver's license or credit cards. We did find an airline ID." He opened a manila envelope that lay on the table and shook the contents into his hand, extracting a plastic ID card. He handed it across the table. I looked at it. It was an old, expired photo ID. She had a newer one in her uniform purse.

"Are you sure it's her?" I turned the ID over in my fingers. Without answering, he lifted a corner of the note pad on the table, revealing a Polaroid photo. He slid the photo across the table until it was positioned in front of me. I was afraid to look, but I was drawn to it.

It was stomach-turning and morbidly fascinating at the same time.

"Oh, God," I murmured. "Oh, God, no." Mary's face was a ghastly gray pallor in the harsh glare of the camera's flash, shaded with dark bruising and speckled with dirt. Twigs and soil matted her tangled hair. She looked as if she might have been asleep except for that. But the longer I looked, the more obvious it became that the light, the life, had gone out of the person in the photo. The decomposing husk in the photo looked almost nothing like the vibrant, warm woman I'd known. No, things hadn't been good between us lately, but at some point they had been. They must have been. Now we'd never have a chance to find out if we still had something to save.

I averted my eyes. "Oh, man!" My stomach churned, and for a moment I thought I was going to be sick. The deputy wordlessly tipped his chair back, reached into the corner to grab a circular metal wastebasket and shoved it toward my chest. I pushed it away and sucked in some air until the nausea passed. Suddenly, I felt my face screw up, and I couldn't stop the tears from rolling down my cheeks, dampening the collar of my shirt. I swiped at them with the back of my hand.

Mankiewicz pulled the photo away. "Could be she was the victim of a carjacking that went bad somehow. Or it's possible she picked up a hitchhiker. Would she be likely to do that?"

I shook my head, sniffled and said, "No way. She traveled for a living. She was careful."

He shrugged. "I wish we could tell you more, but until we get the autopsy report and finish evaluating the evidence at the scene, we just don't know." I held my head in my hands, trying to keep it from exploding. I couldn't think. I could barely breathe, as if an elephant sat on my chest.

"What do I do now?" I raised my head and looked at him, sure he could see the desperation in my eyes.

"Not much you can do," he said. "Go home and take care of your kids. This is going to be hard on them." A wave of sorrow and desolation for my kids wrung a groan out of me.

"Oh, God, what'll I tell them? How am I going to tell my kids they'll never see her again?" My voice broke as a lump formed in my throat, and tears welled up in my eyes again. They watched me in silence until I swiped my eyes with a sleeve and sat up straight.

"I'm really sorry for your loss, Mr. Holm," the detective said. "I'll let you know as soon as I find out when they're releasing her remains. In the meantime, go home. Call your family and friends. You might want to have someone around to help you go through your wife's affairs and plan a memorial service for her. You know?" As distraught as I was, his calm demeanor made an impression. In his line of work I imagined he'd gotten used to dealing with victims of violent crime. But he couldn't have dealt with that many deaths, could he? Especially murders. I shuddered at the thought of the word. It was surreal, just a bizarre nightmare that would be forgotten once awake. We lived in the suburbs, damn it. It was safe here. People didn't get carjacked, and assaulted—and *killed,* for God's sake—in a place like this.

SIX

"SHE'S DEAD." It sounded as listless and unemotional as I felt.

"Who's dead?" Sarah looked at me in confusion.

"Mary. She's dead."

"You're kidding." I shook my head.

"Oh, my God." Sarah put her hand to her mouth. "I'm so sorry. What happened?"

"She was killed. The police found her. They're not sure what happened. Maybe a robbery." The words came out dully. Just the facts. Some were harder to grasp than others.

"Someone killed her?" She looked aghast, her voice full of disbelief.

I nodded. "Assaulted her and then strangled her."

"Assaulted...you mean raped?"

"Looks like." I had as hard a time getting the words out as I did conceding it was even possible that some stranger had forced himself on my wife and then choked the life out of her with his own hands. I didn't believe a typical thief, or even a carjacker, was capable of that, something Mankiewicz was aware of when he'd told me.

"Don't know yet for sure," I went on, "but from what the police said it seems pretty obvious."

"When did this happen?"

"More than a week ago. Probably the same day she disappeared."

"Oh, Jack, I'm so very sorry for you. It must be awful."

I gave her a wan smile that must have looked like a dreadful rictus. *"Be careful what you wish for, right?"* The words tasted as bitter as they sounded. *"It might come true."* Sarah looked shocked, then concerned.

"No, you didn't wish this on her."

"Sure I did." If I could feel anything, it should have been indignation. *"I wished she was dead."* I shrugged.

"You fantasized what your life would be like if she died," she corrected. Semantics. *"You don't really believe that she's dead because of you, do you?"*

"Be careful what you wish for..." I repeated.

"Seriously."

"All I know is that I didn't just think about it. I wished for it, and it came true."

Sarah gazed at me for a moment. *"How does that make you feel?"* she asked softly.

"It's hard to feel anything. It's like I've been shot up with Novocain everywhere. But if anything, I'm miserable. I feel guilty."

"Why? Isn't this what you wanted?" Ah, reverse psychology.

"Not like this. Maybe if it was her fault, like crashing her car after going out drinking with the girls. Or no one's fault, like cancer. But this...I feel like this is my fault."

"I don't understand. Why? Because you wished her dead? How is this your fault?"

"I don't know. Maybe if I'd done more to figure out what was wrong with us. Maybe she wouldn't have been so unhappy. Maybe she wouldn't have started drinking so much."

"A lot of maybes." She paused. *"What do any of them have to do with how she died?"*

I pondered the question. It was so hard to think. Nothing made sense. *"Nothing,"* I mumbled. Somewhere under there, under all those layers of deadening insulation, was a reason why I felt guilty. I couldn't, or wouldn't, go there. Sarah waited. I didn't say anything more, and she didn't press the point.

"How are you holding up?" she asked gently.

"Not too good." I folded my arms tightly across my chest, as if that would prevent the churning confusion inside me from spilling out like entrails from a gutted fish. *"I can't sleep, but when the alarm goes off I want to pull the covers over my head and stay there."*

"But you don't."

"I can't. The kids...I have to be strong for them. They still need me to get them up and off to school, feed them, take care of them. I figure if I just keep moving, stay busy, maybe I won't think about this nightmare so much."

She nodded. *"Probably a good idea. How are the kids taking it?"*

"How do you think?" I couldn't keep the bite out of my voice.

"They've lost their mother, for chrissake—violently. I think they're terrified. Kelsey's closed up tighter than a clam. She hasn't said a word in three days. Tyler comes into our room—my room—in the middle of the night crying and climbs into bed with me. I'm sure he's having terrible nightmares, though he won't say. And I know he misses his mother terribly. It breaks my heart because I don't know what to do. I don't know what to say."

"Just be there for them."

"But I'm not. I'm so confused by all this I don't know how to be there for them."

"Let them work it out their own way, but let them know they can talk to you when they're ready."

"But what do I talk about? I don't know what I think or what I feel. How am I going to help them deal with their feelings if I can't even deal with my own?"

"You will. Just do the best you can. Love them, and listen to them. That's all you can do." She paused. *"If you want help, you can always bring them in here with you."*

"Family counseling?" She nodded. I fell silent, mulling it over.

MY EARS BURNED. I hooked a finger into the starched collar of my dress shirt and pulled to lessen the discomfort it caused. Voices murmured behind me creating a burbling hum. None were distinct enough to make out the words, but I felt sure the speakers talked about me. I felt their pity roll up behind us and envelop us like a shroud.

I sat at the end of a front-row pew, closest to the aisle. Ty sat next to me, unconsciously aping my attempt to loosen my collar. His other hand, barely visible at the end of a sleeve of a navy blazer a size too big, busily rubbed his leg through the stiff fabric of new slacks.

Kelsey sat on his left, also in new clothes. Her first words of the week complained about not being able to find clothes "cute" enough for the occasion. She'd managed to find a relatively conservative black skirt she grudgingly conceded she might wear in the future, and paired it with a white blouse and black sweater.

Next to her, Kelsey's grandmother posed, solemnly resplendent in a tailored charcoal silk suit. A wide-

brimmed hat and veil in a matching color clouded
Letty's carefully made-up face. It didn't hide the composed expression, though, a perfect combination of
sorrow and stoicism.

On the end sat Mary's echo. Bridget's likeness to
Mary elicited double-takes, but on second glance she
was a funhouse mirror reflection, an odd distortion of
the original. She sat taller, took up more space than
Mary had, with features to match—the same as Mary's,
yet coarser. She tucked a strand of mousy hair a tint
lighter than her sister's into the severe bun she wore
like a cap. With her other hand, she nervously fingered
the lace collar of a plain gray dress of some satiny material that looked as if it had come from a dusty trunk
in someone's attic.

Father Manion appeared through a side door leading from the sacristy. The buzz of conversation quickly
wound down, the sudden hush punctuated by random
coughs. He strode to the center of the sanctuary, white
robes billowing at his ankles with each step. I sat
ramrod straight, eyes front, while he intoned a greeting
and began the service. I let myself be lulled by the fa-
miliarity of the Mass. I understood the appeal of Church
ritual, but I'd never been completely comfortable with
it.

Never a particularly religious person, Mary had insisted that the kids be "brought up Catholic." So I'd
attended, as she had, at Christmas, Easter and the
odd Sunday she felt guilty about not having been in a
while. Now, I found myself moving automatically, sitting, standing, kneeling, mouthing rote responses at the
right times, though barely aware of what was said.

Mary's friend Carmen, who had flown out from Chicago, gave a nice eulogy. She told some short anecdotes

about their exploits in the air that elicited muted, self-conscious chuckles from the assembly behind me.

Cathy Whitman, whom we'd met along with her husband, Bill, when we'd first moved here, got up to say a few words about how generous and involved Mary had been in the community. She noted that in addition to being a busy mom, Mary volunteered for everything from classroom parent to organizing a holiday fashion show to raise funds for the local thrift store.

Bridget represented the family by default. Both Kelsey and Tyler declined to say anything. I couldn't blame them. They were both still in shock, and afraid of breaking down in front of all those people, though they hadn't said so. I couldn't—wouldn't—eulogize the woman I'd spent nearly half my life with. I was too afraid of what might come out of my mouth. Letty, of course, thought it her place to suffer in silence and listen to others praise the maternal skills that had resulted in a daughter as wonderful as Mary.

Bridget glided silently up to the lectern like a wraith. In a wispy voice she recited an obscure, abstract poem that I wouldn't have understood even if I'd been thinking clearly. She went on about what a wonderful mother and sister and daughter Mary had been, extolling her virtues in flowery, old-fashioned terms. She finished, though, with an odd invective about what a troubled soul Mary had been, with vague references to unnamed events in her life. The silence when she finally stepped down hung in the air like a question mark, as uncomfortable as new shoes. Father Manion quickly resumed the service.

When Communion began, I let Ty out of the pew and followed him up to the altar, hands gently resting on his shoulders. Ty cupped his hands as he'd been taught. Father Manion gave him a host. When he raised his head, the sadness in his eyes reflected more than my loss. Rather than a host, he offered me his blessing like a consolation prize, making the sign of the cross in the air in front of my face. I moved Ty aside to let Kelsey step up and take our place.

As we turned to go back to our seats, I saw the whole congregation for the first time and paused in surprise. The front half of the church was filled. While the pews weren't packed, there were far more than a hundred people. I could count my friends on one hand. How had we met scores of people in the short time we'd lived there? I scanned the faces in the throng, amazed that I recognized so many. Some gave me smiles of encouragement.

Ty tugged at my sleeve, reminding me to keep moving.

"I DON'T KNOW WHY you had to hire a caterer. It seems like such an unnecessary expense." Letitia Beaumont bustled about our small kitchen like Martha Stewart on crack. She carefully draped her suit coat over the back of a stool, and looped a flowery ruffled apron over her head, expertly securing it with a perfect bow behind her back. She elbowed one of the catering people aside at the counter as she reached for a platter that was ready to take to the dining room.

"We got a caterer precisely so you wouldn't end up doing what you're doing, Letty."

"Well, I don't know why your *friends* can't pitch in like normal folks and bring things and put them out."

"People are busy." I started to explain as she steered around me with the platter. I followed her as far as the doorway to the dining room. "People *will* bring things.

We brought the caterer in just to make sure we had some basics on hand for everyone."

"This isn't anything I couldn't have done." She brushed past me. "I just don't understand why you brought a caterer in."

"Is there a problem with the food?" Another voice chimed in from across the kitchen. A tall, slim blond in a black shantung sheath walked to the counter as she spoke and reached over the food preparer's shoulder to snag a finger sandwich with a perfectly manicured thumb and forefinger. She took a bite and delicately wiped the corner of her mouth with a knuckle.

"No problem, Diane. It's wonderful," I said.

She gave me a tiny nod and immediately turned to my mother-in-law. "Letty, how are you?" she said, her voice reflecting true concern. She moved to buss Letty on the cheek. "I can't tell you how sorry I am for your loss. We're all going to miss Mary so much."

"Thank you, darlin'," Letty murmured.

"I hope you don't mind," she went on, "but I offered to step in and help as soon as I heard. I knew you'd be tired from the flight out, and Jack, of course, has had so much on his mind this week. I know what absolutely wonderful parties you throw, but I thought we should just keep this simple—enough to give people something to eat, but nothing extravagant."

"Yes, of course," Letty murmured. "It's really quite lovely. I just thought I'd help these poor people out. We're about to have a house full of people and there's only one person back here in the kitchen." She reached for another platter on the counter.

I gently put a hand on her arm. "Letty, please. Three more servers are coming any minute." She looked down at the hand on her arm, then at me. I withdrew my fingers. "They'll take care of all this, I promise," I finished.

Diane came up behind her and put an arm around her shoulders. "If you wouldn't mind, Letty," she said lightly, "I desperately need your social expertise. I've been to so few of these things that I get quite confused when it comes to proper etiquette. Carmen and I can't agree, and we need your help." Diane gently led Letty out of the kitchen, plucking Letty's suit coat off the back of the stool as they went, giving Letty no chance to object. When they reached the door, Diane glanced back over her shoulder at me and threw me a quick grin.

"Sorry about that," I said to the woman at the counter.

She turned her head to see if I was speaking to her then replied. "It's no problem, sir." I hesitated, reluctant to leave the safety of the kitchen, then finally turned and left through the door to the dining room. Arrayed on the table were attractively arranged trays of finger sandwiches, crudités with hollowed-out bread bowls of blue cheese and spinach dip, a large cheese tray and a fruit platter. An urn of coffee and a tray of desserts sat on the sideboard. The chairs had been stored in the garage. The caterer had done a nice job. I reached for a piece of cheese as I walked by and popped it in my mouth. It had no taste.

A large cheerful bouquet of flowers brightened the table in the front hall. I stopped to admire them, glad Diane hadn't asked the florist for Mary's favorite—iris. They would have been too dark and funereal. Mary would have liked these, a pretty combination of roses, lilies and alstroemeria in white and shades of pink. I bent to sniff one of the lilies and smelled root beer candy from childhood Christmases. The sound of the doorbell yanked me back to the present.

The woman at the door smiled hesitantly and took a step over the threshold. A few feet behind her stood a man and two boys, one Tyler's age, the other a few years younger. The man had his hands on the younger boy's shoulders the same way I'd stood at the altar with Ty earlier.

"Jack? I'm Jane Adams," the woman said, putting out her hand.

"Of course," I murmured. "Room mother in Tyler's class. Thank you for coming." She gave a hesitant smile of gratitude at being recognized and gestured behind her.

"This is my husband, Al, and my boys, Tom and Joe. We're so sorry about Mary."

"Thank you. Come in, please. There's food in the dining room. Help yourself." I looked at the older boy. "I'm not sure where Tyler is, but you might try the room down the hall there." As the family smiled and moved past me, more people came up the steps to the door. More introductions from those I'd only known as "Terry's dad" or "Jamie's mom" or never met at all. One way or another, they'd all known Mary. More words of condolence that would never feel adequate to those who spoke them, or to me. They wouldn't bring Mary back. More words of gratitude, expressed automatically, a social nicety when I really wanted to scream and cry and rail at the unfairness, the utter waste, the meaninglessness of what had happened.

For hours, people streamed through the front door and circulated through the house like the lazy current of a meandering stream, pooling in spots and swirling in little eddies in others. At times, I found myself caught up in the flow, carried from one room to another without knowing where I'd end up. When someone stopped to say something more than the standard discomfiting apology for something that wasn't their fault, the current parted and flowed around us as if we were boulders in the stream. Moving with purpose—to refresh a drink or help the caterers find supplies—was like diving in and swimming with one eye constantly on the destination, adjusting for the changing current.

"How are you holding up?" I turned away from the cupboard where I was pulling down more glasses for the servers to put out. Diane stood behind me with a plate of food in her hand.

"Not too bad, actually," I replied. "It helps to keep moving. It doesn't seem to catch up if I don't stay in one place too long."

"I know what you mean." She smiled and held out the plate. "Here, I got this for you. You need to eat something."

"Thanks." I took the plate and bit into one of the little sandwiches hungrily. It didn't seem to have any flavor, either.

"No problem."

I swallowed quickly. "No, I mean thanks for everything—the flowers, the food… If it hadn't been for you, we probably would have ended up ordering pizza."

She smiled. "You're welcome. I was glad to help."

"I don't know what I would have done without you. How are you holding up?"

"Fine." She looked surprised. "Actually, I've been having a wonderful time with Carmen and Greg telling 'Mary' stories. They're entertaining Letty."

"Thanks for keeping her busy." She looked at me awkwardly. Movement over her shoulder distracted me. An attractive woman in her mid-thirties purpose-fully made her way toward us through the crowded family room. Her mouth was set in a grim line as if she'd just eaten something distasteful and was looking for somewhere to discreetly spit it out. Diane turned to see what had caught my attention and stepped aside as the woman approached.

"Hello, Julie," I said, summoning as much warmth as I could muster. "Nice of you to come."

"Hello, Jack." The words came out tinged with frost. "We came to pay our respects. We're very sorry for your loss." She spoke not only for herself, but for the man who sidled up a half-step behind her, looking con-trite. He nodded in agreement. He looked a few years older, brush-cut blond hair beginning to thin on top, handsome face grown full from too sedentary a life-style as middle age approached.

"Terrible thing," the man muttered. "Terrible thing. If there's anything we can do…"

"Thanks, Brian, really. I appreciate it, both of you." I paused. "Did you get some food? Can I get you a drink?"

Julie shook her head. "No, we can't stay," she said firmly. "We just wanted to let you know that no matter what, your family—Mary—didn't deserve this. We're very sorry." She lingered a moment longer, eyes flicking across my face, mouth set again. Then she turned and walked the way she'd come without a backwards glance. Brian gave me a forlorn look. I couldn't tell if it was sadness for my loss or his own plight. He turned and followed his wife.

"What was that all about?" Diane asked quietly.

"Nothing," I said, still watching their retreat.

"You looked like you wanted to hit her. Or him." I

turned and looked at her, unclenching the hand in my pocket, and tried a smile.

"No big deal. Honest." She didn't look convinced. "I'm just tired." I took a deep breath.

"People are starting to go home. Why don't you sit down and relax? Have a drink." Kelsey came up to us looking far too grown up, as if she had unconsciously stepped into the role left vacant by her mother's death.

"Hey there," I said gently. She let me put an arm around her shoulder.

"Hi." Her arm circled my waist and she rested her head against my chest.

"You okay?" I felt her shrug.

"Sad," she said. There wasn't much else to say. Motionless a moment longer, she slowly pulled away. "Is it okay if I go over to Amanda's?"

"I guess so." I saw Diane nod. "Sure. People are starting to go home. No reason you have to hang around here. Be sure to say goodbye to your grandmother and Aunt Bridget before you go."

"Thanks, Dad. I will."

"Where's your brother?"

"Up in his room, I think, with a couple of his friends."

"All right. Call me later."

"Is there anything else I can do?" Diane asked when Kelsey left.

I looked around, taking stock. The catering staff was finishing up. One person took the last of the equipment out to the van parked in front of the garage. Another tied up a garbage bag. A third wiped down the counters. They all wore jackets or coats, ready to leave.

"I don't think so, Diane." I faced her. "You've done so much already, I can't thank you enough."

She started to turn. "Oh, I almost forgot. Last time we flew, I grabbed Mary's uniform purse by mistake and she ended up with mine. Could I take it back? I have a trip, day after tomorrow."

"Of course. I think she left it in the laundry room with her suitcase. I'll get it."

"That's okay, Jack. I'll find it. You finish up here with the caterer." I found the head server and did a quick walk-through to make sure they'd cleaned up and taken everything they'd come with. I gave her a large tip to split with the others and walked her out to the van. Earlier, there had still been splotches of sunlight in the yard. Now, darkness settled in and with it chilly night air.

By the time I came back in, Diane and Carmen had put coats on. Diane peered into the purse she'd taken from the laundry room, pawing through the contents.

"What a mess," she muttered.

"Everything there?" I asked.

"I think so." She looked up. "Mary must have panicked when she opened this up and tore it apart trying to figure out whose it was. Oh, well. I'll do it later." She shrugged and closed the purse. "I'll bring Mary's purse back as soon as I get back from my trip."

"No hurry. Bring it with you next time you come visit." I bussed her cheek and turned to give Carmen a hug. "Carmen, it was great to see you. I wish we'd had more time to talk."

"Next time." She smiled.

With Mary gone, would there be a next time? Letty and Bridget stood for a round of hugs and goodbyes. Then they, too, made as if to leave.

"You're going, too?" I asked.

"Mom's very tired," Bridget said quietly. "I thought

I'd take her back to her hotel and get her squared away. That way you can stay here with Tyler."

"Is that all right with you?" I looked at Letty.

"Of course, Jack," Letty said airily. "But thank you for asking." She let me hold her coat for her and slipped her arms into the sleeves. Then she swept past imperiously.

Bridget followed, resignation on her face. "I'll be back in a while," she told me.

I saw them all out, closed the front door and walked down the hall to the family room to collapse on the couch. Tyler got up off the floor in front of the TV. He still wore the dress shirt and new pants, but had shed coat, tie and shoes long before. The pants were rumpled, his shirttail had come untucked and a stain of some sort colored the front of the shirt. He climbed onto the couch next to me and snuggled up under one arm like a puppy. Bridget found us there two hours later, sound asleep.

I SLEPT LIKE the dead. When I awoke I didn't know where I was or even what day it was. The last tendrils of dreams slowly left me, and the room swam into focus. The bedside clock read 5:57. I fumbled for the switch that would prevent the alarm from going off. It wasn't until I turned and saw Tyler curled up in Mary's spot, arm tucked under his cheek, that I remembered. I hadn't even heard him climb in during the night. At once, the crushing weight of despondency pressed me into the mattress. I was tempted to let it force me down deep into a black hole where it was quiet and peaceful.

Ingrained habit took over. I swung my legs over the edge of the bed and pushed myself to my feet. I emptied my head and let my body unconsciously walk through the morning routine—bathroom, running clothes, downstairs, feed the cat, vitamins, shoes, out the door.

Running in the fresh air didn't invigorate me the way it usually did. Nor did the cool light mist that dampened my face. I ran on anyway, one foot in front of the other, ignoring the disjointed thoughts, concentrating on inhaling, two, three, four, exhaling, two three, four… Twenty minutes after I returned, Bridget slipped silently into the kitchen in thick wool socks, probably awakened by the smell of fresh coffee. The guest room was right next to the family room. Her hair was loosely piled on her head and held with a large clip. She wore an ankle-length, thick cotton nightgown buttoned up to her chin. A terry robe covered that, but she stood at the counter with her arms clasped as if she was cold.

"Good morning. Coffee?" I asked.

"Do you have any green tea?"

"I don't know. Let me look." I got up and rounded the end of the counter. "Have a seat." She sat at the kitchen table. I rummaged through a cupboard to find a jar containing an odd assortment of tea bags. To my surprise, a couple of bags labeled "green tea" had been mixed among the orange pekoe, Earl Grey and chamomile. I heated a mug of water in the microwave and put the tea bag in to steep.

"Milk or sugar?"

"Um, honey and some soy milk, please."

I hesitated. "I don't think we have any soy milk."

She nodded. "You do. I bought some yesterday." I opened the fridge. A quart container of soy milk sat next to the carton of regular milk.

"So what are your plans?" she asked when I set the mug of tea in front of her.

"Usual stuff." I slid onto a stool and faced her. "Grocery shopping, housework, maybe a little yard work if it clears up. I'll see if Tyler's up to playing in his soccer game. Life goes on." She blew on the tea, then took a hesitant sip, silent for a moment. "I meant do you know what you're going to do?" she said finally, her voice timorous. "About the children."

"What about them?"

"Well…" She shifted in her chair, looking uncomfortable. "About raising them." I waited, wondering where she was going with this. She searched my face for some sign of understanding. She didn't get it.

"I know you and Mary had some problems," she said slowly. "She was obviously very troubled about something. But she was here. For the kids. How will you raise them by yourself?"

I didn't know how to answer for what seemed a long time. "First of all, you don't know a thing about the problems we might have had." I spoke quietly, smiling to disarm the menace I couldn't quite keep out of my voice. "Second, Mary was *not* here. I'm not sure what was eating at her, but she checked out of this family a long time ago. About the time your dad died, in fact. For your information, I *have* been raising these kids by myself—at least half the time—ever since they were born, while she flew all over the world."

"That was her job."

"Yes, it was." I tamped down the sudden rage that seethed beneath the surface. "She worked hard. She also had a hell of a good time, flying with friends and shopping in Paris and Tokyo."

"What about everything she did? All the volunteering? The things she did for the kids?" Her plaintive voice began to sound whiny.

"You know, Bridget, it's really none of your business,

but I'll be blunt. Mary didn't volunteer for anything that wouldn't reflect well on her. She wasn't a classroom mom so she could spend more time with Kelsey or Tyler. She did it so she'd look like a good mom to the other mothers."

"How can you say that?"

"Look, I'm not saying she wasn't generous, or that her heart wasn't in the right place." I paused, searching for what I really meant to say. "It's just that with Mary it was always about appearances. It wasn't about what the kids wanted or needed, or what I wanted. It was about what she needed. Recognition? Affirmation? I don't know. To tell you the truth, I think she was constantly trying to win your mother's approval." She looked at her tea, hands clasped around the mug for warmth. Several minutes went by before she broke the silence.

"The kids need a mother, a woman, in their lives," she insisted.

"And who would that be?" I said. "You want me to try to find a replacement mom for my kids? What, just move on and act as if she never existed? Are you crazy?"

"Not a replacement," she said hurriedly. "I…they just need a lot of love. They need to feel like a family."

"We *are* a family. There's a big hole in it right now, but hopefully with time that will heal." I looked at her long and hard, her words resonating in my head. "What are you suggesting?"

"Nothing," she mumbled, then in a clearer voice, "I just don't think you can get the children through this alone. I think you need help."

"Whose help?" I began to get an idea of what she was getting at. "Yours? Your mother's? We'll manage on our own, thanks."

"Like you did with Mary?"

"What do you mean?" I suddenly felt defensive.

"Why didn't you *do* something?"

"Do what? She didn't want help. I begged her to go to counseling."

"You could have done an intervention," she said. "She obviously had a drinking problem."

"An intervention?" I couldn't shake the mental image of Mary being spirited away to a stark cell somewhere by shadowy figures, her head covered with a black hood, her arms bound.

"Jack, she was crying out for help. She was just too proud to come out and ask."

I shook my head. "No. You don't just kidnap someone, take them somewhere to dry out for a month and expect them to change. They have to want it. It has to come from inside. She didn't want help. She thought things were just fine the way they were." But I wasn't sure I believed my own words.

"They lost their mother, Jack," she said softly. "There's nothing keeping you here. You lost your job. Sell the house. Move the kids to Savannah where Mom and I can help you get through this. Start over."

"And if I don't?" She looked away and didn't answer.

SEVEN

THE uniformed cop eyeballed me closely as I rolled slowly past. Our eyes locked momentarily. I scanned the lane of cars on my right looking for a hole to swing in close to the curb. It used to be they didn't give you a second look until you'd been parked at the curb for five or ten minutes. More of them patrolled the airport now, and they gave you a second and third look before you came to a stop. The cop looked away, disinterested. I didn't fit a profile.

Fortunately, the summer tourist season was over and traffic at the airport was usually light at that time of morning. Business travelers, especially those headed east, had all taken crack-of-dawn flights to get more productive use from their day than just having an airplane strapped to their butts. I slipped into a spot right in front of curbside check-in for the airline that would fly Letty back to Atlanta and on to Savannah. I quickly hopped out and rounded the front of the van to open her door. She stepped to the curb. I got her suitcase out of the back and carried it to the check-in stand. She followed and handed her ticket to a porter.

"Thank you for being here," I said quietly. "It meant a lot, to the kids and me." She nodded primly. I waited a beat. Nothing. "The invitation for Thanksgiving is still open."

She nodded again. "Thank you, Jack." I was about to turn back to the car, when she pursed her lips, looking as if she had something else on her mind. I waited. "This hasn't been easy," she said, choosing her words, "but I want you to know that I'm sorry for *your* loss." She wouldn't concede any more, but I couldn't blame her. She'd lost a husband and a daughter in the space of a few years. I acknowledged the gesture with a nod and walked back to the van.

Bridget climbed out. "Mom, wait," she called. "I'll walk in with you." She pulled a wheeled suitcase out and set in on the curb, then leaned in to give me a listless hug and a weak smile. "Thank you for letting me stay with you and the kids."

"Better than the alternative." I kept my voice low, but flashed a glance at Letty to be sure she hadn't heard.

"Think about what I said." She fingered the sleeve of my jacket. She looked as if she wanted to say more. Whatever it was, she swallowed it. "If you need *anything,* call me," she finally said, her eyes imploring. "I mean it." Her gaze lingered on my face, as if seeking some sort of reassurance there.

"Bridget?" Letty's voice was impatient.

"Coming, Mom." Bridget grasped the extended handle of her suitcase and joined her mother. She turned and gave me a brief wave. Letty hooked an arm into hers and steered her into the terminal.

On the way out of the airport, light rain dribbled from a sky the color of ashes. It slowly coated the windshield until the world outside was blurred and distorted. I turned on the wipers, but the bleariness remained. I felt a trickle of warm wetness on one cheek. Today was Monday. The kids were in school. We'd returned to normal. As if there would ever be such a thing again.

THE COUPLE CAME DOWN the path from the top of the "Lid," the park that sits atop a nearly half-mile stretch of the freeway on the north end of the island. The park is what money and clout can buy. When the state department of transportation got funds to widen the interstate and add the new floating bridge across the lake, the hue and cry from the island was heard as far away as Olympia. With an indignant not-in-my-backyard attitude, the city said the increase in traffic noise would disturb island residents. State and city officials reached a compromise to cover the freeway at the most populous spot on its route across the island. Massive earthmovers cut a huge trench to accommodate the widened roadway, and when finished, buried it under millions of tons of dirt. Enough for a green, landscaped, twenty-two-acre strip of ball fields, tennis courts, bike paths, playgrounds and picnic areas. Mostly paid for with federal highway money.

They stepped off the path and made their way behind one of the baseball diamonds to the edge of the outfield, now a practice soccer field. Both wore blue jeans, hers flatteringly snug, his baggy, and both wore Eddie Bauer bush jackets, though not in matching colors. They stood at the edge of the field watching and talking for a moment. Then she tossed her head, throwing a mane of thick, wavy hair the color of sun-streaked wheat over her shoulder. She raised a sleek black camera with a big lens to eye level and pointed it at the soccer field one direction, then another.

My attention shifted back to the practice on the field. When I looked up again, the woman's camera dangled at her side on a strap, and she'd moved closer to the small group of moms on the sideline. Her companion was no longer with her. He walked casually toward me around the end of the field, intent on the action. As usual, I stood on the sideline opposite the women.

Tyler hustled after a loose ball and dribbled it up field. Three boys converged on him, and my pulse raced in anticipation of a sure collision. Before they got too close, though, Ty gave the ball a mighty boot and sent it spinning in the general direction of some players who were open.

"They look pretty good," said a nearby voice.

I glanced to the side to see the man now standing a few yards away, hands jammed in his coat pockets. Misery loves company, I guess. The only other men in sight were the coaches on the field with the boys. Up close, he appeared younger, barely old enough to have a kid Ty's age. Long, dark hair pulled back tightly into a ponytail at the nape of his neck gave him a clean-cut appearance from the front, the look of a rebel from the side.

"Not bad," I said, to be polite. We watched in silence.

"They're so fun to watch," he said a few minutes later. I glanced over to see him looking out at the field, smiling. "When they're really little," he went on, "they all move around the field in a gang, like some giant amoeba. Now they understand the concept a little better." I turned back to the field. He was right. A small amoeba crowded around the nucleus of the moving soccer ball. The rest of the kids stood around the field aimlessly, waiting for the wriggling, multi-headed creature to get close enough for its mass to suck them in. The odd sensation of being appraised like a side of beef diverted my attention back to him.

He looked at me curiously, head cocked to one side. "Are you Jack Holm?" I nodded, feeling my mouth turn down at the corners.

"I thought so," he said softly. "Bruce Colvin." The name was familiar, but I couldn't place it. "Man, I was really sorry to hear about what happened to your wife." I mumbled some sort of acknowledgement, wondering why personal loss made even strangers feel entitled to show their pity.

"Hard to believe something like that could happen here," he went on, taking a couple of steps closer. "It must be pretty awful for you."

"Pretty awful," I echoed, nodding.

"That your son out there?" He jerked his head toward the field.

I looked for Ty. "Over there. The one with the dark blue T-shirt." I raised an arm and pointed.

"Looks like he's taking it okay."

It was my turn to look at him curiously. "My guess?" I said quietly. "He's still in shock, like me. He's out there running as fast as he can, playing as hard as he can because he's hoping that it will keep him from thinking about it. Or maybe at least tire him out enough that he can get to sleep and not wake up in the middle of the night crying his eyes out."

"Sorry." He looked chastened. "Must be rough." He had no idea. I didn't enlighten him, and for a moment he fell silent.

"I don't mean to pry," he started in again, reticently, "but what the heck happened, anyway?" I shrugged. "I don't know."

"She was *murdered?*"

"Yes." A knot formed in the pit of my stomach.

"Here on the island?"

"I don't know." I was more insistent this time, hoping he'd take the hint, but no such luck.

"Any idea who did it?"

"Look—Bruce, is it?—I just lost my wife. Some ass-hole *raped* her and then *strangled* her. As far as I can tell from what little the police have told me, she was in the wrong place at the wrong time. I'm trying to figure out how to deal with that." The knot in my stomach was like a white-hot iron fist squeezing my guts. "To tell you the truth, I don't give a shit who killed her. Whoever it was deserves worse, but it won't bring her back. Do you understand that? My children will never see their mother again. I'll never see her again." He took a step backwards and eyed me warily. I unclenched the fists at my side, white knuckles slowly turning pinkish again. I dropped my gaze, suddenly embarrassed, though a small voice inside said I had no reason to be. I turned my hand over. Purple crescent-moon indentations left a track across my palm.

"Sorry, man." He held up a hand, palm out. "I've never lost anybody close to me."

"I don't recommend it." That shut him up, at least for a minute or two. I mindlessly stared out at the boys on the field, wishing I could shut it all out, wishing none of this had happened. I wasn't prepared for what came next.

"So, do the cops think you killed her?" The expression on his face was inquisitive, but guileless. I wondered if I'd misheard him. "I read somewhere that, like, a third of the women offed each year are done in by their partners." He shrugged. "Just wondered if the cops are giving you a hard time. That'd be a bitch on top of what you're already going through." I think I listened as long as I did out of sheer disbelief. By the time he finished, I was already two yards past him.

Ty found me after practice sitting in the van in the parking lot. I'd sorted and rearranged the contents of the glove compartment and the drawer under the passenger seat. Then I'd spent a fascinating half-hour reading the maintenance section of the van's operating manual. Anything to keep from dwelling on the dark thoughts that scuttled through my brain like rats in a sewer. Ty slid open the side door and clambered in, flushed and breathless. I put the manual away. My hand still trembled.

"Good practice?"

"Okay." He shrugged.

I took that to mean good. He sat on the floor and pulled his cleats off. Two days of "Seattle sunshine" had made the field soggy enough that they were caked with mud. The musty smell of decaying organic material filled the van, earthy and pungent. Ty scrambled into the front seat, pulled the seatbelt across his lap and buckled it. I turned over the ignition and pulled out.

"You don't have to stay for practice, you know," Tyler said after we'd gone a few blocks. "You can go back to your office and work or do errands if you want."

I glanced at him quickly. "Thanks, Bud. I appreciate that."

"It's not like it's a game or anything," he said, nonchalant. "Most of the moms don't stay. They don't really watch, anyway. They just, like, hang out and talk."

"Right." I got the point. "Say, you never told me how school was today. I imagine a lot of people tried to offer you condolences."

"Condo-what?" He flashed me a weird look.

"Condolences. When people say they're sorry about what happened to Mom."

"Not really." He stared out the windshield. "People don't know what to say." His tone was factual. "Mostly, they kind of avoid me, like I had a disease or something." Pretty perceptive for ten. I didn't hear any animosity, and wondered why I felt it for him.

"It'll get better." He didn't say anything, but I guess I wasn't all that convincing. We both chewed on it for a while. "Ty, is there a kid on your team named Colvin?" I asked after a bit, my mind switching gears.

"There's Calvin Watanabe."

"No, *Col*vin. Colvin's the last name."

"Oh." He blinked a couple of times, thinking. "I don't think so. Why?"

"Just curious." I put a hand on his shoulder and gave it a light squeeze. I felt him looking at me. I turned my head and gave him a big smile. I lifted my hand off his shoulder and tousled his unruly mop of hair until he smiled back.

"IT'S AMAZING HOW quickly the phone stopped ringing."

"Why?"

"What, we throw a big party and feed everybody and his brother, they say they're sorry, and they all go home and that's it?"

"Why does that bother you?"

I shifted in the chair, unsure of the source of my discomfort. "I don't know. It just seems rude to me. It's like people came because there was free food, and now it's as if Mary never existed. People are already starting to forget her."

"Forget her? Or forget what an enormous loss it is to you, your family?"

"What do you mean?"

"I mean are you upset because you feel people haven't paid enough respect to Mary's memory? Or are you upset because they're not giving you enough

*sympathy?" Sarah watched me patiently while I gath-
ered my thoughts.*

*"Both," I decided. "I don't mean to sound ungrate-
ful, but I remember when my dad died my mother got
cards and letters from people all over saying how he'd
had an effect on their lives. She must have read them all
a couple dozen times over the year after he died. Same
thing happened when she passed away. My sister and
I got a ton of cards. Most of them told some little story
about my mom, and all those stories about the good
times in her life made us forget, a little, how sad we
were."*

Sarah nodded."That makes sense."

*"As far as sympathy goes, what's wrong with that?
Throwing a nice wake might have made all Mary's
friends feel better, but once the party's over and the
lights come back on, I still have to face an empty house.
The kids, too. We have to live with this huge hole in our
world. Sure, we could use a little sympathy."*

"Would that make things better?"

*"Maybe not," I admitted. "But it might make us feel
a little better, a little less abandoned. Mary already did
that. Oh, I know she didn't do it on purpose, but she's
gone. Now it feels like everyone else is jumping ship,
too. Ty said it the other day—it's like people think we
have some terrible disease, so they're avoiding us."*

*She gave it some thought. "Maybe people are get-
ting on with their lives."*

"Easy for them."

*"And it's easy to be bitter," she said gently, "but
maybe you ought to think about how you're going to
get on with yours."*

KELSEY DIDN'T COME HOME after school on Wednesday.
Her last class ended at noon that day. Normally, she

would have been home by twelve-twenty, ready for lunch.

I didn't notice. I'd gotten behind—a week of sheer inertia will do that. Now I buried myself in details. My only client, not counting McAuley and the articles he'd given me, had a major trade show coming up less than six weeks away. I had to pull it together. I had to pull myself together. *Get on with your life,* Sarah had said. Better advice: ignore it and maybe it'll go away.

I picked Ty up from school and drove him to church, then went home for an hour to work. Kelsey still hadn't come home. This time I noticed, but recalled that she had cheer squad practice on Wednesdays. I put it out of my head, assuming she must have spent the afternoon at school studying.

During Ty's soccer practice after CCD, I took his advice and made myself scarce, not averse to avoiding another encounter with Bruce Colvin. I felt odd. As if for the first time in my adult life no one needed me. No boss. No wife. Kids flexing wings of independence. It unsettled me. I wasn't sure what to do with myself. I kicked around the town center, checked out new releases at the video store, treated myself to an espresso drink. And ended up back at the field ten minutes before the end of practice.

I spotted Ty at midfield, and sauntered down the sideline in his direction. He stood with hands on hips, taking a breather.

Alex, playing position for once, shuffled over to him and scuffed the dirt with the toe of one of his cleats. He said something to Tyler, a grin on his face. Tyler stiffened and moved away, eyes on the play. Alex followed, his lips still moving. Tyler moved again, but

Alex dogged him. His voice became audible but not distinct as I drew close.

Suddenly Tyler turned and faced him. "Shut up!" The irritation and frustration in Tyler's voice were perfectly clear.

Alex's laugh was mirthless. He moved closer and murmured again. I feared he'd pushed Ty too far, but play on the field shifted and Ty broke away to chase after the ball. Alex loped after him, getting back into the scrimmage. I was glad they hadn't noticed my approach. The instinct to jump in and referee had been strong. On the way home, I asked him about it.

He flushed and looked away. "No biggie," he said to the passenger window. He glanced at me quickly, then out the windshield with a defiant expression. "It's cool." I let it go. We finished the ride home in silence.

Kelsey still wasn't home by dinnertime. Just about the time I worked up a good head of worry and anger, the phone rang.

"Hi, Dad. It's me. I'm at Jennie's. I know I'm grounded and I should have called, but we had community service this afternoon, and then Jennie offered to give me a ride home from cheer practice, but her mom had to do something important here at her house, so they couldn't drop me off first, and I'm really sorry." She managed it all in one breath, effectively preventing me from unloading a 105mm shell of invective on her. Maybe I was supposed to have known about community service. "When will you be home?"

"Jennie's mom said she could bring me home in about twenty minutes. Or you could pick me up?"

I glanced ay my watch. "I'm making dinner, Kels. I can't go out again right now. It's curriculum night at school. I need you home to watch Ty by seven at the latest."

"Okay. Then I'll ask Jennie's mom to drop me off."

"I mean it, Kels. You should have come home straight from practice. If Jennie's mom can't get you here by seven, I need to know now."

"All *right*. I'll be home by seven."

"Is your homework done?"

She sighed. "Yes, Dad."

CARS LINED BOTH sides of the block-long street leading to the school, which meant an overflowing parking lot. I parked on the street a block in the other direction and hoofed it. By the time I found Ty's classroom and slipped into one of the undersized chairs still available, I was warm. I shrugged out of the jacket and draped it on the back of the chair.

A large clock over the door indicated it was a few minutes past seven. The classroom hummed with conversation as parents chatted in small groups. I recognized several faces. I actually knew the names of a few parents from previous school events and some who'd introduced themselves at Mary's memorial. With three classes of kids at each grade level, a lot of new faces showed up every year.

A couple on the far side of the room seemed familiar. Without thinking, I turned to ask Mary who they were. Putting names and faces together had been her department. I caught myself and closed my mouth before I spoke to empty air. Heat spread rapidly from my neck up into my scalp. I fidgeted, hoping I looked like someone trying to get comfortable, not an idiot.

At the front of the room, a small dark-haired man with a cheerful round face introduced himself as Mr.

Ortiz. For the next half-hour, he enthusiastically walked us through a typical day in the lives of our kids. He used transparencies on an overhead projector as visual aids, most of them typed course outlines. A few whimsical drawings thrown in kept the presentation light.

Parents asked a lot of questions—politely, but every opinion offered was countered by someone else's. It made my head hurt. I felt sorry for Ortiz, but he handled the concerns with diplomatic aplomb. Seemed to me the best we could hope for was to throw our kids into a school with a decent reputation and trust teachers to do their job. I wondered why parents who wanted to micro-manage their kids' education didn't just home-school them.

I listened as attentively as I could. Occasionally, my mind and eyes wandered around the room, watching a parent voice a question, seeing the reactions of others. Every so often, I caught someone's gaze. Each time it happened, though, the person's eyes slid away. I unconsciously rubbed imaginary goop off my nose.

When Ty's teacher finished fielding questions, Jane Adams, the class room mother, gave a short talk about volunteer opportunities chaperoning field trips and organizing holiday parties. That raised more questions. Several people shifted uncomfortably and checked their watches, bolting for the door with expressions of dazed relief when the questions petered out. I straightened up my set of the hand-outs that had been passed around. As I stood up and put on my jacket, the teacher sauntered over.

He stuck out his hand. "George Ortiz. I met your wife at the beginning of the year. I'm sorry about what happened." I still didn't know what to say. When would accepting sympathy stop feeling so awkward?

"Things will probably be pretty rough around your house for a while." He kept his voice low, glancing toward the parents gathered around the refreshments. "I wanted to let you know that I'll keep an eye on Tyler and tell you if things come up." He paused. "Was Tyler okay today when he got home from school?"

"Sure. Why?"

"Kids can be pretty cruel, unfortunately." He shrugged. "I just wondered if he'd caught any flak about what people are saying."

I frowned. "What are people saying?"

"You haven't seen it?" He looked surprised. "Come with me." I followed him to his desk, hands in my pockets.

"This," he said. He inclined his head toward the desk. A neatly folded copy of the local weekly newspaper sat to one side, the main headline and part of the accompanying story and photo visible. I frowned, confused, until the import of the headline sank in—"Island Woman's Murder A Mystery."

"One of the kids brought this in this morning," Ortiz said.

I barely heard the words, barely remember sitting behind the desk. I tried to comprehend what lay in front of me. In my haste to absorb the entire piece, my darting eyes took in only random bits of information—"*...unknown assailant...sexually assaulted...brutally strangled...body dumped...shallow grave...killed here or elsewhere...no suspects...several 'persons of interest'...home alone before her disappearance...several days before she was reported missing...told police she was sleeping...exact time of death indeterminate... 'likely killed sometime Saturday night or early Sunday morning,'...temperamental husband...'I don't give a* *s__t who killed her.'"* The paper had run a two-column photo of Ty's soccer practice with me standing on the far sideline. And then it finally registered. I looked at the byline on the article—Bruce Colvin. I read the entire story again, slowly this time.

Ortiz had been roped into a conversation with some lingering parents. As the stragglers headed for the door, he rejoined me and sat on the edge of the desk, hands clasped in his lap. He nodded toward the paper then looked at me. "True?"

I hesitated, decided not to qualify. "All of it, as far as I can tell. Some stuff nobody's bothered to share with me, of course."

"But…?"

"This—" I started over. "This *jerk* makes it sound like I had something to do with it."

"You didn't, right?"

"Of course not!"

"I thought so." He paused and gave me a wry grin. "I majored in journalism in college—before I switched gears and went for a master's in education. Look, this is probably the biggest story this town has seen in years. When one of the kids brought that paper in today I wondered why. Until I saw the story. This stuff sells newspapers. And gives people something to talk about, even kids."

"So why don't you believe it if it's all true?"

He shrugged. "Lots of innuendo, not a lot of facts."

"And there's nothing I can do about it." Except avoid Colvin and watch what I said, especially around strangers. Some of the disgust and anger I felt was self-directed. Colvin had given me a chance. He'd introduced himself. It wasn't his fault I hadn't known who he was.

I gave voice to a new question. "Why are you doing this?"

He looked thoughtful. "Tyler's a good kid. Bright. Quick. I like him. Losing his mom is going to be tough on him." I stiffened, reminded once more of the enormity of our loss. I feared it, a black hole not even the light inside each of us would escape.

"I know."

"I have a bad feeling this is going to get a lot worse." He reached out and tapped the paper with a finger. "Unless the police catch the guy fast, you're going to get skewered."

"I still don't get it. You don't know me."

"It doesn't always pay to play it safe." He shrugged. "Maybe that'll get me in trouble some day. I don't like it when people jump to conclusions. I thought you ought to know." I regarded him, curious.

"It's happened to you," I concluded. He didn't bother confirming it. "Thanks," I said, then thought to add, "For Tyler."

"Good luck." Class dismissed.

Things hadn't even begun to get worse.

EIGHT

ED MANKIEWICZ waited on the front stoop when I got back from a coffee run the next morning. A caravan of vehicles in the drive left barely enough room to maneuver into the garage. I parked, walked past a phalanx of police officers, and met Mankiewicz on the steps.

"What's going on?" My voice sounded calm, despite the trembling in my knees and the sharp scent of sweat that dampened my armpits. If he noticed, he didn't let on.

"Sorry to bother you, Mr. Holm, but we have a warrant to search the house." He actually looked apologetic. "It's more or less to help rule you out as a suspect."

"A suspect? You're kidding? You think I killed my wife?" The image of Mary's bloated face from the police photo flashed in my head, and my stomach churned.

"We'd like to rule out that possibility," he repeated.

"But why? Why would you think I had anything to do with it?" I swallowed hard, trying to choke back a rising sense of panic. *Colvin's article—maybe that put the idea in his head.*

"Please, Mr. Holm, just let us do our job." He was polite, regretful even.

"Well, of course." Awkwardly, I moved to open the front door for him. "I have nothing to hide. I just don't understand what you're looking for." He motioned to the other officers, and they trooped silently past in single file, disappearing into the house. I followed Mankiewicz inside.

"You did say there was no murder weapon, right?" I asked his back. "Not that it would be here if there was." Mankiewicz conferred in low tones with one of two men in plainclothes, ignoring me. I decided the smartest thing to do was shut my mouth.

Fear stokes the imagination like liquid oxygen on a forest fire. Mine worked overtime. Among the thoughts that sparked and flared like a tinder-dry Douglas fir bursting into flames: the police had never told me how Mary had been strangled. I'd never even considered asking for a copy of the Medical Examiner's report. Dead is dead. I didn't even want to look at the death certificate. Letting my imagination run wild fueled my fear in turn, like a back draft. I took a deep breath.

Mankiewicz turned to me. "This is our evidence technician, Officer Meyer." The man he'd been talking to gave me a polite nod.

"Just to let you know what we'll be doing, we'll try to disrupt things as little as possible. We'll catalog anything we take. You'll get a copy. We're very careful with evidence, and we'll make every effort to see that everything's returned in good condition."

"You and I just need to stay out of the way," Mankiewicz said, taking my elbow. "Why don't we go sit and talk in your office." He steered me down the hall, and gave a nod to the other plainclothes officer who followed us to the den.

Once there, Mankiewicz usurped the desk chair and motioned to a different one. "Have a seat." When I was settled, he gestured toward the other officer. "This is Detective Whelan." Whelan was tall, thin and wiry. A long face with acerbic features gave him a glum look, as if he'd rather be somewhere else—either that or his dog just died.

"What happened to the sheriff's deputy?" I said.

"Sheriff's Department kicked it back to us," Mankiewicz said. He decided to elaborate. "Your wife lived here on the island. You filed the missing person report with us. It's our case. They got involved because they're the ones who found her in unincorporated King County. They let us have it because they have enough to do. They don't need the extra work. Right, Dick?" He threw the question over his shoulder, never taking his eyes off me. Whelan gave a small grunt, but his expression didn't change.

Mankiewicz fished in an inside pocket of his sport coat for a stenographer's notebook. "I know this is difficult, but we really want to get the guy who did this." He leaned forward, lifted a corner of his mouth far enough that his biker-gang face actually looked amiable. "It would really help us out if you'd go through it one more time with us. I know it's a pain, but try to remember every detail, no matter how small or insignificant you think it is."

"You want the whole thing?"

His head bobbed. "The whole thing."

"Where do you want me to start?"

"How 'bout the day before your wife went missing?" He craned his neck to look back at Whelan. "That sound good, Dick?" Whelan must have acknowledged him somehow, because Mankiewicz turned back to me with a satisfied look. I hadn't even seen Whelan blink. "Why don't you start out there? What did you do when you got up?" I thought back, getting my bearings. Had it only been three weeks? I told the whole story again, everything I could remember. When I finished, the room was silent. Mankiewicz stared down at his notebook and gently tapped the point of his pen on the pad. Whelan had taken out a note pad, too, but sat stock still.

"And your wife had no enemies that you know of?" Mankiewicz looked at me from under his bushy brows.

I shook my head. "None that I can think of. She made friends easily. Complete strangers would tell her their life stories. It amazed me how many people came to the memorial service. I didn't know half of them, a quarter of them even."

"You're sure? She got along with everyone at work?"

"As far as I know. Like I said, she usually worked with people she liked, with friends."

"You mentioned that. That include pilots, supervisors—I don't know—baggage handlers?"

I hadn't considered it. "Hard to say. She never mentioned any problems, at least no one specifically."

"Never said she had any hassles with a passenger? Nothing like that?"

"No." I tried to remember the last time Mary had come home with a story about a rude passenger or an overtly macho pilot. In the old days, flight attendants had a standing joke: pilots/passengers sit on their asses so long that half of them have hemorrhoids; the other half are perfect assholes. Nowadays, pilots knew better than to risk sexual harassment suits, and unruly passengers were dropped off at the closest airport to face FAA fines and possible jail time.

He switched gears. "You mentioned you're starting your own business. How's that going?"

"Okay." I shrugged. "Like I told you, I've got a decent project with a guy that could turn into steady work."

"So, keeping the wolves from the door?" He gave a

small smile. "How about your finances in general? Any debts?"

"The usual. Mortgage payment. Credit cards. I always wish it was less, and every time I think I'm getting ahead of it, there's always something else. Braces for the kids. New tires."

"Yeah, I know the drill. For me, it's clothes. And vacations. My wife and I never seem to be able to save quite enough, and we always spend a little more than we planned." His tone was friendly, conversational. He sat back, appearing to savor a pleasant vacation memory. Whelan, by contrast, looked like he'd swallowed a lemon. Other than taking notes, he hadn't moved.

"Your wife owe anybody money?" Mankiewicz said.

I rolled my eyes. Mankiewicz continued to lean back in the chair, but he looked like a retriever that had gone on point.

"She liked to shop," I admitted. "And she liked nice things. So, yeah, she racked up some pretty good-sized credit card bills."

"Must have put a little pressure on you, what with losing your job and all."

"I wasn't happy about it. But it was her money. She had a job, made good money. Sure, I wish she'd put more of it toward the mortgage, or retirement. Or the kids' college fund."

"She didn't see it that way?"

I shrugged. "Like I said, it was her money. Look, Detective, things were—are—a little tight because we can't depend on my steady paycheck anymore. But we're doing all right. I spent enough years putting money into a 401K and paying the mortgage that we have a little cushion. You guys are going to dig all this up anyway. Why bother asking?"

"Some things aren't on the record."

"Like what?"

He stroked his mustache. "Say your wife had a problem with drugs. Or maybe she liked going to casinos a little too often. She might have borrowed money from family. A friend. Or worse." He watched me closely.

"No drugs, no gambling. Her addictions—if you want to call them that—were shopping and white wine. She overindulged in both on occasion. She didn't need to call a loan shark to score a bottle of Chardonnay."

"Just making sure we cover all the bases, Mr. Holm." He consulted his notes again. "Okay, so let's go over your relationship again. You said you two were having problems?"

I felt my face redden. "Not problems, exactly." What had we had, if not problems? "More like being in a rut, I guess. I've been a little stressed out worrying about losing my job and trying to get this consulting thing going. Mary, I think, wasn't happy about having to work more. She was unhappy about more than that, probably."

"About what?"

"I don't know. I got so wrapped up in trying to make sure I could still put food on the table I didn't have time to talk to her and find out. She was gone a lot, too, flying trips. We just seemed to have hit one of those rough spots where we weren't making enough time for each other."

"How was your sex life? Did the two of you still have sexual relations?"

"I'm not sure that's any of your business." I squirmed under his gaze. "Yes, we still had sex."

"How frequently?"

"Not often enough," I muttered. "I don't know. Once a month. Less, maybe. Probably."

"When's the last time you had sex with her?"

I blinked. "The night before she disappeared. Saturday night." He said nothing. Whelan still hadn't moved. They played no "good-cop-bad-cop" routine. Whelan hadn't said a word.

"Did it get a little rough?" Mankiewicz asked after a moment.

"What? The sex? No. No, it didn't get rough. Mary wasn't into that." Then, almost as an afterthought, "Me, neither. Not my thing." As I spoke, I saw where he was going, and my mind worked furiously as the horror of it became more apparent. *Had it been too rough?* Mary'd had too much wine. Sometimes that made her amorous. More often, she would pass through that stage on the way to complete inebriation or just plain passing out, getting me worked up and then let down. *Think.* I'd been unwilling to take no for an answer. I was tired of rejection. We both had needed to feel closer. *Had I forced myself on her?*

No, she'd been reluctant at first. She'd been asleep when I'd come to bed after cleaning up the kitchen. When I'd snuggled up to her naked under the covers, she hadn't wanted to wake up. She'd grumbled and moaned about wanting to sleep. I'd persisted, touching her, trying to excite her. But it hadn't been rough, just determined. And eventually, she'd acquiesced, rolling on top of me, deftly slipping my erection inside her and riding me until we climaxed. She'd lain on me afterwards, head on my chest, until our breathing slowed to normal. Then she'd wordlessly rolled over and fallen asleep. I'd stared at the ceiling until my eyelids shut of their own accord, and had dropped like a stone into that deep well that marked the first few hours of my sleep.

"No. No way." I shook my head emphatically. "Yes, we had sex, but it wasn't rough. And there is no way in hell I would rape my wife. I couldn't do it. I don't care how pissed off I might get that we didn't make love more often. No way I could rape someone, especially my own wife. I'd never be able to look at her again, I'd be too ashamed."

"So, maybe things got a little out of hand. You couldn't live with the shame, so you lost it."

"What, and killed her? You must be crazy." The fact that he could think it, voice it, was chilling. "I didn't rape her, and I sure as hell didn't kill her. She was my wife. I loved her."

He shrugged indifferently. "Was she faithful?" The question brought me up with a start. It seemed like eons before I could bring myself to answer.

"No. I mean, yes. She had an affair. Once. A while ago. It's over."

"You're sure?"

"Of course I'm sure." His eyes widened slightly at the sound of my annoyance.

"It's possible, then, that she could have had an affair without you knowing about it? Maybe gotten back together with this guy?"

"I doubt it." I thought about it. "Well, I suppose it's possible. Anything's possible. I don't think she got back together with that guy, though. His wife keeps him on a pretty short leash."

"But she could have been seeing someone. Someone who didn't want anyone else to know."

"And killed her so no one would find out?" He saw the shock on my face. This all seemed so unreal. Yet, the more I thought about it, the more it accounted for Mary's unhappiness, her moodiness the past few months before her death. *An affair?*

"What about you?" Mankiewicz asked quietly.

"What about me?"

"Did you cheat on your wife?"

"IT WASN'T SO MUCH that she got drunk and let herself get sweet-talked into screwing some guy. I could forgive that. What bothered me was that she was intimate with someone in a way she never had been with me. All the notes and cards, all the flowers and little gifts, all the compliments and affectionate gestures, all the times I tried to show her how desirable she was, how much I wanted her, and she gave herself to someone else. How could she do that? How could she say she loved me, that she didn't want to be with anyone but me and then give something I so desperately wanted from her to another man? I felt so stupid. What a waste. All that effort to make our relationship more passionate."

"You told her all this?" Sarah asked.

"Of course." I considered how to explain. *"When it came out, when Julie called me and told me to keep Mary away from her husband, I was hurt and angry. Like it was my fault. Like I encouraged Brian to fuck my wife. It hurt so much I didn't think I could forgive her or ever want her again. I wanted to hurt her just as much. But more than anything, I wanted to know why. What had I not done? What could she possibly get from Brian that she couldn't get from me?"* I paused. Took a breath. Tried to work it out in my head. *"What's strange is that the thought of her with someone else made me want her even more."*

"You still loved her."

"I suppose. It was more like the fact that someone else found her attractive made me desire her more. But with Mary I always wondered if I just wanted what I couldn't have."

"What happened after you talked with her about it? Did things improve?"

"No. She couldn't—wouldn't—talk about what happened. Or why. She avoided the issue, acted as if everything was all right. At night, she would ask me to cuddle her, the way we always had, as if that would fix it."

"Maybe it was her way of trying to get closer to you."

"More like trying to get back to the status quo." I snorted. *"Don't you see? Nothing changed. She had an affair. That breaks up a lot of marriages. It should have been—I don't know—a catalyst, a reason to figure out what wasn't working for us. But nothing changed. She wanted everything to go back to the way it was."*

"So your sex life didn't get better."

I thought about how to answer. *"You know the joke about the couple with an only child?"* Sarah waited politely for the rest of it. *"They tried sex once and didn't like it. The joke about Mary and me is that we had to try it twice."* She didn't laugh.

"Was Mary satisfied with your sex life?"

"Isn't that the point? I'm the one who wasn't satisfied."

"I meant the quality of it, not the quantity."

"She didn't have any problem reaching orgasm, if that's what you're asking. In fact, she was able to climax pretty easily. It was like role reversal sometimes. Just when I was beginning to warm up, she would get off and

want to stop." She considered me, head tipped slightly to one side.

"No, she wasn't faking it," I said, not sure if that was what she was thinking or not. "We talked about it once or twice. I worried about it. Sex is no fun for me if my partner's not getting off on it. She assured me she was."

She gave an almost imperceptible nod. "Apart from infrequency, what wasn't satisfying about it for you?"

"No passion. No connection. No sense of abandon. No losing ourselves in each other. It was all very prim and proper. Same thing every time—wham, bam, 'thank you, ma'am.' I always felt like she was holding something back. Like I never really touched her soul, or that she ever really wanted to touch mine."

"That must have been frustrating."

"You could say that. I always thought that two people in love were supposed to feel that kind of intimacy, especially when they make love. I always thought there were supposed to be fireworks. You know, the earth moving under you. All that stuff."

"Were you ever unfaithful?"

"No." Oh, what the hell. I'd already told her things I wouldn't confess to a priest. What could she do? Judge me? I paid her not to. "Yes, I've slept with other women."

"How many?" She was composed, but her eyes widened. "Never mind. That's not important."

"I've never told this to another soul." I waited while she mentally pushed aside her prurient interest. "Six. None of them were one-night stands. None of those relationships was fair to the woman involved because I was a married man. But all of them knew that I loved my wife and would never leave her."

"Yet they all ended. Why?"

"Circumstances. One of us would move or change jobs, that sort of thing. Two of them met the men of their dreams and got married. Not one of my affairs ended badly. I loved every one of those women for who they were and what they gave me."

"Did Mary ever find out?" I shook my head. *"Never."*

"How do you know?"

"I just do." I thought of a better answer. *"She would have left me."* Sarah waited until I heard my own words. *"She didn't know,"* I insisted. *"She wouldn't have waited this long."*

"Wasn't that still cheating?"

"Cheating? What did I cheat her out of? I never denied her anything. And I never gave any of those women anything that I didn't give her. Unfaithful? Hardly. I was loyal to a fault. I'm the one who felt cheated. It's like she wanted all the material comforts of marriage without the depth, without putting her heart and soul into it. It felt more like a business contract. We were roommates, not lovers. Friends, not partners. If she'd been there for me, I never would have had a reason to sleep with other women."

"But you loved her." I couldn't help it. My eyes suddenly filled with moisture. She took that for an answer.

KELSEY LOOKED AS SOUR as a jar of dill pickles. "I don't see why I have to go. It's so lame."

"You don't *have* to go," I told her. "I'd like you to go. It's the last time we'll ever go to one of these. It would mean a lot to Ty. It would mean a lot to me."

"Dad, it's just a bunch of screaming little kids running around getting hyper on ice cream."

"I know—boring. But I'm sure that other parents will

drag older siblings there, too, so you'll probably run into some of your friends. You can hang out and be miserable together."

"I doubt it." No one spreads sarcasm as thick as peanut butter on spoken words like a teenager.

"You've forgotten how many of these school socials we went to when you were in grade school. Along with all the choir concerts, plays, fundraisers and whatnot." The guilt trip worked.

When the kids were young, Mary and I thought in terms of firsts—first words, first steps, first day of school. The list seemed endless as they grew and explored the world. Even as they got older, I still had plenty of new things to look forward to—first date, first driver's license, first kiss. Sometimes, the job of parenting Kels and Ty had seemed incessant, interminable. Suddenly, I faced a new kind of milestones. They signaled endings. I had a feeling the ice cream at Ty's school tonight would taste bitter-sweet.

The warm and dry evening pulled people outdoors where they milled about outside the school entrances. Kids played exuberantly on the playground while the light lasted. I steered mine into the generically named multi-purpose room. We remained a family unit until we reached the counter where women dispensed ice cream bars instead of the usual school lunch. Tyler immediately raced off to join some buddies. Kelsey politely stayed with me, though I knew her patience had nearly worn through. I spied Bill and Cathy Whitman at one of the lunch tables and suggested we stop by. Kelsey followed me to their table. As soon as we exchanged greetings, she leaned in close and begged off. I nodded, and she melted away into the crowd.

"It's amazing how much she's matured," Cathy said.

"They grow up fast," I agreed. "I was just thinking on the way over that this is the last of these we'll ever attend."

"Us, too," she said.

"Gosh, we'll miss it," Bill said. His smirk and facetious tone said otherwise.

"Pretty soon, no more field trips, either," I said. "When does that stop?"

"Oh, they have field trips all through high school," Cathy said. "It's just that by the end of sixth grade they don't want to be seen anywhere near their parents." Bill had turned away to scan the faces in the crowd, as if disinterested. He jumped in again.

"They try to pretend they don't have parents until they want money, or car keys or new clothes."

"Well, pretty soon they'll be gone for good."

"I'll believe that when I see it," Bill said.

"Oh, you'll wish they were still here," Cathy said, poking him playfully. "You'll be so bored."

"I just can't believe Mary's going to miss it all," I said. "You know, last science fair presentation, last art fair, graduations. All of it." Cathy looked at me sadly. Bill had already turned away to let his eyes wander again.

"What's going on with that, anyway?" Cathy said after an awkward moment. "The investigation. We heard that the police searched your house. Is that true?"

"Yes." I sighed.

"What on earth for?"

"They said it was to rule me out as a suspect." Bill brought his attention back to the conversation and looked at me with an odd expression of pity and derision. "Rule you in, more likely."

"Bill." Cathy shot her husband a warning look.

"When's the last time you heard of cops searching somebody's place who *wasn't* considered a suspect?" he asked her. He turned back to me. "Seriously, have you gotten yourself a good lawyer? Judges don't issue search warrants unless the cops have a pretty good reason."

"A lawyer?" It hadn't occurred to me. He was already looking somewhere over my shoulder, scanning the crowd again.

"It might be a good idea," Cathy said. Then so quietly I almost couldn't hear her over the din, "Why didn't you tell us?"

I shifted and looked down at the table. "It's kind of hard to admit your wife's gone and you don't know where or why." She looked at me without comment. "What would you have done?" She used the same expression Bill had worn, shrinking me a size or two.

"If it had been Bill, I would have gotten everyone I could possibly think of to beat the bushes until I found him." It didn't matter. Anything I could have done would have been too little, too late.

"The kids and I would still love to see all of you sometime," I said after a moment. "Any chance we can get together soon?"

Bill turned to her and interjected before she could speak. "Hey, there's Joe over there, honey. Remember, we promised we'd hook up and talk about that weekend on the beach before the weather turns?"

"Oh, that's right," she said. Bill stood and waved to someone across the crowded room. Cathy rose, too. "We'll call you," she said. It had a hollow sound.

I sat there a while. Every so often, I waved to people I knew. A few waved back. More simply moved on or turned back to conversations with friends. No one came over to chat. By the time Kelsey and Tyler found me, I felt leprous and more than ready to leave.

NINE

THE office resided in an old loft building on Western Avenue, not far from where I'd worked. I don't know what I'd expected—a whole floor of Columbia Tower, expensive rosewood and beveled glass offices with panoramic views of Elliott Bay, lots of young, strikingly attractive, immaculately groomed, expensively dressed minions coolly tending to the needs of a few craggily handsome older partners in three-piece Italian silk suits, maybe.

Instead, a harried, overweight, plain-faced woman in a slightly disheveled generic black skirt and white cotton blouse held up an admonishing finger while she spoke to someone over a headset perched on her hair like a tiara. I averted my gaze politely and perused the business cards racked in a clear acrylic stand on the reception counter. A half-dozen attorneys shared the space.

The receptionist peeled the headset away from her ear and set it on the desk, pulling a strand of hair loose in the process. She looked at me expectantly. I told her who I'd come to see. She ran her finger down the page of an appointment calendar, her curved, glossy red nail leaving a small indentation on the thin paper in its wake. The finger stopped and tapped the page. She picked up the headset and punched some buttons on the phone, waited a couple of beats, then announced me to someone. I turned and pondered whether to stand or sit while I waited. A couple of empty chairs in beige fabric and light wood—maple, probably—stood in stark relief against the dark brick walls. I eased into one.

Phil Preston presented another surprise. He was small and slight. Diminutive next to me when I stood to shake his outstretched hand. He exuded quiet self-confidence, welcomed me by name without hesitation and looked me in the eye as if there was no difference in our height. Though his hand was small, his grip was firm and dry.

He introduced himself, then said, "Come on back." He had a quiet, calm voice, resonant and commanding at the same time. His eyes never wavered from my face. A shockingly bright shade of blue, they bore no visible edges around the irises to suggest contact lenses. They framed a long, thin nose sharp enough to cut butter, magnifying their intensity.

I followed him down a hall. He walked with the air of a man who knew something the rest of us didn't. It wasn't arrogance or overcompensation for his size. I took stock. Classic clothes. Expensive, but not ostentatious. Wool slacks, not silk, that fell neatly into place with each step, sharp creases a plumb line. Simple tailored Egyptian cotton broadcloth shirt that hung unwrinkled on his shoulders, with no telltale stiffness of starch, not gussied up with anything like a fancy pin collar or monogrammed cuffs. Muted silk tie knotted in a neat half-Windsor. Old-fashioned penny loafers buffed to a sheen instead of Italian tassled slip-ons. About my age, he'd made no vain attempt with hair plugs or a rug to hide a bald head. The perfectly even fringe of dark hair that did circle his head was neatly trimmed.

He led me to a large office furnished more like a study than a work space. There were no file cabinets, no credenzas. The only book case was small. Instead of law books, it held an assortment of contemporary and classic fiction and a few celebrity biographies. Some of the names on the spines stood out—DeLillo, Proulx, Cruz Smith, Theroux, Clinton (both Hillary and Bill), Updike, Irving. A large uncluttered oak desk stood in front of the window, its rich grain visible except for spots covered by a lamp, a matching box for correspondence and a laptop computer.

Preston closed the door and motioned toward a small damask settee flanked by two matching wing chairs against the opposite wall. An antique butler's table stood in the center of the grouping. "Please, have a seat." I chose the settee, putting my back to the wall, and found it unexpectedly comfortable. Preston sat on the edge of one of the wing chairs and crossed his legs. He might have disappeared had he slid all the way into it.

"I had a very pleasant conversation with your friend Jeff Adler this morning," he said with a smile.

"Really?" I wondered who'd called whom.

Bill Whitman's comment had concerned me, but I'd had no more inkling of how to find a good attorney than a paleontologist. There were more than a hundred pages of lawyers listed in the phone directory in my office, the pages edged in blue so they'd be easier to find. More than eight of those pages were devoted to criminal defense attorneys, and that didn't include those who specialized in DUI offenses. I could have thrown darts and then checked names with the Better Business Bureau or the Washington Bar Association.

Instead, I came up with the bright idea of calling Jeff Adler, an old college friend who practiced corporate law back east. He hadn't been able to come up with the name of anyone he knew personally, but he knew Preston by reputation. The call had given me a chance to catch up, too. I realized how easy it had been to lose touch with people who had once meant a great deal.

"It turns out that we have a number of mutual acquaintances," Preston said. "A fellow he went to law school with clerked for the superior court in San Francisco the same time I did—a long time ago." He smiled again. "He became a judge. We still stay in touch. So, tell me how you and Jeff met." I went back in time and pulled out some mental photo albums of happier times. Preston did a masterful job of putting me at ease with interested questions. Only later did it dawn on me that he was sizing me up, not making me more comfortable or establishing any sort of personal rapport. I wasn't even aware of when the small talk shifted to the business at hand.

"I'm sure your children must be taking the death of their mother very hard," he said in a quiet voice. I nodded, swallowed. "My condolences for your loss." He paused. "How can I help?"

"I'm not sure." I began to think I'd made a mistake. "You're aware of my situation." He nodded, even though it hadn't been a question. If he was as good as Jeff said he was, he would have done his homework even in the short time since I'd made the appointment.

"A friend said I should get a lawyer," I went on. "I don't know why. I haven't done anything. I don't understand what's going on."

"You have some concerns?"

"Yes. Why the police searched my house, for example. They said it was to eliminate me as a suspect. Why would I be a suspect? I lost my wife. My kids lost their mother. Someone brutally raped and murdered her.

Threw her in a hole like so much garbage. And they—"
He reached over to an end table, pulled a tissue from
a decorative box and handed it to me with a practiced
move. I started to wave it away, changed my mind and
dabbed my nose with it. He gave no sign he thought it
unseemly, or even unusual.

"I don't know if I need a lawyer or not." My voice
sounded steady at least.

"Why don't you tell me what happened. We'll go
from there." Preston listened attentively, interrupting
gently a few times for clarification. When I finished,
he asked more questions, pressed me to recall specific
details, verbatim conversations, leading me chrono-
logically through my own story. I wondered if he ever
forgot where he put his car keys.

"What evidence did the search warrant specify?" he
asked. He saw my confusion. "The search warrant must
state in detail the area the police intend to search and
the items they're looking for," he explained patiently.
"Did you bring a copy with you?"

"No. Sorry." I flushed.

"Did you read it?"

My face turned even more florid. "I...yes, but most
of it was in legalese. No offense."

He waved a hand. "Perfectly understandable. I can
get a copy."

"I remember it said pretty much the entire house was
fair game." I searched my memory, hoping for a shred
of redemption. "The list actually seemed very general,
now that I think about it—'personal papers, financial
records,' that sort of thing. Oh, and 'leather goods,'" I
said, suddenly remembering how odd it had struck me
at the time.

He looked reflective. "You have an inventory of what was taken?"

"At home, yes."

"And you have no idea why they were looking for those items?"

I shook my head. "No clue. I suppose they hoped to find something that proves I killed her."

"But nothing they took will."

"No. Of course not. A lot of what they took made no sense. Some of it was damned inconvenient. They took the hard drive out of my computer. I had to beg them to copy my working files onto discs. Can they do that? I mean, I had to go out and buy another hard drive to use the computer."

"Unfortunately, yes, they can. If the affidavit and warrant were properly prepared." Deflated, I said nothing. "It's possible they're ruling you out," he mused. "I imagine they already asked you for your fingerprints." My look of surprise confirmed it. "The night they told me they found her."

"Standard procedure when they process a crime scene. Makes it easier to determine who else, besides you and your wife, may have been in her car. From what you've told me, however, there's enough circumstantial evidence to implicate you. They're hoping to shore up a case with whatever they found when they searched your house. I'd like to see the inventory." I nodded.

"And that's everything." He waited.

"Everything I can think of." My eyebrows knitted.

He straightened. "It's natural at this stage, when you're still in the process of looking into representation, to want to withhold information you consider unimportant or tangential. Frankly, I won't know how or if I can help you if you're not completely honest." He paused, saw me hesitate, then went for the closer. "It's the only way I work."

"They took some discs." I felt warmth involuntarily spread once more up my cheeks into my scalp. "From a locked drawer in my desk."

"What was on them?" He ignored my distress.

"Um, erotica. Nude photos."

"Pornography?"

I shook my head. "I wouldn't say so, no. Tasteful nudes. Like you'd see in *Playboy*." It sounded like dissembling, even to me. His blank expression was even more disconcerting, as if he'd never seen a men's magazine.

"I did keep them locked up," I added. I wasn't sure why I sounded apologetic.

"Tasteful," he repeated.

"Yes." I paused. "Look, I don't think enjoying photos of attractive nude women makes me some sort of pervert."

"I didn't say it did," he replied evenly. "I'm more concerned about the implications for your children. You kept them locked up, which is good."

"Of course I did." That was more than I could say about my father, who'd kept a couple of magazines in a dresser drawer. "I'm not dumb enough to think they're appropriate for a ten-year-old. Or my daughter. Though, for that matter, both of them can see a lot worse watching rented videos at friends' houses." The fact was, my kids probably were a lot more sophisticated and had grown up a lot faster than me. I was willing to bet that surreptitious glances at our fathers' copies of *Playboy* was the closest thing to sexual education many men in my generation ever got. Sex-Ed was part of Ty's fifth-grade curriculum.

He held up a hand. "It's not my job to judge you. Assuming you retain me, however, I will tell you how your actions will be perceived, and what that means for you and your children. I'll be blunt. Until I learn more, I don't know where you stand. Given what you've told me, I think there's certainly a possibility that you could be arrested for your wife's murder. If that happens, your children will be taken from you and placed in foster care, at least until your arraignment. When Child Protective Services learns that you kept pornography in the house—" He raised his hand higher to cut me off. "—or what will be posited as pornography, your chances of regaining custody, even if you're acquitted, will be slim."

"I didn't do this." My voice was low, calm, requiring effort.

"I did not kill my wife. And I would not hurt my kids. They know it. I've practically raised them single-handedly. They can't do that. No one is taking them away from me." He regarded me curiously, evidently unafraid of venomous snakes and other cornered creatures.

"It's all about perceptions." He shrugged. "You're willing to fight, at least." I sat in surprised silence.

"I can take you on as a client. I'll get a letter of agreement in the mail to you. If it's acceptable, return a signed copy with a check, and that will effectively put me on retainer. In the meantime, please don't take offense, but I need to have an accurate picture of your financial situation. Could you give me an idea of your net worth?"

"Excuse me?"

"Mr. Holm—may I call you Jack? Jack, if the situation comes to it, conducting a criminal defense is expensive. So is staying out of jail. I need to know what liquid assets you have and what else you can use as collateral." Sweat trickled down my sides. Off the top of my head, I gave him a quick accounting of what I had in retirement savings and built-up equity in the house. Mary's life insurance hadn't paid yet, but the company's policy wasn't very generous anyway. It would barely pay off her credit cards.

He nodded, satisfied. "I'm not trying to frighten you. I just want you to be aware of the realities of this situation. Nothing's happened yet, and perhaps nothing will. In the meantime, I'll get copies of everything to review. I'll also line up a good family law attorney, just in case."

"Family law?"

"Think of us like doctors. It's the same as putting together a team of specialists in an operating room. You wouldn't want an orthopedic surgeon doing an angioplasty, no matter how good. And you probably wouldn't want your cardiologist rebuilding a blown-out knee." I shivered involuntarily, thinking of the mounting costs. We had insurance for an emergency medical team, but not this sort of calamity.

"What should I be doing?"

"You have enough to worry about trying to hold your family together. Concentrate on that."

"What if the police want to talk to me again?"

"Tell them you'll be happy to cooperate, just as you have so far, but that you'd like your attorney present. Tell them they can call me to schedule a meeting."

"But what if they—"

"Don't panic. Stay calm. Be polite." He handed me a card that he pulled from an inside jacket pocket. "Call me immediately. My cell and pager numbers are listed if you can't reach me here at the office. Day or night."

I fingered the card. "Thank you." He stood. "Try not to worry. You did the right thing. This way, we'll be better prepared for whatever happens." I tried to feel as enthusiastic as he sounded.

TEN

ED MANKIEWICZ and Dick Whelan came for me on the following Tuesday at four in the afternoon. Long before the sounds actually registered, I became aware of a car pulling into the driveway, of doors opening and closing. I looked up from the work on my desk and glanced out the window. An empty sedan sat parked in the driveway. A marked patrol car pulled in behind it at the same time the doorbell rang. Ty's footsteps thundered down the hall. I made it halfway to the door when I heard him call, "Dad."

"On my way, Bud." The front door opened wide. Mankiewicz stood across the threshold, folded papers barely visible through his thick fingers. Whelan stayed a few feet behind him on the top step. Beyond Whelan, two uniformed cops stood by the open doors on opposite sides of the patrol car. I recognized one of them, the student resource officer at both the middle school and high school. Tyler looked from me to Mankiewicz and back, his expression blank. Footsteps rumbled down the stairs behind me.

"Dad?" Kelsey's voice. "What's going on?"

"Could you step outside, please, Mr. Holm?" Mankiewicz looked apologetic.

My stomach convulsed at the thought of doing what someone had done to Mary. I choked back the urge to scream some sense into them. Mankiewicz dropped his eyes from my face to the hands at my sides. They clenched, unclenched, clenched again.

"Dad?" Kelsey's voice quavered.

Tyler's eyes were on me now.

"It's okay, sweetie," I reassured her. "Everything's going to be all right. I promise." I reached over and tousled Ty's hair. "Stay here just a sec, okay, kiddo? I'm going to talk with Detective Mankiewicz." He nodded solemnly. I stepped onto the porch. Mankiewicz stepped back, lightly took hold of my elbow and steered me toward Whelan. Schroeder, the SRO, strolled over from the car and stopped at the foot of the steps.

"You've probably guessed what this is about." Mankiewicz kept his voice low, releasing my arm to tap the papers in his hand. "This is an arrest warrant. We have to take you in." He managed to sound as apologetic as he looked. "I don't want to cuff you in front of your kids. You going to be okay with this?" I looked at each of the three of them in turn, then took a deep breath and matched his tone.

"No, I'm not okay with this, but I'm not about to make any trouble." He hesitated, gave a short nod and read me my rights off a card he pulled from his shirt pocket.

"Okay," he said when he finished, "the deal is we take you to the department and process you, then we'll take you to King County jail for the night. Officer Schroeder and his partner will help your kids pack a few things. Then they'll go down to the department, too, and wait for Child Protective Services to come and put them in temporary foster care. I'm telling you this so you don't worry about what happens to them."

"I understand."

"You okay?" Whelan asked.

I looked at him, realizing I'd never heard him speak before. "I'm fine." I turned back to Mankiewicz. "Look, I know you wouldn't be here if you weren't convinced I did this. I didn't. But no matter what, I'm begging you, please don't put my kids in foster care. They need to stay here, on the island. Go to their own schools. Be with their friends."

"You sure you don't want to sit down?" Whelan asked. "You look pale."

"No, I'm all right." I wiped the back of my hand across my forehead, keeping my eyes on Mankiewicz. It came away wet. I shoved it in my pocket. "Please. They're just starting to figure out what normal is again. This is going to be hard for them to deal with. They can even stay with friends. The Thorvahls. Sue and Ken Thorvahl. I know they'd be happy to take them in."

"Hey, Ed?" Schroeder piped up. Mankiewicz turned. "I know them. Good people. I could put in a word with CPS." He raised one shoulder, let it drop. "You know, until the first hearing." Mankiewicz turned back and glanced past me before locking eyes on my face.

"No guarantees," he said finally. "It's up to CPS. If they think it's best for the kids."

"That's all I ask."

"Okay. You can say your good-byes from here. Sorry. Best I can do." As if on cue, Schroeder came up the steps past us and stood between us and the front door. I turned to see Tyler and Kelsey waiting in the doorway. My knees almost buckled at the sight.

"Guys, I have to go with them." I managed to keep my voice steady. "This will all get straightened out soon, I promise."

"Where are you going?" Kelsey took a hesitant step. "Where are they taking you?"

"Down to the police station. It'll be all right, Kels. Just do what Officer Schroeder tells you. He's going to try to fix it so you can stay at Amanda's."

"You're not coming back? Are they arresting you?" Her voice rose, eyes filling with tears.

Mankiewicz had a hand on my elbow again, his tightening grip as confining as any jail cell.

"I'll be back as soon as I can. Maybe a day or two."

"Tell them you didn't do it!" Tears streaked her face now, and she moved toward me. Schroeder put an arm out. "You didn't do it! Tell them!" Schroeder used both hands now to keep her from me. She struggled in his arms, her voice hysterical. "Tell them you didn't do it, Dad! Please! Just tell them." Tyler stood stock still, his face serious, but unafraid. Mankiewicz gave my arm a squeeze.

"I have to go, guys." I blinked. "I love you. I'll fix this. I promise. I'll get us back together again somehow. Take care of each other, will you?" Tyler nodded solemnly. Kelsey just hung on Schroeder's arm, crying so hard that words wouldn't come. Mankiewicz and Whelan walked me to the far side of the sedan before putting cuffs on me. They eased me into the backseat, then got in the front. Whelan jockeyed the car around in a quick three-point turn. As we passed the patrol car on the way out the drive, Tyler patted Kelsey's arm, as if consoling a small child.

"THIS ISN'T GOING TO be easy." Adele Arnold paced the width of the small interview room still in working clothes even at this late hour. She had one hand on the hip of a plaid tweed suit the color of butterscotch pudding. The other was pressed to her forehead as if trying to prevent anything from falling out. Her raised arm had pulled the silk ivory blouse loose from the waistband of her skirt. It formed a little balloon, poking out from under the suit jacket. A line of pale skin showed through a run in her hose on the side of her leg, looking like a scar. It started below the knee and disappeared under the hem of the skirt.

She sat down at the metal table again, picked up a pen and twirled the end of it around a long, loose strand of strawberry-blond hair. Two long tortoiseshell pins precariously held the rest of her hair in a chignon.

"I realize you don't know me," I said. "I'm asking you to accept a lot on faith. My kids need me. I need them."

She shook her head. "I'm not the one who needs to be convinced. We have three days until the first hearing to persuade CPS that the best place for your kids is with you, even though you've just been arrested for killing their mother."

"I didn't do it."

"So you say." She sighed. "It's their job to err on the conservative side. The safety of your kids is their biggest concern."

"And covering their butts," I muttered.

"Take that attitude, and you'll never see your children again in this lifetime."

I blinked. "Sorry. It's been a bad day."

She nodded. "I know, but I'm telling you that you have to be a model father. Polite, friendly, cooperative, sensitive, all those things you claim to be. You show them attitude, anger, anything negative, and you're done." I bowed my head meekly. "As it stands, I think you should prepare yourself for the fact that they're not likely coming home anytime soon."

"I can't accept that," I said softly. "There must be something you can do." The pen twirled some more.

"The easiest way to keep them out of foster care is place them with relatives. Like your wife's parents."

"Her mom? Her dad died a few years ago." I considered it for all of a split second. "Not a chance."

"Why not?"

"She lives too far away, for one. It would totally disrupt the kids' lives, and I'd never see them. Then there's the fact that she doesn't even really like kids."

"Is this just bad blood talking?"

"No. I bent over backwards to be nice to her. She never did like me. The fact is, she always thought my kids should behave like miniature adults. Kids are kids."

"Is this just a difference in parenting philosophy, or is there something we can use here? Is she abusive?"

"I don't know. Depends on what you call abusive. Critical, definitely. When they were little she'd do things like drag them around shopping or sightseeing all day until they were starving and dead-dog tired. Then, she'd take them to a fancy sit-down restaurant and scold them when they whined about having to wait too long for food they weren't going to like anyway." She gazed somewhere past me, pulled the pen out of her hair and tapped it against a legal pad on the table. Then she jotted down a note.

"Anyone else on your wife's side?"

"A sister."

"Any problems there?"

"Besides the disruption of moving out of state?" I hesitated. "I guess not. She's nuttier than a fruitcake. Well, 'eccentric' is a better word, I suppose. But harmless, I think." I hesitated, remembering Bridget's insistence that I move the kids nearer to their grandmother.

Another note. "Okay, what about your side?"

I shrugged. "No one."

"*No* one?"

"My folks are dead. My older brother was killed when I was ten. Vietnam. I haven't talked to my sister in years. Last I heard she was in southern California, getting divorced from her third husband and moving to Las Vegas. To tell the truth, I'd be surprised if she's still alive."

"Drugs?"

I shrugged. "Maybe. Booze, mostly. No way I'm giving my kids to her."

She made another note, sighed, and twirled her hair again. "What are the most onerous conditions you can imagine accepting?" I didn't hesitate. "None. No conditions."

"You have to be realistic." My chest tightened. I sucked in more air. It didn't help.

"My kids had their mother taken away. As if that wasn't bad enough, I get locked up for killing her. Well, I didn't do it, and my kids don't deserve to lose both their parents. I want them home with me. I don't care what you have to do. I'm all they have left. They're all I have left. Don't let them take my kids away."

"You don't even know if you'll get out of here. You could be denied bail, you know."

"Can't happen. It just can't." She watched me swallow hard, blink, sniff. After a moment, she dropped her gaze and studied the pad in front of her.

"A lot will depend on the case worker. CPS will talk to the kids, of course—and you. I'll push as hard as I can to get them to interview anybody you think will vouch for your character and what kind of parent you've been. I'll need a list. Anybody who knows you or has seen you with your kids. We'll get to that in a minute. In the meantime, we need a fallback, a compromise that CPS can live with." She quickly went on before I said anything. "You've got to face it. You're not going to get what you want. But we'll get as close to it as we can. You have to understand these people have a lot to answer for. They have to be able to pass the straight-face test." She paused. "You never heard of it? Whoever the case worker is, she has to face the media when all this comes out. She has to explain why giving you custody of your kids is the right decision—"

"—with a straight face," I finished for her.

She nodded. "If—and this is a big 'if'—we manage to get CPS on your side, we still have to convince a judge at the first hearing." It began to sound less promising. "So, here's what I'm going to recommend. Would your sister-in-law consider coming to live with you?" Something in her eyes prevented me from dismissing the idea outright. She had something up her sleeve. I thought of what Bridget had said at the airport.

"It's possible. I don't know. She'd have to arrange some kind of leave from her job. It's a lot to ask."

She waved a hand impatiently. "Thirty days. That's all we need. If you don't screw up, we'll ask the court at the second hearing to let her go home. I don't know how we'll pull it off. You'll need a letter-perfect report from everyone."

"I just want to be with my kids."

She tipped her head and looked at me for a moment. "If you do half the things at home you say you do, you're far more highly evolved than ninety-nine percent of the men I've ever met." She paused. "Your wife was a lucky woman." I thought of Mary's last portrait. Lucky didn't come to mind.

MY ONE PHONE CALL had been to Preston, and I'd been fortunate to reach him directly. He'd reminded me not to say a word to anyone, then had put all the wheels in motion by asking pointed, yes-or-no questions. He said he'd see me before my arraignment in the morning and told me not to worry. Worry was the only thing I could do.

By the time I'd been booked, taken downtown and processed, it had been after seven in the evening. It had been close to eight-thirty when Adele Arnold showed up. She'd gotten hung up in the bureaucratic tussle with CPS, but the good news was that she'd managed to get the kids placed with the Thorvahls.

Preston, she'd told me, had called them personally to alert them to the situation and get their consent.

Now I was alone, in a strange place, confined, surrounded by hundreds of men I'd spent a lifetime going out of my way to avoid or ignore. It was far worse than the first night away at summer camp. It was the longest night of my life.

WEDNESDAY WENT BY in a blur, a dream, surreal and indistinct. Startled out of a doze by the jail's version of reveille, my first sight was of iron bars. I'd slept in an orange jumpsuit, the uniform worn by guests of the county lockup. Even so, it took me a moment to separate night visions from reality and figure out where I was. The morning wore on in a bewildering schedule of head counts, hygiene, breakfast and work assignments. Most of the men around me fell into lines and moved from place to place with yawning indifference, as familiar with the routine as if they were at home.

I did my best to avoid bumping into any of my nearest neighbors, hoping not to set someone off inadvertently. Guards herded us like cattle during round-up from one activity to the next. They passed me over for a work assignment and sent me back to my cell because I was scheduled for arraignment. I was glad someone knew what I was supposed to do.

At the appointed time, they escorted me from my cell to the courthouse a block over and handed me over to the bailiffs there. The bailiffs stuck me in a small conference room to wait. Sometime later, the door opened slightly. A bailiff stuck his head inside and looked at me, then stepped into the room. He had a bundle of clothes in his hands. He set it on the table, turned and left. The pile contained one of my suits, a pair of shoes, matching belt, a tie, clean socks and briefs. I didn't question how Preston had managed it. Putting on that suit made me feel human again, if a little rough around the edges.

Another interminable wait began. My eyelids kept closing as if weighted. I drifted off when the door opened again, rousing me with a start. The same bailiff was back to take me to the courtroom. We waited again outside the courtroom, then he showed me in and told me to sit. Preston entered through a door at the rear of the courtroom and paused. He scanned the room, acknowledged me with a nod, and sat at the defense table. He pulled papers from his briefcase.

The business in front of the judge concluded. Preston stood, papers in hand, and motioned at me to join him. I looked up at the bailiff for confirmation. He nodded and walked me across the room. I carried the white plastic bag with my inmate uniform like a bag lady guarding her possessions.

"Good morning," Preston said when I joined him. "Get any sleep?" I shook my head. He smiled. "I'm not surprised. You don't look too bad." I managed a grunt. I hadn't shaved. I'd gotten two minutes in a shower, most of it spent watching my back.

"Well, we'll see if we can have you back in your own bed tonight."

"That would be nice." Even in my own bed I would probably sleep with one eye open for the next few nights. He turned back to his papers.

After a moment the court clerk called a case number. Preston stood. I followed his lead. The clerk read the formal charges, some mumbo-jumbo that included the words "murder in the second degree." I caught that part. Preston and the prosecuting attorney identified themselves. The judge addressed me, asked for my plea. I told him in no uncertain terms. Two simple words. Too bad a man isn't always taken at his word. The lawyers wrangled over remand or bail. The clerk set a date for a case-scheduling conference. And suddenly it was over.

"Let's see what we can do about getting you released," Preston said.

He led me out of the courtroom down the hall to a conference room. On the way, another man joined us. He was so stocky that the lapels of his black suit jacket swung like tent flaps in a breeze as he swaggered our way. The rest of his clothes were black, too. A silk shirt with mother-of-pearl buttons opened at the collar. The roll of a double chin nearly covered the next button. He had gray hair cropped close, and his large hooked nose looked as if it had been broken. Maybe twice. Not even a deep tan could hide dark bags under eyes that looked as if they could no longer be surprised.

"Jack Holm," Preston said, "Viktor Kordokova." My fingers barely wrapped around the mitt he extended. It was like squeezing a ham.

Preston gestured at the doorway. Kordokova walked through, eased his bulk into a chair, and rested his forearms on the table. Jewels flashed on two large pinkie rings, diamonds on one, rubies on the other.

"Viktor is a bail bondsman," Preston said as he sat down. "All we have to do is take care of some paperwork, and we'll get bond posted for you. Once that's taken care of, you can collect your personal belongings from the county and be on your way." They handed me papers. I didn't bother to read them, too tired to care. That's what lawyers are for. I signed them, grateful that I wouldn't have to spend another night in jail. When I'd finished, Kordokova was my new best friend, apparently. A thirty-thousand-dollar fee could do that, I suppose. That, and the fact that he now held the deed to my house if I got the foolish notion of chucking it all and skipping town.

Preston had to explain how to get back to the jail and claim my personal effects twice. The second time, I borrowed his pen and wrote it down.

THE HOUSE'S LIVED-IN sounds dominated the silence. The background hum of the refrigerator and rumble of the furnace seemed clamorous without the noisy energy of everyday life to drown them out. The distant rush of passing cars on the main road sounded like waves breaking on shore. Half-full bowls of cat food and water were evidence that someone had been in the house in the past twenty-four hours. The smell of ripe garbage told me it had been kids. No one else could ignore an odor that foul. I took the full bag out of the receptacle, tied it up and walked it to the back door. My footsteps sounded hollow on the hard kitchen floor, echoing as if the house was empty of furnishings.

Kelsey's tortoiseshell cat appeared in the doorway to investigate. Seeing me, she stretched and yawned, then slowly sashayed across the floor, tail twitching like a pennant. She circled between my legs, rubbing herself first against one then the other. I reached down to scratch her behind the ears and stroke her fur. Her guttural purr drowned out the other noises. Content for the moment, she strutted to her food bowl, stuck her nose in it and noisily crunched a few of the dry kibbles in her sharp teeth. Then she sat on her haunches and daintily licked a paw.

"You don't miss them a bit, do you?" The cat looked up at the sound of my voice, stared at me unblinking, and went back to cleaning her paw. "Must be nice. No worries. A little food and water, and you're all set." She ignored me. I was getting used to it.

I called Patti Murphy, the real estate agent who had found us the house when we first moved to the Northwest. She and her husband, Tim, had grown up on the island, but lived in Bellevue now. We'd never been close, but Patti had stayed in touch, and Mary and I had run into the two of them from time to time, usually at fundraisers. When I got her on the line, I asked her to see if she could find out what the house might be worth. Between the bail bond and legal fees, I was going to need money.

After cradling the kitchen phone, I wandered slowly from room to room, taking stock, opening doors and window coverings to let in the light. Each room felt as familiar and comfortable as a favorite bedtime story. Now, everything looked different somehow, as if someone read the story with a different accent, an odd inflection. Each picture, each knickknack, every stick of furniture had some history, some meaning to it. On the walls hung the framed Monet prints we got after an exhibit came to the Art Institute in Chicago—our first "grown-up" artwork. On a table, the Waterford candy dish we received from a long-dead aunt as a wedding present. In the living room, the couch we picked for our first house. Upstairs, the personalized towels the kids got for Christmas one year.

The house was full of her, full of her memories. But already they grew cold and lifeless, fading like chintz curtains in a sunny window. Already, their history was dying. I couldn't remember where the armoire in the den had come from. I couldn't remember why we'd settled on the garish orange Oriental runner in the hall. And only Mary had known where the dozens of vases, knickknacks and baubles had come from. They'd begun to lose their meaning, becoming just stuff, yard sale bargains, littering the house like detritus from a Texas twister. Only this tornado had come from Savannah.

For twenty years she had whirled unpredictably in and out of our lives, bouncing off walls, sucking us into her vortex and spitting us out again. Now she was gone, like a cyclone that had spun itself out, leaving me to try to clean up the mess and repair the damage left in her wake.

I stopped in front of a photo on a shelf in the family room. It was a group shot from Kelsey's middle school graduation a year and a half before, the last family photo we'd taken. We hadn't even been able to get together for a Christmas card photo after that. I picked it up and looked at it more closely. Kelsey stood front and center in a pink chiffon dress looking radiant and very grown up. Mary, Tyler and I stood close behind her, me in the center with my arm around Tyler's shoulders, Mary's hand on Kelsey's shoulder. We all smiled into the camera, looking relaxed. I wondered if we'd been as happy as we looked.

ELEVEN

THE first knock on the door came later that afternoon. A bright light popped on as soon as I opened the door, momentarily blinding me. By the time the big red spot in the center of my vision cleared a woman stepped up within inches of me and thrust a black foam-covered microphone in my face. A man with a video camera on his shoulder stood off to one side several feet behind her.

"Mr. Holm, Kerri Madigan, Channel Four News. Could you tell me your reaction to being arrested yesterday on charges of murdering your wife?" I blinked rapidly. She came into focus slowly. Late twenties, dark straight hair, attractive, her look of concern meant to convey empathy, elicit trust. The way she crowded me and rushed her words said she had another agenda. I drew myself up, ready to snap at her and defend my castle. Something in her eyes shifted, and for a moment she eased off.

"How do you respond to the charges?" she prodded, seeing my hesitation.

I noticed the red light on the camera and Bruce Colvin's story in the local paper came to mind. "I'm sorry, I have nothing to say."

"Don't you want to respond to the charges?" She pressed forward again.

I shook my head and backed up to swing the door shut. "I already did."

"But sir—" She leaned forward, but the closing door cut her off.

I stood stock still, holding my breath until I heard footsteps receding down the steps. When they'd gone, I took a few steps down the hall, stopped to lean against a wall and waited for my knees to stop trembling.

FOUR TELEVISION NEWS TRUCKS sat parked along the shoulder of the street out front when I pulled out of the garage. A reporter slouching against the hood of the nearest one jerked upright at the sound of the van's engine. He waved frantically at someone out of sight, and then strode up the driveway, microphone in one hand swinging at his side. He took a stand in the middle of the drive and turned his back toward me, presumably to face a camera.

I slowed and pulled up several feet away from him, hoping the van was out of the shot. Several other reporters emerged from the other news vans and made their way over to the drive. I turned the wheel to the right and nosed ahead slowly, looking for enough room to squeeze between him and trees lining the edge of the drive. The reporter looked over his shoulder nervously, but stood his ground. I let the van roll forward a few more feet. When it almost nudged him, he turned around and faced me. He mouthed a question, the words unintelligible through the glass. I ignored him and let the van inch forward some more. Another mouthed question. When I didn't bother to roll down the window, he took the hint and backed up a step to let me pass. The tires complained softly as I took a hard right onto the street, and gave the van some gas. In the rearview mirror, I saw the reporters slowly head back to their vans, shaking their heads.

Just before dinnertime I knocked on the Thorvahls' door. An older version of Ty's friend Rory answered the door. Before I said a word, he called over his shoulder, "Mom!" We both heard her say, "Coming," from somewhere inside the house. He turned back to me. "She'll be right with you." He disappeared into another room and left me standing on the stoop.

Sue appeared, wiping her hands on a kitchen towel, a smile of greeting on her face. I saw just the slightest hesitation when she realized who it was, then she put the smile back in place.

"Oh, hi," she said warmly. She pushed open the screen making me back up a step. She didn't invite me in. Instead, she stepped outside, glancing over her shoulder before she pulled the front door partly closed behind her.

"What happened?" she asked in a low voice. "Was it all some sort of mistake?"

I handed her the bouquet of flowers I'd picked up at the grocery store on the way over. "I can't thank you and Ken enough for taking them in, especially on such short notice like that."

She flushed with pleasure. "No problem. Really."

"Are they all right? They're not giving you any trouble, are they?"

"They're fine. Pretty upset when they got here last night. At least Kelsey was. Amanda seemed to help her get over it."

"That's good. I was so worried."

"They're fine here. Ty and Rory have been having a blast."

"I'm glad." I shifted my weight from one foot to the other. "I'd like to contribute, at least. To groceries or something."

"We wouldn't hear of it. Really." She waved it off. "So, what's going on?"

I hesitated. "They charged me, but I was able to post bond, so I'm home." The friendly expression remained, but her eyes flitted across my face.

"So? What? They don't think you did it, do they?" She already knew the answer.

"Look, I probably shouldn't have put your family in the middle of this, but I didn't know what else to do. I couldn't let them put the kids in foster care somewhere."

"Of course not," she said hurriedly. "We're glad to have them."

"I promise you, Sue, I had nothing to do with this. It's all just some incredible nightmare."

"You'll get off, won't you?" I couldn't tell if she was concerned that I would, or wouldn't.

"I've got a good lawyer. We'll see." I gave her a tight smile. "I'm sure CPS probably told you to keep the kids away from me, but can I see them?"

"Actually, they just told us to make sure we didn't leave them alone with you." She smiled, taking some of the sting out of it. "So you won't kidnap them."

"Figures." She looked at me for a moment, then the lines around her eyes seemed to soften.

"Of course you can see them." I let out a breath and wished there was a place to sit down.

"Just so you know, I'm hoping they can come home in a day or two."

"Really? That would be great." I explained the plan Adele Arnold had suggested. Sue agreed it sounded like a plausible compromise. Then she went to get Ty and Kelsey.

"Daddy!" Ty got a running start ten feet from the

door when he saw me, jumped into my arms and wrapped himself around me in a big hug.

"What's up, kiddo?" The feel of his thin arms around my neck and warm breath on my neck as he pressed his face against my shoulder was like throwing a life preserver to a drowning man. Kelsey followed more sedately, almost shyly. She stood a few feet away, watching us. Then she took a hesitant step and awkwardly leaned in, grasping my arm and touching her cheek to my shoulder. It was the closest thing to a hug she'd given me in a long time.

Ty slid down me like a fire pole, landing on his feet. He jammed his hands in his pockets. "Can we come home now?"

"Not quite yet," I said. I watched Kelsey's face fall. "You'll have to stay here a couple more days. Is that okay?"

"Cool." Tyler tossed it off as if it didn't matter one way or the other. "Rory and me are having a good time."

"Rory and I."

"When can we come home?" Kelsey asked softly.

"I don't know. A lot of it depends on you guys."

"On us?" Tyler's eyes widened.

"I have to go to court and ask a judge to let you come home. Tomorrow or the next day, someone is going to come and ask you guys a lot of questions about what life is like at home, what I'm like as a parent, stuff like that. The judge will get a report and decide what's best."

"Can't we just tell him what's best?"

"I wish we could, kiddo. It doesn't work that way. But the judge may want to meet you and talk to you personally."

"What if we say the wrong thing?" There was fear in Kelsey's eyes.

"As long as you tell the truth, there is no wrong thing to say. Just answer as honestly as you can, even if you think it isn't what they want to hear." I wondered what she would say about her relationship with her mom, about the differences in our parenting styles. I wondered what she would say about us, about Mary and me. Kelsey wasn't blind or stupid. Surely she'd seen Mary's drinking, her unhappiness. She'd probably sensed the trouble we'd been having before I did, though she might not have been able to articulate it. I still couldn't.

"Actually, this will work out great," I said. "You guys get to hang with your friends, and I get the house all to myself. Ahh, peace and quiet."

"Da-a-d." They both turned on me accusingly. I couldn't help smiling.

"Dad, is it okay if I go see what Rory's doing? We're building this really cool Ferris wheel out of Legos."

"Sure, kiddo." He started for the door. "Hey, forget something?" He turned. I got down on one knee and he came over for a hug. "I'll come over and see you sometime after school tomorrow."

"Okay. See ya." He dashed back into the house.

Kelsey stood quietly, eyes down, nudging a brown leaf with the toe of her shoe. "So, what's going to happen?" she asked quietly. She kept her eyes on the ground. "Are you going to jail?"

"No, sweetie. Not if I can help it." She looked at me then. The question still hung in her eyes. "I didn't do anything wrong," I said. "They can't put me in jail." She didn't look convinced.

THREADING MY WAY through the media vans, I made it into the garage intact. The doorbell rang as soon as I was in the house. I thought to ignore it, but it rang again insistently. A lone man stood on the porch facing the drive. No cameras. No microphone.

I frowned as I opened the door. "Yes?"

He turned. "Jack. Got a circus out here." A huge smile lit up his face, crinkling his eyes nearly shut. The broad nose and straight, square-cut salt-and-pepper hair falling across his forehead finally registered.

"Tim. What are you doing here?"

"You know." He shrugged, his grin widening, if possible.

"Ready-Fire-Aim said you called this afternoon and told me you're in trouble, so here I am." Barrel-chested and stocky, Tim Murphy reminded me a little of Pete Rose. But looks were where the slight resemblance ended. After studying to be a teacher at Notre Dame, Tim had come home and ended up driving a Coke truck for ten years before learning he had a tumor in his chest the size of a baseball. Hodgkins disease. They took out the tumor, along with his spleen, and zapped him with radiation for ten weeks. A year after he found out he had cancer, he ran the Portland Marathon. When Coke laid him off not long after, he took a job teaching Phys. Ed. at Sacred Heart in Bellevue and hadn't looked back. I'd never met a guy more devoted to helping other people, especially kids.

"Well, come on in."

"Wish I could." He stuck his hands in his pockets. "I've got to run to a planning meeting for our Tijuana mission trip this summer. But I thought I'd stop by and see if there's anything I can do."

"You've heard…" I saw him nod. "They want to take

the kids away from me. Maybe you could put in a word when the time comes?"

"Sure. Be happy to if I can. How you holding up?" The weight of the day suddenly pressed on my shoulders, and I felt them sag.

"It's been…rough. I just don't understand why, you know?"

"I always figured that my getting into Notre Dame was the twenty-first Mystery of the Rosary. Maybe this is the twenty-second. You know I don't think God gives us more than we can handle, Jack. You'll get through this." I shook my head slowly.

"Sometimes I wonder."

"You might think about doing what I do. I always pray to the Blessed Virgin Mary because moms always seem to do right by their sons, and get them to do what they want. Couldn't hurt." He stuck out his hand, and I met his firm grip. "Call me if there's anything I can do," he said, and turned down the steps into the darkness.

I SPENT AN HOUR ON the phone that night with Bridget, coaxing, wheedling, cajoling, everything short of actual begging to persuade her to help me. She countered every ploy with a wishywashy "I don't know" or "that might not work for me" in her whispery voice. I tried bribery, offering to make up any lost wages. She sounded offended, saying she could never do it for money. I tried blackmail, reminding her she'd said I could ask her for anything. She turned it back on me, making me feel guilty for asking her to make such a huge sacrifice. I appealed to her sense of charity. I took a page from her book and tried guilt, reminding her that Ty and Kelsey were the only close family she had left, other than Letty. In the end, after I assured her that she wouldn't have to stay any longer than thirty days no matter what, she relented. I suspected I would feel like Pyrrhus long before the month was up.

Two more reporters knocked on the door after that, looking for on-camera quotes. I turned them away as politely as I could.

TRISH NELSON, THE CPS caseworker, grilled me more thoroughly and asked harder questions than any job interviewer. Of course, she had a lot more latitude than a prospective employer. If she wanted to know the color of my underwear I'd be obliged to tell her. I could sick the EEOC on her for asking that question if I was applying for a job.

She wasn't the unattractive, harried, cynical, shiftless, uncaring bureaucrat I expected. I assumed she had too many cases and too little time to learn enough about us to make an impartial judgment. She seemed in no hurry to get to another appointment. Relatively young, she approached her job with energy and enthusiasm. But she was evidently old enough to have a lot of experience. She told me that caseworkers had to have six years' experience in the field or a master's in social work to work in her department.

When she first showed up, casually dressed in khakis, white blouse and a bush jacket, dark blond hair pulled back into a ponytail, I pegged her for late twenties. She was slender, but athletic, with a cute, tomboyish face covered with freckles. Friendly and easy-going, she quickly put me at ease and got me talking about my personal history. The effect was disarming. I wanted to like her, wanted her to like me. I reminded myself that she was a professional, not here to make new friends.

From what little she revealed about herself, I gathered that she was a little older than I'd thought. Early thirties, maybe older. The lack of a wedding band suggested she didn't have kids of her own, but that didn't mean she couldn't figure out what was best for mine.

She asked about my relationship with Mary, about the division of household labor, about how we'd handled parenting issues. She asked about the kids, how they'd been conceived (planned, more or less, from Mary's point of view); who they'd been named after (no one—Mary had just liked the sound of the names); what sort of babies they'd been (Kelsey: active, vocal; Tyler: quiet, content); how they did in school (no complaints); how they got along (as well as can be expected); how well they got on with us (better than expected); if they had friends (lots); and more.

She told me to walk her through the kids' daily schedules; I gave her the weekly schedule. She asked me how I handled school emergencies and other work-day interruptions. I indicated that the benefits of working at home included flexible hours, availability and close proximity to the kids' schools. She wanted to know the name of their doctor (Jim Schultz) and their health history (excellent other than the usual childhood ailments like colds and chicken pox, and the time Ty was hospitalized for a respiratory infection when he was six months old). She asked me how I would handle "female" questions from Kelsey (as honestly as possible, with help from a friend's mom, like Sue, if necessary).

She took a tour of the house, checked the food in the pantry and the fridge, the closets in the kids' rooms, the books on the shelves. She asked about dating, curfews, homework, television, chores, rules and discipline. She asked the names of their dentist, orthodontist, teachers and friends. I hit every pitch she threw. A few went foul—I could think of only one of Kelsey's teachers—but at least I got wood on every one.

Before she left, she set an appointment to spend time observing us as a family the next day. When she'd gone, I realized she'd given me no clue of her impressions. She'd shown interest, concern, curiosity, but not a single reaction to any of my answers. She'd even managed to make the whole experience pleasant, sort of like being convinced, once she had me on the rack, that I was into "light bondage." Yet she'd given nothing away. I had a sudden urge to stake her at poker. Or take her to dinner. I wasn't at all sure where that last impulse came from.

I ENDED UP TAKING HER to dinner, sort of. She showed up at the end of the day on Friday, almost an hour late, and came with me to the Thorvahls' to pick up the kids. Ready and waiting when we pulled in the drive, they looked freshly scrubbed and neatly dressed. I stole a glance at her, certain that she would see through the ploy to impress her. The kids climbed in the back of the van guardedly, and politely said hello as they strapped themselves in. Trish twisted so she could see them, gave them a smile and asked how their day had been. As I pulled away, she already had Tyler chatting away about school. A glance in the rearview mirror told me Kelsey remained cool to the whole idea.

Back at the house, I invited Trish to sit at the counter. "You said you wanted us to try to follow our normal routine. Since it's already late, I thought maybe you wouldn't mind having dinner with us." She looked startled, and uneasiness flashed across her face. I wondered if I'd made a serious blunder.

"I don't know…"

"It would be no trouble." I gave her what I hoped was a reassuring smile. "We have plenty."

"It's not that. It's—well, I guess I *was* late for our appointment. It's just very unusual to socialize with clients."

I shook my head. "Strictly fact-finding. It's either watch Tyler sit in front of the TV and Kelsey talk on the phone, or eat dinner with us."

She hesitated. "Okay, then, dinner."

"You're not getting anything fancy."

"Good!" Tyler piped up. "I don't like fancy food." Trish's sudden laugh surprised me.

"I used to hate it when my parents took us out to dinner," she told him. "Having to dress up, sit still and mind our manners, and eat fancy food. Yuck. I know just how you feel."

"Well, this definitely won't be fancy," I said. "Can I get you something to drink?"

"A glass of water would be fine." I pulled a glass down from the cupboard and filled it with ice and water from the dispenser on the refrigerator door. As I set it down in front of Trish, I noticed Kelsey hanging back on the couch in the family room.

"Hey, Kels? Why don't you tell Ms. Nelson about the community service projects you're working on with Jennie?"

"She wouldn't be interested."

"Well, then why don't you tell me? It's been a while since you've given me an update."

"Actually, I'm very interested," Trish said. It sounded so genuine that I saw Kelsey's ears perk up ever so slightly. She stood and walked into the kitchen.

"Well, we do a lot of things." An awkward start.

"Which is your favorite?"

Kelsey looked thoughtful. "There's this café downtown that serves food to homeless people. I really like working there. It's fun. The people are really nice. When you see them on the street, they look real scary, but in the café they're just glad to be treated like normal people. They're, like, so appreciative." I worked while she talked, falling into my normal dinner prep routine.

"Hey, Ty, how about giving me a hand? Why don't you set the table?" He scooted off to the dining room to get silverware, surprising me. We only used the real silver on holidays and for special guests.

"So what's your least favorite?" I heard Trish ask.

Kelsey made a face. "Working in the thrift store. We hardly ever get to do fun stuff like work the register. Usually, they just make us move stuff around, or sort clothes. It's hard work."

"Hard work is good for you," I said, smiling.

"Then why don't I ever see you down there?"

"You're right, I should volunteer more," I said. "I just seem to find plenty to do around here. It's hard to find the time." Tyler came up to the counter and stood next to Trish.

"Want to see the science project I did at school? It's really cool." He led her down the hall and out of sight.

"She seems really nice," I said when they were out of earshot. Kelsey's shoulders traveled up and down, a half-inch each way.

"I guess."

"You're doing great, sweetie. Just relax and be yourself."

"But what if she doesn't like us?"

"What's not to like? We're nice people."

"She just makes me so nervous."

"She seems pretty laid back to me. Pretty sympathetic, too. I thought she was going to be horrible. You know, come in here with a checklist and flunk us on everything."

"Yeah, well, she might. Maybe we're doing everything wrong and we just don't know it."

"You're not doing anything wrong, Kels. I promise. Don't worry so much." I heard Ty explaining the pictures on the walls as he and Trish came back down the hall. "Dinner's ready," I announced when they walked into the family room.

Trish stepped over to the table, hesitated, then pulled out the chair at one end.

"Not there!" Ty said sharply. She looked up startled. I frowned, then realized the source of her confusion. Ty had set five places at the table. He patted the chair next to his. "Sit here."

I silently let out a breath. "That's a great idea." I watched Ty pull out Trish's chair for her as he'd seen me do countless times for his mom. Secretly pleased, I wondered if we were laying it on a bit thick. I waited until Trish and Kelsey sat down before taking my own seat.

"Hang on," Ty said. "I have to get Kelsey's drink." I passed food to Trish while he scooted into the kitchen. He came back in a flash with a large glass filled to the brim with juice. He watched it intently as he started to put it down. I saw his hand waver and sensed catastrophe too late. The glass slipped, fell with a crash on the table and dumped its contents onto Kelsey's plate and into her lap.

"Shit!" She jumped up, tipping her chair over backward. "Look what you did, you little—" She caught her-

self and looked around to see all of us staring at her. She
reddened. "Sorry, Dad," she said, her voice subdued.

Suddenly, I felt all eyes on me. Ty's face screwed
up as he fought back tears. "Hey, no big deal," I said.
"Accidents happen. Ty, why don't you get some paper
towels? Kels, if you run up and change real quick, we
can get those clothes into the laundry so they don't
stain." They both threw me grateful looks and hurried
off. I couldn't bring myself to look at Trish. I excused
myself and went to the kitchen to wet a dish towel with
hot water. I helped Ty blot up the spilled juice with
paper towels, then wiped down the table and floor.
Kelsey reappeared in clean sweatpants and top, detour-
ing into the laundry room to throw her clothes in the
washer.

When she sat down, Ty walked up to her and said in
a low voice, "I'm really sorry, Kels."

"That's okay, squirt. No biggie." She glanced at me
nervously. I forced a smile.

"Hey, let's eat before it gets cold."

NO ONE SPOKE ON the drive back to the Thorvahls.
Though still early evening, darkness had settled in
hours earlier, days so short now that it felt late. Ty
yawned sleepily in the backseat. Kelsey looked out the
window. Light rain fell. Droplets on the windows spar-
kled like diamonds every time we passed beneath a
streetlight.

When we pulled up to Sue's house, I got out with
the kids and walked them to the door to say goodnight.
I gave Tyler a hug, then turned to Kelsey. She didn't
move.

"Hey, how about a hug?"

"Dad, she's watching us," Kelsey hissed.

"That's the point. Give me a hug." She hesitated, then stepped in and wrapped her arms around my waist. I kissed the top of her head. "That wasn't so hard, was it?" I grinned at her. She threw me a look. "I love you."

"Me, too." She turned to the door. "Come on, squirt, let's go."

"I'll see you tomorrow." I waited until the door shut behind them before turning for the van.

I'd driven halfway back to the house before Trish said quietly, "Thanks for dinner."

"Hey, sorry about all the excitement."

"They were nervous. It's completely understandable."

I worked up the courage to say something else. "Um, thanks for taking the time to get to know us a little better."

"It's my job." It wasn't what I wanted to hear. "I enjoyed it," she said after a moment. "I think your kids are coping remarkably well, considering they just lost their mother."

"Thank you." I left it at that. I'd heard a huge "but" buried somewhere in there, and now I had the whole weekend to worry about it.

TWELVE

MONDAY morning, I met Adele Arnold in family court. She wore another tweedy suit, conservatively cut, but she looked fresh and buttoned up this time. She was somewhere around fifty, and attractive enough that with more flattering clothes she could have turned a lot of heads. Her appearance, I surmised, was calculated. She went for the matronly look. She wanted to look like someone's mom. She probably was. I hadn't asked.

"It's touch-and-go," she told me on the way into the courtroom.

I jammed my hands in my pockets, discreetly trying to wipe the sweat off my palms. "What do you mean?"

"I petitioned for full custody without supervision. Opposing counsel won't buy it, but I've almost got him sold on a compromise plan. There's just one sticking point."

"What's that?"

"Your caseworker."

I swallowed hard. She didn't seem to notice. "I thought we all did so well."

"You did. Her report is pretty positive, but she still recommended against leaving the kids with you."

"Why? I don't understand? She saw how good I am with them."

She tilted her head and cocked an eyebrow. "Think about it." We sat down at the defense table. It took me a moment.

"Oh. So, what do we do?"

"Play it out."

"Does that mean I have to testify?"

She shook her head. "The petition states our case. The A.G. will present DCFS' position. I'll get to cross-examine your caseworker. Her report puts you in a pretty good light. We'll present a compromise plan and hope opposing counsel helps us sell it to the judge. You won't have to say anything unless the judge or prosecutor wants to ask you questions for some reason." She put a hand on my arm and lowered her voice. "Okay, here we go."

The clerk called court into session, and introduced our case. As Adele predicted, the attorney general refuted the grounds for our petition, and called Trish Nelson to testify. When Trish sat down after being sworn in, she glanced coolly at our table, unafraid to meet my gaze.

"Ms. Nelson," the A.G. started. Trish turned her attention to him. "Would you please summarize your investigation in this case?" Trish took a breath and succinctly recounted the numerous phone and personal interviews she'd conducted with friends, acquaintances, neighbors, teachers and family, not once referring to notes. She'd been thorough, if nothing else.

"What conclusions did you reach as a result of your investigation?" the attorney asked when she finished.

"Mr. Holm is an attentive and loving father," she said simply. "He has a good relationship with his children, and appears quite capable of caring for them."

"Yet you've recommended that Mr. Holm's children be placed in foster care. Why is that?"

She didn't hesitate. "Despite his abilities as a parent, I can't overlook the fact that he's been charged with his wife's…death." Adele put a hand on my arm again, making me aware that I was crowding the table, legs tensed, laced fingers white at the knuckles. I slowly eased back from the edge of my chair.

"My first concern has to be the safety of his children," Trish went on. "The only way I can guarantee their safety is to place them in someone else's custody."

"Thank you." The A.G. returned to his seat.

"Ms. Arnold?" The judge looked our way expectantly.

"Thank you, Your Honor." She stood up and approached Trish. "Ms. Nelson, in your investigation, did you find any indication that Mr. Holm ever hurt his children in any way?"

"No, I didn't."

"He didn't spank them, or verbally abuse them?" Her tone was casual, curious.

"The children said that he raised his voice on occasion, but they didn't feel he ever did so inappropriately."

"And to the best of your knowledge, he never publicly humiliated them or did anything else to cause them emotional or physical harm?"

"No."

"Mr. Holm and his family have lived here for just three years. Did you investigate Mr. Holm's behavior toward his children prior to their move?"

"Yes, I did."

"Could you elaborate?"

"I spoke to a number of people in Chicago who knew the Holms before they moved here. None of them suggested he was anything but a good father."

"These were friends? Family?"

"Friends, mostly." She shrugged.

"Anyone else?"

She hesitated. "I also spoke with the director of the school his children attended."

"Go on."

Trish took a breath, let it out. "She said that he was one of the few fathers who volunteered time in the co-op nursery classrooms when his children were younger." It seemed to take effort to get the words out. "She said he served on the school's board of directors for several years."

Adele looked as if this was news to her. "Really? For several years? I assume the school found his contributions valuable then?"

"Yes."

"Don't most organizations involving children have to screen prospective board members?"

"I don't know what the law in Illinois is, but most organizations do, to avoid potential liability."

"Did this school screen Mr. Holm?"

"Yes. There were several references on file as well. Copies are attached to my report." Adele nodded, ignoring the dig. She looked down, musing, before addressing Trish again. Watching her, I realized good lawyering had more to do with great acting than encyclopedic knowledge of case law. It was about winning arguments. Being persuasive was all about how she presented information, not just the facts themselves.

"Would you say Mr. Holm is a typical father?"

Trish looked at me for the first time since she started testifying, then back at Adele. "No."

"Why not?"

"Judging from what I've learned, I'd say he spends more time with his children than the average father. And given the nature of his wife's job—late wife—he's more involved in actually raising them."

"You mean the day-to-day chores of making meals, doing their laundry, taking them to doctors' appointments, that sort of thing?" Trish inclined her head slightly, looking pained.

"Do you think he's over-protective or obsessive about his kids?" Adele went on.

Trish hesitated, then shook her head. "I didn't see any evidence of that, no."

"So, for all intents and purposes he's a kind, loving father actively involved in his children's lives as well as their care. Yet you don't think it's in their best interest to live with him."

"No. I'm concerned for their safety. There's no telling what he might do if he's capable of killing his wife."

"Allegedly," Adele said quickly. "Isn't Mr. Holm innocent until proven guilty?"

She shook her head. "In my job, I can't take that chance."

"Ms. Nelson?"

She hesitated. "Yes, but—"

"Thank you," Adele said quietly, cutting her off. She walked back to the table.

Trish looked over at the attorney general. He moved his head slightly to the left and back. She stepped down and collected her purse and briefcase. Glancing at her watch, she hurried out of the courtroom, her mind apparently already on the next item on her schedule.

"Ms. Arnold?" The judge's voice brought my eyes back to the front. "Anything else?"

"No, Your Honor."

"All right, then. Closing statements?"

The A.G. stood. "Our concerns are obvious, Your Honor. Mr. Holm has been charged with a violent and serious crime. In cases like this, children are usually put in foster care. We recommend it here." He looked over at our table as he sat down.

Adele glanced at him, then looked at the judge and stood, resting her fingertips on the table. "Your Honor, this is *not* a typical case. There is no evidence, let alone history, of domestic abuse. Mr. Holm has not only proved highly capable as a parent, his children have depended on him equally as much as their mother all their lives.

"These children have just lost their mother, lost her violently. They have no other family close by. To take them away from their father and the only home they've known here, and place them in a strange environment, especially now, would cause them irreparable harm. Ms. Nelson herself attested to his capabilities as a parent. Since he now works from his home, he also is physically available to his children whenever they need him. We ask that the court grant our petition and keep this family together."

The judge waved a hand as if dispelling an offensive odor. "I can't just overlook the charges against your client." Adele's tone became businesslike. "The children's aunt—Mrs. Holm's sister—has indicated she's willing to come live with the family. In addition, we're willing to accept a safety plan." I sat up.

Adele's hand moved slightly in my direction along the table's edge, her eyes still on the judge. I waited.

"What did you have in mind?" the judge said.

"Special safety instructions to the kids. An alert to teachers, coaches or any other adults directly involved in their activities to report signs of violence or abuse. Mr. Holm's sister-in-law makes daily voicemail reports to Ms. Nelson, assuming she remains the caseworker. And Ms. Nelson makes semi-weekly visits to check on the children." She made it sound as if I was something growing in a Petri dish, subject to microscopic inspection. I dreaded the thought. It would be like prison. No, on second thought, it definitely wouldn't be that bad.

Adele turned and looked at the other attorney.

The judge did, too. "Mr. Cassidy?"

"It's unusual." He fidgeted in his seat. "But I think it would satisfy our concerns." I sagged in the chair, exhausted. In a daze, I listened to Adele and the attorney general hammer out the details of the agreement. He suggested that weekly in-home visits would be adequate in light of the daily phone reports. Adele stipulated that the agreement last only thirty days until the next hearing. When they finished negotiating, the judge turned to me.

"Mr. Holm, do you understand this agreement?" I nodded. "Yes, Your Honor."

"And it's acceptable to you?"

"Yes, if it means keeping my kids with me."

She leaned forward, her face turning hard. "Mr. Cassidy is correct in saying that this is very unusual. I'm not inclined to award custody to a parent charged with a crime this serious. But according to all reports you're an exemplary father, and there's nothing to suggest that you would harm your children. I'm going to grant your petition with the changes made here. Don't make me regret it."

"Thank you, Your Honor. I won't." Adele started putting papers back into her briefcase. "That's it?" I asked her.

"Until the next hearing." She shut the clasps on the case and gripped the handle. Then she leaned over and spoke in a low voice, "You've got thirty days. Don't mess up."

THE PHONE RANG as we walked in the back door. I dropped Bridget's suitcase on the floor in the family room and hustled into the kitchen to answer it.

"Mr. Holm, this is Carol Atkins, the secretary down at school. Mr. Ortiz asked me to call you."

I turned my back toward the family room. "Yes?"

"Tyler got into a fight at recess after lunch. He's all right," she added quickly.

"Nothing too serious, then?" I said it lightly, but kept my voice low anyway.

"Oh, no. Not too bad. But you know our policy. Violence is an automatic suspension. He's here in the office. Could you pick him up?"

"Of course."

"Mr. Ortiz said he would call you after school to talk about it. He had to give Tyler a referral, so you'll be getting a letter in the mail about the incident. It'll tell you if and when Tyler has to do detention."

"Thanks."

"Oh, that's quite all right," she said cheerfully. "I'll see you when you get here." I hung up the receiver and turned around. Bridget stood in the family room, looking at me curiously.

"Is anything wrong?"

"No, not really."

She didn't let it go. "Who was that?"

"School. Ty's not feeling well, so I'm going to run down there and pick him up."

"I hope he's all right." She looked concerned.

"I'm sure it's nothing to worry about."

"I could come with you."

"No, that's okay. Why don't you stay here and relax? You must be tired after the trip."

"A little. I guess I'll just start unpacking my things."

"Make yourself at home. You know where everything is?"

She nodded. "I'll be fine. If I need anything, I'll ask you when you get back."

Tyler sat in the waiting room adjacent to the secretary's office, arms folded across his chest, eyes narrowed, mouth turned down. His feet dangled a few inches above the floor. His upper lip was puffy at one corner, as if he was hiding a grape between his lip and eyetooth. There was a red blotch high on one cheekbone that might darken to purple later. His pants were streaked with dirt and his shirt was pulled out of the waistband. When he saw me, his eyes grew wary, but showed no fear, only defiance.

Sprawled on a chair opposite him was another boy, head thrown back, expensively sneakered feet sticking out on the floor waiting to trip an unwary parent. He held a wad of red-stained tissues to his nose, elbow pointed at the ceiling. His other hand dangled over an arm of the chair. A shock of dark hair was mussed. One side of his face was grimy with mud. Pale skin showed through the front of his shirt where two buttons had popped off. His eyes were closed.

I stepped up to the counter. The secretary gave me a sunny smile, inured to the bumps and bruises of other people's children, and slid an open three-ring binder across the counter. I signed Tyler out, glancing up at the clock on the wall to note the time. I contemplated the space marked "Reason." Hastily scrawled "Dr.'s Appt.," "Orthodontist" and "Sick" filled in the lines below. I wrote down "Injury." I turned and motioned to Tyler. He pushed himself out of the chair and shuffled after me, head down. The kid in the other chair never moved. Outside, I heard the slow scrape of Ty's rubber soles on the asphalt behind me, sounding like the bluster had gone out of him. I got in the van without a word and waited while he wearily climbed in the back, either too afraid or too defeated to ride up front with me. The silence as we pulled out slowly filled the space between us like a dirigible inflating, squeezing uncomfortably, pushing the very air out of the van.

I gave in first. "Well?" The mirror showed him squirming in his seat, a pained look on his face that the bruises had nothing to do with. He didn't say anything.

"I thought we talked about this sort of thing." Silence. "You told me you could handle this sort of situation. 'Tell a teacher or walk away.'"

"He's an a-hole, Dad!" he blurted out.

"Excuse me? I thought we talked about that, too."

"Sorry." He mumbled through the swollen lip, eyes downcast.

"You going to tell me what the fight was about?" Nothing. "Who was the other kid? Looked like you gave him a bloody nose."

This time his expression in the mirror was incredulous. "You didn't see?" I shook my head. "It was Alex."

I turned in surprise to look at him, then jerked back to keep my eyes on the road. "I thought you were going to give Alex a wide berth from now on. I'm a little disappointed."

"He started it." His voice rose defensively. "He called you a rock killer." His face was flushed with anger.

"A 'stone killer'?"

"Whatever. He said you killed Mom. I couldn't let him get away with that." I didn't know how to respond. I should have known people wouldn't keep their suspicions to themselves. It was another few blocks before either of us spoke.

"You okay?"

Some of the tension went out of him. "Yeah. He hits like a girl. I think he feels a lot worse." I wanted to cheer, give him a congratulatory clap on the back, maybe buy him a beer.

"You know what you did was wrong."

He sighed. "Yeah, I know." Our eyes met in the mirror. "How much trouble am I in?"

"Enough. You're suspended from school today. You'll probably get detention."

"What about at home?"

I didn't answer at first. Then I said, "Aunt Bridget's here."

"That's cool." After a moment, he said a quiet "Oh." It was another block or two before he thought it through. "What are you gonna tell her?"

"I don't know." When we pulled onto our street, I spied two television trucks a few blocks down near the house. I took my foot off the gas.

"I want you to get down on the floor, Bud." I kept my voice low and even. "Right now. No questions. Just do it." I heard the rasp of the seatbelt, and when I glanced in the mirror, he'd disappeared from view. I pressed down on the accelerator gently.

"There are a couple of TV crews up near the house." The top of his head started to pop up. "Uh-uh! Keep your head down, kiddo. I know you want to be on TV, but now's not the time."

"How come?" His voice sounded muffled.

"Remember what I told you about the deal I made in court? About how they want to make sure you and Kels are safe? If those TV cameras get a load of you looking like that while riding around with me, somebody might think I'm the one who hurt you."

"I'm not hurt." He sounded indignant.

"I know that, tough guy. But it's what people might think." We rolled slowly past the TV vans, and I pulled into the drive. One of the reporters walked up to the door with a cameraman in tow. I quickly lowered the window. They both turned at the sound of the van in the drive.

"Excuse me," I called, "but you're on private property. Please leave."

"The public has a right to know—"

"But you don't have a right to be here. Please, just leave us alone." I rolled the window up without waiting for a reply and pushed the button on the garage door remote, edging the nose of the van inside before the door was completely open.

Tyler's voice sounded softly behind me. "Boy, that guy really made you mad, huh?" Inside, Bridget's maternal instincts kicked in as soon as she took one look at Ty's face. Even Ty had shrugged it off. Not long before, bumps and scrapes would have sent him running to Mary or me with tears in his eyes. He'd earned these. He'd accepted the risk when he responded to Alex's taunts.

"What happened?" Without waiting for an answer, she dropped to her knees in front of him, looking shocked. Taking his face in her hands, she gently turned his head one way then the other, inspecting the damage.

"Oh, your lip. That could have loosened a tooth." Her wispy voice belied her concern. "Open your mouth, let me see. These aren't baby teeth, are they? And your cheek. You could have a fractured cheekbone, maybe even have damaged your eye. Not to mention concussion. My goodness, you're almost certain to have at least a mild one." She looked at me, eyes narrowing. "He needs to see a doctor, and have a set of X-rays taken, I should think, to make sure he hasn't caused permanent injury to the eye socket or jaw."

"I'm fine," Tyler insisted in a small voice.

Bridget ignored him, waiting for a response from me.

"He's fine," I echoed. "It's just a fat lip. We'll put some ice on it, and on his cheek, and see how he does. If it swells up any more I'll call the doctor."

Her look was defiant, but she didn't argue. "How did this happen?"

"A little scuffle on the playground." She quickly turned to look at Tyler.

"It was no big deal," he said. "Just some pushing and shoving." Her gaze shifted from Tyler to me and back again. She got to her feet and put her arm around Ty's shoulders.

"Let's get you an ice pack."

PHIL PRESTON LEANED forward, elbows resting on the arms of the chair, fingers laced in front of his chest, up-turned thumbs touching at the tips to form a little triangle. He considered me, but there was no reading his expression. I'd just spent the better part of a half-hour recounting Mary's last day—again. A month's distance made the telling only slightly easier now, as if time had softened and blurred the shock and horror of losing her, of seeing that photo of her decomposing body. I doubted that image would ever fade entirely from memory.

"You had intercourse with your wife the night before she disappeared," he said. It was our first official attorney-client meeting. He didn't refer to notes.

"Yes. I told the police."

"That's consistent with the DNA evidence. And you weren't overly aggressive?"

I shook my head. "Neither of us was into rough sex. And I didn't force her, either."

"That's *in*consistent with the evidence."

"Which means someone *else* killed her. Not me." I took a deep breath and sat back.

He waited a moment before responding, watching me. "We have to give twelve people a plausible reason to believe that."

"So, I have to prove I'm innocent?"

"No, not prove it. Simply present facts which support the possibility that someone else could have done it."

"It's not a 'possibility.' I didn't do it. Someone else did. Period."

He gave me another curious look. "According to your statement to the police, your wife was in bed, sleeping, when you went running the day she disappeared."

"That's right."

"And when you went to check on her around ten-thirty, she was gone."

I nodded. "I went over all this with the police." He raised a forefinger without unlacing his hands. I closed my mouth.

"The medical examiner's report estimates the time of death sometime after midnight on Saturday night." He waited until it had sunk in.

"But that…I couldn't have…" I tried again. "She…" Preston rose and stepped over to a sideboard in the corner. I heard the clink of a heavy glass, the rising pitch of water filling it. A moment later he handed it to me. I took it numbly, sipped without tasting, pressed the cool glass against a flushed cheek.

"It's an estimate, though. Right?"

"It's an estimate."

I cleared my throat. Took another sip of water. "That means she could have been killed Sunday morning. Maybe later." My voice was lower this time.

"It's possible. Unfortunately, the estimate puts the time of her death between one and three a.m. Sunday morning."

"But they're not certain, right?"

"No, but the forensic pathologist obviously was confident enough to establish a window of time in which she was killed. It would be difficult to dispute without investing a lot of money in our own experts. Even then, another pathologist may not want to impugn the M.E.'s report. I'd rather consider other possibilities first."

"Like what? That *I* killed her and have absolutely no recollection of it?" He gazed at me coolly without replying. "Well, what other explanation could there possibly be? I didn't get it before. I couldn't understand why the police thought I had anything to do with it. But now it's pretty obvious that for them it's a slam dunk. I've got no alibi. They think I lied about when she disappeared. So, what? We go for an insanity defense? I lose my kids forever?"

He waited silently until I wound down. "It's problematic," he said quietly, "but it's only the first of what I expect will be many setbacks. Don't let yourself get thrown every time we run into an obstacle. If you want to get out of this intact, with custody of your children, you have to be willing to fight. I thought you were. And, at all costs, you have to maintain an even disposition. You cannot, even for a moment, give anyone remotely involved in this case the impression that you have a temper or can be goaded into a rage of any kind. Do you understand?" I blinked and swallowed, then nodded slowly.

"Now *think,* Jack. Things are not always the way we perceive them. We could assume the medical examiner is wrong and spend countless hours and dollars trying to prove it. Or we can take the report on good faith. If your wife was killed when the report says she was, then something about your recollection of the sequence of events is flawed. Somehow, your perception doesn't match reality, if we are to believe the facts in evidence. So, *think,* damn it."

THIRTEEN

SINCE Bridget's arrival, Ty had gone quiet the way a nuclear submarine does on Yellow Alert or Def-Con Whatever. Mostly, he got by doing things for himself, avoiding the need to communicate. Otherwise, he managed pretty well with sign language and grunts. He could talk, but the few times he actually spoke during the next week occurred when Bridget did something that angered him.

The first time was a repeat of our dinner with Trish Nelson. Ty set five places at the table for dinner Bridget's first night. Unlike Trish, Bridget exhibited no confusion about where to sit. She went straight for the place at the end of the table opposite mine.

"That's Mom's place," Ty told her quietly.

"Your mom's not here." Bridget spoke softly, but her voice held no gentleness.

"That's her place," Ty said firmly.

Bridget looked around the table. Ty stared at her unblinking, his face open. Kelsey hung her head, doing her best to cloak herself in invisibility. Finally, Bridget shot me a look of exasperation. I said nothing. She *harrumphed* like an old woman and sidled around the corner of the table and sat next to Ty.

THE SECOND TIME, I heard Ty shouting from my office. I spun the desk chair around and bolted for the door.

"Put it back!" Ty's angry voice came from the living room.

I pulled up short in the doorway. Bridget and Ty squared off in front of the fireplace, staring each other down across the coffee table. Ty stood rigidly, skinny arms protruding straight down out of his short sleeves like pipes, small clenched fists knobbed at the ends. Bridget had a hand on her hip. A silver picture frame dangled from her other hand, knickknacks piled on the table in front of her.

"Ty?" I said. Neither of them moved. "Tyler, don't you have some homework to do?" He turned slowly, as if coming out of a trance, and his eyes focused on my face. I nodded knowingly. "I'll take care of it," I said.

He hesitated, then stalked past me, rancor shimmering like heat waves in his wake. Bridget's eyes followed his retreat then shifted to me. She thrust out her lower jaw.

"What are you doing?" I said.

She looked at the picture in her hand and set it down quickly, jerking her hand away as if it was hot. She straightened, pulled in her chin and smoothed her dress with her hands. "There's just so much clutter in here. I was trying to weed out a few things. Simplify. Make it easier to dust." Her face soured as she glanced around the room.

"Just leave it. I'll clean. You don't have to bother."

Again her face pinched. "I'm just trying to help."

"What did you expect? You can't just go put her life in a box and store it away."

"She's gone. Mary's dead, Jack. Tyler has to get used to it."

"He knows she's gone. I just don't think he wants to get used to it. Not yet."

"He has to. It isn't healthy for him to go around pretending she's going to sit down for meals or admire her things. He needs help."

"Oh, come on, Bridget. He's fine. He has to work through it his own way. You're not being very sensitive. He just needs time."

She managed to draw herself up even straighter, as if a steel rebar had been shoved up her spine from tailbone to the top of her head. "I didn't have to come here. But since I agreed to this, the court has made me responsible for the children's well-being."

"That's not true, and you know it. You're here as an observer only."

She folded her arms across her chest. "Don't you get snippy with me, Jack. Whatever you call me, you still need my stamp of approval to get custody of these children."

"Don't do this."

"I'm just saying that you ought to consider counseling for Tyler. He needs to face reality."

I looked out the window for a long minute, avoiding her stare. "I'll consider it," I said.

"Good." She gave a quick nod, unfolded her arms and took a step toward the door.

I stopped her. "But you have to leave Mary's things alone. We're not ready to erase her from our lives just yet."

Silent for a moment, she tipped her head slightly. "I suppose a little more time won't hurt."

THE THIRD TIME OCCURRED at the dinner table again, a few days later.

"Tyler, would you please pass the potatoes?" Bridget said. Ty took another bite of chicken, paying her no attention. The bowl of mashed potatoes sat in the middle of the table in front of him. "Tyler, did you hear me? Please pass the potatoes." Both Kelsey and I looked at Ty. He ignored us, studying something on his plate while he slowly chewed.

"Hey, Bud, you want to wake up?" I said gently. He looked at me reluctantly.

"Your Aunt Bridget asked you to pass the potatoes."

"They're for Mom," he said.

"Aw, jeez, get a clue!" Kelsey said. She got to her feet, jostling the table as she stood, grabbed the bowl and extended it to Bridget. Ty made a grab for it, but she held it out of his reach until Bridget took it from her. "You are such a dork," she said, and sat down heavily, her face dark as thunderclouds.

Tears welled up in Ty's eyes. Before anyone else could see them, he jumped up, knocking his chair over backwards. "They're Mom's favorite," he yelled, bolting from the room.

I called after him. "Ty, come back. We've got more." Muffled thumps sounded their way across the ceiling above our heads as he ran to his bedroom. I sighed.

"Well, don't look at me." Kelsey's eyes widened. "He *is* a dork."

"Jack," Bridget said. She had her somber schoolmarm face on. "It's time." Kelsey's head ping-ponged from me to Bridget and back, an unformed question on her lips. She didn't give it voice.

"I DON'T KNOW what to do with him."

"He's here now?" Sarah said.

I nodded toward the door. "In the waiting room, reading magazines. He didn't want to come in. I didn't want to push him."

"That's okay. I understand. So, what's the problem?"

"He won't talk. Well, hardly ever, except to criticize his aunt, or protect his mom's turf."

"What do you mean?"

"He pretends she's still here. Like she's just gone to the store and she'll be right back. He won't let anyone touch her things. He sets a place for her at dinner..."

"Does he believe she's still there? Or pretend?"

"Pretend. I think. A month ago, he told us he just wants things to be normal again."

She looked thoughtful. *"That could mean he's created a fantasy world in which his mom's still alive. Or, as you said, he's pretending, to create the illusion that things are normal."* I scratched my head.

"That doesn't help you, does it?" she said. *"Does it bother you?"*

"It doesn't bother me, but he's driving his sister nuts, and his aunt insists he get counseling to help him through the grieving process."

"She's Mary's sister? She's there to monitor the situation for DCFS?"

I nodded. *"And it's not going so great."* She paused. *"It's natural to be afraid. Don't let it get you down, though. You can't control everyone else's feelings. Just do the best you can."*

"What does that mean? What am I supposed to be doing? Tyler's shut himself off. I can't seem to reach him. I don't know what Kelsey's problem is. I can't tell if she's angry, or resentful, or sad or what. All I know is she gets moodier by the day. And if I can't convince Bridget in the next three weeks that I can handle them, I'll lose them."

"You don't know that."

"What else am I supposed to think?"

"I'm sure Bridget will realize that despite the challenges you face, they're better off with you than anyone else."

"Tell her *that."*

"I think you should."

"I'm trying to."

"She doesn't have children, does she?" I shook my head.

"So, tell her you have too much work to handle the household chores right now, and let her take over for a few days."

"Are you crazy?"

"Why? What would happen?"

"The place would fall apart."

"Maybe. Isn't that the point?" She looked at me. *"So far, it sounds like you've been treating her like a guest. Let her run the house for a few days and get an idea of what your job is like."*

"What if it backfires?" She shrugged. I weighed the potential risks. *"What about Ty? What should I do?"*

"Bring him along with you. Tell him he's welcome to join us anytime he has something on his mind. Even private stuff he doesn't want to share with you."

"What if he doesn't want to?"

"Look at it this way. At least you can honestly tell Mary's sister you're taking him to therapy."

I LOST KELSEY THE FOLLOWING week. I suppose she'd been straying further and further from the confines of home and family and childhood since Mary died. Probably longer than that. Now, though, she was in strange territory, shadowy terrain she'd never considered venturing near before.

It wasn't just her attitude, which was surly and uncooperative most of the time. Other parents—those who'd been speaking to me before this nightmare had begun—had assured me she exhibited typical teen behavior. I'd always responded, "Not my daughter." Maybe I'd been in denial, but I'd been secretly grateful that Kelsey had always seemed content to follow the rules.

She came home from Randi's half an hour after curfew that night. I finally collapsed on the couch in front of the television to wait for her. She let herself in the back door and gave me a cursory wave. I gave her a look of disapproval. Her mouth tightened and she flipped her hair with a little toss of her head as she passed me on the way to the kitchen for a drink. I let it go.

She was late getting up the following morning. When she didn't come down for breakfast at the usual time, I went upstairs and found her still asleep. I put a hand on her hip and shook her gently. She grumbled and moaned and told me to leave her alone. I shook her again and told her to get up, talking to her until she opened her eyes. She asked what time it was. When I told her, she scrambled out of bed, whining that she wouldn't have enough time to get ready for school. She was dressed and downstairs ten minutes later.

Late that afternoon the phone rang. When I answered it, a recorded message from the assistant principal at the high school informed me that my "son or daughter missed one or more class periods." I called Kelsey on it. She hemmed and hawed and mumbled an excuse about being late to first period because she'd slept in, but that it was my fault because I hadn't gotten her up in time. I let that one go, too.

Two more calls came that week. Both times, Kelsey

blamed a teacher who marked her absent for being a few minutes late. I suggested she make more of an effort to be on time.

BRIDGET MADE A VALIANT show of running the house for a few days. It wasn't a fair test. Anyone thrown into a strange house would have at least some difficulty adjusting to schedules, learning where things are kept, finding the ways around town. The idea of giving up control, especially to Bridget, terrified me. The only way I could make it work was to give it up cold turkey. I locked myself away in the den, ostensibly to write an article, and came out only for bathroom breaks and meals.

I finished the article. Then, with too much time on my hands to think, I read—magazines, books, whatever would keep my mind occupied. I cheated some by making up excuses to come out for coffee, water, snacks (all falling under the category of meals), reading the mail and one or two other things. In fact, I took no small pleasure from watching Bridget stumble in her quest to show me how a household ought to be run. Again, it wasn't fair. She didn't have children. She'd never taken care of anyone but herself. The amount of dirt, mess, laundry and food in a house with four people was as incomprehensible to her as the number of zeroes in a zillion.

There are no awards for parenting, or housekeeping, or even being a responsible adult. There's a general belief, however, that women are good at these things. Expectations for men, especially when it comes to domestic chores and raising children, are pretty low. The fact that people like Trish Nelson were surprised to find my home clean and my children well cared for without a woman around offended me. As if in my hands—a man's care—we would devolve into Neolithic creatures dressed in animal skins, huddled around the electronic fire of the television, communicating in grunts, sitting in our own garbage and subsisting on Chinese take-out and pizza delivered by pimply high school geeks.

Three days proved enough. Three days of grimaces around the dinner table as we politely tried to choke down culinary oddities like tofu lasagna and brown rice and eggplant casserole. Three days of listening to Kelsey call loudly down the stairs to ask Bridget what she'd done with her clothes or where she'd put her books. Three days of hearing panicked complaints about being late. Three days of watching Bridget's patience wear thin and her proper bearing come unglued. Long enough to frustrate her, but not so long that she got used to the routine.

After that, I reinserted myself into home life a bit at a time. I got up early enough to make lunch for Tyler after my morning run, before Bridget was up. I popped out of the office at convenient times to offer to run an errand or pick up one of the kids from school or an activity. Bridget never said anything, but more than once I saw what could have passed for gratitude cross her face. I couldn't exactly call it a ringing endorsement, but I thought I'd made my point.

"Tyler, why don't we play a game of cards or something?" Bridget's voice—the sort of high-pitched, coddling noise women reserve for babies and puppies—made her suggestion sound like wheedling.

Tyler sprawled on the floor in front of the television, chin resting on his palms. I glanced up from doing dishes to see him shake his head without taking his eyes off the screen.

"Come on, Tyler, I'll bet you're good enough to beat me." She fawned, trying to divert his attention. "It'll be fun." He wasn't swayed. She hesitated a moment longer, hoping he'd change his mind. When he didn't relent, she straightened and came into the kitchen. I finished rinsing a pot, put it in the dish rack and started scrubbing another.

"I'm worried about him," she said. "He never talks, Jack. That just isn't normal."

"He's fine." I scrubbed harder.

"I just don't think therapy is doing him any good. Who is this person you're taking him to?"

"It's only been two weeks."

"Yes, but…"

"But what?" I stopped scrubbing and faced her. "You're as bad as he is. No, worse. He's just trying to figure out what normal is without a mom. You want all of us to pretend it never happened."

Her eyes widened. "That's not true. I just think he should talk about it. He shouldn't bottle everything up inside."

"He's fine. And for your information, his behavior is nothing unusual given the circumstances."

"Is that what the therapist says?"

"Yes." I clamped my jaw.

She looked as if she wanted to say something else. The dining room door banged open. She turned with a start to see Kelsey breeze into the kitchen.

"I'm going to Jennie's." Kelsey stopped and eyed the two of us. "What?"

"Nothing," Bridget said. "We were just talking about what you kids might like to do over Thanksgiving break."

Kelsey looked at me again, then shrugged. "Nothing to do."

"Oh, there must be something you'd be interested in. A visit to the art museum. A hike up in the foothills. Maybe we could drive up to Vancouver one day."

"Been there, done it, Auntie B. We've kinda maxed out on the touristy stuff." Bridget's hand started toward her mouth. She lowered it, smoothed her dress, then twisted the fingers of her other hand.

"Well, why don't you think about it. I'm sure we'll come up with something."

The corners of Kelsey's mouth twitched up, then down. She looked at me. "I'm going to Jennie's," she repeated.

"Who's picking you up?"

"Some friends." She shifted her weight under my gaze. "Ray, Bobby and some girls, okay?" I shook my head. "Dad! What's wrong with that?"

"I'm sure they're perfectly good guys, Kels. But they're, what, juniors? Seniors? You're a sophomore. Not happening. Besides, that's too many kids in the car."

"Now what am I going to do?"

"If you need a ride, I'll take you."

"Yeah, right. I can't wait to get my license." She gave me a withering look, spun on her heel and flipped open her cell phone. She stopped a few steps away, her back to us. "Hi, it's me," she said into the phone. "Change of plans. Can you pick me up?" She listened for a moment, then shut the phone and put it in her purse. She still looked irked when she turned back to face me. "Jennie said she'll pick me up," she said. I must have looked surprised. "She's sixteen. She has her license."

"Fine. I assume her parents will be there."

"I'm sure. They usually are." She was getting the knack of this teen thing—the sneering lip, the disdainful voice.

"Don't stay out too late," I said. She didn't bother to reply. I was up to my elbows in dish suds again by the time the back door slammed.

"Well, that was rude," Bridget said. "Why do you let her get away with that?"

I rounded on her. Droplets of water flew from my wet hands, staining her dress with dark spots. "What would *you* do?" Her mouth worked. Nothing came out. "Exactly what I thought—nothing." I turned back to the sink.

"I'd talk to her," she finally said in a small voice.

"By all means, go ahead."

"She's so angry."

"Gosh, do you think so?"

"But I can't imagine why."

"Maybe because life sucks? Because it isn't fair?"

"That's my point. There's nothing she can do about what happened. Why carry around all that anger? It isn't good for her."

"Maybe she just hurts."

She flinched. "Well, I hurt, too, you know. I don't take it out on everyone else, though."

"You're an adult, Bridget. She's a teenager. A confused, angry, vulnerable teenager." I considered her. I never thought there had been much love lost between Mary and Bridget, but Mary's death must have affected her somehow. I sighed. "Talk to her if you think it'll do any good. I sure don't know what to do."

"I HATE THIS."
  "What?"

"Having her in the house. Having her judge what sort of parent I am. As if she has the faintest clue what being a parent is all about."

"Doesn't she?"

"Well, I suppose none of us really does, but at least some of us have had practice. She's smart, but she has about as much common sense as a doorknob." Sarah waited.

"Once, when Kelsey was just a baby, we spent Christmas in Savannah with Mary's parents. Bridget was there, too. One day, Kelsey was in her carrier, and Howard—Mary's dad—was playing with her. Kelsey was tiny, less than two months old. All of a sudden Howard says, 'Oh, look, she's smiling. Bridget, come look.' I could see Kelsey smiling from where I sat. She was staring intently at Howard's face. So, Bridget walked over to his chair from the dining room and looked over his shoulder. 'That's not a smile,' she said.

"Howard said, 'Sure it is. She's smiling.' He made a face and some goo-goo sounds and Kelsey's smile got even bigger. Bridget got all serious and insistent and said, 'That's not a smile, Dad. It's probably gas.' So Howard said, 'Gas? I don't know about you, but gas doesn't make me look like that. Passing gas, maybe.' By this time I could hardly keep from laughing, but Bridget didn't even crack a smile. She said, 'Dad, it can't be a smile. Babies that young don't smile.' Howard told her 'It sure looks like a smile to me,' but she said, 'I've been reading a very well-known book on childrearing, and the book says that babies that young aren't emotionally capable of smiling.' So, Howard turns to her and puts on this serious face just like hers, and says, 'Well, Bridge, I guess she hasn't read that book.'" Sarah chuckled. "That's a cute story."

"Yeah, but you see my point? She's always doing stuff like that. Drives me nuts."

"What choice do you have? Don't let it get to you. You only have two weeks, right?"

I shivered. "I hope."

"How's Tyler?"

I shrugged. "The same."

"Think he'd like to talk?"

"I doubt it."

She nodded. "I won't push it, then."

"COME ON, AUNTIE B," Kelsey called. "We're waiting."

"I'll be right there." Bridget's voice sounded muffled and distant.

The three of us sat at the dining room table, hands in our laps. A wisp of steam rose from the gravy boat parked in the center of the table. A platter of sliced turkey, bowls of mashed potatoes and green peas and a basket of dinner rolls surrounded it, rapidly cooling. I thought about what to be thankful for.

Tyler's head jerked and he looked at something over my shoulder. His face went white. Then curiously, like one of those charity thermometers showing rising donations, it slowly filled with red. "Take it off," he rasped.

Startled, I swiveled to see Bridget stop in mid-stride halfway into the room. She wore a satin dress in a festive red-and-green tartan that seemed all too familiar. She looked confused.

"Take it off," Tyler yelled.

Bridget looked fearful now. Kelsey got to her feet and stood with a hand on her hip, taking Bridget in from head to toe, looking disgusted.

"I—I just…" Bridget stammered. Then she said, "It's Thanksgiving," as if that was explanation enough.

"Take it off," Tyler yelled again. "You are not my mother! You're nothing like her! Stop pretending to be her."

"This is fucked!" Kelsey said.

She got my attention. "What?"

"I said, 'This sucks,'" she replied quickly, all innocence.

"I don't know what you're so upset about," Bridget said. "I—"

"Take! It! Off!" Ty bellowed.

"Enough." The three of them looked at me. I turned to Bridget and spoke quietly. "You had no right to go through Mary's things without permission. Please change into something else and put the dress back where you found it. *Now.*" She started to object, then turned and walked from the room. I faced my children. Kelsey's disdain evaporated and Ty's anger turned to wide-eyed surprise.

"Do you want to end up in a foster home? Is that it?" They shrank from the words. I looked at Kelsey. "Of course this is fucked, as you so eloquently put it. There's nothing about this situation that's good in any way, shape or form, except for one thing. We're still together. Your mother's gone. It stinks. It sucks. It isn't fair. But I can't fix that. I'm trying to save what's left of this family. And I'm begging you two, just try to keep it together for four more days. Let's just try to get through this probation period. Please. All right?" They nodded nervously, their pale faces drawn with fear. I wiped my mouth with my hand, then stuck it in my pocket to keep it from shaking.

FOURTEEN

"*WHAT'S WRONG?*"

"*I don't know. Nothing, really.*"

"*I've never seen you this down.*"

I shrugged and managed a wan smile. "*Bad hair day.*"

"*Nothing's happened, has it? You haven't gotten any bad news?*"

"*No.*"

"*So, you have work. And you're not in jail. And you still have the kids.*"

"*Yes.*" *I nodded, though I didn't find Sarah's attempt to cheer me up all that amusing. I gazed out the window. A sky as gray and heavy as a tombstone darkened the landscape and drained the color from trees and shrubs, leaving them a dull and drab green the color of army fatigues. Light rain fell steadily, the widespread drops plinking relentlessly onto roofs and pavement and leaves and grass, creating their own syncopated symphony. Clouds of steam rose from a chimney on a building across the office complex and disappeared into the leaden sky.*

I shivered. "*I don't know what to do about the kids. It's like we managed to keep the family together for nothing.*"

"*I thought things were getting better.*"

I shook my head. "*Worse. Oh, they did a great job of convincing Bridget that we're one big happy family.*

Finally. But they're more miserable than ever. At least I am. Ty seems to withdraw more and more every day, and Kelsey is getting out of control."

"It isn't easy. They need time."

"How much time?"

"It takes a broken leg a couple of months to heal. Don't you think a broken heart takes a little longer?"

"Well, yeah." I shifted uncomfortably in my seat. "That's not what I meant."

"Have you talked to them?"

"About what? Of course I talk to them."

"About how they feel about their mother's death."

"Well, I—I guess not. Not really."

"Have you told them how you feel?" She saw the helplessness in my eyes. "Because you're not sure how you feel?" she said softly.

"I guess." I paused. "It just seems so personal, so selfish to talk about how I feel. They're the ones who really hurt."

She looked at me for a moment. "They'll talk about it when they're ready. But you have to find a way to let them know you're there to hear it. It sounds like the three of you are so lost in your own pain you can't share it with each other. You need to let them know they're not alone."

I turned and looked out the window. "I don't know if I can do that," I said finally.

She watched me for a moment as if waiting for a more positive commitment. "You might try joining a single parents' group."

"What? You mean one of those groups that organizes activities for singles?"

She laughed at my look of surprise. "No, I mean a support group. Where single parents get together to talk

*about some of the challenges they face." I must have
had a dubious look. "Honest," she said, "it could help.
You could use a little support, and you might get some
good ideas on how to handle the kids."*

"Maybe."

BRIDGET GRASPED THE HANDLE of her suitcase, then hesitated. "I'm still not sure this is what's best for the kids,"
she said.

I looked over her shoulder at the people walking into
the airline terminal while I composed a reply. "Have
you changed your mind?"

"No, I'll stand by what I said at the hearing."

I considered her. "Why?"

"It's what the kids want. I'm not sure they're old
enough to make that decision, but I asked them where
they thought they were better off. They want to be with
you, Jack. I'm not surprised. It's all they know, now that
Mary's gone. That doesn't mean it's right."

"As you say, it's what they know."

I paused. "They're my *kids,* Bridge. You think I'm
not going to do everything in my power to take care of
them, to make them feel safe and loved after this?"

Her eyes searched my face. "I don't know, but I'll be
calling Trish every once in a while to find out."

I nodded. "You do that."

She turned away, then paused. "I did this for Mary.
No more favors, Jack. Don't call me again." She waited
for my nod, then disappeared into the crowd inside the
terminal.

More than a dozen people gathered in the meeting
room at the library, all but two women. Ranging in
age from late twenties to early fifties, they came in all
shapes and sizes, from a leggy, drop-dead-gorgeous

blond in jeans and a sweater to a frowzy redhead who obviously couldn't have cared less about her looks. Pale plump arms splotched with patches of red overflowed a white short-sleeved blouse that barely reached her waist after following the contours of two rolls of fat around her middle. The rest of the outfit consisted of cargo shorts and sandals worn over tan socks. I felt chilly in khakis and a turtleneck.

Four long tables had been arranged in a square in the center of the room. The large room filled with voices as the women engaged in several conversations around the table. I took a seat along one side as unobtrusively as I could. I needn't have worried. The other male at the table, a small Asian who looked about my age, paid close attention to the conversation of the two women who flanked him, his head swiveling back and forth. He stopped long enough to look at me when I sat down and give a small nod. The only other person who acknowledged me was a woman who still stood behind her chair. She flashed me a smile, then loudly cleared her throat.

"Let's get started, please," she said. The conversations slowly trickled to a stop. "It looks like we have a newcomer tonight." She looked at me. "Would you like to introduce yourself, and tell us what you do and the ages of your kids?" Heads turned my direction. I sat straighter.

"I'm Jack. I'm a marketing communications consultant. I have a fifteen-year-old daughter and a son who's ten." My face felt warm.

"Welcome, Jack," said the woman at the head of the table. There were murmurs around the table, and everyone quickly shifted their attention back to the group leader. A sharp-faced woman swiveled to look at me again with narrowed eyes. Between them was a long, thin nose that appeared as if someone had pasted an arrow on her face. It pointed at a tight-lipped mouth.

"Weren't you arrested for killing your wife?" she said.

The room went deathly still. My face now felt hot.

"I was released." She held my gaze a moment longer, then shrugged and turned back to the woman in front. I turned my attention there, too, and slowly felt everyone else's eyes uneasily turn away. I tried to make myself a little smaller in the chair.

"So, anyone have a burning issue today?" the group leader said. Her cheeriness sounded forced.

"I've got one." The speaker was in her mid-thirties with dark, almost jet-black hair in a pageboy cut. The rich contralto of her voice sounded incongruous coming from the petite frame and elfin face. "How do you get an ex to cough up child support on time?"

"Good one," someone said. There were low chuckles around the room, relieving the tension.

"I mean," the woman went on, "when you're married, they constantly bug you about how *you're* the one who's always late. But as soon as those papers are final, they're never on time for anything anymore."

"I'll say," the woman next to me muttered.

"I send him an e-mail to remind him," someone said. "He usually just forgets. He always gets it to me right away if I remind him."

"I let him know that if he can't get the payments in on time, he's welcome to take the kids and pay a nanny to watch them while he goes to work," another person said. "It'd cost him a heck of a lot more than he's paying in support." Heads nodded in agreement.

"How late is he?" the sharp-faced woman asked.

"Two weeks."

"Two weeks?" the frowzy redhead said. "Honey, if he does that all the time I'd drag his ass back to court and make them garnish his wages."

"That'd work," Sharp-Face said.

"If it's an ongoing problem," the group leader said, "you can get the state to help you go after him. There's a special department that goes after deadbeat dads. I have the number here somewhere. I can give it to you later if you want. Okay, who's next?"

"It's not much, really," said a quiet voice, "but does anyone have a problem with laundry?"

"Honey, I've got more problems with laundry than the Maytag repairman," the redhead said, provoking hoots of laughter from the table.

"No, what I mean is always ending up being the one who has to do it. It seems like every time my kids come home from visiting their dad, their clothes are always dirty."

"If you ever get their clothes back," someone chimed in.

"That's right," said the woman with the pageboy. "They're always losing stuff at their dad's, and he can never seem to find it. Guess who ends up buying them new stuff?" Nods and murmurs said they all were familiar with the drill.

"How old are your kids?" the group leader said.

"Nine and eleven."

"That's not too young to teach them how to wash their own clothes."

"Really?" She looked skeptical. "I can't see my nine-year-old doing laundry."

"Believe me," the leader said, "they can do it. It might not be pretty, but they have to learn to chip in."

"But isn't the real problem at their dad's?"

"Honey, if he didn't do laundry before he left, he's not gonna start now." The redhead again.

"It's true," the leader said. "Things about your ex that irritated you when you were married will probably irritate you as much or more now. That's not to say you can't calmly remind him that you'd like the kids to come home with clean clothes. But you might find it easier to focus on a solution at home."

"I guess I could try it." It went that way for another hour. More vitriolic discussion about the bad behavior of ex-husbands. Some decent advice and strategies for raising kids, most geared toward younger ones. And a fair amount of gossip and chatter about everything from the high price of manicures on the island to the best place for a *chai* latte.

I needn't have worried about being obtrusive. Once the initial shock faded after I'd been "outed," it appeared our gender had rendered the other fellow and me invisible. We both sat quietly, taking it in. No one consulted us for a male perspective on any subject or encouraged us to air our problems. Every so often, he and I caught each other's eye. His face had no more expression than the thoughts in my head.

Refreshments—two plastic bottles of juice, foam cups and a plate of store-bought cookies—had been set up on a table along the wall. When the hour ended, he and I found ourselves standing next to each other a few feet away from the cookies. He looked at me timidly.

"You kill your wife?" His voice was heavily accented. His Ls came out sounding like gargled Rs, so "kill" became "kirr." No matter. I understood perfectly. My ears burned, and I forced myself not to jerk my head around to see who might have overheard.

I shook my head. "No. I've been accused of killing her. I didn't."

"But police arrested you? And you not in prison?" I shifted my weight and stole a quick glance around. Any other time, I might have found his pronunciation of "po-reese" amusing. Not now. No one paid us much attention, but I tried to think of a polite way to extricate myself anyway.

"No. Here you're presumed innocent until proven guilty." My voice must not have held a lot of conviction.

He looked confused. "Sorry. My English not so good."

"It's a lot better than my Mandarin," I said.

"You speak Chinese?" His face brightened then fell when I shook my head.

"Just bad French. Most Americans don't bother learning another language. They figure they should be able to speak English anywhere in the world and be understood."

He nodded earnestly. "In China, you would be in prison." A look of consternation darkened his face and he waved his hands back and forth, palms down, as if polishing furniture. "No, no," he went on. "I not mean you. Just someone in my country." My forehead unfurrowed and I nodded. He looked relieved.

"Jack Holm." I put out a hand. He shook it with enthusiasm and tipped his head in a tentative bow.

"John Woo," he said.

He pulled a business card from his wallet and handed it to me. I glanced at it before putting it in my shirt pocket. My fingers hadn't even let go when I pulled it out to look at it more closely. The name at the top was Jian Wu. His title read "senior systems engineer" for a high-tech firm on the east side of the lake.

"Have you been here long?" I said.

"About six months."

"With your family?"

"My daughter. My wife still in China."

"It must be difficult for you. How old is your daughter?"

"Fifteen."

"Mine, too. How is she adjusting?"

He looked rueful. "Too good. Her English very good. Already she thinks she is American girl, not Chinese."

"Right. The music, the clothes, the makeup…"

He nodded vigorously. "She is like wild animal sometimes. Hard to say what to do."

"Hard to tell?"

"Yes, 'to tell.'" He struggled with the word, then paused once he got it out. "You are from Seattle?"

"No, Chicago."

"Ah! Al Capone." He held a pretend Tommy gun and sprayed imaginary bullets around the room. I couldn't help laughing. He grinned at my amusement. "You like Seattle?"

I shrugged. "It's beautiful. I love the water, the mountains and trees, and that it's green year-round. I even like the weather. The people aren't very friendly, though. Polite, but not friendly."

He nodded. "Like in China."

"It's been hard to make friends here. Has it been the same for you?"

"Yes, but also because my English not good."

"Your English is fine." I was already getting used to his substitution of Rs for Ls.

"Pardon me," a voice said behind me. I turned to see Miss Pageboy. "I couldn't help overhearing, and I don't know what you're talking about. I've lived here all my life and I've had friends here since I was six." Her expression dared me to come up with a response.

It took me a minute. "Maybe that's the point. You already have friends, so you don't bother making new ones." She didn't have a ready comeback. She looked at me a moment longer, then spun on her heel and walked away. When I turned back to Jian, he looked at his watch.

"I must go home," he said. "I enjoyed very much to meeting you."

"I enjoyed talking with you, too," I said, surprised that it was true.

"I will see you the next time?"

"Yes, I believe you will."

THE RINGING PHONE jarred me out of a trance. Shaking it off like a dog coming out of the rain, I glared at the phone. Indifferent, it rang again. I picked it up. It was Scott Carlson, my trade-show client. We talked for a few minutes about his objectives for the show and some general strategies. He gently probed for details to see if I'd come up with any ideas. I hedged. When it became apparent I wasn't going to reveal anything even if I did have something brilliant in mind, he fell silent.

After a moment, he said, "Look, Jack, the reason I wanted to find out where you are on this is that I didn't want you to get too far along." He paused. "I hate to be the one to tell you, but we have to let you go." My mouth went dry, and the room dimmed. "Jack?"

"Yeah." It came out a croak. I worked my tongue around and tried again. "What's the problem? No budget?"

"Well, things are tight, but no, that's not it."

"What, then? You brought in someone else?"

"Nah, I wouldn't do that to you," he said quickly, his voice placable. "It's just—it's just that this *thing* you're mixed up in…Joe just thinks it isn't good for the company's image to have you as a spokesperson while this is hanging over your head."

"Jeez, Scott, if it's bad PR you're worried about, I can stay behind the scenes. I'm not really your spokesperson anyway. I'll just set it all up for you guys."

"Won't work." I could hear him shaking his head. "Joe's made up his mind."

"Just let me put together the plan and do the upfront work. I can get someone else to cover the details on site. I'll be invisible."

"I wish we could work it that way, Jack. I really do. The decision's been made."

"That's it?" I heard my voice crack through the roaring sound in my ears. The room slowly revolved first one way, then the other.

"Sorry, but yeah, that's it. Call me, though, if you get this all cleared up. You do good work. I mean that."

"Thanks." My mouth tasted bitter. I let the receiver fall limply to the desk and heard a click as he disconnected. Disjointed thoughts whirled through my head— the growing size of my debts and mounting legal bills, the shrinking amount of respect I had for that pinhead Carlson and his gutless boss, the complaints of the pissant man-haters in the meeting the night before… Another bell jarred me back to the present. The door this time. I dragged myself out of the chair. A faint voice coming from the phone, reminding me to hang up and try my call again.

I didn't recognize the man on the porch. He looked pleasant enough, dressed neatly in khakis and a button-down shirt partially covered by an unzipped windbreaker. A late-model sedan stood in the driveway behind him. Frowning, I opened the door.

He smiled. "Jack Holm? I have something for you." He extended his arm until the envelope in his hand was a foot from my chest.

I took it from him. "What's this?"

His smile broadened. "All yours." He turned and skipped down the steps.

I watched him go, then looked at the envelope in my hand. I tore it open, shoving the door shut with a foot. I took it to my office, and sat down to read. My mother-in-law, in her infinite wisdom, had filed a petition for custody of the kids. *My* kids.

I reached for the phone and fumbled through papers on my desk looking for Adele Arnold's business card. My fingers drummed the desktop as the phone rang once, twice... The receptionist picked up on the seventh ring, then promptly put me on hold. My watch loudly ticked off the waiting seconds. She finally came back on and put me through to Adele's office.

"Have you seen this?" I said.

"Yes, I got a copy of the papers this morning."

"What the hell is it?"

"Just what it says. A custody petition."

"I thought this was all settled at the hearing last week."

"You got through the probationary period. That doesn't mean your former mother-in-law doesn't have the right to file for custody if she wants to."

"Christ, Adele, this is crazy. Does she have a shot at this?"

She hesitated. "To be honest, yes. You've still got this charge hanging over your head. DCFS isn't happy about you having custody. They acquiesced to letting you have the children during the probationary period because someone else was in the house with them."

"But Trish Nelson still checks up on us. What's the problem?"

"The problem, apparently, is your dead wife's mother. She doesn't want you to have the kids. I'm sure this is making the folks at DCFS breathe a little easier, though."

"They don't know Letty Beaumont. We can't let this happen. You have to stop this, Adele."

"Take it easy. She doesn't have custody yet. And we're not going to make it easy for her. There's another hearing in a month or so. Standard procedure in most cases to decide if a trial is necessary. I'll argue against it, but this new petition almost makes a trial a certainty. We can stall that, hopefully until after your other case is resolved. In the meantime, we do some digging."

"For what?"

"Anything we can find. You did say you thought she was unfit to care for your kids, right? So, we find out what sort of parent she was to her own daughters."

"I don't know. Mary's dead. So's her dad. Bridget probably wouldn't talk about it even if she knows something terrible about her mother. Who are you going to talk to?"

"We'll find something." Her voice held confidence I didn't feel.

"I'm going to lose them, aren't I?"

"You haven't yet. Come on, now. Be optimistic. Just hang in there." I didn't reply. "I'll call you before the next hearing," she went on. "Okay?"

"How much is this going to cost? Trying to get something on Letty. What'll this cost me?"

"I don't know. Why?" She sounded surprised.

"I can't afford it, is why. It's costing me just to talk to you, Adele. Between you and Phil Preston, the fees are piling up. I don't know how I'm ever going to pay them all."

"Don't worry about it. It'll work out, I'm sure. You want to get out of this mess, right?"

"Of course I do."

"Then you focus on what you have to do there at home. Let me worry about the legal stuff, at least as far as your kids are concerned." She paused. "Tell you what. I know this guy, owes me a favor. I can probably get him to help out *gratis.* So, don't even think about it, okay?" I hung up wondering how my day could get any worse.

FIFTEEN

HIGH SCHOOL locker-room trash talk paled in comparison to the stream of invective coming out the mouths of the women around the table. Five minutes earlier, the session had devolved into a puerile discussion of male shortcomings—literally. They made light of the subject, laughing at their own ribald banter, but many of their voices held a bitter undertone that suggested for them it was personal.

More surprising still, even after my third or fourth time with the group, was the ease with which they carried on in front of Jian and me. Men can be crude, boorish, thoughtless. But this…I suppose some of them figured we deserved a taste of the female perspective, to walk a block or two in Manolo Blahniks. I'm not sure any of them gave it that much thought. We were insignificant, unseen.

Debbie, the group leader, finally put a lid on all the frivolity and got the discussion back on track. When the group quieted down, Jian surprised me by quietly weighing in.

"I have question." His face was serious. "How you say 'No' to clothes?"

"Why, Jian," said Lara, the one with the pageboy, "are you thinking of baring all for us?" Some around the table snickered.

Jian looked at her, uncomprehendingly at first, then with annoyance. "No, I mean what to tell my daughter when she ask for clothes." He threw up his hands. "Always new clothes."

"Are they things she needs?" Debbie said.

"Too expensive," Jian said. He made a face. "Not for a proper girl."

"Sounds like you have two issues," Debbie said. "Are you worried that what she wants to wear is too revealing? Or that it costs too much?"

"Yes, both."

She nodded. "Okay, let's talk style first. Any thoughts, folks?"

"Thank God there's a dress code at the middle school," the redhead said.

"There isn't one at the high school, though, Pam," Debbie reminded her.

"Well, hell, there oughtta be. Especially for girls," Pam said.

"I think what the girls wear these days is cute," Lara said.

Pam snorted. "If you're a hooker, maybe." She turned to Jian. "Honey, you just gotta lay down the law is all. Are you the boss, or what?"

Lara shook her head. "It'll never work."

Pam turned on her. "Why not?"

"She'll rebel. I did. The more my mother complained about what I wore, the more outrageously I dressed."

"It's the peer pressure," I said. A bunch of heads turned in my direction, surprised, I guess, that I could talk. "Same deal with Kelsey. If her friends have Juicy, she's gotta have it. If everyone's into A&F, then that's where she has to shop. If Uggs are in, she's gotta have them."

"You can't blame her," Lara said. "It's no fun being

on the outside looking in." She looked around the table. "You remember high school."

"Some parents, like Jian, don't want their daughters wearing provocative clothes."

"It's the style," Lara insisted. "It's only provocative to men with nothing but sex on their minds."

"Sorry," I said with a wry smile, "but what do you think high school boys have on their minds? Calculus?" There were a few chuckles. "Look, all I'm saying is that Pam's right; sometimes you have to take a stand." I looked over at Jian. "The thing you have to know about kids, especially girls, is that they all want to feel important and included. They act the same, talk the same and wear the same clothes as their friends so they'll fit in. What sometimes works with Kelsey is to remind her that if she knows what it's like to feel *un*important and *ex*cluded, then she should work just as hard at making other people feel included as she does herself. Encourage your daughter to look outside herself and see the bigger picture." The room fell silent. A few women glanced my way with thoughtful expressions. Others pointedly looked away, as if uncomfortable. One woman held my gaze longer than necessary. She had yet to join in any of the catty conversations, and it made me curious. I took in her pretty face. I'd never paid her much attention before. She had a strong jaw, graceful neck and high, round cheeks that lent her eyes a mischievous twinkle. Long chestnut hair tucked behind her ears spilled over her shoulders. She gave me a small smile before finally averting her eyes.

Debbie tried to jump-start the conversation again. "Something else you can try is compromising a little. Say, if she keeps up her grades, let her get a blouse she likes. Or maybe something you can both agree on."

"You can always make your daughter pay for her own clothes," another woman said. "Tell her she can wear what she wants, but only at certain times. Like after school. And only if she earns the money to buy it."

"Good luck with that," Lara said, eliciting more chuckles, and the conversation moved on.

Afterward, Jian and I marshaled forces as usual, picking a quiet corner to sip a glass of juice and chat for a few minutes before getting back to reality.

"Why so angry?" he said when we'd retreated far enough not to be overheard.

"Me?" I said. His eyes darted to the other side of the room. "Oh, you mean the women? They're not all that bad." I glanced at the woman who'd caught my eye earlier.

"So many so angry."

"My guess? They feel used. They gave their ex-husbands children, made a home for them. Then they were traded in for newer models like old cars. I think they feel robbed—of their youth, their social stature, their standard of living. They blame it not just on their exes but on men in general. It's depressing."

He waggled his wrist, pointing a finger at my middle then his own. "We two are different."

I snorted. "I'll say. We're a little outnumbered here, partner."

"Ah, so." He flashed a smile. "Not only because we are men. Also because we did not choose to be alone, yes? My wife in China. Yours..." He shrugged. "All these others choose not to be married anymore."

"Some of them had the choice made for them, but I see what you mean."

"I miss my wife." He uttered the statement without emotion or a change in expression. That he said it at all,

I sensed, conveyed the depth of his feelings. He looked at me. "You?" I looked away and didn't answer. When I met his gaze again, he nodded, mistaking my discomfort for concurrence. It was more complicated than that.

I TUCKED TYLER IN BED when I got home, and peeked into Kelsey's room on the way downstairs. It looked more foreign than usual, as alien as my daughter was becoming. Clothes lay strewn on the floor, the bed was unmade, and stacks of magazines, school books and papers obscured the desk. The wastebasket next to the desk overflowed with empty bags, tissue paper, tags and other remnants of recent shopping expeditions. I sympathized with Jian, but Kelsey earned her spending money. I sighed, unsure if the clothes or the condition of her room were worth the fight.

When the phone finally rang shortly before ten, I snatched it up savagely, ready to growl.

"Dad?"

I stiffened, anger replaced by concern. "What's wrong, Kels?"

"Can you come get me?" She sounded on the verge of tears. "There's been an accident."

"Are you hurt? Where are you?"

"I'm okay. I just want to come home." Her voice was plaintive this time.

Something else was wrong. Forcing patience, I asked more slowly, "Where are you?"

"I'm not sure. East Mercer? No, West—no, East Mercer. Wait a minute." The phone crackled in my ear. I frowned. Kelsey was speaking slowly, but it was more than just confusion. I felt my heart racing and took a deep breath. "East Mercer," she said, coming back on the line. "'Bout Fifty-sixth or -seventh, or something. I don't know."

"I'll get there as fast as I can. Is anybody else hurt, Kels?"

"I don't think so."

"Did you call for help?"

"Just come get me. Please?" I took the stairs two at a time and raced down the hall as quietly as I could. Panting, I looked in on Ty. He was fast asleep. I carefully pulled the door shut and ran back downstairs, left a note on the counter in case he woke up, and grabbed my jacket on the way out to the garage.

The wipers slapped at the rain splattering the windshield on the way down to East Mercer. My sweaty palms slipped on the steering wheel, and I wiped first one then the other on my pants. The van strained around the first turn, and I forced myself to slow down. A ways further, lights flickered against the trees across the road. As I came around a sharp curve, the blue strobe lights of a police cruiser reflected off the glistening black pavement. Red flares on the road sizzled with each drop of rain. The patrol car sat parked halfway on the shoulder. A uniformed officer standing next to it waved me into the other lane. Another patrol car parked a hundred feet beyond faced the opposite way. Between them, illuminated by their headlights and searchlights, a dark sedan had careened off the road. The car lay on its side at an angle in a deep ditch, its right wheels off the ground.

Past the scene, the road ahead darkened. I turned around in a driveway, then let the van roll slowly back toward the accident. When I found a spot to pull onto the shoulder, I stopped and climbed out to walk the rest of the way.

A dome light illuminated the interior of the first patrol car. An officer sat in the driver's seat, bent over a clipboard. A girl scrunched down in the backseat. I couldn't see her face. Just past the first car, a boy sat on his haunches by the side of the road, arms clasped around his knees. He looked miserable, but not from getting damp in the light drizzle. As I approached the officer in the road, I saw another boy behind him sitting on the pavement in front of the patrol car's bumper. The car's dark interior silhouetted someone in the backseat.

"Is it bad?" I said as I walked up.

"Not too bad," the cop replied. "Kids are just shook up. Hard to see what shape the car's in, but I don't think it's totaled."

"Officer Schroeder?" I had a better look at his face now that I was closer. "It's Jack Holm. My daughter Kelsey called me. Sounded like she was mixed up in this."

"That would be her." He jerked his head toward the car behind him.

"Can I take her home?"

"I dunno." He craned his neck to look in her direction, then turned back to me. "We already got her statement. I don't think we're charging her. Let me go check." He sauntered over to the other patrol car and rapped on the window. When the driver rolled it down, Schroeder rested his elbows on the door and stuck his face in. They talked for a minute or two, then he ambled back.

"I don't think we'll need her anymore tonight," he said. "She seems to be okay aside from being a little tipsy, but you might want to keep an eye on her."

"Tipsy? There was drinking involved?"

"Looks like it. We didn't find any indication there

were drugs, but our accident investigator hasn't gotten here yet."

"Look, is there any way you could keep her out of this? She wasn't driving, I hope."

"Nope. Kid over there was driving." He nodded to the boy behind me.

"I wouldn't ask, but you seem to care what happens to her." I swallowed hard. "Despite what this looks like, I care, too. We've just been going through a pretty rough patch. And no matter what you think of me, I really am trying to keep my family together. I'm doing the best I know how. I just don't want anyone to take her away over this."

He looked at me a long time, then made up his mind. "I'll see what I can do." He walked back to the car and leaned in to talk to her before taking a step back and letting her slide across the seat. He helped her out and took hold of her elbow as she walked toward me. In a moment, I saw why—her feet refused to travel in one direction and her knees wobbled. She stumbled once, but Schroeder hauled her back up on her feet. A few yards away, she broke free and took the last few steps by herself. She planted her feet and stood in front of me, swaying slightly.

She looked at the pavement, then slowly up at me from under the hair falling into her eyes. "I'm okay. Really. Can we go home now? Where's the car?"

"Just up the road." I pointed.

She set off determinedly. I quickly fell in step and took her arm, but she shrugged me off. I didn't press it, but stayed close in case she stumbled.

"Thanks," she said to the officer over her shoulder. She had manners, at least, if not sense.

Kelsey faced away from me on the ride home and

stared out the window, head bobbing loosely on her shoulders each time we hit a big bump. When we pulled into the garage, she fumbled with the latch and nearly fell out the door when it opened. She slammed it shut and went inside before I could help. When I caught up with her, she yanked her coat off and threw it on the floor in the direction of the coat tree. She flopped on the couch as I hung up my jacket.

"So, yell at me," she said.

"You're drunk."

"Am not." She pouted.

"I lived with your mother long enough to know drunk when I see it." I could see the comment sting through the anesthetic haze of the alcohol.

"So why don't you yell at me?"

"I know better than to argue with someone who's had too much to drink. We'll talk in the morning."

"Fine."

"I'm going to bed."

"Fine. I'm just going to sit here for a while." She leaned back and closed her eyes. Suddenly they snapped open and a look of surprise washed over her face. She leaned forward, grabbed the arm of the couch and pulled herself to her feet. "Oh, God, I'm going to be sick." She moaned and stumbled to the bathroom. Moments later, the pitiful sounds of retching wafted through the door.

I stood unmoving. Mary would have followed her in, run a washcloth under cold water in the sink, wrung it out and held it to Kelsey's forehead while she threw up. No matter that Kelsey had done this to herself. I'd done the same for Mary on too many occasions. Mary had gagged at the smell of her own or anyone else's vomit, but when it came to her kids she'd fought the reflex.

Leaving the sounds behind, I climbed the stairs and went to bed.

"YOU'RE GROUNDED FOR life this time." Kelsey sat at the kitchen table cradling her head in her hands. Unbrushed hair fell in her face, partially obscuring darkened eyes and a pallid complexion.

"Yeah, right," she muttered.

I walked over to the table and set down a plate of plain toast in front of her. She made a sour face and pushed it away.

"What the hell were you thinking?" I said, sitting across from her.

"What difference does it make?"

"A big difference. The Kelsey I know wouldn't have done anything quite that stupid."

"Maybe you don't know me very well."

I shook my head. "How long have you been drinking?"

"I don't *drink,* okay? I just had a few sips."

"You had more than that. And this probably wasn't your first time, I'm guessing. Was it?"

She squirmed on the stool despite the look of impudence. "I may have tried it once or twice. So what?"

"Because it's dangerous, especially at your age."

She sat up and fixed me with a stare. "You drink. Mom drank."

"And you think that made her any happier?" I paused. "I'm an adult, Kelsey. And when I do have a beer or glass of wine with dinner, I rarely have more than one."

"It was an accident," she said, sounding less sure of herself.

"You don't get it, do you? Aside from the fact that you're only fifteen and shouldn't be drinking, you could have been seriously hurt or even killed. What the hell were you doing getting into a car driven by some kid who'd had a few?"

"Brian's not a kid," she retorted, face flushing. "He's eighteen."

"Worse. He's old enough to know better. You're not even supposed to accept rides from guys his age. You know, if you'd bothered to even pretend to be sorry, maybe I wouldn't be so hard on you. But as it stands, no TV, no phone, no extracurricular activities."

"Dad! Not fair!"

I shook my head. "I'll tell you what's not fair. It's not fair that you're trying to screw up what's left of this family. We're just lucky the media weren't camped outside last night. If the police report this or it gets back to Trish Nelson, you and Tyler end up in foster care or at your grandmother's. Is that what you want?"

"Better than this," she shot back. "In case you hadn't noticed, this isn't a family anymore."

"It is, damn it, and I'm doing everything I can to hold it together. I'll tell you what else isn't fair—you thinking you're the only one in the world with problems. You think you're the only kid who's ever lost a parent? You don't think Ty misses her, too? Get over it. Life goes on."

Her eyes narrowed and filled with wetness. "I hate you," she said. "I really hate you." She stood up swiftly, shoving the chair so hard it tipped over and skittered across the floor. She marched out.

"Get ready for school," I called to the empty doorway. I stared at the toast on the table and felt my shoulders slump. I wasn't hungry anymore. I turned my head and pushed my plate away. It banged into Kelsey's with a clink.

"I DON'T GET THIS." I stared at the papers in front of me.

Phil Preston glanced up from the other side of the round Queen Anne table in his office. "I'm not surprised," he said. "It gets quite technical. What can I help you understand?" He insisted on meeting every other week to discuss my case, review information related to it and develop strategy. I didn't see the point. Nothing seemed to change. He'd finally convinced me to go through the documents supporting the prosecution's case, starting with the medical examiner's report. I couldn't get past the death certificate that sat on top. It seemed so odd to relegate someone's life to a few statistics on a piece of paper—name, sex, address, date and place of birth, date of death...

"Do you have a calendar?" He went to his desk, picked up a slim leather-bound date book and brought it back to the table. After opening it and riffling through the first few pages, he handed the open book to me.

"Here. This is what I mean." I put my finger on the page and rotated the book toward Preston. He rose and leaned over the table to look. "The death certificate says this is the day she died, but it's the day her body was found. That's a week later."

"That's correct. On the death certificate, the medical examiner lists the date and time the body was discovered as 'date of death.'"

"But I thought you said the M.E. determined that the time of death was sometime the night before she disappeared."

He looked at me curiously, then sat back down. "Then I mis-spoke," he said.

"You misspoke?" I blinked. "You're not going to do that in front of a jury, are you?"

He was unfazed. "Read the Medical Examiner's report. Then let's discuss it." I started to object, but he raised a hand. I bowed my head and read. The report was nine descriptive pages about the condition of the body when discovered, the trace evidence at the scene, and the findings of the autopsy and laboratory tests. Most of it was in medico-legal jargon that would take years of experience or a few advanced degrees to understand. Like reading French after only three years of high school study, I figured out enough to think I got the gist without really being sure. The file also contained an envelope of crime-scene photos. I didn't have the courage to open it. When I finished, I sat back and waited as Preston made some notes.

"Let me see if I got this straight," I said when he looked up. "According to the report, Mary's body had been there for a while." I paused and swallowed the bile that rose in my throat, then took a deep breath and tried to shake the macabre images out of my head. I tried again. "Because she had been buried, her body was in—what did the report say?" I shuffled the pages. "Here it is—'an excellent state of preservation.' So, the M.E. couldn't determine whether she'd been dead for two days or two weeks."

Preston nodded. "That is correct."

"So the M.E. didn't determine a time of death."

"Not exactly. The prosecutor is drawing some conclusions based on the report. Did you read the sections on stomach contents and toxicology?"

I nodded, swallowing hard again. "Well, sort of."

"Stomach contents suggest that she ate sometime within four or five hours of her death," he said, "though using stomach contents as a guide to time of death involves an unacceptable degree of imprecision. Toxicology tests show that there was alcohol in her blood, which would be consistent with having wine or a drink with a meal. Her stomach contents matched the menu you told the police you prepared for her that night. You also told the police she had a few glasses of wine. Since the M.E.'s opinion is she died within five hours of eating, the police and the prosecutor took it the next logical step and concluded that she died shortly after the last meal you made for her."

"Which means she was killed sometime early Sunday morning," I said slowly.

He finished my thought. "Before you say she disappeared." Oxygen seemed to have been sucked from the room, and I wondered why they had the heat up so high. I stuck a finger in my collar and loosened my tie.

"That's just an assumption, right?"

"Yes, it's an assumption."

"I mean, she could have eaten a meal like that any time the week she disappeared."

"She could have." His expression said he didn't think it was likely.

"So, they don't really *know* when she was killed."

Preston exhaled with a short puff of breath, not quite a sigh. "There is other evidence." He motioned to the file folder visible under the autopsy report. I pulled it out and opened it. In it lay a sheaf of eight-by-ten glossy photos, maybe four or five. I stared at the first one, turning the photo this way and that until I recognized what I saw. It showed an aerial view of a large tract of land criss-crossed with even rows of trees.

"What is this?" I held up the photo.

"A Christmas tree farm."

"This is where she was found?" I'd never asked for the particulars, nor had any morbid desire to see the site where she'd been killed. I think it would have given me nightmares, as if I didn't already have them almost nightly.

He nodded. "Her car was situated far back on the property, well out of sight of the road. The tree farm's owner had an ongoing property dispute with a neighbor. He wanted a visual record in addition to a survey, so he hired an aerial photographer."

"I don't get it."

"Look at the rest of them." The first two were similar, but taken on passes from different directions. The third one appeared the same, yet distinct from the first two. It took a moment to see that the light was altogether different, meaning the photo had been shot at another time. Then I noticed something else, a blob in between rows of trees. The next photo showed an enlargement of the blob—a car, parked among the trees. "Mary's car," I said.

"The photographer took the first set that Saturday afternoon. Apparently, he wasn't satisfied with them. Too much contrast between the portions of land in sunlight and those in shadow. So, he went back up to take another set the next day. Those were taken around ten on Sunday morning. The camera timestamped the film."

I looked at the photos again. They were like a David Copperfield illusion—now you don't see it, now you do. "How did you get these?"

"The property owner is the person who discovered your wife's car. He reported it to the Sheriff's office. They asked him how long the car had been there. He didn't know. Apparently, Christmas trees don't require much attention at that time of year. He hadn't been on the property for some time. But when he saw the photos he called back and offered the Sheriff copies."

"You've got to be kidding."

He shrugged. "The police got lucky. It happens. The problem, Jack, is that the forensic evidence alone is enough. Don't forget, your semen was found in the victim."

"My *wife* and I had sex that night. Isn't that what husbands and wives do?"

"The physical evidence says she was assaulted, Jack."

"I didn't rape my wife." I carefully enunciated each word. "Why doesn't anyone believe me?" I felt my eyes grow wet.

"There's more."

"More? Good God! How could there be more?"

He raised an eyebrow and said nothing until I settled back into my chair. "If you had read the police report carefully, you would know what I'm referring to."

I dropped my gaze. "What's the point?"

"The point, Jack, is that this is quite serious business. I cannot defend you properly if you will not aid me in that defense. You must participate in this process if we are to be successful. We will need to take advantage of every inconsistency we can find. You are the only one who can say for sure what is consistent with the evidence and what is not."

I stared at the hands in my lap. "So, what else?"

"When her body was recovered, the police found her cell phone in the pocket of the coat she wore. Naturally, they checked the record of her incoming and outgoing calls. The last call was made to her voicemail box shortly before three a.m. Sunday morning. The phone company determined the call was routed through a cell tower two miles from where she was found." I didn't want to think of Mary struggling, trying to fend off her killer, desperately reaching for the phone in her pocket to call for help. I didn't want to think of how terrified she must have been.

"Why didn't she call nine-one-one?" I said, my voice husky. "Why call voicemail?"

"The police suspect she was already dead. They believe the redial button on the phone was activated by accident. Probably when the killer dumped her body in that grave." I squeezed my eyes shut tight, but images of Mary's dead face still floated in my mind. I took a deep breath and opened them.

Preston was still looking at me, expressionless. "What *did* happen, Jack?" he said finally.

"I don't know." It came out a whisper. "Honest to God, I don't know."

SHAPES OF DARK GRAY with indeterminate, shifting edges moved slowly across a backdrop of lighter gray. Scattered drops of rain fell as the shapes passed overhead. Unfazed, small birds flitted from branch to branch on the trees outside the window, their songs barely discernible through the glass.

"Are you okay?" Sarah's question slowly registered. I turned to look at her. "Anything you want to talk about?"

"I might as well say I did it." I found myself thinking out loud. "Everything points to me. I might as well just admit it, say it was me all along."

"Jack?"

"I mean, no one believes me anyway."

"What are you talking about? Are you talking about Mary?" I focused on Sarah's face as a horrible thought scuttled into my head like a large gray house spider racing across open floor for some dark corner.

"Oh, my God." My hand went to my mouth. *"What if I really did it? Oh, God, what if I actually killed her and just don't remember?"*

"No, Jack, you couldn't have." I saw Sarah shaking her head, but I couldn't chase the thought away. Like the spider that suddenly senses a presence, the thought sat frozen, refusing to budge. It was black and ugly and more chilling than any I'd ever had in my life.

SIXTEEN

I DRIED my hands and walked into the bedroom. Mary's favorite nightshirt, the pink one that said "Kiss all frogs—one may be your prince," lay carelessly thrown over the back of a chair. Like so many other things, a cloak of invisibility had covered it. I'd taken it for granted, overlooked it. Now it suddenly asserted itself, demanding attention. It didn't occur to me to wonder how it got there, only what to do with it. I tipped my head and looked at it, weighing options—hang it up; fold it and put it in a drawer; toss it in the laundry… I walked over to the chair and took hold of it, changed my mind, let go of the fabric, the lingering impression of its softness, its scent, stirring memories like sediment at the bottom of a pond. I stood still and let them settle back into the darkness.

The house felt devoid of life. Three people, the ghost of a fourth and a cat lived there, but it might as well have been empty. All the happiness that had filled the nooks and crannies, and imbued the pictures and knick-knacks and furnishings with memories, had somehow drained away. As fast as I tried to patch the hole left by Mary's death, cracks and fissures opened it up again. All that remained was a shell.

Quiet prevailed now. Kelsey shut herself up in her room when she wasn't at school and refused to acknowledge that Ty or I existed. Ty had suddenly traded television for books. I saw it as a positive development, but it deprived us of even background noise. I don't think he'd uttered a word since the Thanksgiving fiasco with Bridget. Even the cat disappeared, disgruntled no one paid any attention anymore. It probably adopted a more animated and cheery family somewhere.

The only thing that occupied my conscious mind now was this nameless dread that nothing mattered. It didn't matter what I did or didn't do. Doubt tinged everything. It seeped in, cold and damp. It settled into my bones to the point where the possibility that I had killed Mary became more convincing with each passing day. Even if I hadn't, my fate seemed a foregone conclusion. I would be found guilty of the crime, whether I'd done it or not. And I would lose everything. No, nothing much mattered anymore. Still, I blindly stuck to the routine, stubbornly getting up each morning and putting one foot in front of the other.

WHITE ITALIAN LIGHTS glittered in the bare branches of the trees lining the downtown streets. They were one of the few things that made the short days heading into the depths of winter a little less depressing. City workers had strung them two weeks earlier. I hadn't noticed until now. Houses all over the island were festooned with similar lights, and colored ones as well, along with other signs of Christmas cheer. Stores had been decorated and stocked with holiday merchandise in the weeks before Thanksgiving. Most years, I did my best to ignore the commercialism, at least until Thanksgiving dinner had been digested. With Christmas less than two weeks away I had no more holiday spirit than a Maori. The lights looked cheery, though, compared to the sad rain that smeared the windshield.

I'd gotten so involved in the details—getting kids to

and from, meeting schedules, taking care of things—
I didn't know what anything looked like anymore. I'd
forgotten to notice the things that matter. The blue-
ness of the summer sky. The smile on the face of the
woman behind the bakery counter at the supermarket.
The smell of just-cut grass, or new rainfall damping
down dusty earth. The sound of a contented baby burbling and cooing in its stroller, or birds singing early,
almost before there's any other signal that day's about
to begin. The sight of the season's first big snow dust-
ing the tops of the distant mountains. Or the feel of
freshly washed, crisp, cool sheets, or someone's hand
gently touching my cheek. There are hundreds—no,
thousands—of them. Impressions that make a life.

Ty sat in the passenger seat, staring out the side
window at the passing lights. I wondered if a lifetime of
good impressions—of Christmas mornings, and loving
embraces, and days of joy and wonder and laughter—
would ever outweigh the awful burden of knowing his
mother had been brutalized and murdered.

"You thought about what you'd like for Christmas?"
I asked, breaking the silence.

He didn't reply. I glanced at him. He hadn't moved.
The wet, black street slid beneath the van's wheels,
carrying lamp posts and street signs and buildings with
it.

I tried again. "Can't think of anything you want?"
This time I saw his shoulders rise and fall. I sighed
and rubbed a hand across my mouth. "Say, who was
that mom I saw you talking to when I picked you up
today?" He glanced at me quizzically, then shrugged
again. I was sure he knew who I meant, but I didn't
push him. At school, kids either waited in the bus shelter to be picked up or on the playground right behind
it. When I rolled up to the pick-up spot earlier, Ty was

on the playground, listening earnestly to a woman who crouched in front of him. The scarf on her head concealed her profile. When Ty saw me, he ran over. The woman never turned our way.

We rode on in silence. Colored lights spiraled the height of a fifty-foot evergreen in the park at the south end of town. After that, the street grew dark and dreary again, lonely pools of yellow light dotting every other corner.

"MEN ARE SUCH PRICKS," Lara said.

The support group meetings had become repetitive bitch sessions. "Excuse me?" I said.

Her head jerked in my direction, surprise on her face. "Sorry. Present company excepted," she said hurriedly.

"No." I shook my head. "'Sorry' doesn't cut it. You know what? I've got the same problems you do. I cook and clean and raise my kids by myself. I worry about bills and work and a million other things. And I did all that long before I lost my wife. I've got more problems than you, really—you all suspect I killed her, and I can't turn around without the media hounding me and my kids, even though I didn't do it.

"I've been coming here for weeks, listening to you berate us. All you do is trash the men in your lives. If you're not happy with what we're doing, you're unhappy with what we're *not* doing. Not all men are total assholes, you know. Some of us are assholes only half the time, and that's only because we don't know any better." A couple of very soft chuckles eased some of the tension, but most of the women stared at me in shock. I plowed ahead. "We think differently than you do. We're built differently. We *are* different. Things you take for granted don't even occur to us. But that doesn't mean we're vindictive, or that we're out to hurt you or screw you over. We just don't know what you want. Or don't understand what you want. Or why you want it. Give us half a chance. Tell us what you want in the first place. Don't make us try to read your mind. More than likely we'll do it happily. Throw in a reward, like a little affection, or—God forbid—physical intimacy, and we'll leap at the chance to do it. Well, as long as it doesn't involve too much talking, I guess. But this venom, this hatred of the male species, is unwarranted and unproductive, and I'm sick of it." They gaped at me silently. I felt my face flush. It was too late to exit gracefully with my foot stuck in my mouth, but I slid my chair back and stood up. "I don't need this. I don't know why you call this a support group. Lack-of-support group, maybe. I'm out of here."

Halfway to the door I heard a voice say quietly, "He's right, you know. I've seen him with his kids." I didn't stop, but when I got to the door I paused and turned. The woman still spoke, drawing the group's attention. "He's really good with them. Not all dads are deadbeats. Some of them really pitch in." I still didn't know the woman who came to my defense. We hadn't yet spoken, but since that first time, I'd caught her looking at me more than once during meetings, her expression inquisitive, but cool. She looked up now and our eyes locked. I felt something indescribable in that moment, some sort of connection, as if she'd passed me a message. I nodded in thanks and slipped out the door.

The air outside tasted good—crisp and cool. I stood on the curb, drinking it in. Blood coursed through me in rhythmic pulses that matched the thudding of my heart. A cold ember somewhere down deep knocked itself free of its coating of ash. Now exposed, it began to glow. Its warmth dried the dankness inside, shrank my depression.

The door behind me opened. Curious, I turned. Jian rushed toward me with a broad smile. He grabbed my hand in both of his and pumped it energetically. "Thank you, thank you."

"For what? I—" But he'd already let me go and taken a step toward the library. He looked back, the grin still on his face. "I go take notes," he said.

I laughed, the first one I could remember in a long time.

"Hey," I called after him. "Come to dinner next week. Bring your daughter."

He nodded as he pulled the door open. "Yes, yes." With a wave, he disappeared.

KELSEY FLOUNCED ONTO the couch in the family room and turned on the TV. I turned off the water in the sink. "Aren't you grounded?" I said. "Besides, don't you have homework?"

"I don't know." She didn't take her eyes off the television. "Maybe."

"Then I suggest you get yourself upstairs and get it done."

"I don't believe this."

"Believe it. Even if you weren't grounded, you know that's the rule. Homework first."

She got to her feet and stabbed the remote with a finger. The screen blinked and went dark. "This is such bullshit." She stomped up the stairs.

Shaking my head, I returned to cleaning up the kitchen. Ten minutes later, thumping overhead and the slam of a door spurred me down the hall. Kelsey trod heavily down the stairs and headed straight for the front door. I quickly inserted myself in her path. She stopped and looked at me defiantly, her hand on her hip.

"Where do you think you're going?" I said.

"Out." She moved to go around me.

I blocked her path. "You're not going out, and that's that."

"I've been grounded long enough, and I'm getting out of here." She skipped a step to her left and tried again. Once more I barred her way. She swayed back and forth, looking for an opening.

"Stop this. It's almost eight on a school night. You're grounded, and you're not going anywhere."

She stood still and looked at me, hands clenched into tight fists at her sides, eyes brimming with wetness. "Why are you doing this? This is so unfair."

"You did this to yourself, Kels," I said quietly. "You can't expect to behave the way you have been lately and not pay the consequences."

Her expression was unlike anything I'd seen, anger and hate so focused, so personal, it smoldered. "I have paid. Every day I pay in this place."

"What's that supposed to mean?"

"This is all your fault!" She threw herself at me, shoving me with all her might. "Mom wouldn't let you do this to me."

"Mom's not here." I struggled to stay upright. Her strength was surprising.

"'Cause you killed her!" she shrieked. She hit me now, flailing at my shoulders and chest and face with her fists.

"I didn't," I protested, shocked by her sudden eruption of emotion. Too slow to avoid the first hail of punches, I got an arm up just in time to ward off a shot to the nose. I took half a step back and braced myself.

"You killed her!" she screamed again. "I hate you! You killed her!" Anger contorted her pretty face into an ugly mask, and tears rolled down her cheeks.

"I didn't, Kelsey. I swear I didn't. Stop it!"

"You might as well have. You drove her away! And now she's never coming back." She punctuated every accusation with another round of windmilling arms, raining blow after blow on my arms and shoulders.

I staggered back under the onslaught until I felt the wall at my back. In self-defense, I got my arms around her shoulders and pulled her in tight against my chest. "I didn't do it, Kelsey. Honest. I loved her. I couldn't do that to her." She struggled, trying to wriggle out of my grasp with cries of frustration. She pounded her fists against my chest, ineffectually now. I held on even tighter. Suddenly, she stopped fighting and went limp. She pressed her face into my shoulder and sobbed loudly. I sagged under the weight and slid down the wall until I sat on the floor. She ended up in my lap, clinging to me tightly the way she had as a child when she was hurt or scared. Her tears burned my skin as they rolled down my neck under my collar. I tentatively put a hand on her head and stroked her hair.

"Why?" she sobbed. "Why did she have to get killed?" I didn't have an answer. I held her and rocked her for a long time until she quieted in my arms. A small noise made me glance up. Ty squatted on the top stair, hanging on to the banister with one hand, face covered with fear. I silently mouthed, "It's okay." The tension slowly drained out of him and he nodded seriously. Then his little face disappeared.

Kelsey's sobs slowed and stopped. Her breathing returned to normal except an occasional shuddery sigh.

Finally, she went still, making no move to extricate herself from my arms.

"Did you really love her?" Her small voice sounded muffled against my chest.

"Yes, I loved her." She didn't say anything. "Kels, look, I'm not going to lie. Things weren't good between us. But not because I was driving her away. Your mom had her own issues, her own demons to wrestle with."

"Why did you move us out here? Things were fine when we lived in Chicago." I heard the accusation in her voice.

"They weren't all that great, Kels. We moved for lots of reasons. One, because I thought it was a terrific job offer."

"You didn't do it for us. You did it for yourself. It was all about your ego."

"Hold on a second." For some reason, the barb stung. "Where'd you get that idea?"

"That's what Mom said." She sniffed. "She said it was because you wanted to be a big shot, and you couldn't do that at the place you worked."

I shook my head. "Not true, Kels. It wasn't just for me. As a matter of fact, the last thing I wanted was a more stressful job. We needed the money. And I thought maybe I could get to the point where Mom wouldn't have to work anymore. I think she resented the fact that she couldn't be a stay-at-home mom."

She tipped her tear-stained face up to look at me. "But she would have hated that."

I nodded. "I know. And the more money I made, the faster she—we—spent it. She couldn't have stopped working. Not only couldn't we afford it, she would have hated giving up the freedom of traveling all over the world with her friends."

"She would have hated *housework*." Kelsey managed a small, wry smile. "But I still don't know why we had to move so far away."

"I thought it would give us a chance to start over, Kels, maybe fix what had gone wrong."

"But you took us away from all her friends, from all *my* friends." There suddenly, out in the open, as plain as day, lay the depth of Kelsey's grief. She didn't just grieve for her mother, which would have been bad enough. She grieved the loss of her childhood and the only life she'd ever known. Guilt knifed me in the heart.

"I'm sorry, sweetie. Really, I am. I was just trying to do the best I could for everybody." She said nothing for a long time, quietly resting her head on my shoulder. When she finally spoke, it gave me a small start.

"Were you guys going to get divorced?"

I thought a moment before answering. "I don't know. Maybe. It never came up. We hadn't even gotten to the point of talking about it." She seemed to be digesting that. "That was part of the problem," I went on. "We weren't talking about much of anything."

"I guess a divorce wouldn't have been so bad," she said.

"No, it might not have been too bad."

"Not like this."

"Not like this," I echoed.

A FEW DAYS LATER, I had a visitor. The kids were in school. I worked in the office on another article that Terry McAuley had thankfully thrown my way. He'd become a steady source of income. It didn't make up for the loss of Scott Carlson's business, but it helped pay the bills. The sound of the bell startled me. The few times it had rung in the past several months hadn't signaled good news. I wasn't sure I wanted to answer it.

The person standing on the front stoop startled me even more. "Diane."

"Hello, Jack." She looked nervous.

I swung the door open wide. "Come in." She poked her head in first and looked around before stepping inside. I wondered if she expected to see wholesale changes now that Mary was gone. We'd made hardly any. Ty had clearly informed us that he didn't want us disturbing anything. I wouldn't have known where to start even if I had a notion to do something with Mary's things. I closed the door and gestured down the hall. She preceded me into the family room, swinging a shopping bag at her side.

"Would you like some coffee?" I stepped around her into the kitchen.

"Um, tea, if you have it." I watched her gaze around the room as I filled a kettle with water. She finally settled on a stool at the counter.

"How have you been?" I said, filling the silence before it became awkward. "Still flying, I assume. Are you still working Tokyo trips?" I retrieved mugs, milk and sugar while she caught me up on life at work and news about friends. While she talked, I steeped the tea, set it in front of her and poured myself some coffee. After a few minutes, the conversation petered out. I prodded her with questions, racked my brain for names of Mary's coworkers. Soon she ran out of gossip and fell silent. She idly scraped the handle of her mug with a brightly painted fingernail. Finally, she looked up, her face uncertain.

She opened her mouth, closed it, opened it again. "You really look like shit." Her face turned serious. "I wanted to apologize. This is hard to say." She paused and looked at her mug again. "I promised I'd stay in touch after Mary died. I didn't, and I'm sorry. At first, it was just too painful. I didn't want to be reminded. As much as I adore the kids, I didn't think I could be around them, or all the things that might remind me of Mary, without bursting into tears. It was just so sad. I really felt like I'd lost my closest friend in the world." She rested her forearms on the counter, and wrapped her hands around the mug. She stared into her tea, divining what to say next. I kept still.

"I blamed you, Jack," she said softly. "I knew how unhappy Mary was, and I was sure it must be your fault. She never said, but I figured what else could it be? When you were arrested, I was convinced you must have done it." She finally looked up and her eyes met mine. "I'm not proud of that, but you can't really blame me."

I shrugged. "Most people figure the police know what they're doing. If they arrest you, odds are pretty good you must have done something."

"I hated you after that. It was pretty easy to lay the blame on you. I was so angry about what happened to Mary. I wanted someone to suffer. I wanted *you* to suffer." She dropped her gaze.

"Why are you telling me this?"

"I was wrong. I don't know, maybe you did what they say. But I was wrong to jump to that conclusion just because everyone else did. The more I thought about it, the more I realized that I just didn't believe it. After all these years of knowing you two, I just don't think you could do such a thing. And whether you did or didn't is neither here nor there. Unless they prove you did it, it isn't fair to the kids—or to you, I guess—to treat you this way. You deserve the benefit of the doubt, at least. So, I just wanted to tell you I'm sorry."

I let it sink in a minute. "Thank you. That means a lot."

"You're welcome. Just don't prove me wrong. You better not be guilty."

"I'm not," I hurried to reassure her. "But that doesn't mean things are going to go my way necessarily."

Her eyes widened. "What do you mean?"

"There's not a lot that proves it *wasn't* me. So who do you think a jury will believe?"

A look of guilt flashed across her face. "What are you going to do?"

"I don't know. Pray my lawyer comes up with a hell of a defense." We both fell silent.

"I better get going," she said after a moment. "I've got errands to run, and I'm sure you have work to do." She stood up and took a step away from the counter. Suddenly, she turned and bent to retrieve the shopping bag on the floor next to the stool. "I almost forgot. I promised to get this back to you the week after the funeral." Curious, I took the bag from her and looked inside. Mary's uniform purse lay there, along with what looked like a scarf and a sweater.

"I borrowed the clothes a long time ago," she explained.

"Then you should keep them."

"Oh, no. No, I couldn't." She held her arms out straight as if to push the bag away. "Why don't you see if Kelsey wants them?" I walked her to the front door. She paused before stepping over the threshold. When she looked at me, her eyes glistened. "Tell the kids I said 'hello.'" She turned and walked away.

Back in the office, I realized I still had the shopping

bag in my hand. I sat down and pulled out Mary's purse. I stared at it for a minute, then slowly went through every compartment and placed the contents, one by one, onto the desk. There wasn't anything particularly extraordinary or even personal about them. Arrayed across the desktop were a flashlight, corkscrew, oven mitt, lipstick, compact case, two tampons, ballpoint pen, sewing kit from the Hotel Nikko in Tokyo, travel-size bottles of hand lotion and shampoo, also from the Nikko, a plastic spoon, assorted bobby pins and hair clips, breath mints, mascara, eye-liner pencil, emery board, three postage stamps, some scraps of paper covered with scribbled to-do lists and an unlabeled CD.

I looked at the assortment for a long time, wishing it held some insight into the person I'd spent the last twenty years with. It was so frustratingly normal, I wanted to scream. It could have belonged to practically any woman in the Western world—except for one thing.

I stared at the CD. It sat unblinking, a round silver eye in a slim plastic case, staring back indifferently until I grew smart enough to figure out why it seemed out of place. We had a CD changer hooked up to the stereo in the family room. There was a DVD player hooked up to the television. But Mary had never owned a CD player.

I slid the CD into a drive on the computer and opened the directory. The files on it didn't look like music files. I'd never seen the file type before. It looked like a Chinese pictogram. I clicked on one of the files. A message box popped up asking me what program I wanted to use to open it. I didn't have a clue. The box listed available programs. I highlighted one and clicked "Open." Nothing happened. I tried another one. Again, nothing. I tried every program on the list with no success, then sat back, stared at the monitor and rubbed the days-old stubble on my chin.

Whatever the disc's contents, it wasn't going to give them up easily.

I TALKED JIAN INTO COMING to dinner with his daughter the following week after the start of Christmas break. He seemed eager to spend time with us and grateful for the invitation. He probably felt as socially isolated in some ways as I did.

"I don't know why we have to have them over for dinner," Kelsey said, looking peeved as she arranged flatware on the table. Quiet and subdued since her cathartic meltdown, she acted far less contrary. But the girl I knew the summer before had disappeared. Now she looked at me warily whenever we were in the same room, like a skittish cat.

I turned off the faucet and sighed, wishing she'd figure out how good she had it. My wet hands dripped in the sink. "Because they're nice people." She turned back to what she'd been doing. I lifted a colander of fresh spinach out of the sink and shook it to drain the excess water. "Where is Ty, anyway?"

She shrugged. "Upstairs, I think." She didn't look up.

"Well, when you finish that, would you go tell him to come down? They'll be here any time." She huffed to let me know what an imposition it was. The bell rang. I went to answer it while Kelsey trotted upstairs to get Ty. I swung open the door to see a strikingly pretty young Asian woman standing on the stoop. Then it registered that Jian stood behind her with his hand on her shoulder, a big smile on his face.

"Hello, hello," he said. "We are here."

"Yes, you are." I couldn't help a smile. "Come in. Please." I stepped back to let them in. On a second look, I realized that makeup is what had made Jian's daughter appear older. He introduced her as Mei Lei when they were inside. Sensing Kelsey and Ty on the stairs behind me, I reciprocated. Jian and his daughter stepped closer and Kelsey murmured a hello. Ty straightened his shoulders, stepped up to Jian and stuck out a hand. Jian gave him a two-handed shake and bowed.

"How do you do? So pleased to meet you." Ty flushed with a combination of embarrassment and pride, and stepped back. Prodded into remembering her manners, Kelsey shook his hand next, awkwardly imitating his bow. Then she backpedaled and shoved her hands into the pockets of her jeans. Mei Lei did the same. I was struck by how alike they were, and how different. Light and dark. Yin and yang. They eyed each other warily, legs crossed, heads tilted curiously.

"You wanna come up and see my room?" Kelsey said.

Mei Lei nodded. Jian beamed. I led him down the hall to the family room. Ty tagged along behind like a puppy.

I once read a story about the friendship of the two poets Coleridge and Wordsworth. Wordsworth walked into his friend's cottage one night and sat down in front of the fire without a word. After three hours of silence, he got up, thanked Coleridge for a perfectly enjoyable evening and left.

While the girls disappeared upstairs to talk, giggle, try on clothes, trade secrets or whatever it is girls do, we guys had as close to a perfect evening as you could get. After exchanging a few pleasantries with me, Jian happily performed sleight-of-hand tricks for Ty while

I prepared dinner. Ty silently marveled as Jian pulled quarters out of his ears and made them disappear into thin air. Jian did more tricks with one of Ty's shoelaces and a few with a deck of cards. Never once did he question why Ty remained mute.

Mei Lei's animated patter about the differences between Chinese and American culture made dinner lively. Kelsey feigned boredom, as though it was all old news, but her eyes sparked with interest, and she prompted Mei Lei with more questions about life in China. The answers surprised me, demonstrating more similarities than differences between our families. Jian's family had a lot more freedom and higher standard of living than I imagined. Jian smiled throughout, pleased that the girls seemed to be getting along.

I offered Jian tea while the girls cleared the table, then joined him when it was ready. The kids disappeared. I asked Jian more about his job and how he'd been able to come to the States. He said the company he worked for was American, but had a big contract in China, and that he was actually on loan from the Chinese company he'd been working for.

I had a sudden idea. "Hey, I hate to make you talk shop when you're off work, but maybe you can help me with something."

"If I can, yes. It is something with computers?"

"Sort of. Come on, I'll show you." I led the way to the den and pulled a spare chair up to the desk. I held up the disc that had been in Mary's purse. "I'm trying to figure out what's on this." Jian settled into the chair in front of the computer monitor while I slid the disc into the CD drive. I pulled up the directory.

He peered at the list of files. "And you cannot open?" I double-clicked on the top file to demonstrate. "I may see, please?" I let him slide into the desk chair and watched over his shoulder while he rapidly moved the mouse and opened dialogue boxes showing file properties and other information. Finally, he opened a box with a black background and started typing furiously, filling the screen with white letters and symbols. He stopped typing suddenly, peered at the screen, and closed everything.

"I am thinking they are maybe pictures," he explained as he opened another program and tried again. Nothing happened. He frowned and went online, quickly clicking through web pages until he found what he wanted. After downloading it, he launched a new program, and used it to try opening one of the files again. A dialogue box popped up and requested a password.

"Ah, so," Jian said knowingly. He leaned back in the chair. "These files are what we call encrypted. How do you say it? Password-protected. I do not have password. I am guessing you do not, either?" I shook my head. He looked at me curiously. "Where did this come from?"

"It was in my wife's purse. The one she takes— took—to work."

"It is most curious. You do not know where she got it?" He pointed to the screen. "Those are *hiragana.*"

"Is that Japanese?" I saw him nod. "You know what they mean?"

"Some. They are not like Chinese. Or *kanji,* which Japanese borrowed from China. They are just sounds, not words."

"Can you figure out the password?"

"Not sure. Could be very simple code. Or..." He lifted his shoulders and looked apologetic.

"Could you try?" When I saw him hesitate I added,

"It could be important." His eyes flicked across my face, then he nodded.

He turned back to the computer, looking at his watch as he did. *"Ai ya!"* he said. "The time. I must be going home." He rose. "I will come tomorrow, yes? Tomorrow we will see if we can find the secrets of these files." He smiled.

JIAN SHOWED UP a little before noon the next day with Mei Lei and a large grocery bag.

"Is Kelsey here?" Mei Lei said shyly. Her face was scrubbed free of the makeup she'd worn the night before. She seemed to have lost some of her self-assuredness with it.

"Probably upstairs," I said. She looked at me questioningly. "You can go on up. It's okay." I turned to Jian. "Can I take that for you?"

"Ah, no. It's okay. Come, I show you." He took a step toward the hallway. "Is okay, yes?" I nodded and he led the way back to the kitchen. He put the bag on the counter and started pulling white food cartons out of it. "Is lunch." He grinned. "Mexican." He opened a carton and tilted it to show me the burritos inside.

We arranged the food on the counter and when it was ready called the kids down to eat. Once they settled at the table, we took plates into the den and parked in front of the computer. He inserted a CD he'd brought with him, and went to work on the keyboard.

He explained what he was doing as he went along. "First, I am installing program to unlock password. Is very powerful decryption program, but could take days. Weeks, even. Computer must try millions of combinations to find the correct one." He tapped his temple with a finger. "Is challenge I cannot ignore. Always to be smarter than computer. Disc from Japan, yes?"

I shrugged. "I don't have a clue. That's as good a guess as any."

"Files are very secret," he went on. "If person who does this is from Japan, I am thinking password is Japanese."

I gestured at the monitor. "Well, does that program understand Japanese?"

The smile spread across his face. "In a manner of speaking." He chuckled at his own joke. "Program is made to try groups of keys on keyboard, no matter what is written on them."

"You mean combinations of any letters and numbers."

"Yes, and symbols, too." He pointed at punctuation keys on the keyboard. "Like this, and this. In Asia, many computers use same keyboard as this. Too difficult to use Chinese. Each character is a word. Keyboard must be big as house for all our words. But in Japan, some computers use symbols like alphabet called *kana.*"

"I thought Japanese characters were called *kanji.*"

He gave me an impatient look. "Yes, but *kanji* is like Chinese. Characters come from China. Like in China, each has meaning. Special characters, like alphabet, are *kana. Kana* are symbols for all sounds in Japanese language. But there are two kinds. First comes *katakana.* Later comes *hiragana.* In Japan, they call it 'women's writing.' Is softer and rounder than *katakana.* See?" He pointed to the computer. The screen showed two sets of Japanese symbols, one very angular, the other more flowery. "They mean the same thing," he said. "On computer in Japan, when you push key with *hira-*

gana, computer give you choice of *kanji* you wish to use."

"You type a letter and it asks you which word you want," I said.

He smiled. "Yes. Now you see. So, I have taught program to read *kana.* If password not totally random, then maybe… Ah, so. Is not, as I thought." I followed his gaze. A box had popped up with a string of Japanese characters in the password line. He murmured something, engrossed in the screen. "I think maybe we are lucky. It is difficult combination," he said over his shoulder. "Maybe random. Maybe mean something if you know right *kanji* for each *kana.* Computer would take much longer without knowing *kana.*" He copied the password, closed files, opened the mystery CD, and pasted the password into another program as he called up one of the protected files. The screen filled with a high-resolution photo in lush tones with subtle dramatic lighting. No amateur snapshot, it showed an ornate red velvet couch set against a deep blue textured backdrop. On the couch a figure reclined entirely nude except for a colorful silk scarf casually draped over a shoulder. Blond hair spilled over one of the blood-red cushions, framing an angelic face accentuated by startlingly deep blue eyes. A hint of uncertainty—or fear—combined with innocence made the face more alluring.

I absorbed all this in an instant, but another second passed before it registered that the figure was a pre-pubescent girl. She was maybe nine or ten.

"Ta ma de!" Jian said.

"Shit!" I exclaimed at the same instant.

I quickly stabbed the eject button on the disc drive with a finger. Before it had opened, I shut off the computer, then fell to my knees, reached under the desk and yanked the surge protector's plug out of the wall socket. The room went silent.

SEVENTEEN

THE image seared itself into my brain. I bucked like a horse with a cat on its back to shake it off. Then I rocked back off my knees and sat on the floor, my back against the desk.

Kelsey had been just about nine when she'd decided that she no longer needed my help washing her hair. Until then, neither of us had felt self-conscious when I gave her a bath. I hoped she never felt ashamed of her body or even being nude in front of others if she chose. But I had a hard time imagining a child that age posing in such a fashion. It made my skin crawl. I suddenly felt as if I needed a shower.

I glanced at Jian. He inspected his shoes intently, looking decidedly uneasy. "What did you say?" I asked.

"What?" He looked at me, then put his hand up to his mouth and bowed his head. "Oh, so sorry. It was not nice thing to say."

I waved away his concern. "Don't worry about it. I was just curious."

"Oh." He brightened. "I say what you say—*ta ma de.* It mean, 'oh, shit.'"

"Then you saw it, too."

He nodded. "Little girl made to look like *biao zi.* Um, what we call courtesan. Very bad."

"Hooker? You don't know the half of it." My shoulders slumped.

"You not feeling well? You not look so good. Pictures make you sick?"

"We've got a problem, Jian. That stuff is poison." I nodded toward the computer. "If all the files are like that, you can go to jail for a long time just for having them in your possession."

"I am not saying—telling," he said with a serious look. "I promise. But we cannot find out about where disc comes from unless we look at it."

"What if that image is on my hard drive now? What if a hacker gets into my computer and downloads it? Good God, you can get life in prison for distributing child pornography."

He reached over and put a hand on my shoulder. "Is okay. Breathe. Like this." He held his cupped hands at his waist, closed his eyes, then sucked air deeply into his nostrils and slowly exhaled through his mouth. He opened his eyes and looked at me. "Now you," he said. "No, is not foolish. You try." I did as he said, and felt some of the tension in my neck and shoulders ease as I exhaled. I opened my eyes.

"Is better, yes? Why you so worried? You have firewall, yes?" It came out sounding something like *hire-war*.

"I'm sorry. What? Oh, sure. Firewall. Sorry." I paused. "It's not just that." He looked at me curiously. I met his gaze and rubbed my chin for a moment. Then I told him everything. About Mary's murder and the evidence that finally led the police to arrest me. How they had come in with a warrant and searched the house. And about the computer discs and hard drive they'd taken. Once again I was embarrassed to admit, even to another guy, that some of the discs had contained photos of nude women.

I don't know why I felt guilty. Looking at erotica occasionally seemed pretty harmless. Mary had pretty much lost interest in physical intimacy years before anyway, despite my best efforts to keep the romance and passion alive. It was ironic, I thought, that I'd been able to talk her into having sex the night she'd been killed. Only because she'd had too much to drink. And now it was being turned against me, evidence that I'd raped and strangled her. And now... If anyone learned of this disc, on top of what the police had already collected as evidence... Jian looked at me with a very strange expression. I wondered when I'd stopped talking. "What is it?" he asked.

I looked away. "Nothing. I was just thinking." Jian waited patiently. "You never met Mary, but do you think a wife and mother could have anything to do with this?" I jerked a thumb toward the computer behind me.

"Do you?"

I hesitated. "I don't know what to think. I guess even after twenty years I didn't know her." I thought back. "I believed she was asleep the night she was killed. I thought she was here safe and sound, but for some reason she got up in the middle of the night and went out. I never heard her, never knew she was gone. I can't believe she had anything to do with this, though."

"Then you must find out how this has happened," he said. "I will help."

I hesitated. "I can't ask you to do that."

"You did not ask," he said. My surprise must have shown. "You are my friend when no one else would be. I will help."

JIAN SAID HE NEEDED A FEW things from home, so we took a break. The girls asked if they could walk to the shopping center at the south end, and left cheerfully when we said okay. Sue Thorvahl called—for the first time since I'd reclaimed the kids—and asked if Ty could spend the night. Though not speaking yet, he brightened considerably when Sue and Rory picked him up.

Jian returned with a small notebook computer and more CDs. We settled in the den and rebooted my desktop computer. First, he tracked down all the temporary files on my hard drive and deleted them. Then he wiped the hard drive clean. A really sophisticated computer geek might be able to reconstruct a portion of the temporary file, he told me, but likely not enough to generate a clear image.

He inserted the mystery disc in his notebook computer and opened the file we'd glimpsed before. As soon as the image filled the screen, hairs on the back of my neck rose and my stomach felt queasy. I forced myself to look. Not at the subject itself, but individual details, searching for clues to where and why it had been taken. I spotted an odd string of alphanumeric characters in the lower left, and an unusual pictogram in the lower right.

I turned away. Most disturbing about the photo was its allure, the fact that it aroused my prurient interest. But the photo's truth was too horrifying to contemplate.

Jian sighed. "Is enough, yes?" He closed the file. "Is sad." He sat motionless for a moment, then sighed again and opened the next file.

Again I avoided looking directly at the subject, confining my gaze to the periphery, taking in only small portions at a time, never the whole. Similar in nature, it featured a different backdrop, different set pieces, different child. Another alphanumeric sequence appeared at the lower left, and the same tiny pictogram in the lower right. Jian left this file open a fraction of the time we'd looked at the first. That was still too long. I looked away.

He clicked through the remaining files at a faster pace, spending less time on each photo. There were close to thirty of them, about equally divided between males and females, all essentially the same. I could scarcely bring myself to think of them as boys and girls. I had trouble accepting the fact that someone had co-erced that many children into such poses.

Jian ejected the disc and shook his head. He held it up. "This is very bad. Did you see *kanji* on pictures? I see symbols like these in China. I think this one is symbol for Japanese *yakuza*."

"What? You mean gangs?"

"Is more like tongs in China. Or the Mafia. You know—*The Godfather*."

"How do you know all this? I thought China censored stuff like movies from America."

He smiled at my naiveté. "You think we not eat at Pizza Hut before we come here?"

I gave a short laugh. "Man, that is sad. To think the ambassadors of our food culture are fast-food chains. I don't think I've had a really good pizza since I left Chicago."

"No? Is okay. Chinese food here not so hot, either." After a moment his face sobered. "How your wife get this? Yakuza not something you joke with. You still not think she have something to do with this?"

"God, no. I can't even imagine it." I didn't tell him how prudish Mary had been. "She could have gotten it anywhere."

"But why? She would not take if she knew what is on it, yes?"

"Never. It would make her sick."

"Then why she take if she *not* know what it is?"

"I don't know," I said. "Mary would have taken it from a complete stranger if she thought the person had a nice smile. Maybe she took it as a favor, to give to someone else."

"Or maybe she not know it was in her purse."

"Someone slipped it in there?" I thought about it. "It couldn't have been there long, then. She would have noticed it."

"Perhaps." He steepled his fingers, touched them to his lips, and gazed at something unseen.

"I'M LONELY." The admission startled me. Not because I gave it voice, but because I'd taken so long to recognize the truth of it.

"You miss her."

I turned away from the window and looked at Sarah. "Actually, no, I don't think I do." I shrugged. "At least, not the way you're thinking. I miss what might have been. But that's the problem—I never had it. I think I've been lonely for twenty years. It just took me this long to realize it." She tipped her head and looked at me curiously.

"Oh, I loved her. And I know she loved me in her way. But it was never what I expected love to be. It just wasn't anything like what you read in books or see in the movies. We seemed to be more like friends, or roommates." I paused, and looked out the window again. "The kids miss her, though. A lot."

"It's a good thing you have this new friend, then. Jian?"

I faced her with a wry smile. "I like him, but he's not exactly my type."

*"Ah." Awareness flashed in her eyes. "Maybe it's
time you got out there again and met some people. Get
back up on the horse, as it were."*

"Maybe," I mused.

I LEFT A FEW VOICEMAIL messages for Diane. She finally
called back at the end of the week. "I need a favor," I
told her. "A big favor. Two of them, in fact. I need you
to think back to the last flight you and Mary worked
together."

There was silence, then a tentative, "Okay. I'll try.
What about it?"

"Was there anything unusual about the flight?"

"No-o. I'm not sure what you mean."

"Did Mary spend more time with any of the passengers than usual? Did any of them single her out?"

"Not that I remember. She acted the same as always.
Joking. Laughing. A little flirtatious with the guys. I
mean the older gentlemen. You know how she was."

"Yeah, I know." I paused. "You're sure there was
nothing strange about the trip?" She heard the disappointment in my voice.

"Sorry. Except for grabbing each other's uniform
purses, I really can't think of anything."

"How did that happen anyway?"

"I don't know." She sounded puzzled. "Wait, I remember now. Right before we landed Mary asked me
if I had any lip balm. I handed her my purse. She put
it on the counter in the galley next to hers. When she
stowed them both before strapping herself into her jump
seat, she must have gotten them mixed up. What's this
all about, anyway?"

"Something in her purse didn't belong to her. I
thought maybe it belonged to a passenger." I paused.

"Which leads me to the second favor. Is there any way you can get a copy of the passenger manifest for that trip?"

"I can't do that, Jack." She sounded shaken. "Even if the company kept them this long, I can't just pull up a manifest. It's against company policy. They don't make those public."

"Diane, please. It's important."

She was silent. "I know a fellow in Operations," she said finally. "He's sort of sweet on me. I think I might be able to get him to do it for me."

"Thank you."

"So, are you going to tell me what this is all about?"

"When I know. Not just yet."

WE HAD DINNER AT JIAN'S house the week following Christmas. His small, unassuming house was near the library, an easy walk from the high school. Though sparsely furnished, it felt surprisingly homey. More than big enough for the two of them, they improvised to accommodate the three of us. They pulled a couple of living room chairs up to the wooden table in the kitchen.

Mei Lei assumed a much more traditional role than she had at our house. She helped Jian prepare food and played hostess before dinner. After we ate, some signal must have passed between them. Her solemn face and stiff demeanor vanished. She broke out in a smile as she took Kelsey's arm and whispered something in her ear. Giggling, they disappeared into another part of the house.

Jian excused himself and brought back an ornate wooden box from the living room. He opened it and placed a beautifully carved Chinese checkerboard on the kitchen table. Ty's face lit up, and the three of us jumped into a spirited series of games. When Ty tired of it, Jian found some puzzles he thought Ty might enjoy. Ty settled on the floor in the next room with them.

"He is smart boy," Jian said as he came back to the table.

I nodded. "Thank you. He is, even though he doesn't say much."

"Kind of like us at parents' group." He grinned.

I joined him. "God, I hope not all single women are like that."

He gave me a curious look. "You are thinking of meeting someone?"

"I don't know. It's probably too soon. And with all the uncertainty in my life, I'm probably not ready. I mean, what woman wants to date someone who's waiting to go on trial for murder?"

"But you are thinking about it, yes?" he said. I looked away. "Maybe you try when ready."

WHEN WE GOT HOME from dinner, I asked Ty to head upstairs and get ready for bed. Kelsey went up, too, saying she had homework to finish. A few minutes later I went up to tuck Tyler in. I caught him coming out of the bathroom, scooped him up with an arm around his waist and tickled him in the ribs. He squirmed and laughed as I carried him to the bed, trying to pry my arm loose so he could get away from my tormenting fingers.

I dumped him unceremoniously on top of the covers.

"I had fun with you tonight, kiddo." He grinned, looking devious. "Oh, no you don't." I grabbed him just as he was about to spring a counterattack and tickled him with both hands this time, sending him into a paroxysm of laughter.

I stopped to let him catch his breath. "Hey, remember that time we drove down to Gamma's and Pop's house in Florida?" I asked. He looked at me blankly. "We stayed in that little motel room, all four of us? We barely had enough room to turn around." The blank look gave way to a worried expression that bordered on fear.

"Oh, sure you remember," I said with a smile. "We were going to spend a day at Disney World, and you couldn't wait to meet Goofy. Not Mickey, but Goofy." I kept my tone light, wondering what bothered him. "Anyway, we were all crammed in that motel room, and something I ate turned me into the Tickle Monster. You and Mom laughed so hard I thought snot was going to come out your noses." Ty's face took on a look of panic and tears started rolling silently down his cheeks. Half-formed thoughts and images churned in my head like bubbles in a hot tub.

"It's okay," I said. "It's no big deal. It was a long time ago, and you were pretty little. It's okay if you don't remember." But his tears flowed even faster, and his small face reflected despair so bleak that it rent my heart. I hugged him tight and rocked him, as if I could somehow squeeze all the pain and sadness out of his thin body. "I know, I know, I know," I crooned. "You miss her. We all miss her, Bud. You miss her so much that sometimes it scares you. It's okay. It's okay to miss her. And it's okay to be scared." I stopped rocking and looked at him. "That's it. You're scared, aren't you? But not because you miss her. It's because you don't remember. Is that it? You're scared that you'll forget her. That's why you want everything to stay just the way it is. That's why you always set a place for her at

the dinner table and why you don't want us to touch
her things. Oh, Ty."

I cupped his cheek in the palm of my big hand. "Ty,
you won't forget her. You can't forget Mom. She'll
always be a part of you." He tipped his tear-streaked
face up to look at me. The tears stopped, but he looked
uncertain, as if unsure whether to believe me.

I had an idea. "Hang on a second. I'll be right back.
Will you be all right?" He nodded solemnly. I brushed
his cheek with my hand and stood up. He made no attempt to stop me, so I hurried downstairs and rummaged
through a cupboard in the family room for an old photo
album. When I found it, I carried it back upstairs. I sat
on the edge of Ty's bed. He swung his legs over the edge
and sat next to me. I opened the album across our laps,
and flipped through the pages until I came to the pictures
of the vacation I'd been thinking of.

"See?" I put a finger on a photo. "There you are at
Gamma's house." I pointed to another. "And here's
Mom." He drank the photos in eagerly, studying each
one closely. He slowly turned the page. And there was
the memory he hadn't been able to find. A snapshot
at a crazy angle of me as the Tickle Monster stalking
a laughing Mary and the giggly boy in her arms. Another shot of the three of us on the bed in the tiny motel
room. Then a picture of Kelsey and Mary in the midst
of a pillow fight with Ty caught between them. More
pictures of the motel. A turn of the page revealed the
sights of Disney World and Ty's meeting with Goofy.

As he looked at each new photo, a widening smile
slowly replaced the sadness and fear on his face. When
he closed the album, though, he looked at me with uncertainty in his eyes again.

"You still a little scared?"

He nodded, then said in a small voice, "Sometimes I forget what she looks like." He'd spoken. I wanted to jump up and down, and shout with relief and glee. I wanted to grab both his hands in mine and dance wildly around the room with him. I wanted to ask him to tell me his name, anything, over and over and over again, never tiring of his little voice. I acted as if nothing had happened.

"That's okay," I said. "It's normal for some memories to fade with time. That doesn't mean you'll forget her. And it doesn't mean that you don't love her anymore. She'll always be in your heart." I touched his chest with the tips of my fingers. "Even if you can't see her face clearly in your mind. The cool thing is, any time you get worried that you're going to forget, you can just look at pictures like these and she'll be right there with you." He sat lost in thought, his face scrunched up with the effort. As if someone pulled a mask away, his face abruptly lightened. He rolled onto all fours and bounced his way up toward the head of the bed, and slid under the covers. He let me tuck them under his chin, then reached for a book on the nightstand.

At the door, I turned. "Good night, kiddo. I love you." On my way out I heard him say, "Love you, Dad." Downstairs, I sat at my desk in the den for a long time and slowly thumbed through the photo album. Mary's cheery face looked out at me from page after page, in scene after scene, with and without the kids. I smiled at the memories. I laid it aside and reached for the anniversary photo of Mary and me on the shelf over the desk. I looked at it closely, then put it in a desk drawer and let her go.

I began to shut down the computer, changed my mind and checked e-mail. Junk, lots of it. Spam promising lower mortgages, cheaper prescription drugs, harder erections, bigger breasts. And one e-mail.

Jack,

You probably don't remember me—support group, last time you were there. I just wanted you to know that I don't believe what they say about you. I'm not sure why I'm doing this. My life is so busy I barely have time to eat some days. But I don't think I'm too busy to explore the possibility of spending time with the right person every once in a while.

Anyway, I thought you should know we're not all bitches, and not all of us think men are jerks. Amy

EIGHTEEN

I READ the e-mail again, and a third time, trying to figure out how to respond. Questions flitted through my head like Monarchs in migration. But I couldn't help remembering how Amy had looked at me my last night at the support group. I hadn't even known her name until now. I finally worked up a pithy response saying I thought she obviously needed a good home-cooked meal, and providing them happened to be one of my more accomplished skills. I asked a couple of inane questions, like where she worked and what she did for fun, what turned her on, and signed it "Your turn, Jack."

WHEN DIANE EVENTUALLY called to tell me she had the passenger list from Mary's last flight she didn't sound happy about it. I made arrangements to drive into Seattle and pick it up at her apartment.

I found a spot on the street less than a block from her building on Capital Hill and when I rang her intercom she buzzed me in. I took the elevator up. She met me at the door, but didn't invite me in. The list was in her hand. She gave it to me without comment. When she swung the door shut, I put up a hand and stopped it.

"Look, Diane, I'm sorry if this was a hassle to get." I wasn't quite sure what the cool reception was all about. "I wouldn't have asked if it wasn't important, and I really appreciate it." She said nothing, her mouth set in a grim line, but she released her pressure on the door.

"If you could just think back one more time to that day," I went on. "Are you sure Mary stayed in first class? She didn't work business class or coach at all?" She gazed somewhere over my shoulder, then shook her head. "That narrows it down. You don't remember her spending time with anyone in particular?"

She started to shake her head, but hesitated. "Four-B," she said.

"You're sure?"

She threw me an acrid glance. "She talked to everyone, Jack. That was just Mary. But I do remember the guy in four-B being very attentive. No one sat next to him, so he talked to Mary whenever she came by."

"Where did you and Mary stash your stuff? You know, your suitcases and purses?"

"Behind the last middle row of seats."

"What is that, row five? Six? D, E and F?"

"Four. D and E. There are only two seats in the middle. Just don't ever let anyone know I gave you that."

"Thanks. I won't." I started to tell her I'd make it up to her, but she'd already closed the door.

"Ito Takeshi." I showed Jian the list. "That has to be the guy."

"But you say she would have taken from any nice person. She could have gotten disc any time she in Tokyo." I felt Jian's eyes on me. "What is it?" he said. "You are angry."

"It's nothing." I shook my head. "I'm fine."

"No, I see this in your eyes. Is same thing when you say to women in our group 'Qu ni de.'"

My head swiveled toward him. "What's that mean?" He looked off into middle distance. His face turned defiant, and he thrust out his arm, giving the wall the finger. He flashed me a smug smile.

I couldn't help a snort of laughter. "*Qu ni de,* huh? I'll have to remember that." I fell silent for a moment and tried to make sense of it. "What if this Takeshi guy *did* put the CD in Mary's purse? What if he wanted to bring it into the country so he could burn copies and sell them? What if he got scared and thought customs might find it? He figures, slip it into the flight attendant's purse. She'll breeze through customs, and he can get it from her later. But what if he misses her outside customs? This is hot enough that he'd track her down to get it back, right? Hell, Mary probably let slip where she lived." Jian watched me work it out. Snippets of memories curled around the edges of my consciousness like the tendrils of dreams. *Phone calls from a man who thought I had something he wanted. A stranger in a car talking to Ty in the parking lot. Someone standing on the embankment overlooking soccer practice. A creepy guy staring through the windows of the high school commons. All the same person?*

"And this makes you angry," he said.

"Yes." I couldn't even begin to enumerate how angry I was, or with whom. I only knew that somehow it felt not good, exactly, but familiar. Something that had lain dormant inside was now stirring. The ember glowed brighter. It was as if I'd awakened after a long sleep.

"Jian, what if someone—it doesn't matter who— what if he came looking for this? What if Mary was killed for this?" His eyes widened, but he didn't say anything. I tapped the paper in my hand with a finger. "This could be the guy."

"I think maybe you are—how do you say it?—grasping at straws," he said slowly.

I waved a hand impatiently. "That's not the point. The point is that I *did not kill my wife.* A lot of people are convinced I did, and I started to believe them. But I didn't do it. Someone else murdered her, snuffed her out like a candle. Whether it was this guy or some crazy off the street, whoever it was didn't just take away her life. He took our lives away from us, too." I stood and paced the room, then faced him again. "Angry? Yes, I'm angry. I've been letting this guy win. I let him destroy me and my family a piece at a time. No more. I want my life back. I have to find a way to prove that I didn't do this. This is a place to start." He sat expressionless, as if still undecided.

I pressed on, hoping to tip the scales. "I could be all wrong. But this changes everything. Don't you see? Mary had something she wasn't supposed to have. This…this noxious, perverted filth is like poison. It's dangerous. But somehow it ended up in Mary's purse. And three days later she was dead. It's too much to be coincidence."

He gave a short nod. "Maybe you are right." I met his eyes. They seemed to acknowledge my unspoken thanks.

"So, how do we find out who this guy is?"

"Internet," he said brightly. "Is answer to every-thing."

AFTER TY WAS TUCKED into bed and Kelsey had gone to her room to finish homework, I stopped in the den to check my calendar and organize my to-do list for the next day. Before I shut down the computer for the night, I checked e-mail once more.

Jack,
Answers to your questions: Work—shop owner, designer (I design and sell dishware). Fun—to be

determined (let's talk later, if you're willing to give me your phone number). Turn-on—your wit.
Amy.

I sat back, suddenly aware of a feeling I couldn't describe, as if life had somehow changed.

WHEN THE KIDS WENT back to school after the break, I spent time poring over copies of all the reports that were pertinent to my case. The ones I'd ignored for so long. "Inconsistencies" were what we were looking for, Preston said. Hard enough deciphering the scientific and technical jargon let alone figuring out what *didn't* make sense, I slowly got the gist of it all.

The autopsy report was pretty straightforward. As ghoulish as it read, the terminology rendered it largely impersonal. The descriptive language explained the science of what had happened to a thing and all its parts. It contained none of the emotion involved, no narrative of events, only the resultant changes to Mary's body. Reading through the material, I tried to do the same. I blocked out memories of her, the sound of her voice, the smell of her perfume. I concentrated on the details, pushing the image of her face out of my head.

I'd accepted the fact that someone had choked the life out of her. The report detailed the evidence that led to the M.E.'s conclusion—fractured hyoid bone, pinpoint hemorrhages in the conjunctivae of the eyes, bleeding in the strap muscles of the neck. The report also noted the bruising on the inside of her thighs and the small vaginal tears that indicated she had been sexually assaulted.

The lab reports, however, confused me. Preston had warned me that the science behind them was compel-

ling, but not exact. That's where he hoped to make a
case. It all seemed a little fuzzy to me. The Medical
Examiner's sexual assault tests showed the presence
of semen. The state crime lab had conducted DNA
tests. The semen was mine. I already knew this. But
the M.E.'s report stated that the number of morpho-
logically intact sperm suggested that sex had likely occurred several hours before death. But the bruising and
other signs of assault had been inflicted "close to the
time of death," according to the report.

Reports on the analysis of trace evidence were just
as confusing. The police had collected evidence from
her car, so much of it that the crime lab had simply
identified and logged it. Kelsey, Tyler and I had been
subjected to the minor indignity of being fingerprinted
shortly after her body had been found. As messy as
Mary's car had been, the only fingerprints not belong-
ing to one of the four of us had been on the doors and
windows in the backseat, and were too small to be an
adult's.

Trace evidence found under Mary's fingernails was
determined to be her own skin, probably from scratch-
ing her throat as she struggled to relieve the awful pressure from the killer's hands. A tiny piece of dyed leather
also was found, as well as a substance of some sort. The
lab analysis identified it as a combination of oils from
different sources and plant glycerides derived from
some specie of the genus *Rhus*. None of which meant a
damn thing to me. Since traces of the same substance
had been found on Mary's neck, however, the Medical Examiner had concluded there was a possibility the
killer had worn gloves recently treated with some sort
of leather conditioner. Explaining why the search war-

rant Mankiewicz served me with had referred to leather goods.

There was another bit of confusion for which there was neither explanation nor conclusion. Among the trace evidence recovered from Mary's body were hairs. Pubic hairs, to be exact, two loose matching hairs found on Mary's body, entangled in her pubes. They weren't hers. Another was found on her clothing. It didn't match the others or hers. No further tests had been conducted. I wondered why.

I LOCKED UP AND HEADED into Seattle, carefully checking to see if anyone followed, ready to shake any paparazzi I spotted. I chewed an antacid to calm the butterflies in my stomach.

Amy and I had traded e-mails and phone calls for the better part of the week. I couldn't deny that I liked the way she expressed her thoughts in e-mails, and I liked the sound of her voice on the phone. It was Amy who suggested lunch. Lunch, not coffee. A bold move on her part, more risky. A bigger commitment of time and money than meeting for coffee. She recommended a place near Green Lake so we could walk after lunch if we felt like it. I liked her assertiveness and confidence, but I broke into a sweat at the thought of not hitting it off well enough to survive both lunch and a walk. And wondered why she was interested in the first place.

I found a place to park on the street half a block from the restaurant twenty minutes early. A block down, the lake glinted brightly under a clear blue sky. I strolled down to the park and found the path that circled the lake. An odd assortment passed by taking advantage of the break in our usual February rain—mothers with strollers, couples, roller skaters, joggers and bikers whirling by.

Calmed by this oasis in the middle of the city, I headed back up the street toward the restaurant. Mid-block, my cell phone rang. I recognized the incoming number, glanced at my watch and decided to take the call. Terry McAuley asking about the last article I'd turned in. I had the answer to his question, but it led to a long discussion. When I finally hung up, I hurried to the restaurant, nervous again, compounded now by embarrassment that I was late.

Sunshine streamed in the restaurant's front windows, making it difficult to see into the dim interior. As my eyes adjusted, a tall, lanky woman with dark hair rose from a booth and strode toward me, her hand outstretched. I recognized her. She had the same small confident smile. But there was a touch of uncertainty in her eyes, as if I might not be who she was looking for. Her gait reminded me of a thoroughbred, leggy and awkward in tight quarters, but graceful and beautiful given room to run.

"Jack," she said.

I put out my hand. Her touch was electric. I murmured some sort of greeting, but didn't even know what I said. I was too surprised by the odd current that coursed up my arm and spread through me, making even my toes tingle when I shook her hand.

She led the way back to the booth. I remembered my manners and waited until she was seated before sliding in across from her. I didn't remember much of anything else. I didn't remember what I ordered, or even eating it. We talked about ourselves—vital statistics, our families, where we grew up, what we did for a living—but

I didn't remember what we said. The words registered somewhere, but sensations, not thoughts, consumed me.

Lunch went well enough that we agreed to walk around the lake. We sauntered slowly down to the path, but once there she set off with purpose, swinging into a graceful easy stride that nearly matched my own.Without even being aware of it, I found myself falling into step. We talked more, this time about even taboo subjects like politics and religion. We compared likes and dislikes in movies, music and books and found enough similarities to feel kinship, and enough differences to keep things interesting without feeling at odds. We talked about our passions and some of our dreams and a little of what we hoped to find.

From time to time, I glanced at her, took in her face, her expressions, the way she moved. She seemed familiar. Three-quarters of the way around the lake, I took her hand. She laced her fingers in mine. We walked the rest of the way like that, as if we'd been friends all our lives. When we reached our starting point and stepped off the lake path, our pace slowed as if neither of us was quite ready for the walk to end. I went with her to her car, and waited while she opened the trunk and traded her athletic shoes for a pair of ankle-high boots with two-inch heels.

"I really enjoyed this," I said.

She leaned over to place her sneakers in the trunk, then straightened and turned. "Me, too." For the first time since we'd met in the restaurant, we shared a moment of awkwardness. She saw my hesitation and took a step closer. "Could I have a hug?" Her voice was soft.

I stepped into her embrace and pressed my hands against her back, holding her close. She felt warm, the muscles in her back strong under my fingers. Every inch of her melded into me, fitting me like a well-tailored shirt that's been washed and worn to a comfortable softness. Something inside me let loose. As if I found myself in safe harbor for the first time in months.

I DROVE SLOWLY through the center of town on the way to Kelsey's dance class. Despite several construction projects that would bring hundreds of new residents and dozens of small businesses to the island, the town center was quiet and sleepy. Primarily a bedroom community, an affluent suburb of Seattle, the only times the town center was truly busy were when it was filled with morning and evening commuters, employees on their lunch hour, or locals doing Saturday errands.

The fact that it was an island insulated it even more from outside influences. Despite easy access to Seattle and Lake Washington's east side, people didn't get off the freeway and stop without a reason. Every so often, someone showed up with malicious intent, but the weekly newspaper's crime sheet usually noted items no more serious than noisy dogs, stolen bikes, minor vandalism and the occasional car prowl.

The island didn't look dangerous. But I had my own theory. In a way, it was more dangerous than the inner city. No, there were no drive-by shootings, no gang violence. Not yet, anyway. There was, however, complacence, a sense of false security. As if nothing bad could ever happen in a nice place like this. A lot of kids had too much money and time on their hands. They drove expensive cars fast, did drugs, held after-school drinking parties while their parents worked.

Every so often tragedy struck, like the girl who drove drunk following one of those parties, lost control and died when her car rolled down an embankment. Or the sixteen-year-old kid who killed an elderly woman out walking her dog because he drove too fast. There were desperate people who would do anything to solve a perceived problem. Like the fellow who tried to raise rent money by snatching a fifth-grade girl off the street on her way home from school and holding her for ransom. Or the person who had, for whatever reason, killed Mary.

Jian stood on the curb at the community center when I dropped Kelsey off. He waved enthusiastically as Kelsey got out of the van and stepped around the front.

Pleasantly surprised, I rolled my window down. "Hey, Jian. What are you doing here?"

"Ah, I am bringing Mei Lei to dance, yes?"

"She talked you into it?" Kelsey had encouraged Mei Lei to come to hip-hop class with her. She, in turn, had been working on Jian for weeks.

He shrugged his shoulders. "She need the exercise."

"You want to get some coffee while the girls are in class?"

He hesitated, then his face broke into a smile. "Yes. Why not?" I drove to the closest Starbucks—even our small town had six. The place was quiet that close to dinnertime, so we had our pick of places to sit.

"I have news for you," Jian said when we were settled. He looked pleased with himself. "I have found out more about your mystery person." He paused, drawing it out. "Ito Takeshi a businessman from Tokyo. He run a big conglomerate there. Very important man."

"Maybe he's not our guy," I said, disappointed.

He shrugged. "Most interesting thing is Takeshi's company not make anything. Not like Mitsubishi or Sony. Takeshi's company a holding company that own pieces of many others. In some cases, it own subsidiaries outright. Those companies make things, like cleaning products."

"So, Takeshi does what, exactly?"

"Manage company investments, mostly. But I am curious about this kind of company." He flashed a Cheshire grin. "When I am child, school teach us evils of Western capitalist society. We learn holding company is like trick I show your son—what you call 'shell game.' So, I look for shells."

"I'm not sure I understand."

He leaned forward. "Best way to hide something is confuse the eye. Make you think it is in a place where it is not. The more shells, the easier to hide something. So, I look for Takeshi companies that make nothing. If you keep turning over shells, maybe you find something, yes?"

"You found something?"

"One of subsidiary companies own other company in entertainment business. That company own companies that make video games, music, concerts. One of these also own nightclubs. Not just any clubs. These are, how you say, stripper clubs. In Las Vegas and Reno, in Nevada."

I felt the grimace on my face and wiped it off with a hand. "A tough business that I wouldn't want to be in, but not illegal."

"No," he said, "but very profitable. Especially for Japanese company. Japanese businessmen who come to this country are used to geisha tradition in Japan. They pay much money to go to stripper clubs when they come here."

"I still don't understand why you think this is so important."

His face lit up. "Ah, I am coming to this.You must be patient. Because this is such profitable business, many such clubs pay protection money to Yakuza. But Yakuza realize they make more money if they own these clubs. And Japanese businessman find much more in these places than pretty girls to look at. Yakuza sell them whatever they want if they know how to ask right questions."

"'Whatever' meaning…?"

"*Biao zi,* drugs…" I was afraid to ask. "Child pornography?"

He nodded. "Not just pictures."

It took a moment to register. "They would actually…? Then that disc is…"

His head bounced like a bobble-head doll. "Is maybe a catalog. But not just for pictures."

The way he said it—*cat-a-rog*—normally might have made me smile, but I felt too sick. If Jian was right, Takeshi had watched my children, spoken to them.

If it *was* Takeshi, though, he'd stopped calling, stopped threatening. *Why?* Because he thought I didn't have what he was looking for? Or because he knew I'd been charged with, and would likely be convicted of, a murder he committed?

AT DINNERTIME, I CAUGHT Kelsey looking at me several times with a strange expression while I bustled about in the kitchen. Each time, she quickly turned her attention elsewhere. I called Ty in from the family room and asked Kelsey to help me take plates to the table. The two of them sat down while I made one more trip into the kitchen for a couple of last-minute things.

"What is with you?" Kelsey asked when I sat down.

My face must have reflected surprise. "Don't tell me you don't know what I'm talking about."

"No, what?" I said.

"You're, like, all hyper and stuff. And it's like you're forgetting to breathe or something."

"Really?" I looked at Ty. "You think I'm acting weird?"

He shrugged. "Uh-uh. You look okay to me."

Kelsey looked skeptical. "I don't know. You just seem...different. You sure it's nothing?"

"Nothing I know of," I said, trying not to stray too far from the truth. "I'll let you know, though, if something comes up."

"Right." She let it drop, but she checked me out once or twice more before dinner ended.

I thought I would burst with impatience waiting for Ty's bedtime. I found myself moving from one task to another, unable to sit still, suddenly spying dirty counters and disorganized cupboards and a dozen other chores that had somehow escaped attention for months. If I hadn't known what Kelsey was talking about before, I did now. It was hard to take a breath, and my stomach was doing that fluttery thing again.

I forced myself to sit patiently through a short bedtime story for Ty, glad that he let me read to him again every so often. As soon as I tucked him in, though, I hurried to the den full of anticipation. I had e-mail.

J,
I haven't felt so many feelings with someone in ages. Slow and steady would be practical now, wouldn't it? But how can one resist feeling so good? Fast? A little crazy? Yes, but we haven't done anything except feel, imagine, wonder...no

harm. I enjoy you and want to know more. Am I scared? Yes. Do I want to retreat? Not a chance. How about coffee and a walk, day after tomorrow? By the way, the last name is Thwaite.

AMY WAS LATE. AFRAID she'd changed her mind, I paced the floor of the coffee shop from an entrance on one side to another hoping I hadn't missed her. Suddenly, there she was, walking up the steps. For a moment, I had an urge to turn and walk the other way before she saw me, certain I'd made a mistake. She was a stranger, someone whose faults, like mine, would only lead to disappointment. Indecision rooted me to the floor. Then the door opened and she stepped inside. She headed my way with a smile, walked into my arms and held me close. Any lingering doubt vanished like morning mist under a warm sun.

Armed with paper cups of coffee, we walked the lake path again, counterclockwise this time. She settled into the same purposeful stride. We slipped into the same easy conversation, eager to learn more, yet unembarrassed by occasional lapses into silent reflection.

"We need to test ourselves," I said after one such pause.

She looked at me curiously. "What do you mean?"

"This is almost too good, right? Maybe because we're putting our best faces forward. I want you to like me; you want me to like you."

"But I *do* like you." She smiled.

"Likewise. But just to make sure, so we don't waste each other's time, let's both think of the most horrible thing about ourselves. I'll tell you mine and you tell me yours. And if we don't both run away screaming, then maybe we've got a chance."

Her laugh sounded deep, throaty, unself-conscious.
"The most awful thing we can think of?"

"Yeah, like maybe you sleep in rollers and snore."

She laughed again. "Wouldn't you like to know?"
She sobered when she looked at my face. "All right, I'll
go first. I was never married. You look surprised."

"I shouldn't be." But I was. "You have kids, though."

She nodded. "I have a daughter. Grace. When I got
pregnant, I saw right away that things between me and
her dad just weren't going to work. I left."

"That's not so awful. You did what you had to." I
paused. "Are you still going to group meetings?"

"Some of it's helpful." She smiled at my disbelief.
"She's seven. A real doll. Maybe someday you'll meet
her."

"I'd like that," I said. Then after a pause, "We can't
keep avoiding it, you know." For the first time, I saw
something approaching fear in her eyes. "Look, I don't
know why you're interested in me, given the circumstances. If the media see you with me, your life will
become a living hell. Why are you so convinced I didn't
do it?"

"I've seen you with your kids," she said simply.

"That's it?"

"Maybe I'm nuts. I just know you didn't do it, that's
all. I've watched you." She flushed. "Well, not like that.
I'm not a stalker. I see you around town. I notice how
you act around people, like the cashiers and clerks in
the grocery store. You're nice. Most people don't give
them the time of day."

"You must have a lot of faith in human nature." I
paused, but she didn't reply. So, I told her the whole
story, from the morning Mary went missing to the trial
coming up. I told her about feeling so lost and over-

whelmed by guilt and the pain my kids were going through that I started to believe what people were saying. I told her about meeting Jian and finding the disc in Mary's purse and realizing that she'd probably been killed because of it.

I explained the dilemma I faced of having evidence that might exonerate me but not being able to take it to the police for fear they would use it to incriminate me further. I told her how certain I was that Jian and I were right about Takeshi, yet how much I feared this one chance at freedom would turn out to be wrong.

When I finished, I glanced at her. She hadn't missed a step, and now shrugged out of her light jacket, tying the sleeves around her waist. It was another beautiful, sunny day, and the air had warmed considerably since early morning. The brisk walk had heated us up, too. It suddenly occurred to me that she hadn't run away screaming.

"Wow," she said quietly. "That's a lot to deal with." I didn't know if she meant for her or for me. She showed no fear, no overt concern.

"I'm telling you this because I want to be totally honest with you up front. I want you to know what you're getting into if you decide you want to spend time with me."

"I appreciate that," she said.

"Look, I don't know what's going to happen between us. We don't know much about each other. We have no history yet. Some e-mails and phone calls. A couple of walks. I don't know if you're 'the one,' the person I'm supposed to stick with long enough to find out if fairy tales really do come true. All I can tell you is the moment you took my hand the other day, I felt something. Some connection that makes me think I want to know you. Know you well enough, care for you enough, to be open to all the possibilities."

She was silent for a while. "That's fair enough," she said finally.

My steps felt lighter. The day brightened. Sunlight dappled the blue water of the lake, its surface riffled by the breeze. I smiled at all the people passing us in the opposite direction, took note of a man fishing on the shore, a toddler taking top-heavy steps in the grassy park, a dog happily chasing a tennis ball thrown by its owner.

Amy took my hand, and I laced my fingers in hers.

I PULLED INTO A PARKING space and scanned the playground for Tyler's unruly mop of hair, but saw no sign. Flustered at being a few minutes late again, I headed for the office and caught sight of Ty with a woman, walking the opposite direction, past the portable classrooms. The woman had her arm around Ty's shoulders. I recognized the scarf.

"Tyler," I called. He hesitated, but kept walking. "Tyler Holm!" He glanced over his shoulder this time. The woman didn't look around, just tightened her hold and guided him away from me.

I quickened my pace. "Ty?" Dark thoughts scuttled through my head and my stomach tightened. I remembered again the phone calls, the man in the car... Ty wriggled free of the woman's grasp, and skipped out of her reach. He appeared to say something to her. She hurried away, and he ran to me. I crouched and gathered him in my arms.

"Are you all right?" I held him at arm's length. "What was that all about? Who was that woman?"

"No big deal, Dad. One of the moms."

"What did she want?"

"She didn't think I was supposed to be out here by myself, and wasn't sure who you were." He answered glibly, but looked guilty. "I told her you're my dad." I searched his face. Something didn't smell right, but I let it go.

"Don't scare me like that."

NINETEEN

I WALKED briskly past Preston, set my briefcase on the small conference table and pulled out reports with my notes scribbled on them.

"I have a bunch of questions and concerns we need to discuss," I said, taking a seat. He didn't reply. I looked up and saw him standing near the door, mouth agape. "Something wrong?"

He gave a small shake of his head. "No, nothing. Let's get started then." He joined me at the table and tilted his head to get a look at the top document on the stack in front of me.

"I've got a real problem with all these time estimates," I said.

"Which ones?" He riffled through his papers, still trying to find the right document.

"Look, let's say she *was* killed sometime that night. It still all seems a little iffy. Take the assault, for example. The Medical Examiner's report says that due to the minimal amount of visible bruising, Mary was assaulted shortly before she was killed. We had sex hours before that. If I had raped her, then there would be more visible signs of bruising."

"I told you the science isn't exact. The Medical Examiner will testify these are soft findings, estimates only. The fact remains her assault and murder took place some time that night, when you have no alibi."

"I still say it's a discrepancy. I mean, what if this guy

wore a condom? He rapes her, but leaves no semen. And because Mary and I had sex earlier, my semen is still present."

He looked thoughtful, then jotted something on a legal pad. "All right, go on. What else?"

I flipped through pages, looking at my notes. "Okay, what about this business of leather gloves? The police never found any leather gloves or leather conditioner in the house because I don't *own* any leather gloves. They took shoe polish and some other stuff from under the kitchen sink. Obviously nothing that matched the substance they found on Mary."

He waved dismissively. "The prosecutor will simply claim you threw the evidence away."

"But if there's no evidence, doesn't that create *some* doubt?"

"It depends. The jury could see it either way. I think they are more likely to believe that you simply disposed of anything that might incriminate you."

"I was smart enough to do that, but not smart enough that I left evidence of rape?"

"Let me explain something, Jack." His tone was patient. "I believe the prosecution is going to present this to the jury as a crime of passion. That's why the charge is murder in the second degree, not first-degree murder, or even aggravated murder. The prosecutor will suggest that while the crime itself may have been committed in the heat of the moment, without rational thought, the succeeding concealment of the crime was carefully calculated. You will be painted as a very cold and unsympathetic killer." I said nothing.

He went on. "I know it sounds discouraging. I just want you to be prepared for what will happen in that courtroom. My job is to present your side and make the arguments you have just laid out in as favorable and persuasive a manner as possible. My hope is that we will cause at least one or more jurors to have doubts."

I waited a moment, then flipped to another page. "How about this, then?"

He peered at the document from across the table. "What are you referring to?"

"State crime lab analysis of trace evidence submitted by the Medical Examiner." I paused, then continued while he shuffled papers. "Pubic hairs were found on Mary's body. They don't match each other, or hers. And none of them were tested for DNA, so there's no indication who they might belong to."

"Yes, I remember that." He found the page and scanned it quickly. "What's your point?"

"Doesn't that suggest that someone else besides me may have come into contact with Mary? Rather intimate contact?"

"The hair was found on her clothing. It could have come from anywhere—a public restroom, an airplane lavatory."

"For *chrissakes,* the hair was found caught in her underwear. Do you honestly believe she was in a public restroom that night? Or hadn't changed her panties since the day she last flew? Are you out of your mind?" His mouth set in a straight line and the muscles in his jaw worked. He sat back and let his eyes wander. Finally, he leaned forward putting a forearm on the table, and looked me in the eye.

"The jury still won't believe you because they will perceive that you lied to the police concerning the time that Mary disappeared."

I frowned, then understood what he was referring to. "I've thought about that a lot. The fact is, I don't know if Mary was there or not that morning. I just assumed she was."

"What do you mean?"

I looked up at the ceiling, thinking of a way to explain. "When I fall asleep at night, I sleep so heavily for the first few hours that you could set off a siren in the house and I might not hear it. The kids will even tell you that. After that, though, I'm a very restless sleeper. I wake up every twenty minutes or so. When I got up to go running Sunday morning, I didn't really even look over at Mary. The covers were rumpled and it appeared as if she was there, but I never actually looked. Why would I? She'd never left the house in the middle of the night before. Why wouldn't I assume she was there? That's where she was supposed to be. Besides, it was early. The shades were drawn. The room was still dark."

"You wouldn't have awakened if she got up in the middle of the night?"

I shook my head. "Not for those first two or three hours. After that, maybe. Probably."

"And your children can attest to this?"

"Yes. They've been up enough times during the night—whether from nightmares or a sick stomach—to know who will wake up to help them. Late at night, it was always Mary. Early morning, always me." He sat back again and touched a forefinger to his lips, his elbow on the arm of the chair. After a moment, he exhaled loudly.

"Taken altogether, it might be enough to do the trick."

"You mean create reasonable doubt." He nodded. "That's not enough."

"It will be enough to get you acquitted."

"And still have everyone think that I did this? No." I

pushed back from the table and stood up quickly. I ignored Preston's surprise and paced a few steps away, then turned. "You don't know what it's been like. I lost all my friends. My kids are treated like pariahs. Everywhere we go people stare and whisper. The state wants to take my kids away from me." He watched me silently.

"I want to know who did this," I told him. "I want to know who was with my wife that night. Don't you see? I have to prove that I didn't do this. There is no such thing as presumption of innocence. As soon as your face is plastered across newspapers and TVs, people assume you're guilty. Not me. I can't live like that. If we have to prove someone else killed her for people to believe I didn't do it, then that's what we'll have to do."

"What do you propose?"

"Test those hairs, for starters."

"That won't tell you whose hair it is. Nor will it prove she came in contact with anyone else." He paused. "It will be expensive."

"I don't care."

"And it will be difficult to get the state to move very quickly."

"Just do whatever you have to."

He looked at me appraisingly. "I'm pleased to see you participating, finally." His voice held little inflection. I couldn't tell if he was being sardonic or complimentary. He didn't let me bask long in the glow of his admiration.

"There's something else you should know," he went on. "A trial date has been set, and though I might be able to eke out a continuance, it isn't likely without very good grounds."

"When?"

"The middle of March. Not much time." Less than

two months. My shirt grew damp under the arms. Time wasn't my only problem.

"Something else on your mind?" he said.

I forced myself to meet his gaze, hoping my face was impassive. "Hypothetical question: if you were given evidence of a crime, would you be compelled to turn it over to the police?"

"Not compelled, exactly. But as an officer of the court, I imagine that I would be ethically bound to do so, yes. Why?"

I ignored the question. "Would you have to reveal the source of the evidence or who gave it to you?"

He answered slowly. "I suppose that could depend on the circumstances. If doing so violated attorney-client privilege, then perhaps not." I thought about it. When I didn't say anything more, he didn't pursue it.

THE PHONE RANG, DISRUPTING my train of thought. I wanted to finish an article before deadline, and the writing had been going slowly.

"Kelsey? Tyler?" I called as the phone rang again. "Would someone please get that?" There was no answer from either of them. The phone rang a third time. I scowled at it. Calls coming in after three or so in the afternoon were rarely for me. By then, the east coast had already gone home for the day and folks in the Midwest were getting ready to, so business calls stopped coming in. I snatched up the receiver and answered in the middle of the fourth ring.

"I, uh—" A woman's voice sounded confused, hesitant.

"Hello?" I said.

"Is Kelsey there, please?" This time she was brisk and businesslike.

"Letty?" I was sure I recognized her Southern-belle voice. The line was silent. Caller ID displayed a local number I didn't recognize. I frowned. "I'll go get her." I set the receiver gently on the desk and went looking for my daughter.

"Who is it?" she said when I found her in the laundry room, of all places.

"Gamma, I think." She gave me a funny look, then shrugged and followed me out of the laundry room. She took the call on the kitchen phone. A half-minute later, she poked her head into my office.

"There wasn't anybody there," she said. "Are you sure it was Gamma?"

"Pretty sure." I wondered if I'd been talking to a dead phone.

"Call her back and see." She lifted one shoulder, let it drop, and disappeared. Twenty minutes later, she was back, softly tapping on the door frame. I swiveled the chair around at the sound and leaned back.

"Gamma said she did try to call, but got disconnected," Kelsey said.

"Ah. So, how is she?"

"Fine."

"That's good. Hang on a second, okay?" I got up and squeezed past her through the doorway into the hall. "Hey, Ty?" I called. "Come down here a minute, will you?" A muffled, indistinguishable reply came from somewhere above us, then the sound of feet thumping overhead and down the stairs.

"Yeah, Dad?"

"Come on in, both of you." Kelsey stepped aside so I could go back in the office. "Family meeting," I said. "Have a seat." They tentatively sat in the den's other two chairs. I swung the office chair all the way around to face them. I looked at Kelsey. "So, how long has Gamma been calling?" She flushed and looked guilty. "Hey, sweetie, you're not in trouble, and I'm not mad. I'm just curious."

"A while, I guess," she said.

"Since right after Thanksgiving," Ty said brightly. "After Auntie Bridget went home."

I turned to him. "Ah, that was my next question. So, you've been talking to her, too?" He nodded. "And all this time, I thought you weren't talking to anyone?" Now it was his turn to be embarrassed. Kelsey came to his rescue.

"He didn't," she said. "When Gamma called, I put him on the extension. She'd talk, and if she asked him a question, I'd answer for him."

"Very clever." I smiled. "Okay, so here's the deal. No more keeping it secret. If you guys want to talk to Gamma, you can. Any time you want."

Kelsey looked at me warily. "I thought you and Gamma hated each other."

"To be honest, I don't think she cares much for me, but she's your grandmother. Whether I like her or not is beside the point. She should be a part of your lives. What I object to is that she wants to split us up."

"But I don't want to live with Gamma," Ty said, looking frightened.

"You don't have to, kiddo. Don't worry."

"But what about the custody thing-y?" Kelsey said.

"She's not going to get custody. The reason Gamma asked the court to let her take you is because she thinks I'm going to jail, and she doesn't want anything to happen to you two. She's worried about you, that's all."

"But what if you do go to jail?" Ty said in a small voice.

"I won't. Your grandmother may think I had something to do with Mom's death, but I know I'm innocent."

"But how will you prove it?" Kelsey said.

"Because I think I have an idea of who did this."

"You know who killed her?"

"What if he finds out you know who he is?" Ty swallowed hard, fighting tears, now more than a little scared. "Won't he come after you?"

I shook my head firmly. "No. I don't want either one of you to worry or be scared. No one's coming after us. I promise. But I am going after him. I have to."

"For Mom?" Ty said.

"For all of us."

"You'll be careful, won't you?" Kelsey said. She wore a brave face.

"Promise." I held up three fingers in the Scouts' salute. Suddenly, puzzle pieces clicked together in my head. "She's here, isn't she?" They both looked guilty. "Ty, the woman on the playground. That was Gamma, wasn't it?" He nodded.

I looked at Kelsey. "How long has she been here?"

She hung her head and spoke to her shoes. "Since before Christmas."

"Where is she?"

TWENTY

I BANGED on the door of the motel room with the heel of my fist. Hard enough to show I meant business, but not loud enough to attract unwanted attention. The media had long since decamped, returning only when there was a hearing or development in my case. But it paid to be careful. I'd learned to spot the cars of a couple of freelance photojournalists, and kept an eye out.

"Who is it?" The voice sounded muffled through the door.

"Open the door, Letty. It's me, Jack. We need to talk." Silence stretched on so long, I raised my hand again to knock only to hear the sound of the knob turning. The door opened a crack, light from the room illuminating my face. She peered at me, and slid the security chain off. She swung the door just wide enough to step into the opening and looked at me expectantly.

"I understand why you filed that petition," I said. "I get it. I know you have the children's best interest at heart. I don't blame you. But here's a little advice. Drop it. Don't pursue this any further. There's no way in hell you're going to get custody of my kids."

"I'm calling the police now." She turned away, leaving the door open.

I called her bluff. "No, you're not." She paused. I stayed put. "Look, I don't care what you think about me, or even if you believe what they say I did. I'm not unreasonable. If you want to see the kids, that's fine.

Call first. Visit with them as much as you like. Just don't even think about trying to take them away. Are we clear?"

She said nothing for a moment, then looked at me. "We'll see."

"YOU SEEM DIFFERENT."

"I'm angry."

"Really?" Sarah looked surprised. "You don't seem angry."

"Trust me, I'm angry."

"Hmm, that isn't what I'm sensing, but let's talk about that, if you like. Why are you angry?"

"Because I almost convinced myself that it was no use fighting it."

"Fighting what?"

"Everything. The system. What people think."

"So what are you going to do?"

"I want my life back. I don't want to go to jail. I don't want to worry about my kids being taken away by DCFS or their grandmother. I want out of this mess. I have to fix it."

"Ah, that's what's different."

"What?"

"You're back." She smiled.

"I DON'T HAVE MUCH TIME," I said.

Jian slid into the chair opposite mine and handed me a short latte. He sipped carefully from his own cup and winced when the hot liquid burned his tongue. "What you want to do?"

"I don't know what to do. I don't even know if Takeshi is the guy. But I have to figure out a way to find out, and soon. I think maybe you were right; I'm grasping at straws."

"You will not know until you try."

I shrugged. "But try what?"

Jian looked thoughtful. "You need proof that Takeshi do this, not you, yes? What about fingerprints?"

His face brightened as I sat up, then fell when I slumped back in my chair. "The police said whoever it was wore gloves."

"Not when he put disc in your wife's bag."

"Yeah, but we've had our hands all over that disc."

"Not on case disc comes in. You put in bag when you get home. Give to me. I hold for you. Just in case." He still looked hopeful. "You say your attorney get state to test hairs found on body for DNA, yes? So, you need Takeshi DNA to see if it match."

"Now, how would I get that?"

"How the police get yours?" He raised his eyebrows.

It had been more than four months. I had to think. I hadn't volunteered it, yet DNA evidence had been one of the reasons Mankiewicz had been able to get an arrest warrant. It took a while before it came to me. "They offered me a drink when they brought me in to tell me they found Mary's body. They gave me a cup of water. They must have taken a sample off the cup."

"So, we do same." He smiled.

"Right. We fly to Japan, track this guy down and ask him if he's thirsty? Come on, Jian."

"Not Japan," he said, unflustered. "Las Vegas. He go there two times each month. I call company in Tokyo and ask." I stared at him. "Why you so surprised?"

"Why would you do that?" I said.

"To find out if he pay special attention to stripper

clubs. If not, maybe he is just Japanese businessman coming to Seattle. If so, maybe he is Yakuza boss."

"I mean, why would you do that for me?"

"Why not? You would do same for me as my friend."

"I don't know what to say." I swallowed the lump growing in my throat.

He looked down at the table and waved a hand in front of his bowed head. When he looked up, his face was flushed. "So, when we go to Las Vegas?" He grinned.

For a moment, I actually began to think it wasn't as crazy as it sounded.

His grin faded. "What's wrong?"

"I can't go looking for this guy. If Takeshi *is* the guy who slipped that disc into Mary's purse and then came after it, he knows who I am. He was in our house, for *chrissakes*. He knows what I look like, who my kids are. He called and threatened them." He watched me silently. "What if it doesn't work? If he figures it out, he might come after Kelsey and Tyler to get the disc back. No, I couldn't let that happen." I shuddered.

"I will go," he said softly.

"By yourself? No way. I can't let you do that, Jian. Too dangerous. It'd be asking too much."

"How then to get this guy? You say yourself you cannot go to police."

"Well, you're not going alone."

"Then we go together, yes?" His face lightened again.

It looked like it might be my only shot. I had to pursue this, as crazy as the idea was. Like I'd told Preston, it wasn't enough to suggest someone else could have murdered Mary. I had to find the guy or I would lose everything. And I was running out of time.

"Yes, we go together," I said firmly. "I've got an idea how we can handle this." I dialed Adele Arnold to ask if we could meet. Her secretary said she wasn't available until my court date the following week. I sighed and said I'd talk to her then.

TIME OPERATES DIFFERENTLY in a courthouse, as if the judicial system exists in a different dimension. Court appearances scheduled for eight-thirty in the morning might be called sometime before noon. Unaware of when I would actually have to appear before a judge, I showed up at family court in a suit and tie a little before eight-thirty and waited. Attorneys obviously understand how time works in this other dimension. Adele appeared a few minutes before ten. She stopped and scanned the room until I caught her eye, then briskly headed my direction. I rose to meet her.

"We should be up any time now," she said, perching on the edge of the seat next to mine.

"What's this about, anyway?"

"A formality." She sniffed. "The judge will ask if we're ready for trial. I'll ask for a continuance."

"What if the judge says no? Letty might be here." I told her about my visit to the motel.

She sniffed again, but didn't answer. She looked away. Apparently, she got some sort of signal. She patted my knee and said, "This is us. Let's go." I followed her to the courtroom, my palms clammy. Inside, another hearing finished wrapping up and we took our seats. Letty sat with opposing counsel across the aisle. She gave me a prim nod. I almost didn't have time to get uncomfortable. The clerk called the case and the judge asked where we stood. Adele moved for a continuance, arguing that a trial now would be unfair.

"How so, Ms. Arnold?" the judge asked.

"Mr. Holm's attention and efforts are focused on asserting his innocence at his criminal trial, Your Honor. He can't reasonably be expected to defend himself on two fronts at once while he's taking care of his children." I stared at her slack-jawed.

"What do you propose?" the judge said.

"Hold the trial date over to the end of April, Your Honor. When Mr. Holm is acquitted, he'll have time to prepare adequately for trial in this court."

"And if he's found guilty?"

"Then the state will have saved the cost of a trial."

"Makes sense." The judge turned to the shark Letitia Beaumont had hired to take my kids away from me. "Any objection?"

"Your Honor, it's our contention that the longer these children are left in the care of this man, the more irreparable the harm done to them. In addition, my client is here at great personal expense. It would be unreasonable for her to stay, or to keep flying back and forth across the country. We'd like to see this matter go to trial as quickly as possible."

"Then I suggest your client stay home until an actual trial date is set." The judge turned to the attorney general representing DCFS. "Any evidence that he's not meeting requirements?"

"We share Mr. Watkins' concerns," he said, indicating Letty's lawyer. "We don't think—"

"Is there any evidence he isn't complying with DCFS terms?" the judge interrupted. The A.G. hesitated, then shook his head. "Any objections to Ms. Arnold's motion?" the judge said.

"Not as long as Mr. Holm's caseworker is satisfied that the children are adequately cared for, Your Honor."

"So noted." The judge deferred to the clerk for a trial date, and we were done.

I purposely kept from looking at Letty. I didn't want to see her reaction, nor appear to gloat. Outside the courtroom, I hurried to catch up with Adele and leaned in close as we walked.

"What the hell was that?" I said in a low voice.

"Good strategy." She glanced at me and smiled, never breaking stride. "I got a continuance. That's what we wanted. Don't worry."

"Easy for you to say," I muttered.

She turned into one of the small conference rooms lining the main foyer and closed the door behind me. "So what was it you wanted to talk to me about?" She slid into a chair.

"The guy you said would look into my former mother-in-law."

"What about him?"

"He's good?"

"Very."

"What is he? A private investigator?"

"Yes. Used to be a cop. A detective. Retired after twenty years with SPD and took a job as an insurance investigator. Did that for another ten years and got bored, so he quit and went out on his own. Why?"

"I want to hire him." She looked at me sharply. "I can't tell you why," I said.

"Can't? Or won't?"

"Won't. Look, I know you're not supposed to violate attorney-client privilege. It's better if you don't know. It's nothing illegal," I said hurriedly. "I just need him to do some investigating." She finally relented and pulled a PDA out of her briefcase. She found the right entry, and copied his name and number on a scrap of paper. When I reached for it, she pulled it away.

"Are you sure you know what you're doing?"

"No, but I'll figure it out." She puffed through her nose and rolled her eyes, then gave me the name.

TOM FARLEY WAS A BIG fellow. Jian bowed reflexively when Farley introduced himself and almost clocked himself on Farley's belt buckle. I extended a hand and watched it disappear inside a paw as big as a catcher's mitt. If not for his shambling gait over to the table and an aw-shucks attitude, he would have been intimidating. His close-cropped hair was graying on the sides, but still thick. Physique that had once been solid was starting to go soft, but he wasn't fat, just big. I guessed he was in his mid-fifties, but he hadn't let himself go to seed. He hitched a chair to one side so he could cross his legs, stuffed one hand in his pocket and draped the other arm on the table.

"Thanks for coming," I said. "Can I get you something? Coffee?"

"Nah." His bulk spilled over the sides of the chair. "I'm good. So, what can I do for you?" Down to business.

"I want to find out if someone was involved in a crime. I need help obtaining evidence."

"What sort of evidence?"

"I need to know if this person was at a crime scene, so fingerprints and a DNA sample."

"What was the crime?"

I wet my mouth with a sip of coffee to help get the words out. "Rape and murder."

One of his eyebrows rose a notch. "Why?" I looked over at Jian, then at my coffee and finally back at Farley.

He still regarded me with a vacant face. "You don't want to tell me," he said.

"You could find out easy enough, I suppose, but I'd rather not. I'd rather you stayed as impartial as possible. Since you were a detective, I assume you know all about preserving the chain of custody, and—"

"Chain of possession," he said. "It's called 'chain of possession.' You want this treated like evidence in a police investigation. Who is this person?" He saw me glance at Jian again. "I have to know who and what I'm dealing with. It's my ass." I suddenly realized from the tone of his voice and the shrewd way he'd been looking at me that his bumbling nature when he'd first approached us was a facade.

"Japanese businessman named Ito Takeshi." I gestured toward Jian. "We think he may be a Yakuza boss."

His eyebrow went up again, but his expression didn't change. "That's not good." He studied me for a moment. Without taking his eyes off me, he made a fist and waggled his thumb at Jian. "What's his part in this?"

"Jian's my friend. He offered to help. Takeshi—if he's our guy—knows who I am, so I can't get too close or he might suspect something. Jian can help you."

His mouth tightened. "Not a good idea. Things could get screwed up. He could get hurt."

Over Farley's shoulder Jian's face fell. Farley's eyes were still on me. "He's really helped me out on this," I said. "He deserves to be in on it if he wants to."

"If I do this, I don't want to be responsible for amateurs," Farley said.

I shook my head. "We know the risks. It's why we called you in, but you can use us. Jian speaks a little Japanese, which could come in handy. And with three of us working him, he'll be less likely to think anyone's onto him. Plus, we can watch each other's backs."

His eyes flicked over my features. "You've given this some thought. Whatever you think this guy did must've pissed you off."

"You might say that."

"What did you have in mind?" Jian and I leaned in and hunched over at the same time, elbows on the table. I started telling Farley what we'd mapped out so far.

"Uh, Dad?" I glanced into the rearview mirror. Ty's face reflected nervousness under the usual untidy mop of hair. It reminded me that I had to get him a haircut.

"Yeah, kiddo?" I checked the road, then leaned down and felt for the pad of note paper in one of the dashboard cubbyholes.

"Uh, you wanna slow down?" Surprised, I looked at the speedometer, and glanced in the mirror again. He really was nervous. I eased my foot off the gas. The van slowed to something closer to the speed limit. When I glanced in the mirror again, he was looking out the window.

"You nervous about today?"

"Not really. I'd kinda like to be alive when I get there, though."

"Funny. I'll try to pay more attention to my driving from now on." I found myself increasingly preoccupied with thoughts of the impending trial. "You sure you're not going to miss baseball? You can do both, you know, if you want."

"Nah. This'll be way better."

"So, how come you didn't want to play baseball this year?"

"It's not really my thing. I think *tae kwon do* is going to be way better, that's all."

"You're probably right." I thought *tae kwon do* classes were a great idea. Given my present state of anxiety, I wondered if I should join him.

We rolled through town to the martial arts studio, and when we pulled up in front, I asked him if he wanted me to stay and watch.

"Thanks, but I can handle it." He hopped out and slid the door shut firmly. I watched him walk to the door, head up, back straight, without looking back. It occurred to me as I drove away that my ten-year-old son was a lot braver than I.

JIAN AND I TAG-TEAMED dinner in the kitchen. Dinner with Jian and Mei Lei had turned into a regular affair, at least once or twice a week. Kelsey and Mei Lei seemed to have become fast friends, and Ty, though he was odd man out, seemed perfectly content most of the time to hang out and listen to Jian and me talk or watch TV close by.

"Takeshi will be going to Las Vegas soon," Jian told me. I took a moment to digest the news. "Is good time to go. Is holiday week. Winter break. No school."

"I don't know. That's coming up awfully fast."

"So is your business with judge in court." I didn't need the reminder

"Are you sure about taking the kids? I still think we should just let Farley handle it."

"We can find out more than he can by himself. And is important you go. You see Takeshi, you will know if he does this to your wife." He thumped his chest. "You will know in here."

"Then we better get busy making plans. We need to

get plane tickets, make hotel reservations, maybe rent a car. And we need to make sure Farley can do this."

"We must talk to children."

"That, too." I'd almost forgotten.

We told them at dinner. Jian took on the fib, telling a half-truth about wanting to meet someone there to talk business. But we positioned it as a chance to take a short, fun-filled vacation and put it to a vote.

Kelsey looked skeptical. "It's Vegas, Dad. Is there really anything for kids to do there?"

"There will be a pool at the hotel for starters." She began to open her mouth. "And Vegas has some of the world's best shopping." Her mouth closed. Mei Lei's eyes grew round.

"What about me?" Ty said.

"Jian says that there's a really good magic show at one of the hotels. David Copperfield or David Blaine. One of those Davids." I glanced at Jian for help.

"Not David. Is Lance Burton." He shrugged.

"Sorry. Anyway, we'll all go to a show one night. It'll be fun."

Ty raised his hand. "I'm in. I want to go."

Mei Lei shyly raised hers. "Me, too."

"Well, yeah," Kelsey said, "I guess I'll go, too, as long as everyone else is." She didn't sound eager, but her eyes glinted with excitement.

"Very good," Jian said with a small smile. "We go, then."

AMY AND I WERE EAGER to see each other. Maybe too eager, but this felt like no ordinary courtship. We weren't dating in the traditional sense, either—that endless stream of activities a couple does before a guy gets invited in for a cup of coffee. Both of us knew somehow we'd end up as lovers. It was far more than simple physical attraction. We sensed a connection that had little to do with dinners in fancy restaurants or weekend trips to romantic country inns. It wasn't about impressing each other. It was about spending as much time together as we could spare from busy lives of raising children, earning a living, maintaining a home.

If I'd still had friends around, some would no doubt have warned me that it was just a stage. That initial phase of any relationship—especially one fueled by pheromones, hormones and any other "-mones" there are—when two people can't stand to be away from each other for a moment. Dodging the press and avoiding public scrutiny gave our relationship an added shot of adrenaline. Friends would have told me it was too soon after Mary's death. That I hadn't given myself enough time to grieve. That I was on the rebound.

Seeing Amy filled me with joy. Parting was like having some unseen organ ripped out of my chest. I wondered how that could be after so little time. I wondered how that was possible when even I recognized that we didn't know each other well enough to have discovered the irritating little habits that would grate on us until they drove us screaming in opposite directions. A part of me said that she would hate the way I chewed my food, or I would hate the way she brushed her teeth. But all I could think of was when I would get to see her again.

We carved out chunks of time to be together. Time when we could fill each other up with light and gladness. Time when we could share our worlds and introduce each other bit by bit to those things that shaped us, moved us.

She invited me to come by her shop, a cute little

storefront in Fremont that was cheery and brightly lit. Artful displays accentuated the whimsy of her designs. She let me browse alone, absorbing the patterns and colors and the moods they evoked. Then she led me into the back. The single large room served as storage area and design studio. Large, multi-paned windows let in lots of natural light. Sturdy wooden work tables and shelves held a range of earthenware projects in varying stages of completion as well as raw potter's clay, paints, supplies. Two pottery wheels and two small kilns helped fill the space.

Here, too, she let me wander, refraining from giving me a guided tour, letting me form my own impressions. I noted small details—flowers in a bud vase on a corner desk, jazz CDs on a shelf next to a compact stereo system, aprons streaked with clay and paint neatly hung on a brass coat tree. They reflected her personality, her creativity. I glanced at her, face suffused with pride and a touch of uncertainty, like a child awaiting the outcome of room inspection. A flash of heat rivered across the floor from her, flaring incandescently through me. The intimacy of the space suddenly was vividly apparent, more personal in some respects than her bedroom.

I gave her an appreciative nod. She relaxed, as if releasing a breath she'd held too long. She led the way back into the shop and introduced me to the woman working the register, then told her she was leaving for the day. The woman flashed me a knowing smile behind Amy's back.

We took Amy's car. She gave me running commentary about the neighborhoods we passed on the way to her apartment. Once there, she parked on the street out front. I got out and went around to open her door. She swung her legs out and unfolded herself, then hesitated.

"Let's walk." She looked at me. "Is that okay with you?"

"Sure." She silently led us through side streets to an arterial that wound down a steep hill. She didn't seem tense, but I wondered if nerves had caused her to suggest a walk. She took my hand, and we descended wordlessly, comfortable in the stillness. Toward the bottom of the hill, the trees thinned, allowing a view of Puget Sound. We came out on level ground in a large waterfront park and strolled along a path parallel to the shore. A gull soared overhead on motionless wings, giving a small cry of greeting. It slowly glided lower and landed on the beach a dozen yards away among its flock.

"There's so much I want to tell you," I said. "About how good it feels just to be in the moment with you. About how much better life is with you in it. It just seems so much brighter, so full of possibility."

"I love being with you, too. I like being surrounded by your presence—sensuous, safe, strong."

"I worried, you know."

"About what?"

"That we'd quickly learn things about each other we didn't like. But there's not one thing about you, inside or out, that I don't like. I adore your face, your voice, the way you walk, the way you think. I want to keep discovering something new about you every day."

"I feel that way, too," she said. "You excite every fiber of my being. Sometimes just the way you look at me makes me tremble." She squeezed my hand, and I leaned into her, pressing my arm against hers as we walked.

"A few months ago," she went on a moment later, "I was talking with a friend of mine, lamenting the scarcity of men of passion and depth in my life. She

very wisely said that when the time was right someone would come along and unlock my heart. Someone
who would be willing to see beyond life's facade and
appreciate what's important." She stopped and faced
me. "The time is right, and you, dear Jack, have made
that happen." I enfolded her in my arms and held her
close, my face pressed into her hair. Gulls patrolled
the narrow strip of sand along the shore. Off in the
distance, white sails flitted like butterflies across the
blue surface of the sound. A cargo ship slowly churned
north, its white wake dissolving quickly behind it as if
it had never passed. Far beyond, low hills rose out of
the water, growing into mountains on the horizon. Snow
still frosted the highest peaks.

"I don't want to lose you," I whispered. She pulled
away, still holding me, eyes searching my face. "I think
you were meant for me," I said. "I think I was meant to
find you. Now. At this time in my life. And now that I
have, I couldn't bear it if we couldn't be together. It's
my only fear."

She put her finger to my lips. "Then don't think about
it."

"How can I not?"

"You're not guilty." She said it simply, as if it explained away all my problems.

"Ah, but I am." I saw her eyes widen. "I'm guilty of
loving you." She smiled and pulled me close again. We
held each other for a long time. I got lost in her, and the
last thing I wanted was a roadmap out. I wanted to stay
there forever. Poets, bards, romance novelists, lovers,
greeting card writers all had spent millennia attempt-
ing to describe those feelings. None had yet succeeded.
I cupped her face in my hands and kissed her gently.

"I promise you two things. I promise to take you

as you are, every day in the moment. I'm not going to project or worry about what the future might hold." She shook her head, but I held up a hand. "And I promise I won't ever take you for granted. I want every day to be one of discovery for us. I will do everything in my power to keep this feeling, this passion, alive."

She kissed me by way of an answer, and nuzzled my neck. "One day at a time would be good," she murmured.

TWENTY-ONE

FARLEY wasn't thrilled about going out of town on a holiday weekend, but since it was a paying job and we were running out of windows of opportunity, he agreed. I told him what flights I'd found for us, and offered to book him, too. He said it would be better if he made his own arrangements and billed me so it wouldn't look like we were traveling together. I didn't tell him we were bringing our kids.

I couldn't help wondering if I was doing the right thing. A burning anger in my gut told me Takeshi had everything to do with Mary's death. And a tightening constriction in my chest signaled my growing sense of desperation as the days left to the trial clicked by. Yet I suddenly had an impulse to talk it all out with someone, seek validation. I had this overwhelming urge to get someone's advice. And the one person who kept coming to mind was a woman named Amy.

"I'VE MET SOMEONE."

Sarah was surprised, but she recovered quickly, her face smoothing into an expressionless mask. "How do you feel about that?"

"Like a kid."

"How so?"

"Excited. Uncertain. Nervous. Happy. Silly. I don't know. I keep walking around the house with this goofy grin on my face."

"Is that good or bad?"

"Good, I guess. I'm not sure. I have all these crazy, mixed-up feelings I had when some girl in eighth grade decided she liked me. It's thrilling, but there's this fear that it won't last."

"Who is she?"

"A woman I met from the support group. I never knew there were so many unattractive, unhappy single women out there. Amy's different. We just seem to fit."

"In what way?"

"All ways. We like a lot of the same things. We think alike. I think we want the same things in life, the same things in a relationship. She feels good. We even fit physically." I saw her raise an eyebrow, and hurried on.

"We haven't slept together or anything like that. She likes to hug when we see each other. And hold hands when we walk. It just feels right."

"Do you think you're ready?"

"For a relationship?" I paused to consider. *"The timing couldn't possibly be worse. My life is in limbo on the way to potential disaster. A month from now, I could be in jail and my kids could be in the custody of a woman who will likely do anything to keep me from seeing them again. But am I ready? Yes. I've been waiting for this all my life. I want the storybook romance. Love, passion, I want it all."* Sarah looked at me askance.

"Call me crazy." I couldn't help a short laugh at my own joke. *"I used to wonder, when I was with Mary, if I was just having a mid-life crisis. I thought about what it would be like to be with a younger woman. Someone with flawless skin and a body not yet affected by gravity. Someone with boundless energy and the desire to*

*make love all night. Someone passionately in love with
me. I mean, I still feel young. Why shouldn't a young
woman be attracted to me? Mary always thought it was,
I don't know, undignified to feel that way. She made me
feel old and dirty for wanting her."* Sarah nodded.

I went on. *"The women in the single parents'
group—I saw how bitter some of them are because
their husbands left them for younger women."* I shook
my head. *"That isn't it.That's not what I want. It's not
a mid-life crisis. I haven't traded in the van for a sports
car. I don't mind the gray hair, not even the fact that I
can't physically do things I did when I was twenty. Or
thirty. I don't know how to describe it. I look at Amy's
face, at the lines and the character it has. Not just because of her age, but because of all the life reflected
there, the life she's led. And each time I realize how
much I like it, how beautiful it is, more beautiful than
anything in the world."* I paused, searching for the
words. *"When I'm with her—when I even think of her—
it's as if someone has flipped a switch somewhere inside
me and lit me up like a Christmas tree."*

WE DESCENDED IN THE darkness with nothing below us
but more of the same, like being lowered into a vast
cave with no bottom. The plane arced in a tight turn,
and suddenly Las Vegas winked and glittered against
the black desert floor like a carnival in the middle of
an asphalt parking lot.

Getting the kids packed up and ready to go after
school had been no easy task. Kelsey had kept vacil-
lating on what clothes to take, and Ty had outgrown
most of his summer clothes from the year before. Once
packed, we'd picked up Jian and Mei Lei and driven to
the airport. Farley had told me he'd get in touch with us

at our hotel, so I didn't have to worry about him. But I'd herded our posse through the airport and onto the flight like a border collie on speed.

I'd spent most of the flight chasing the same thoughts through my head, wondering how much trouble I could be in for leaving town, and how much trouble I might be getting us into by bringing everyone along on this fool's errand.

"Earth to Dad. Earth to Dad." Ty's voice sounded from across the aisle. The girls next to me giggled. "Uh, we're on the ground, Dad. You want to come down here with the rest of us?" Thirty minutes later, we crammed into a taxi and "ooh-ed" and "aah-ed" over each new display of lights along the Strip as if they were bursts of fireworks on the Fourth of July. Though late, I had the driver take the Strip all the way through town, slow as it was, to impress the kids. I couldn't remember the last time I'd been to Vegas, but it had been before the last wave of big hotels went up. The sheer excess awed me as much as Jian and the kids.

We rented two rooms at Circus Circus. I should have found an inexpensive all-suites hotel with no casino somewhere off the strip. But the covered amusement park at Circus Circus might keep the kids busy for a day at least. And I'd gotten a deal on room rates. Management had no way of knowing they weren't going to make it up from us at the casino. I didn't know about Jian, but I didn't have any spare bills to drop at the tables. The airfares alone had pushed one of my credit cards to the limit. The hole was getting deeper—even if I didn't end up in jail, my debts could swallow us alive.

The hotel sat at the opposite end of the Strip from the airport. We checked in, the clamor of bells, jingle of coins and flash of lights from the casino assaulting our senses even from a distance. The clerk assigned us adjoining rooms in one of the low-rise buildings to the side of the main tower. It had more of a motel feel to it, a little quieter away from the action. Even with a map and directions from the desk clerk, the complex was so big we got lost trying to find the right building.

The hotel brought to mind an eccentric elderly aunt, a dowager gone a bit dowdy. Despite taking great pains to still look the part, the makeup ends up caked on too thick, the lipstick a little crooked and the perfume applied too liberally. Everything looked a little tired and worn behind the bright facade, a little outdated. Jian and the kids were too excited to notice, but I found it depressing and oddly discomforting, as if beneath all the cheeriness something dreadful was going to happen.

By the time we found our rooms, the kids were tired but jazzed. While my two explored our room, I unpacked. Kelsey wasn't happy about sharing a room, but grudgingly agreed when I told her she could have her own bed and Ty and I could share the other. Ty didn't look thrilled with the arrangements, so I called housekeeping and ordered a cot.

We had just decided to order something from room service when someone knocked at the door. Ty scampered to answer it, straining on tiptoes to look through the peephole. He opened the door for Jian and Mei Lei. Smiles covered their faces.

"Is some place, huh, Jack?" Jian said, about to burst with excitement.

I smiled. It was hard not to be infected by his enthusiasm. "This is slumming compared to some of the hotels in town."

"Yes, I go see some now," he said. "Much too excited

to sleep. If not too much trouble, Kelsey could stay with Mei Lei for short time?"

"Could I, Dad?" Kelsey piped up. "We could watch a movie on TV and order room service. We'll be right next door."

"Sure. It's fine with me. Ty and I can hang out here."

Jian gave a short bow. "Thank you. I just take short walk. Get some air to breathe."

SOMETIME LATER, THERE was a soft tap on the door. I looked up with a start, realizing I'd dozed off. I rubbed my eyes. The bedside clock said it was well after midnight. I saw Jian standing in the hall through the peephole and let him in. He tiptoed past me.

"I sorry to be so long," he whispered.

"It's okay," I said in a low tone. "Ty's a pretty sound sleeper. You haven't been gone that long. An hour or so. You can't have gone too far." I gestured toward a chair.

He plopped down on the empty bed instead. "Not far," he agreed. "I see hotel next door with big tower."

"Paris?" I had no clue.

He shook his head. "Stratosphere. And I walk past hotels across street. Many lights. And many people. I never see so many on street at night except at special time. New Year, maybe."

"There are probably more people out at night here than during the day." Ty stirred, breathed a shuddery sigh and rolled over, still asleep.

Jian turned back to me. Leaning forward, he lowered his voice. "I not want you to worry, but I go to club. Just to see."

"Takeshi's club? You went in? Did you see him?"

He shook his head. "Takeshi not there. I ask. They

say he is at club in Reno." He saw my face fall. "Is okay. He is coming back tomorrow."

I scolded him, hiding my relief. "That could have been dangerous. You don't want to draw too much attention to yourself."

"I am careful."

"I hope so. I feel guilty enough getting you mixed up in this."

"I choose this, yes?" The question lingered on his face until I gave a short nod of acknowledgement.

I changed the subject. "What's it like?"

He reflected for a moment. "Very big. Very fancy. But not nice.There are many women—very pretty—but when I see them I think of our daughters. In China, they would bring much shame on their families. It is different here, but here they are also someone's daughters, someone's sisters."

"You don't have to do this, you know."

"Is good for me to see this for myself," he said. "I enjoy our time in America very much. You have many freedoms we do not. But you have problems just as we do." A low murmur of voices issued from the television, and muffled sounds of traffic drifted in from the Strip.

"We sleep now," Jian said, getting up. "I go and send Kelsey to bed." I stretched and put my hand over my mouth to cover a yawn.

"Thanks. That's a good idea."

"Tomorrow, we have some fun." Jian's infectious smile was back. "Then we get to work." I walked him to the door and stood with one foot in the hallway for a minute while he rousted Kelsey from the room next door. She shambled past me sleepily. Jian waved cheerfully from his doorway and turned to go inside.

I stopped him with a loud whisper. "Jian." He looked at me expectantly. "Thank you."

BY LIGHT OF DAY, THE Las Vegas stage set became more readily apparent. Far more substantial than a Broadway backdrop or even a detailed Hollywood facade, it still wasn't quite real. Despite the opulence and grand scale, without the magic and mystery of lights at night it was harder to suspend disbelief, to get caught up in the city's make-believe. Under the desert sun, it took on hard edges, a harshness that hinted at its utter lack of concern or compassion, its callousness.

A sense of something inherently evil nagged at me as we made our way down to breakfast and later as we took a little sightseeing trip down the Strip. We ambled from one hotel to the next, stopping to watch the extravaganzas staged out front to draw people in. With eyes wide and mouths agape, we fell under the spell and allowed ourselves to get sucked into a couple of the vast entrances. Agog at all the lights and sounds, we stood motionless for a time in each until our senses overloaded and we staggered out again into the heat and sunshine.

After the third one, after absorbing the sight of people mesmerized by the spinning wheels of the slot machines, the hypnotic motion of dealers' hands, the allure of the exotic trappings—white tigers and pirates and gondoliers—it made an odd sort of sense. The city was soulless, indifferent. The malignance that seemed to lurk beneath the veneer was in ourselves. The glitter, the games, the entertainments were simply temptations that brought out our baseness.

I gave my shoulders a hard shake, sloughing off the narcotic charm of lights and bells. There was a strange light in the kids' eyes, a feverish look of hunger for more. They drooped in the heat, tired from walking, yet their faces reflected a yearning so consuming that they had forgotten everything else. Even Jian looked glazed.

"Who's up for a swim?" I said loudly.

"I wanna keep going," Ty said, his face eager.

"Hey, I'm hot," I said. "I think we ought to go back to the hotel and jump in the pool. We can see more later when it's cooled off."

"We haven't even had a chance to check out the shops in any of these places," Kelsey said.

Jian looked at me curiously, then at the girls. He suddenly jerked to life, as if he, too, had shed some spell, and he waved his hands.

"No, no," he said. "Your father is right. We have plenty time to see more later. Now is good time to swim. And then we eat." With a little more cajoling, we herded the kids back to the hotel. On the way, I wondered what had possessed me to subject them to this. I didn't want them to be seduced, to aspire to this. But maybe, just maybe they saw through the sham. Maybe they saw it for what it was—a giant amusement park. Maybe it was only adults who succumbed to all the city's vices.

The message light on the phone in the room blinked when we got back after swimming. I retrieved the message and heard Farley name a time and place, nothing else. No phone number. Not even where he was staying. I told Jian on the way to lunch. We spent the afternoon in the hotel's amusement park, watching the kids run from ride to ride laughing, just being kids. A little before five, we put Kelsey and Mei Lei in charge and went to meet him.

We found him in a lounge not far from the hotel. Despite the bright sunshine, endless night clothed the interior of the lounge, like most of Las Vegas. Even this early, men occupied half the stools at the bar, most of whom gazed lackadaisically at a baseball game on television. More patrons sat at a half-dozen tables, mostly couples in dim booths around the perimeter. Farley had a tall glass of something on ice in front of him. It was nearly empty. I wondered if he would present a problem. Adele had said he was good.

He nodded as we sat down across from him. "Good trip?" he said. Without waiting for an answer, he turned to look toward the bar and raised his arm. A waitress lifted her chin in recognition, then turned a wad of gum over in her mouth and started to saunter over.

"It was fine," I said. "We spent most of the day playing tourist."

The waitress stopped a foot from Farley's shoulder. He glanced up, then gestured at us. "Anything for you, gentlemen?"

"Coca-Cola," Jian said. "Very hot outside."

"I'm fine, thanks," I said.

Farley craned his neck to look up at the waitress. "I'll have the same again."

"Club soda? You got it, honey." She strode away, putting a little emphasis into the sway of her hips.

"I hate this town," Farley muttered. "Too many ways to get into trouble." He went on before I had a chance to respond. "So, tonight we'll just get a feel for the club." He waggled his wrist, pointing his finger back and forth between Jian and himself. "If our subject is there, we'll see if he has any sort of routine. More than likely, he spends most of his time in a couple of favorite spots—one of the private rooms if he's entertaining VIPs, a spot at the bar, or near the door where he can watch the action." He fell silent as the waitress approached with a tray. She served Jian's and Farley's drinks, picked up the empty glass and left. Farley stirred the ice cubes in his glass with a straw, but didn't take a drink.

He looked at Jian. "I want you to look like a real customer tonight, okay? It's okay to look around and get a feel for the layout. But I want you to concentrate on the show. Ogle the girls. But pay attention to the routines, the timing. And try to stay in one place. Don't keep moving around like last night."

I looked at Farley. "I thought you got in today."

He shook his head. "I wanted to get as much of a feel for the subject's routine as I could. We only have one shot at this."

"But Tak—" Jian caught himself and looked around furtively. No one paid us the slightest attention. "Subject not there last night," he said.

"Yes, he was," Farley said quietly. "He came in late."

"Where were you?" Jian looked puzzled. "I not see you." I leaned forward to hear the answer. Farley was hard to miss.

"Here and there." He flashed a smile, then his face turned serious again. "That's the point. You have to blend in. Look like you belong."

"What should I do?" I said.

"Keep an eye on your kids," Farley said. "This isn't a good place for them to be left alone."

TWENTY-TWO

WE TOOK the kids to dinner and a show, as promised. We had just enough time after meeting with Farley to hustle them to a casual restaurant in the hotel. Then we caught a cab to the Monte Carlo, down the Strip.

Not even ninety minutes of jaw-dropping, head-scratching illusions, though, managed to keep my mind from meandering. I was glad to see Ty and Kelsey smile again, act like normal kids. They hadn't really cut loose and had fun like that since losing Mary. For a little while at least they could forget and be transported to worlds of delight and fancy. Maybe Disneyland would have been my first choice, but Vegas, for all its sins, was just the dose of magic and fantasy they needed.

"Wasn't that awesome?" Ty said in the cab on the way back to the hotel. He tugged on my sleeve. "Dad, didn't you think that was cool?"

I turned away from the lights flashing by the cab's windows to look at him. "Sorry?"

"The show, Dad. The show," he said with annoyance.

"Oh, right. Yes, it was very cool." I gave him a smile and fell silent again while they all rehashed the evening's highlights.

MY HAND HOVERED OVER the phone. Ty's breathing was even and heavy, a soft snore. Kelsey was next door with Mei Lei again. Jian had gone to the club. The sheers covering the window blinked blue, red, then blue again in time with the ticking of my watch, a constant reminder that Vegas never closed. I picked up the receiver and dialed.

"Hi," I said in a low voice when the call went through. "It's me."

"Hello, me," Amy replied.

"Sorry I didn't call you last night. We got in late, and by the time the kids had something to eat and went to bed, it was too late to call." We'd talked on the phone every night since we'd met.

"That's okay. I missed hearing your voice."

"This is so weird. I'm here in this bizarre fantasyland with the kids and Jian and his daughter. I'm not even sure I did the right thing coming here. I've got a million things on my mind. But I feel so connected to you, every other thought I have is about you."

"Wow, that's a lot of thoughts."

"Tell me about your day." She recapped the highlights, making me laugh with a couple of stories about odd customers who had come into her shop. The sound of her voice soothed me. Listening to her talk about the normal, mundane routine of getting through her day helped put the world back into perspective. What mattered wasn't so much the reason why we were in Las Vegas as the wonder in Ty's eyes during the magic show, the delight on Jian's face at each new sight, the giggles the girls shared.

We talked for a long time about everything and nothing. When we finally hung up, some of the restlessness I'd been feeling all day was gone.

JIAN DIDN'T COME BACK until nearly two in the morning. I unfolded myself carefully from the chair at the sound of his knock, joints stiff from sitting so long. My eyes were dry and grainy from reading. Jian unsuccessfully tried to stifle a yawn as he came through the door.

"How did it go?" I whispered.

"Is okay." He looked dazed. "Is too much."

"Too much what?"

"Everything. Too much music. Too much lights. Too much women with no clothes." He shuddered. "Very tired. Is okay I sleep here? Kelsey asleep in my bed. I not want to wake them. I write note for Mei Lei."

I shrugged. "Sure."

"Good." He heaved a tired sigh and shuffled into the bathroom.

When he came out, I traded places with him, and brushed my teeth. By the time I slid gratefully between the sheets, Jian was asleep in the next bed, covers pulled up under his chin.

WE MET FARLEY IN ONE of the hotel lounges the next day. This business of meeting in different places seemed overly cautious, but Farley was the pro, so I didn't question it. He barely glanced up when we arrived. Coffee and orange juice sat on the table in front of him this time.

"Breakfast?" I raised an eyebrow.

"You might say that." His hair was damp, and he looked freshly shaved.

"Any trouble last night?"

He glanced at me. "Nope. Pretty dull." He gestured at Jian. "Your friend left around one-thirty. I stayed until closing at six."

"In the morning?"

A corner of his mouth lifted. "Yeah, this is breakfast." Then to Jian, "What do you think?"

"Very…interesting."

Farley chuckled. "I guess that's one way to put it. A little over the top, huh? What else?"

"Very expensive."

"No, expensive is when you get a room for private dances and order bottles of champagne for the girls. You didn't even get a lap dance."

"How much did you spend?" I said.

Jian put his hand on his chin, adding it up in his head. "One hundred dollars, I think."

"That much?" I figured maybe half that for drinks and cost of admission.

"That's about right," Farley said, "if you were tipping with singles. The guys in the private rooms tip with twenties and hundreds. Some of them drop thousands a night."

"I wonder if any of this is tax deductible," I grumbled. "Expenses for this trip are going to kill me."

Farley appraised me. "Maybe. No harm in checking." He turned back to Jian. "Notice anything else?"

"Girls who serve drinks move around. I get new waitress every time I order drink."

He nodded. "They're working the room, hoping some customer will request a dance."

"Men also switch places—after every show," Jian said.

Farley looked at him keenly. "You noticed that." He saw the puzzlement on my face. "Security. The bouncers in the club rotate to keep them sharp. Your guy did the same thing. He moved between sets, checking different areas of the club."

"That's good?"

"It means he's somewhat predictable. It'll depend on whether there are VIPs in the club, but he sticks to a routine. Anything could screw it up, though. Sunday's usually a quiet night, but because it's a holiday weekend they're running the same schedule as last night. They do three big shows on the main stage—at nine, eleven and one. In between they've got girls dancing all over the club, not just the main stage. That's when the subject moves, so that's when I move. We'll try after the early show first." He waited for a reaction. It sounded so simple.

"Too risky," I said. "What if someone sees you? They'll stop you and ask a lot of questions."

"That's what he's supposed to watch for." Farley nodded at Jian.

"And do what? Try to intervene?" I shook my head. "You need a diversion. Take people's eyes off you."

Farley looked at Jian. "You can do that, can't you?"

Jian puffed out his chest. "Sure. No problem."

"I'm coming with," I said. They both turned to look at me. "This is my problem. If this guy is guilty, then he really screwed things up for my family. I have to do this for Mary. She didn't deserve this. I have to do this for her, for the kids. I have to do this for myself."

"So, you're in," Farley said.

Jian nodded agreement.

WE TOLD THE KIDS I WOULD be going with Jian that night over an early dinner in the hotel.

Kelsey didn't bite. "What's going on?" She looked at me suspiciously.

"It's just business, Kels."

"But why do you have to go meet Mr. Wu's friend? You don't know anything about computers."

"Jian thought I might enjoy getting out, so he asked me along. Without kids," I added.

"What are you going to do? Go to one of those chicken ranches or something?"

"Kelsey!" I tried to look stern, hoping she mistook my reddening face for anger.

"A chicken ranch?" Ty piped up. "What do they do, dress chickens up like cowboys?"

"No, dipstick," Kelsey said sharply. "It's where they *raise* chickens so they can turn them into chicken strips and stuff." Jian and Mei Lei looked thoroughly confused, but they stayed mute.

"Look, it'll be fine," I told Kelsey. "We might be out late, but you guys can all just sleep in our room. Jian and I will bunk in Jian's room if we get back late."

"I guess it'll be okay." She looked dubious.

"It'll be fine. And yes, I expect you to keep an eye on your brother the whole time, and be responsible."

She put an injured look on her face. "Did I say anything?"

"Besides," I went on, "it'll be almost bedtime when we leave, so you won't have much time to worry about it." She finally accepted it grudgingly, but I tried to keep her from noticing that I barely picked at my food after that.

After dinner, we watched the circus acts in the hotel's big top. Like the brochures promised, aerialists plied their craft high above the floor on wires and ropes and swings, putting our hearts in our throats and giving us reasons to gasp. Clowns created madcap mayhem in the center ring, leaving us breathless with laughter. Jugglers and cyclists and gymnasts amazed us with feats of strength and agility.

Tyler's head began to droop despite the smile painted on his face. I signaled Jian, and in the face of half-hearted protests, we gently urged the three of them to their feet and made our way out. I changed while the kids settled in my room, then Jian and I went next door to Jian's room. While he got ready, I called Amy.

"Hi," I said when she answered. "I just wanted to give you a quick good-night call."

"Kind of early for you, isn't it?"

"We probably won't get back 'til late. Too late to call."

"We? You're going out?"

"This is our last night. We have to try to pull it off tonight."

"Getting the evidence you need, you mean? I thought that investigator and your friend were going to do this. Aren't you going to stay with the kids?"

"I have to do this, Amy." The phone was silent. "The kids will be fine. We won't be gone that long."

"Isn't it dangerous?" Her voice was hesitant.

"Nah. Piece of cake. We'll be in and out."

"I wasn't talking about getting the evidence," she said lightly. "I meant isn't it dangerous going to a strip club?"

"I'm not going to look at girls. I'll close my eyes. I'll be good, I promise. Besides, you're the only one I'd like to see do a striptease."

"Maybe someday."

"Ah, well, you've got the tease part down." She laughed. Jian came out of the bathroom and signaled that he was ready.

"I have to go," I said into the phone. "Call you tomorrow?"

"You better. And please be careful." Outside, I turned toward the main lobby where we could catch a cab. Jian grabbed my sleeve and motioned the other direction, then started walking. I shrugged and followed,

quickening my step to catch up. He led the way over
to Industrial Boulevard. Judging from the neon, it was
a different sort of strip tucked behind the enormous
facades on the more famous Strip. A long block from
our hotel Jian veered off the sidewalk toward the entrance of what could have been an upscale restaurant or
nightclub. There were no neon outlines of nude women
or flashing strip lights to announce the building's purpose. Instead, white Italian lights brightened a tastefully
landscaped walkway to a canopied entry. A small, discreetly lit plaque near the front door read "Club Cristal."
As we approached, a well-dressed young man stepped
forward and greeted us with a smile. He looked like a
fresh-faced senior on some college football team.

"Welcome, gentlemen," he said, sticking out his
hand. "Glad you could join us this evening." The personal touch impressed me, even though I knew it was
meant to make me feel good about parting with my
money. We stepped into a softly lit, quiet, elegantly
appointed lobby. Plush carpeting covered the floor. A
circular settee in the center and upholstered chairs scattered around the perimeter provided comfortable seat-
ing. On opposite sides of the room were a coat check, a
box-office and his-and-her restrooms. Double doors at
the other end led into the club. I stepped up to the box
office window and paid admission for us both.

Through the doors, the main showroom was busy
and boisterous. Loud music pulsed from the sound
system, and the babble and buzz of conversation and
laughter rose over the music. A bar flanked one wall of
the cavernous room. A glass-walled private room ran
the length of the other. Dim booths and tables filled
the back half of the room. More brightly lit tables with
groupings of comfortable chairs filled the half in front

of the main stage. A broad staircase on one side climbed to a mezzanine balcony and doors that probably led to the private rooms.

Two dancers worked opposite sides of the stage under bright spotlights. Small circular stages ringed by easy chairs dotted the room. Solo performers in various states of undress undulated on half of them. Despite a puritanical flush of embarrassment that made the club feel far too warm, the atmosphere was surprisingly benign. While not exactly wholesome family entertainment, the club was far from the dark, seedy den of iniquity and guilt-ridden angst I'd expected. It was surprisingly light, with elegant, contemporary furnishings. Spot and recessed lighting created an atmosphere that felt more romantic than furtive. While the clientele was predominantly middle-aged men, quite a few mixed groups of younger people in their twenties and thirties appeared in a festive mood.

As Jian and I parted company inside the doors, he murmured out of the corner of his mouth. "Takeshi sitting at end of bar." I headed into the relative dimness in the back to see if I could find a table with a good vantage point. Jian made his way toward one of the small stages near the front of the room. Almost as soon as I settled into a chair, a pretty young woman in an elegant evening dress stopped to ask if I'd like something to drink. I ordered a beer in hopes that it might calm the trembling in my hands.

Shadowed and sheltered from direct view of the bar by one of the solo stages, by shifting slightly to the right, I could see Takeshi at the far end of the bar. He sat facing the room, eyes taking in the main stage. A pool of light fell on the bar behind him. A tall glass of something liquid sat at his elbow, and blue smoke curled upward in the light from an ashtray next to it.

He looked unremarkable. Not much distinguished him from most of the other men his age in the club. He wore a dark suit, white shirt, dark tie, but so did several other patrons. Even the most casually dressed men wore nice slacks and dressy shirts. Not even his ethnicity set him apart. Quite a few Asian faces dotted the crowd, many of which were Japanese. But I knew that profile. It was the same man I'd seen watching Ty's soccer practice months before.

My palms grew moist, and I felt my shirt grow damp under the arms, glad that I'd worn a blazer over it. If Jian was right, I sat nearly face-to-face with Mary's killer. With that realization came sudden fear, and I started shaking so badly I nearly knocked my beer off the table. *He knows me. And my kids. This was a bad idea.* I desperately wanted to bolt, to cut and run. To go find my kids and take them as far away from this man, this monster, as possible. I mustered every ounce of willpower I had and stayed put.

Songs and dancers came and went. I paid little attention. When the waitress realized I wasn't much interested in her, or any of the dancers who took the small stage in front of me, she acted much less friendly. It barely registered. I watched Takeshi, afraid he would recognize me. After a while, it became apparent he didn't just focus on the dancers. His sharp gaze took in the whole club, checked the door, scanned the audience, monitored the service on the floor. The few times he looked in my direction, I slumped in my seat below the level of the stage in front of me, out of sight. When he did look at the strippers, it wasn't with the same hungry expression on the faces of most customers. He looked detached, emotionally disinterested, as if appraising their technical prowess, not their sensual appeal.

Half an hour later, the stages went dark and the music died, replaced by a house announcer promoting upcoming acts. The lull lasted a few minutes, during which a few men walked up to Takeshi and held short conversations before moving off to some other part of the club. Security, I assumed. I paid close attention, committing each face to memory and noting where they took up positions. One of the conversations became so animated that Takeshi got off his stool and let himself be drawn a few feet away from the bar. The man towered over him, gesticulating excitedly.

Movement beyond them caught my eye. Around the corner of the bar next to a waitress station a man appeared, visible for a brief moment in the cone of light illuminating the corner of the bar. *Farley.* I'd wondered when he was going to show up, but he'd been here all along.

Takeshi crooked his finger. The bouncer bent down and leaned in to hear Takeshi speak. He nodded and walked away, but Takeshi didn't follow. Instead he turned and climbed back onto his stool. He took a sip from the glass on the bar, lit another cigarette and assumed his former position. Behind him, Farley stretched innocuously and sat down, disappearing into the shadows.

The music began again, and an announcer introduced the main show, getting the audience revved up. The lights came up on the main stage, and as the music rose to a crescendo the stage erupted in activity. The next hour was a kaleidoscope of color, motion and sound. Far from the bump-and-grind I expected, the show consisted of a series of tasteful, well-choreographed acts ranging from aerialists hanging on silk ropes to Vegas-style dance numbers with showgirls in sequins and feathers. Like a very sensual version of Cirque du Soleil, most of the acts ended up being performed almost entirely in the nude. Titillating at first, the tasteful performances seemed so natural they were no more erotic than a romantic ballet or modern dance routine.

Takeshi remained motionless through the whole show except to light more cigarettes. When it ended, the house music faded into the background and the club's staff moved around the floor. Waitresses took drink orders—I switched to seltzer—and bouncers moved from one station to another. Dancers in sexy evening wear mingled with the guests, striking up conversations at tables around the room. Again, several people stopped to chat with Takeshi, but he seemed disinclined to leave his spot and check other areas of the club.

I squirmed with impatience, wondering how Farley managed to remain immobile, unnoticed. I couldn't see Jian, but I imagined he was as nervous as I. When the music came up for a solo dancer on the main stage, I began to worry. Takeshi hadn't moved. The song ended and another started with two dancers taking the place of the one onstage. Another duo came on at the beginning of a third song, this time dancing together, not separately. Still, Takeshi looked settled in. The crowd, however, became more raucous, rocking in time to the music, cheering and whistling as the dancers removed articles of clothing.

Suddenly, a group off to the left grew even more clamorous. Catcalls and jeers rang out along with the hoots and whistles. Along with everyone else in the club, I sat up and craned my neck to see the commotion. Across the room in the glare of the spotlight, Jian worked the pole on a circular stage in time to the music. He danced alongside a buxom brunette stripper almost a head taller than him. Even from a distance I saw the goofy grin on his face as he tucked a bill into her thong. A good sport, the girl brought him into the act, but some people around the stage voiced their displeasure.

Whether alcohol or inspiration put him on stage didn't matter. Bouncers converged on the stage from different parts of the room. Takeshi rose to his feet, but didn't look too concerned. Farley stood behind him in the shadows.

Onstage, Jian nimbly skipped out of the reach of one bouncer's grasp. He planted himself behind the dancer and mimicked her moves. Half the group surrounding the stage burst into laughter, but several men shouted angrily at Jian to get off. I took a quick look around the room. Almost all eyes that weren't glued to the other dancers valiantly going on with their routines were drawn to the ruckus. Takeshi stepped away from the bar, a look of annoyance on his face.

The world changed then for me, as if the earth wobbled on its axis, shifting half a degree into a different dimension. Colors flowed around me like the smoke that drifted upward in the circles of light. Music pulsed like blood through my veins, sounding from within. The sinuous energy of the dancers filled me with its rhythm, and the long ropes of muscle in my arms and legs thrummed like the taut strings of a cello. Edges, contours, dimensions all grew clearer as if by a change of light. I suddenly read faces as easily as first-grade primers—lust there, rapture on that one, guilt on another. Takeshi's reflected hidden cruelty. I knew what to do.

Legs trembling, I pushed away from the table and slowly worked my way over to the bar. Lots of people had gotten to their feet now, and the crowd seemed to be siding with Jian. A bouncer climbed up on the stage and lunged for him. When Jian ducked out of the way, the crowd roared its approval while a few men close to the stage jeered. I swung my gaze back to Takeshi. He stood riveted by the scene, but his face now displayed anger.

Another roar went up. I turned to see the bouncer on the stage swing his arms wildly. He lost his balance and fell into the waiting arms of a group of guests like a rock star caught by fans in a mosh pit. Takeshi pushed his way through a throng of customers toward the stage. I casually moved down the bar, scanning the faces there. The action across the room held their attention.

Farley stepped out of the shadow, his eyes on Takeshi, and moved slowly around the corner of the bar, hands in his pockets. The din of the crowd rose again. I ignored it this time, and kept my eyes on the people around Farley. My heart pounded in my chest, and my mouth went dry. I licked my lips and pushed past a few people, making my way closer. When Takeshi was swallowed up in the crowd, Farley turned his attention to the bar.

He was good. In one motion he pulled a hand from his jacket pocket, reached for the glass and tipped its contents behind the bar. Then he swiftly put it in a plastic bag that appeared in his other hand. He slipped it into his pocket, already reaching for the ashtray with the other hand. His hand glowed whitely in the light over the bar, and I realized he wore latex gloves.

Movement beyond him made my breath catch. A

waitress watching the commotion on the floor now side-
stepped toward the bar, as if to turn in a drink order.
She turned just as Farley bagged the ashtray and tucked
it into his coat. She hesitated, her face uncertain. I
stepped up my pace, and looked directly at her, hoping
to catch her eye without saying anything that might attract the attention of others.

Farley stepped away, momentary surprise on his face
when he saw me approach. I focused on the waitress. He
must have sensed something was wrong, but he didn't
hesitate. He kept going without turning around. A pro.

The waitress followed him with her eyes, and as I
passed him she opened her mouth. "Hey!" I pulled out
all the cash I had left and held it up. One more step
toward the bar and the color of the bills popped in the
light. Her eyes flicked to the money.

I gave her a big smile. "Sorry. He likes souvenirs."
I reached over the corner of the bar and handed the
folded bills to her. "This ought to cover it. Hope it's
no trouble." Before she could reply, I headed for the
door, hot on Farley's heels. The crowd cheered now,
and as I made my way out the door I caught a glimpse
of Jian with his arms and legs wrapped around the pole,
holding on for dear life. Two very large men tried to
peel him off. I pushed through the lobby doors, and
strolled past the doorman out into the neon-tinged night,
fighting the instinct to run like hell.

I pasted a smile on my face, hoping I looked like a
satisfied customer. "Great show," I said.

"Have a nice night, sir," he said. "Come back again."
Halfway down the walk two valet parking attendants
came to attention. "Get your car for you, sir? Call you
a cab?" one of them asked. I shook my head.

And then I was out on the street, sucking in great

gulps of dry desert air, trying to slow my heart. There was no sign of Farley. I walked down the street to the closest intersection and crossed to the far side. My breathing evened, my pulse slowed as I walked off the adrenaline. I stopped when I drew abreast of the club and waited for Jian. Several minutes passed, and he still didn't show. I paced nervously and wondered why. My phone rang.

"Where are you?" Farley asked. I told him. "Get out of there now!" he said. "Get your kids and go straight to the airport."

"Why? What's—?"

"Shut up and listen! Take the first flight you can get. Go, now! Call me when you get through security." He hung up.

TWENTY-THREE

I RAN, forcing back the panic that threatened to invade every cell of my body. Something had gone horribly wrong, and Farley thought we were in danger. I'd been stupid to think I could take on a Japanese crime boss. Now my family, Jian's family, would pay. Pay dearly, the way Mary had. I couldn't let that happen. I pushed myself harder, ran faster.

Kelsey and Mei Lei stared at me wide-eyed as I burst through the hotel door, their faces reflecting blue from the television screen in the darkened room. A lump under the covers of one of the beds stirred and shifted, revealing Ty's shaggy head against a white pillow.

"We have to go," I said. "Right now." I kept my voice low, but they heard the urgency in it.

"What happened?" Kelsey looked frightened.

"I'll tell you later. Right now, we need to grab our things and leave. I really need your help, girls. Just do as I say and please don't ask questions."

"But where's my father?" Mei Lei said.

"He's coming," I lied. "He'll meet us later. Now, please, get your things. No time to be neat. We have to walk out of this room in three minutes." Without waiting for a reply, I walked to the bed and gently shook Ty awake. In gentle tones, I told him to get up and get dressed. He rubbed his eyes and yawned, but did what I asked.

"Where we going?" he said.

"Home, I hope."

THE RIDE TO McCARRAN seemed endless. The silence in the cab amplified the tension, and a pall of fear shrouded us all. The children couldn't bring themselves to meet my gaze, afraid to read the emotions that showed on my face. I caught Kelsey peering at me out of the corner of her eye and tried to paste on a smile.

We piled out in front of the main terminal, and trooped up to the ticket counter. I checked the departures board. Only two airlines had non-stop flights to Seattle. The airline we came in on had a flight out at midnight, barely enough time to get through security. Nervous, I herded the kids toward the ticket counter, swiveling my head to check the faces of passersby. I don't know who I expected to see. Ty grumbled sleepily when Kelsey bumped him with a suitcase. Kelsey snapped at him. I hushed them both and moved them along in the line. Mei Lei followed silently, head down. The line moved slowly, the airport still busy even at this time of night. Finally our turn, the kids slid the bags up to the counter as I stepped up and handed our tickets to an agent. He compared our IDs to the names on the tickets and typed on his keyboard.

I turned and scanned the crowd again, stunned to see a face I recognized this time. The man's size registered first—big, like Farley—then his face and clothes. A bouncer from the club. Another man accompanied him, smaller, with Asian features. Japanese, like Takeshi. Their heads stayed in constant motion as they slowly walked through the terminal, eyes scanning the crowd. I quickly turned back to the agent, fighting the rising alarm that twisted my stomach in knots. *They couldn't be looking for me. How could they know?*

"Heads up," I said softly, tapping the kids' shoulders to get their attention. I turned to keep the agent from overhearing. "I want you all to be ready to move if I tell you to. Whatever I say, do it. Don't hesitate. Do you understand me?"

"Dad?" Kelsey's voice was plaintive.

"I can't explain now. Just be ready." I straightened and checked on the two men. They'd moved past us, headed toward the end of the terminal.

"How many bags?" the agent asked.

I turned. "What? Oh, sorry. Four." The two men reached the end of ticketing, did an about-face and slowly worked their way back. I averted my eyes and slouched over the counter. While the agent printed baggage claim checks, I tucked my chin into my shoulder and glanced back to mark their progress. The agent slid boarding passes into a sleeve along with the claim check stubs and handed it to me. The next time I dared peek, the big man had gone on point. He tugged at the other's sleeve. I followed his gaze, and froze.

Jian stood at a terminal entrance craning his neck to look over the sea of constant motion. The moment he spotted me, his face lit up. I shook my head frantically and held my hand in front of my chest, pointing to my left. His smile faltered as he glanced in that direction. He looked at us again, puzzled. The two men stopped to watch, and their faces turned toward us, too.

"Come on, kids," I said quietly, keeping my eye on the men. I spread my arms and steered them away from the counter. "Stay close to me. Mei Lei, your dad is here. This is important. Act like we don't know him. Do you understand? All of you, we're going to walk right past him. Don't even *look* in his direction." We walked toward the opposite end of the terminal to find the tram that would take us to our gate. Jian started toward us, still uncertain. I risked a glance behind and saw the pair from the club heading our way with purpose. They'd figured it out. Jian had led them to us.

"Faster, kids," I urged. "Jian's coming. Don't look. Just keep moving." Just yards away now, Jian searched my face. I gave one last shake of my head, praying he understood. Something behind me diverted his attention for a brief moment. Suddenly, the veil of confusion lifted from his face. He broke into a smile again, raised his arm and waved excitedly. *That sealed it, for sure. We're done for.*

But as we drew close, Jian kept waving and smiling at something over my shoulder. When we passed each other he didn't even glance at the kids. They watched his antics, mouths open, heads rotating as we walked on by.

"Keep moving," I growled under my breath. "Don't look back. Go, go." Halfway down the terminal, I risked a look back. Jian had cornered an unsuspecting family at the ticket counter and jabbered away while they attempted to get away from him. The club bouncers stood off to one side and watched, momentarily confused. When the family finally broke away from Jian, the two looked at each other, then scanned the crowd again, turning our way. They broke into a trot.

"Run!" I said. "Follow me! Now!" I grabbed Ty's hand and pulled him along behind me. He felt the urgency in my grip and churned his little legs to keep up. The girls hesitated but sprinted after us. I led the way over the pedestrian bridge to baggage claim. If Takeshi's men had made us, then we couldn't fly out.

Even if we beat them to security, they would know where we were headed and simply have someone meet us at the other end. No, we had to find another way out. I wracked my brain.

"Kelsey!" I called over my shoulder, breathing hard. She pulled abreast. I huffed the words in spurts as we ran. "We have to get away from those men behind us. We're going outside. Past baggage claim. Get into a cab. I'll draw them away. Tell the driver to drop you off at Avis. I'll meet you there." Shouts rose behind us. I glanced back long enough to see Jian catch up to Takeshi's men and fling a luggage cart in their path, sending them both sprawling.

I egged the kids on. "Move it!" *We might just have a chance.* The four of us raced through baggage claim and out the other side onto the street. I looked wildly in both directions until I spotted a cab stand and steered the three of them toward it. I pulled money from my pocket and pressed it into Kelsey's hand.

"Go! Run!" I said. "I'll see you soon. I promise." They sprinted for a cab, and I ducked back into the shadows. The two goons burst through a door as the cab pulled away. They pulled up short and scanned the passing cars, heads turning like spectators at the U.S. Open. The Japanese fellow spotted the cab first and pointed. I saw Ty's face peer out the window as it flashed by, but couldn't make out anyone else. I hoped they couldn't either.

The short one stepped into the roadway. If he got the cab's license number, Takeshi might be able to trace its destination. By then I hoped we'd be long gone. I pressed myself against the building, farther into the shadows. Finally, they turned and went back inside. I pulled out my cell phone and called Farley.

"What the hell is going on?" My voice broke and shifted up an octave like a teenager's.

"Are you getting on a flight?" he asked.

I forced air into my lungs. "A couple of bouncers from the club showed up at the airport. They spotted us! We can't fly out. I'm going to try to rent a car. How'd they find us so fast?"

"You got away?"

"I think so. They saw my kids drive away in a cab. I'm hoping they figured I'm with them."

"And your friend? Jian?"

"He's here somewhere. I don't know where." I took a breath. "What happened?"

"Security at the club detained Jian instead of simply giving him the boot. They checked his ID. I figured if Takeshi found out where he was from, he might put two and two together. So I called you and told you to skedaddle. Looks like he figured it out faster than I thought."

"Do you think he knows what we did?"

"Maybe. If not yet, he'll figure that out too, eventually. He'll talk to all the employees, maybe review the security tapes."

"The waitress…"

"Yes," he said. "Nice move, by the way. You bought me enough time to get out."

"Then how did you know Jian was questioned by security?"

"I stuck around to make sure you two got out."

"What about the evidence?" I felt sweat dribble down my sides. Panic squeezed my chest.

"Safe," he said. "Already on its way. I passed it off to a colleague. Now, get out of there while you still can." The phone went dead. I didn't have time to think about who Farley had roped into helping him, or how he would preserve the chain of possession, or even how much this new wrinkle was going to end up costing me. I had to move quickly. I had to find the kids, and Jian, and get out of Dodge.

I moved cautiously to a door and peered inside. No sign of the two. Fighting the impulse to run, I strode purposefully to the shuttle bus waiting at the curb and got on.

The kids sat huddled in a corner of the car rental office. I made them wait there until I signed the papers for a big SUV. They followed me out to the car, faces full of questions, but I held up a hand while I pulled out my phone and called Jian. He sounded out of breath.

"You okay?" I asked.

"Yes, yes, fine. Where are you?"

"I rented a car. I'll pick you up." I told him where to meet us and described the SUV.

Five minutes later, we pulled up to the curb in front of Departures. I hopped out and scanned the sidewalk for Jian. I finally spotted him a couple of doors down and waved. He waved back and hurried toward us, wheeled suitcase in tow.

"Dad?" Kelsey's voice came from the car. "Uh, Dad?" Louder this time and more shrill.

Through the windshield I saw her point to something up high behind me. I turned. Above the street ahead hung the pedestrian bridge. Takeshi's men stood behind the glass looking down. They broke into a run.

"Jian!" I waited long enough to see him quicken his pace, then raced around to the driver's side and clambered in. I had the car in gear and rolling when Jian climbed into the backseat and heaved his suitcase into the cargo space.

WE WERE FIFTY MILES outside of Las Vegas before anyone spoke. Jian cradled Mei Lei in his arms in the backseat. She looked like she'd fallen asleep. Next to them, Ty pressed his face to the window, staring out into the darkness.

"Who were those men?" Kelsey said softly. Her face glowed dimly in the dashboard light.

"Security guards from a club in Las Vegas."

"Why were they chasing us?"

I hesitated. She deserved to know. They all did. "They were after *me*. I was trying to get evidence to prove I didn't have anything to do with Mom's death." I heard stirrings in the backseat. In the rearview mirror I saw Ty lean forward. His eyes widened, and fear shone in their depths.

"That's why we went to Las Vegas? The man who killed Mom was there?" His hands gripped the edge of the Kelsey's seat. "Are you crazy?" His voice rose to a shrill pitch. "You followed some psycho killer to Las Vegas and took us along?" Mei Lei started and sat up. Jian put his hand on Ty's shoulder and murmured soothingly, but Ty shrugged him off. His knuckles whitened from gripping the seat, and his thin shoulders trembled. His eyes glistened in the light from the dash, but he wouldn't let go of any tears.

"What are you? Freaking nuts?" His high squeaky shriek quavered, but struck me dumb with all the power of a blow to the solar plexus. "Do you have a death wish or something?"

"Whoa!" Kelsey said. "You want to chill out a little, squirt?" She squirmed in her seat and looked at Ty, still red-faced and shaking. Her eyes narrowed.

I breathed deeply, exhaled. "Ty, you have every right to be angry with me. But if you'll calm down, I'll explain. To both of you. You, too, Mei Lei." Ty thrust an obdurate jaw toward me, but didn't protest. Kelsey looked perplexed, but said nothing. In the mirror, I saw Jian nod. I took another deep breath. "Yes, I took you to Las Vegas under false pretenses. I hired a private investigator to help get evidence that would prove who killed Mom. Jian helped."

"You were part of this?" Mei Lei pushed away from her father.

"Yes," he said firmly. "Friends help each other. This man has been my friend, *our* friend." Though I still didn't understand it, I felt grateful for his loyalty. Mei Lei looked betrayed.

"We brought you kids along because we couldn't leave you home alone," I said. "We thought it would be a fun sort of mini-vacation. And it was. I had a great time. Didn't you?" Kelsey nodded reluctantly. Ty remained silent, still unsure. "If I'd thought for a minute that you guys were in any sort of danger, I never would have done it."

Kelsey's gaze shifted from my face to Ty's and back again. "That's not what he's afraid of, dummy." I recoiled. She ignored me and bravely went on. "He's afraid of losing you, too. Like Mom." She paused, summoning another ounce of courage with a deep breath. "So am I." I put my hand on her arm, the ache in my chest like an anvil's weight on my ribs. Neither of them moved. My hand fell to my side.

"I won't let that happen. I promise." The words came out with a fierce rush. "That's why I had to find this guy. Not just so I don't go to jail. But so he won't hurt anybody else. He has to pay for what he did. Do you understand?" I saw Ty nod hesitantly and avert his eyes when he saw me looking. I glanced at Kelsey.

"You lied to us," she said quietly. "We trusted you."

I nodded. "I won't do it again. From now on, we keep everything out in the open. If any of us has a problem, we can call a family meeting."

"Even me?" Ty said.

"Even you."

Kelsey looked leery. "Everything?"

"Well, you don't have to share private stuff. But anything that affects the family, yes."

"That means you, too, right?" She looked at me curiously, reticent even when I nodded. Then she just blurted it out. "Are you dating someone?"

"Why?"

She peered at me. "You are, aren't you? I knew it. Well?" she said, raising an eyebrow.

"I've met someone," I said haltingly, already regretting my promise.

"Is it serious?" she demanded.

"I don't know yet. I know I enjoy being with her." Kelsey crossed her arms. She pursed her lips tightly, and squinted through narrowed eyes.

"How did you know?" I said.

"You've been acting really weird the last couple of weeks." She paused. "I hope you don't expect me to like her." Her nostrils flared.

I waited a beat. She backed down just a little, letting her expression soften some. "That will be up to you," I said. "Look, I'm not trying to replace Mom. I'm not trying to forget her, either. But it's time for me to get out and meet people."

"Why? What's wrong with things the way they are?"

"Nothing's wrong. It's hard to explain. I love you two, and I'm glad that we're starting to feel like a family again, even though we all miss Mom. It's just that I want companionship, too."

"What's wrong with Jian? He's your friend, isn't he?"

I flushed, and glanced at Jian in the mirror. "Yes, he is. And I'm very glad he and Mei Lei are our friends. It's just not the same thing, Kels. I'm not sure you'll really understand it until you're older."

"I'm not a child." She tossed her head.

"I know that." I took a breath. "Look, no one can take your mom's place. No one else can fill the hole she left. But she's not coming back. I'll never forget her, but I can't sit around wishing things had been different. I have to move on. I have to start living again."

"So, what? To heck with us, is that it? Don't you give a damn about us? What if she turns out to be horrible?"

"Of course I care about you, but I like this person. She's pretty special. I think you'll like her, too, but no one's going to force you to. I do expect you to be polite, though. I expect you to give her the same respect I'd give any of your friends."

"She's not, like, moving in, is she?" Panic flashed across her face.

"No, not now. I don't know. Maybe someday. I just meant when you have the chance to meet her."

"We'll see." She folded her arms across her chest. "I doubt it."

"I doubt she's ready to meet you, either." I felt my patience thinning. "We're just getting to know each other, Kels. Nothing's going to change. At least not for a while. I'll take it slow, I promise."

"Where are we going, anyway?" The abrupt change of subject caught me off guard.

"I'm not sure. I'll let you know when I figure it out."

"Fine." She tossed her hair over her shoulders and turned toward the window.

I focused on the road ahead, watching the white stripes of the lane divider blink on and off in the headlights. After a few minutes, I checked the mirrors out of habit and came upon the reflection of Ty's watchful face with a start.

"Hey, sorry if I scared you," I said. "Are we okay?"

He hunched his shoulders and raised his eyebrows. "What's her name?" He'd moved on, apparently.

"Amy."

"Is she pretty?"

"Very."

"Prettier than Mom?" His tone was curious, not concerned.

"No, just pretty in a different way."

"Is she nice?"

"She's one of the nicest people I've ever met." He mulled that over, evidently finding it acceptable. His face brightened and he leaned back in his seat with a small smile.

A LITTLE MORE THAN SIX HOURS later, I stopped in Provo, Utah, for gas. On the way out of the airport in Las Vegas I'd made a split-second decision to stick to big interstate highways instead of deserted back roads. I had only two choices, really—southwest to Bakersfield or northeast to Salt Lake City.

Jian was awake when I got back in the car after filling up the tank, but the kids still slept soundly. Ty lay stretched out in the back, giving Mei Lei room to lie across the middle seats, her head in Jian's lap. Kelsey lay curled up in the passenger seat. Jian caught my eye.

"You have plan?" he said softly.

I shook my head. "I think we should get rid of this car. They could still be looking for us. I don't know how far this guy's reach extends."

He looked thoughtful, then nodded. "When you tired, I drive." We traded the SUV in for another one at the Salt Lake City Airport. The rental agent gave me a funny look, but didn't argue. Jian took the wheel this time, and Kelsey moved back to sit with Mei Lei. We got a drive-through breakfast somewhere near Ogden, and after wolfing down some food and a cup of coffee, I fell into a restless sleep in the passenger seat.

Just outside Boise, Jian indicated we needed gas again. Ty said he was hungry, and the girls complained that they needed a bathroom. After a short pit stop and more junk food, we got on the road again. Bolstered by gallons more coffee, I drove, using the miles to think, wondering how I'd gotten us into this. And how we were going to get out of it.

"Hi," I said TIREDLY into the phone.

"Where are you?" Amy asked. "I tried calling a couple of times."

"Sorry, I turned the phone off. We're just outside Yakima."

"Yakima? What are you doing there?" Jian walked up to me, waggling his hand, concern on his face.

"Just a minute," I told Amy, and held the phone away. To my surprise, Jian snatched the phone out of my hand and cut the connection.

"Bad idea," he said, shaking his head. "I underestimate Takeshi. No more. He know too much about you. If he know your cell phone number, he can trace phone location. Use pay phone. Over there." He pointed to the side of the gas station.

"How do you know all this stuff?"

He shrugged. "Is not important." I walked to the pay phone and called Amy back.

"Sorry. I had to get off the cell phone."

"What's going on, Jack?" I heard the worry in her voice. If there was anyone I could trust, it had to be Amy. I told her everything. She listened silently.

"Why are you doing this?" she said.

"Because I don't want to go to jail. I don't want my kids to end up in foster care. Because I want a future with you." I paused. "And now, because I have no choice."

She responded with silence. Then, "What will you do now?"

"I'm not sure. Hole up somewhere. We can't go home. Takeshi will have the house watched. I'll call Preston tomorrow and see if he got the evidence. We'll go from there."

Again she was silent, as if making some decision. "I have a place," she said hesitantly. "My parents left it to me. It's not far from you."

"I couldn't ask that of you, Amy."

"You didn't. I'm offering."

"No, I can't put you in danger, too."

"You won't. This Takeshi person doesn't know about me. You'll be safe there. It's up past Roslyn. You know, where they filmed that quirky TV show, *Northern Exposure*? I watched them film a couple of times when I visited my parents there. A long time ago." I had to think a minute before I remembered the show she was talking about. She gave me directions and told me she'd have the woman who looked after it open it up with a spare key.

"I can't thank you enough," I said. "You're a lifesaver. The kids will be happy to have a shower and a real bed."

She laughed. "As long as you promise to go back with me sometime."

"Absolutely." I smiled. Then, like I did with my kids nearly every day, I tossed off an "I love you" without thinking. And realized as I hung up how much I meant it.

I WOKE THE NEXT MORNING to sunlight streaming through the windows of a log cabin. It had been nearly midnight when we'd finally found the place in the hills above Cle Elum Lake, twenty-four hours after our escape from Las Vegas. Too late and dark to see our surroundings even if we hadn't been too tired to care.

I walked to the windows. The lake spread out below, a slash of cobalt nestled among green tree-covered hills. The Cascades rose behind them. Normally frozen this time of year and dusted with snow, the warm winter and lack of precipitation had left the water open, the hills bare. Home was only an hour and a half away, but it might as well have been on the other side of the world.

I turned at sounds of someone behind me. Jian quietly rustled through cupboards in the kitchen. I joined him to make a list of things we'd need from town. Twenty minutes later, I found a pay phone in Roslyn and called Preston's office.

"You got the package okay?" I asked.

Preston snorted, peevish. "Yes, I got it. I personally delivered it to a lab yesterday. You couldn't have bothered to let me know in advance to anticipate receipt of material evidence?"

"If I'd told you, you never would have approved."

"Was it obtained illegally?" he said sharply.

"No." Someone as good as Preston could argue that

Farley had committed petty theft, but since I'd left money to pay for what we took my conscience was clear.

"Who is this person?"

"I can't tell you that. Not yet." He went silent for a moment. "But you think whoever it is might have something to do with your wife's death. May I ask what?"

"I think this person killed her."

"And you obtained this evidence where?"

"In a public place." He waited for the rest, but I was reluctant to volunteer more.

"Farley indicated that he came directly from the airport when he showed up early yesterday morning," he said. "A holiday, I might add." I ignored the tetchy comment.

"We traced this person to Las Vegas."

"You risked forfeiting your bail to leave the state on some capricious notion that you've somehow learned the identity of your wife's attacker?"

"I knew you wouldn't approve."

"My approval should be the least of your concerns. Either you've been very busy since the last time we met, or you've withheld quite a bit of information. Care to enlighten me?" He didn't sound happy.

"I've been busy."

"Hmm, yes. Farley says you ran into a bit of trouble. This person knows who you are?"

"Yes." I wasn't sure how much I could trust him, but I told him about the phone calls, the man watching Ty at soccer and Kelsey at school.

"Why didn't you mention this earlier?"

"I was a little preoccupied," I said, unable to keep the anger out of my voice. I took a breath and went on more calmly. "I didn't connect it with Mary's death until later. I found something I think this man wants. Bad enough to kill her for it. Only she didn't have it at the time."

"And you can't tell me what this 'thing' is or who wants it."

"Not until I'm sure."

He grunted, then paused. "The good news," he said, "is that the state crime lab finally sent back results of the tests we asked for. The hairs found on your wife's body are yours. The hair found on her clothing, however, doesn't belong to either of you, as you suspected." It wasn't surprising, but I felt disappointment.

"That's something, at least."

"As unlikely as it seems, the prosecuting attorney can still argue that it could have gotten caught on her clothing almost anywhere." His tone warned me not to get my hopes up.

"Unless we know whose it is."

"Yes," he said simply.

"How long until the lab tests come back? You did put a rush on it, didn't you?"

"Thirty-six hours depending on your sample."

"Tomorrow, then?"

"I doubt anyone worked on it yesterday—the holiday, remember?" President's Day. The kids were off school all week, fortunately. I'd almost forgotten what day it was. "Why don't I call you when the results come back," he said.

"You can't," I told him. "I'll call you."

WAITING WAS HARD. We managed to keep from going stir-crazy in the cabin. Jian and I took the kids shopping for clothes in Ellensburg, since our luggage now sat in baggage claim at Sea-Tac. Ty and I explored the woods around the cabin on an old logging road. We found a cupboard full of board games and played a few in front of the fire after dinner. But I still couldn't keep my mind off all the questions running through my head.

I called Preston again late Wednesday afternoon from the pay phone in Roslyn.

"The DNA came back a match," he said. I thought I hadn't heard him right. "DNA on the glass and cigarette butts Tom Farley gave me matches that of the hair found on your wife's clothing. Care to fill me in now?"

"Not over the phone."

"I'll come to you. Where are you?"

I deliberated. "You know what can happen if they find us?"

"Of course. I'll be prudent." I gave him directions. "I can find it," he said. "Give me about two hours."

PRESTON SAT ACROSS THE cabin's kitchen table looking as if he'd eaten three bites too many. I finished telling him everything I knew or surmised about Ito Takeshi.

"Do you want to see...?" I left the thought unfinished.

He turned his head to the side and waved both hands at me, souring like old milk. "No, no. It's better if I don't have specific knowledge of what's on the disc, I think. In retrospect, you were smart not to tell me. Not right, perhaps, but smart."

"Well, do you want it?"

"Good God, no. If its contents are what you suggest, mere possession of that disc is punishable by up to ten years in prison. I would be compelled to turn it over immediately."

I blinked. "Ten years?"

He nodded. "Hang on to it. I'll make some calls tonight and see if I can set up another pre-trial conference tomorrow. You don't want to sit on it any longer than you have to. Besides, what you turned up is important enough to warrant a call to the prosecutor—the judge, even."

"What will you tell them?"

"Enough to get a conference scheduled, no more." He paused. "I will have to bring law enforcement in on this as well. You can't simply give this to the court. They will no more want to accept responsibility for it than I. You'll have to turn it over to federal agents."

I hesitated. "If that's what you think we should do."

"The FBI is probably best equipped to investigate this." He paused. "This is all very positive, Jack. I'm confident this will cast enough doubt on your alleged guilt to assure you an acquittal. But much of what you've told me is supposition, as circumstantial as the case against you. There is evidence that, on the face of it, could place this Takeshi person in proximity with your wife. But the fact he was on the same plane could cause the prosecutor to see it otherwise." He watched me chew on it like cud. When I didn't reply, he levered himself out of the chair. "The sticky part is that you have nothing that directly links Takeshi to this disc except a theory."

Jian had thought of something that would connect them. Preston started for the door. I held up a hand. "Wait. The CD case. Takeshi handled it." I grimaced. "So did we, but it's possible…"

He paused, then nodded. "Bag it. Bring it along. We'll turn that over, too. I'd rather not take chances with a lab. I think we should let the FBI handle it. Then no one can accuse you of manufacturing whatever's found."

"Okay." I rose and followed him to the door. "You'll call me?"

"As soon as I hear."

"There's just one problem," I said. "I don't have the disc."

TWENTY-FOUR

I AGREED to meet Amy at the art museum downtown before the conference Preston set up. She told me she needed to see me, and I found I couldn't bear being apart from her any longer. I drove into Seattle early the next morning, parked in a nearby garage and waited inside the museum entrance. Clothing and umbrellas flapped wildly on the sidewalk, ravens' wings beating against gusts of wind that blew the light rain sideways. She appeared suddenly, dashing the last few steps to the entrance, laughing as the wind threatened to pull the umbrella from her hands. She shook her hair back over her shoulder and brushed away drops of water from her eyelashes with the back of her hand. I felt incandescent, so brightly lit from within that my face shone and my fingertips glowed red.

She paused for a quick embrace before we stepped up to a counter to check our umbrellas. An aura surrounded her, shimmering like waves of heat off black tarmac. I felt its pull, a magnetic vibration tuned to a frequency intended for one. I took her hand as we walked up the wide staircase to the exhibit hall, our talk on the way unbridled. But once in the hall, we became players in an elaborate and intricate dance. One moment we were so close we seemed fused from shoulder to knee, the immediacy of it as startling as it was comforting. The next moment we drifted apart to contemplate paintings that caught our eye. Near or far, I was always aware of her presence. The two of us glided around museum patrons as if they didn't exist, two celestial bodies in a gravitational waltz that brought us together, pushed us apart.

Our time together quickly disappeared. On the way down the stairs, I felt an impulse to grasp her by the shoulders, press her up against a wall, crush my lips against hers. I wanted to feel the warm weight of her breasts against me, the heat between her legs on my thigh. The way her breath caught said she harbored similar thoughts. A stairwell door opened above us, reminding me we didn't have the museum to ourselves. We hurried the rest of the way down, and I walked her to her car.

"Aren't you scared?" she asked as we turned into the parking garage.

"Of course I am."

"You don't have to do this."

"You know better than that."

"You don't," she insisted.

I held the elevator door for her and pushed the button for her floor. "Look, I know I'm in over my head here. I'm not trying to be stupid, but I need to make sure. There's more, actually. I need to take my life back."

"I don't want to lose you." I looked deep into her green eyes, losing myself in their depths, trying to fathom what lay there.

"Don't worry. Forty or fifty years from now, we'll look back on this and laugh."

"Is that a promise?"

I nodded. "As long as you'll be my girl." I pressed her against the elevator wall, took her face gently in my hands and kissed her. The hunger with which she responded sent my heart leaping against my ribs. My head spun, and I melted into her, a river cascading over a deep cleft of a mountainside into the calm, vast pool of her. And then she was gone, the imprint of her body, her lips, indelibly burned on mine.

I DROVE DOWN THE STREET past Jian's house. Slowly enough to take note of cars at the curb and the lack of pedestrians, but not so slow as to attract attention. Weeks earlier, when Jian had insisted I bag the plastic case Takeshi's CD had been in, I'd done it just to humor him. Now it might end up being the piece of evidence that saved me. Only I had to figure out a way to get it. And the disc itself.

I didn't think Takeshi would have someone watch Jian's house, but I couldn't take any chances. I circled the block and wheeled into the parking lot at the high school and sat there for five minutes. Then I drove past the house in the opposite direction, faster this time. I saw nothing out of the ordinary, but that didn't slow my rapid heartbeat. I parked two blocks over and walked to the house this time.

With school closed for the week, many families had left on vacation. Quiet reigned in the neighborhood, and nothing stirred. I pulled the baseball cap down tight over my ears. My eyes flicked back and forth behind dark glasses, checking parked cars in driveways for occupants. No sign of a soul. I walked up to Jian's front door as if I owned the place and slid his key into the lock. With a last look behind me, I opened the door and stepped inside. Jian had told me where to look for the CD case. I found it without much trouble and was back on the street in less than five minutes. Heart pounding, I retraced my steps to the rented SUV and climbed in. No one followed me or raised an alarm.

I took several deep breaths before driving across the middle of the island toward my house. I felt odd, as though coming home after months away and finding everything changed. *Had it only been less than a week?* I turned off Island Crest, drove past the church on the corner, then past the turn to my street. I quickly looked both ways for signs of anything unusual. A few parked cars, all empty. No one on the street. I continued on past the intersection and followed the road as it curved down a hill and ended in a circle. I swung the SUV around, pulled to the curb and waited several minutes before returning the way I'd come.

Again I slowed as I approached the street leading to the house, absorbing all the details, taking a mental photograph. Something *was* different. By the time I rolled up to the stop sign at Island Crest I had it. A cable company van. Parked up the street from the house, not in a driveway. I threw the SUV into reverse and backed up far enough to pull into the church's front lot. I got out and walked across the lawn to the side of the church and rounded the end of it, staying close to the building. From there I had a view across the lower parking lot and the street below. Two men sat motionless in the van, faces pointed down the street toward my driveway.

I returned to the SUV, thinking furiously. The house behind mine butted up against the church's lower lot. I could get there through my neighbor's backyard, but the men in the van still might spot me. The answer stared me in the face. Through a copse of trees in front of the church, I saw a familiar car parked on the opposite side of the upper lot. *The paparazzo.*

I crouched low and came up on the driver's side of the car. He sprawled in the front seat, head back, mouth open, eyes closed. I rapped on the window. He jerked awake and cringed when he recognized me. I held my hands up, palms out. He looked at me suspiciously, then rolled the window down.

I crouched next to his car. "What's your name?"

"Frank." He waited.

"Frank, you want a story, right? You've been after me for months. What if I agree to give you an exclusive? What'll it buy me?"

He hesitated. "What are you looking for?"

"See that cable van?" I pointed it out. "What's it been doing?"

He shrugged. "Nothing. Sitting there."

"And how long's it been there, Frank?"

He thought about it. "Why?" I saw his expression change, as though he already knew the answer.

"A while, right? Day or two? Don't you think it's odd those two fellows aren't doing anything except sitting?"

"One of them goes up the pole next to the truck every so often."

"Makes it look good. They're watching." I paused. "They're not cops, Frank."

"Who are they?"

"Yakuza. Bad guys." I told him enough of the story to whet his interest. He still looked skeptical, but said he'd play along if I was serious about the exclusive. Dead serious, I told him.

Two minutes later, he sauntered up to the cable van and knocked on the driver's window. I cut through my neighbor's yard, slid down the embankment behind my garage, and quietly let myself in the side door. I paused to let my eyes adjust to the darkness and took a step toward the minivan, promptly tripping over Ty's bike on the floor. I went down in a tangle and cursed softly, hoping the noise hadn't carried outside. I stood the bike against the wall, popped the locks on the minivan and eased into the driver's seat.

The dome light helped me quickly find what I was looking for—the case for The Eagles' *When Hell Freezes Over* concert CD. It was the only CD I could think of that Ty and Kelsey would be certain *not* to listen to. I slipped it into my jacket pocket. Suddenly, a square of light appeared from the door into the house, across the garage. *Someone was waiting inside.*

I hopped down into a crouch next to the van and slammed the door, extinguishing the dome light. I moved quickly to the rear, taking a chance that whoever was there would try to cut me off at the side door where I'd entered. Something brushed my leg in the darkness, nearly causing me to leap out of my skin and yawp in fright. The cat, out in the garage to use the litter box, no doubt. I reached down and ran my fingers through its fur to calm my nerves.

I took a breath and silently rounded the end of the van head down, then sprinted to the open door leading inside the house. A figure at the side door stopped and whirled at the sound of my footsteps. I pushed the button on the wall that triggered the garage door opener. The sound stopped my pursuer in his tracks.

I didn't hesitate, throwing myself through the doorway into the house. I heard the cat yowl as if stepped on as I raced through the laundry room and slammed the door behind me. I sprinted to the back door in the kitchen. A door opened behind me as I burst into the backyard and scrabbled up the slope to my neighbor's yard, ignoring the blackberry brambles that caught at my clothing and tore into my skin. I looked back once to see a man dressed in white overalls start to follow then change his mind and disappear back into the house.

I didn't have much time before he called in reinforcements.

My lungs burned as I cut across the neighbor's property and pounded up the asphalt lot to the SUV. A glance down the hill showed Frank the paparazzo still yakking at the pair in the van. But they paid him no attention, their focus on the shouts coming from my driveway. The driver turned. And saw me. As I rounded the corner of the church out of sight, he reached out the window and shoved Frank aside.

I leapt into the SUV and threw it into gear, wheeling out of the lot with tires squealing. Turning north onto Island Crest, I realized I had little chance of trying to outrun them on the island's main drag. So I took the first left, catching a glimpse of the cable repair van pulling onto Island Crest a block behind me. As soon as I turned the corner, I took another left onto a side street and gunned it down the block, coming out only yards away from the startled paparazzo still standing in the street where the van had left him. Without even a wave, I cranked the wheel hard to the right, accelerated to the next corner and turned right there, too. The cable van was nowhere in sight, but I didn't slow down. I went left at the next corner, down a half-hidden narrow street that emptied out onto West Mercer Way. Barely tapping the brakes at the stop sign, I swerved around the corner and sped up the curvy road as fast as I dared. I didn't breathe easy until I turned onto the I-90 floating bridge without any sign of pursuit.

THE EIGHT MEN AND TWO women around the table seriously outmanned us. They made the small conference room feel as close as a rush-hour bus. Whiffs of cologne, perfume, deodorant, perspiration, tobacco and someone's fetid breath intermingled, creating a single scent reminiscent of a piano bar on Sunday morning. The *pirr* from the tiny vent in the ceiling barely disturbed the thick air, unable to counteract the heat from all those bodies.

I sat unmoving, elbows pulled in, knees knocked, hands in my lap. The fellow on my right grunted apologies for bumping my chair as he wedged a briefcase under the table at his feet. I recognized him from previous pre-trial conferences—the prosecuting attorney on my case. A couple of beefy-looking men leaned awkwardly against a wall, fidgeting with their hands. One was dressed in a suit, the other only in slacks, shirt and tie. A younger woman in a charcoal suit stood quietly against the opposite wall looking tense and very serious. She patently ignored me, peering instead over the shoulder of the P.A. In the corner beyond, an older woman perched on a folding chair with a steno pad in her lap, apparently waiting for a signal to begin chronicling. Next to her, looking uncomfortable, stood Mankiewicz.

I leaned closer to Preston. "What's he doing here?"

He murmured back, "D.A. invited him. He's the arresting officer. It's his case."

"Mr. Preston, you want to get us started here?" the judge interrupted.

I straightened. The judge I recognized, too. He sat across from me in shirtsleeves, his gaze moving impatiently from face to face. The men on either side of him were unperturbed. Both wore crisply starched white shirts under gray lightweight wool suit coats. One looked close to my age, with a square jaw on a lean face and close-cropped hair. The other appeared in his mid-sixties, his well-fed face turned jowly over time by gravity's inexorable pull. Preston sat on my left, also heedless of the heat and cramped quarters. A small smile played at his lips making me wonder what he knew that I didn't.

"Certainly, Your Honor." He looked around the small room. "Thank you all for coming on such short notice. New evidence has come to light in Mr. Holm's case—"

"What evidence?" The P.A. spoke sharply. "We received no notification of new evidence." Preston looked at him, the small smile of amusement still on his face.

"Let the man speak, Mr. Ryobi," the judge said. He waved a hand at Preston.

Preston addressed Ryobi. "Consider this notification. These are recent developments, which is why I asked for this conference." He looked around the room. "Our investigation of this case has turned up substantial evidence that someone other than Mr. Holm perpetrated the attack on his late wife." I looked down at my hands to hide a wry smile at Preston's inclusive comment. As long as he took responsibility along with the credit, it was fine with me.

Ryobi looked skeptical. "Another suspect? Oh, please." He turned to the judge. "Your Honor, this is a transparent attempt to delay trial."

"He's entitled. Let's hear it. Mr. Preston?"

"Your Honor, forensic evidence collected by the Medical Examiner's office included pubic hairs found on Mrs. Holm's person. We asked the state crime lab to perform DNA tests on those hairs, which the prosecutor's office apparently deemed unnecessary. Two of them belong to Mr. Holm. The third, however, belongs to a Japanese citizen named Ito Takeshi." Ryobi's mouth opened in surprise. He shut it quickly. The younger man sitting between the judge and Preston straightened almost imperceptibly, seeming to grow more alert.

"How could you know that?" Ryobi asked, flustered.

"We tested a sample of DNA provided by Takeshi. The results matched those of the hair tested by the crime lab." Preston handed out stapled copies of what I presumed were lab results. I took a stack, placed a copy in front of Ryobi and handed the rest to the woman behind him. I guessed she was his assistant prosecutor.

"So, who is this guy?" Ryobi said.

"A prominent member of the Japanese Yakuza, we believe. Further, we are convinced that Takeshi was involved in the distribution and sale of child pornography and possibly in child prostitution as well."

"You have evidence?" Ryobi said.

"Yes, we do." Preston gestured toward the man on his left. "That's why we invited Special Agents Thomas and Yomura. Mr. Holm wishes to turn it over." I took that as my cue, took the CD out of the Eagles case and gingerly handed it across the table to the fellow I assumed was Thomas. He grasped it by the edges between his thumb and two middle fingers, throwing a glance over his shoulder at the man standing behind him. Yomura reached into a suit coat pocket, pulled out a plastic bag and held it open.

Thomas swiveled and dropped the disc into it. "What's on it?"

I looked at Preston, who nodded. "Digitally encrypted photos of children in erotic poses," I said. "All numbered."

His face was unreadable. "That's it?"

"Each photo is marked with a Yakuza symbol. The file index on the disc is in Japanese."

He appeared satisfied. "How did you break the password?"

"A friend who knows computers. He also speaks a little Japanese, so he taught a decryption program to read *kanji*. I imagine you want the password." I held out a folded piece of paper.

"That would help." He reached over to take it, and quickly unfolded it, glancing inside. A smile passed across his face like a flash of sunlight through clouds when he saw the *kanji* characters. He folded the paper and passed it over his shoulder. Yomura snuck a peek, and a corner of his mouth also lifted when he saw the joke.

"Am I to understand that there is child pornography on that disc?" the judge asked, eyes boring into me. "You know it's a federal crime to possess child pornography?"

"Yes, sir."

The judge leaned forward on his elbows and looked at Preston. "You were aware of this?"

"Not until two days ago, Your Honor. At which time, I placed calls to Special Agent Thomas to arrange a meeting so my client could turn it over, and to Mr. Ryobi to set up this conference." The judge *harrumphed* and sat back in his chair.

"What's this all about?" Ryobi said, frowning. The woman behind him looked even more serious, if that was possible.

Thomas took the lead. "Ito Takeshi is an officer in a large Japanese corporation with business dealings here in the U.S. One of his company's affiliates owns several gentlemen's clubs in Nevada and California. We've been aware of him for a long time. He takes a personal interest in the business."

"What's the FBI's interest?" the older man next to the judge asked.

"Just what this man has uncovered, sir—prostitution. More specifically, child prostitution. We've suspected for a long time the clubs were a cover for this sort of activity. Frankly, we thought his organization was using the Internet, but we could never trace anything back to him or the company. Apparently, this is how they got the word out about what was, um, available."

"Sorry, I don't get it," Ryobi said. "What's the link between Takeshi and the victim?"

"My client found that disc among his wife's possessions," Preston said. "Takeshi was a passenger on the last flight she worked before her death. We surmise that something spooked him, so he slipped the disc into her bag to circumvent the possibility of its discovery by customs agents. No doubt he intended to retrieve it somehow before leaving the airport, but Mrs. Holm's bag inadvertently was switched with a coworker's. We believe Takeshi tracked her to her home. She likely surprised him while he was searching for the disc, so he killed her."

"And you believe the disc is Takeshi's because...?" the older man asked.

"Besides the fact that it has Japanese gang insignia on it and Takeshi had access to Mrs. Holm's bag on her last flight, we're hopeful that there's a more direct link." I placed the plastic bag containing the CD case on the table in front of me and shoved it toward Thomas. I saw Mankiewicz follow it with his eyes as Thomas picked it up.

"In this case, fingerprints," Preston continued. "We obtained some from Takeshi. If the FBI can match any prints on that CD case to what we have, I imagine that will be fairly conclusive."

Ryobi weighed his options. "What do you want?" he said gruffly.

"I have a motion here to drop all charges against Mr. Holm." As if by magic, a folded legal document with a blue cover appeared in Preston's hand. Ryobi's mouth worked, but nothing came out. He looked around for help.

The older man next to the judge shook his head and finally spoke. "Can't do it, Phil. We did you a favor by not upping the ante and upgrading the charge to aggravated murder. You've got a lot of supposition here."

"Looks like he's got a lot of evidence to back it up, too, Dan," the judge said.

The mention of his name finally triggered recognition—Dan Culver, assistant district attorney. Ryobi's boss.

Culver tented his fingers and touched them to pursed lips. "I suppose we could look into it, depending on what the folks at the FBI find out. I'll go along with a continuance, if that's what the defense wants."

"We want Mr. Holm exonerated," Preston said.

"Then let's present what we've got to a jury and see what they decide," Culver said.

"I know a way," Thomas said quietly. All eyes turned to him. He looked at each face in turn. "We'd be more than happy to put Takeshi out of commission. He can help." He inclined his head in my direction.

"A sting?" Culver said.

"There's no reason to put my client in that sort of jeopardy," Preston said. "We have more than enough now. He's already put his family in danger by pursuing evidence that should have been investigated by the police and the prosecutor's office. Not only do I think charges against my client should be dropped, I have half a mind to file suit for false arrest and—"

"I'll do it," I said. I looked at Thomas. "I assume you want me to bait him with the disc."

He nodded. "If he goes for it we'll know it's his."

Preston put a hand on my arm. "Are you sure this is what you want to do?"

I swallowed hard and nodded. "I'm not living with the ambiguity anymore. Life's already hard enough. The only way this man will leave us alone is if he's put in jail." Thomas's mouth twitched briefly, and I thought I saw sudden respect in his eyes.

"Acceptable to you, Dan?" the judge said. When Culver nodded, the judge turned to the fellow quietly standing against the wall all this time. "Give us a new trial date, Charley. Say, six weeks out." He looked around the table. "That enough?"

"We'll set it up as soon as possible," Thomas said. "If Takeshi takes the bait, we can wrap this up fairly quickly."

"HE STAYS," I SAID. I didn't let Thomas's annoyance faze me.

"I can't take responsibility for—"

"You don't have to." My irritation surpassed his. "He's perfectly capable of taking care of himself. You wouldn't be here if it wasn't for him."

"I know that." Thomas paused, letting his face settle into a smooth mask. "We'd just like to keep things simple, that's all."

"Look, I get that you guys have a certain way you like to do things. But he has a right to be here if he wants. And I want him here."

"No one faults you for being nervous." Now he sounded conciliatory.

"Damn right, I'm nervous. But I'm not just looking for moral support. He can help." Jian had been sitting quietly while we talked as if he wasn't there. Now he nodded eagerly. Yomura flashed a glance at him, then at Thomas, and turned his attention back to fiddling with wires that connected a tape recorder to the phone in the cabin.

"It just makes things more complicated," Thomas said patiently.

I shook my head. "He speaks Japanese."

"So does Agent Yomura."

I ignored him. "He's seen Takeshi, knows a little of how he thinks. And he can back me up."

"That's what we're here for." Thomas and Yomura had arrived early that morning, surprising me. I didn't think they'd get approval that quickly. But I was eager to get it over with.

"No offense, but I want all the back-up I can get with this guy." His eyes drifted. "This guy killed my wife," I said more sharply.

"I know what he's capable of." Thomas looked thoughtful. "What are you thinking?"

"I want Jian on the line. He doesn't have to say anything unless he needs to. I want insurance. Stashing a copy of the disc somewhere in case anything happens to me isn't enough. Takeshi could still try to kill me, or use my kids as leverage. I want him to know that someone else knows about him."

He hesitated, then nodded. "That's acceptable."

"We're set," Yomura said quietly.

Thomas's eyes stayed on me. "You ready?"

"Give me a minute." I took a deep breath and rubbed my hands on my thighs.

Outside, fluffy cumulus clouds liberally clotted a blue sky, and the distant patter of rain signaled a quickly passing shower. An eagle cried high overhead as it lazily drifted in the breeze. I took another deep breath. How many people around the world at that moment found themselves in situations so desperate they would do the unthinkable? I wondered. People so hungry, so frightened, so angry they would risk everything. Thousands? Hundreds of thousands?

Jian had rehearsed it with me, going over all the possibilities dozens of times before Thomas arrived. I picked up the receiver and dialed the number written on the piece of paper in front of me. Thomas donned headphones. Yomura already wore a headset with the microphone turned off. He motioned to Jian to pick up a cordless handset. Our eyes shifted from one to another for several seconds while the call went through. A woman's voice answered in Japanese. Yomura peered at me. I turned and nodded at Jian.

"Konnichiwa," Jian said, followed by something unintelligible to me except for "Takeshi-*san.*" She put us on hold. Seconds dragged by in the quiet room, the ticking of my watch sounding as loud as someone walking across a hardwood floor in tap shoes.

"Takeshi." The low growl startled me.

"Mr. Takeshi, I have something of yours."

"Excuse, please?"

"I have your CD, Mr. Takeshi, your disc."

"Who is this, please?"

"You know who it is."

"Sorry. You must have wrong number." From the corner of my eye, I saw Thomas waving frantically.

"You put a CD in my wife's purse on an airplane," I said in a rush. "Last fall. Tokyo to Seattle. You never got it back." There was silence on the line. Thomas cranked his hand in a circular motion. "I have it, Mr. Takeshi. I think you want it back." I pressed the phone harder to my ear to keep my hand from trembling.

"A CD?"

"Not music. Pictures. Photos."

"Ah, so. Then it must not be mine." He sounded relieved.

"I think it is. Pictures of your *children,* maybe."

"How would you know this?" The relief was gone.

"Because they were so well protected. Encrypted, in fact. Sound familiar?"

"You've seen these pictures?" He sounded baffled now.

"Yes, in great detail. They're not something you would want others to see, I'm sure."

There was silence again for a moment, then, "I'll have to call you back. Give me your number." I glanced at Thomas with raised eyebrows. He hesitated a fraction of a second, then nodded. I rattled off the number, and when the line clicked I cradled the phone.

"Now what?" I said.

"I don't think we lost him," Thomas said. "He probably doesn't want to talk on the club's phone. So we wait." Less than a minute later the jangle of the phone made me jump.

"Number's blocked," Yomura said, looking at a readout.

"It's him," Thomas said. He motioned to me. "Go." I picked up the phone and said hello.

"What do you want?" Takeshi's voice was gruff.

Anger raced through me like a jet of flame, igniting

an urge to scream at him. I swallowed hard and said through gritted teeth, "I want my children to have their mother back." He didn't reply. Thomas waved a warning at me. "You can't give me that, though, can you, Mr. Takeshi? So, I want money. A lot of it."

"And if I don't do this?" He said it slowly, as if taking time to think through his options.

"I give the disc to the police. Along with evidence you killed my wife."

He went quiet again. "How much do you want for the safe return of these pictures?" His English had improved dramatically.

My insides continued to burn, but my mind was as clear as it had ever been. "I can't begin to put a price on what your disc has cost me, Mr. Takeshi. My legal fees alone are more than a hundred thousand dollars. And what price do you put on a person, Mr. Takeshi? How much for the mother of my children?" I saw a storm roil in Thomas's eyes. He pulled the edge of his hand across his throat. I turned away. "Probably not worth much in your world, but worth a lot to me. Let's say half a million. Plus expenses. Oh, what the hell, let's round it up to an even million."

"You assume a great deal," he said calmly. "That the disc is mine, first of all. And that it is worth so much money to the person who misplaced it."

"Oh, I know it's yours."

"So you say."

"It shouldn't be difficult to match the fingerprints on the CD case to yours."

He thought about it. "And if I agree to pay you for the return of these pictures?"

"You get the disc, and you never hear from me again."

"Why should I believe you?"

"I don't want anything to happen to my children."

The room went still while we waited for his answer. "I believe I can meet your terms," he said slowly.

"That's good. That's very good." I took a breath. "Here's what I want you to do." I gave him instructions we'd worked out ahead of time. "I've taken precautions," I told him when he agreed. "I made one copy of the disc."

"No copies."

I ignored him. "I put it in a safe deposit box. If something happens to me, the disc goes to the police. If I live to be a ripe old age, the disc will be destroyed."

"No. That's no good. Accidents happen, you know."

"I guess you better hope that doesn't happen."

"Omae o korosu," he muttered.

I looked around. Jian's eyes widened. Yomura frowned. I lifted my shoulders in a silent question.

"Bakani sunjya ne!" Jian said suddenly.

"So, you speak Japanese?" Takeshi said.

"No," I replied. "That's my other precaution. I have a friend who knows about you."

"I will know if he has accident, too," Jian said eagerly. *"Urusai, kono bakayaro!"* Takeshi sounded annoyed. *"Tameguchi kitten ja ney o."* Jian's voice was calm, but there was menace in his eyes.

Takeshi fell silent.

"Do we have a deal?" I swallowed, trying to ignore the gnawing in my gut.

The response was grudging. "Yes." I hung up and fought the urge to race to the bathroom, squelching nausea.

Thomas glanced at me with reluctant admiration, as pleased as he was ever likely to look. "You okay?"

I nodded. "Nerves." I turned to Jian. "What did he say to you?"

"He say he will kill you. I say—for you—I'm not so stupid."

"Then what?"

"He call me idiot and tell me to shut up." Jian shrugged. "I tell him to be more respectful."

Yomura grinned. "Actually, he said, 'Don't disrespect me, you fuck.' You were right. His Japanese is pretty good."

TWENTY-FIVE

No BACK-ALLEY MEETINGS late at night for me. No lonely pre-dawn vigils down at the docks. I told Thomas I wanted to make the exchange in as public a place as possible. In Seattle, that would be somewhere like Pike Place Market or Seattle Center, popular places teeming with tourists and locals alike. But Thomas thought they were too open. It would be too easy, he said, for Takeshi to cut and run, even though nearly a dozen agents would take part in the operation.

Instead, they picked Pacific Place, an indoor four-story shopping mall on Sixth Avenue. With only a few entrances, it would be easier to contain, they said. It was plenty public with a lot of foot traffic. I just wanted it to be over. The nightmare had gone on far too long already. I wanted the bastard Takeshi to be in my shoes for a change. I wanted to look forward, not back.

Pink clouds slowly changing to gold heralded a good beginning to the day. Birds kept up a constant chatter, but didn't disturb the peacefulness. I went for a quick walk before breakfast. The tranquility and steady rhythms of my heart thudding in my chest and feet slapping the pavement soothed my fears, replacing them with free-floating thoughts. *Tyler's going to need braces soon. Kelsey needs a ride to a job interview next week. My God, when did she become old enough to work?* By the time I got back to the cabin the sun cleared the tops of the trees and took some of the chill out of the early morning air.

At breakfast, I told the kids the plan. They looked fearful, and Kelsey tried to talk me out of going. I told her that I was scared, too, but that if I didn't do this, I'd be fearful for their safety the rest of my life. They finally said they understood, but their good-byes were tearful.

Someone on "the team" called me on my cell a little before ten to tell me Takeshi was in town. Thomas made sure his people were at the airport to keep Takeshi under surveillance when he arrived. I called Amy from the road to let her know it was almost over. She admonished me to be careful. I assured her that Thomas said he'd do everything he could to protect me.

"We should celebrate," she said. "I'll drive up to the cabin. We can have a party."

"Are you sure?" I thought it was premature, but I didn't want to dampen her enthusiasm.

"Of course. It's time I met your kids. I'll bring Grace. It'll be fun."

Thomas, Yomura and several other men, including Mankiewicz, waited for me in a room at the Sheraton. Thomas saw me scowl at him and shrugged, as if to say it wasn't his idea. They had me strip down to my briefs. Two of the men hovered around me, carefully wiring me for sound. One of them used a disposable plastic razor to shave patches of hair on my sternum and just below my navel. Then he secured a tiny microphone to my chest with a wide strip of duct tape, and stuck the trailing wire to my stomach with another piece of tape. The other man squatted behind me and attached a transmitter to the small of my back the same way.

When I finished putting my clothes back on they

looked me up and down, inspecting their handiwork. A light windbreaker covered the slight bulge at waist level in back. They told me to walk around the room and talk to myself to test the transmitter and sound level. Then instructed me to walk down the hall to the elevator and talk the whole time. Halfway there, a door opened and a man emerged. I lowered my voice and relayed that bit of information in a mutter. The man turned and walked to the elevator. He glanced at me dispassionately as I approached.

"Morning," I said brightly. He grunted and looked away. "Beautiful weather we're having," I said, reaching the doors just as a *ding* signaled the arrival of a car. The man flashed me a look meant to discourage conversation and faced the door as it opened. "Have a nice day." I waved and turned, hurrying back up the hall.

A collection of barely suppressed grins greeted me inside the room. "Works fine," one of the techies said. He started packing up the equipment.

Thomas came up to me. "You're good to go."

"So what happens now?"

He jerked his head toward the technicians. "We give these guys time to get set up. Once everyone's in place, you go over." He looked at his watch. "Plenty of time. You're not supposed to meet for half an hour. So, say twenty minutes." He peered at me. "You still with us?"

"I'll be fine." I rolled my head on my shoulders, easing the tension in my neck.

"Any questions?"

"What if he doesn't bring the money?"

"Tell him the deal's off. Walk away." He saw the look on my face. "Don't worry. He wants that disc. He'll bring the money."

"You really think he'll bring a million in cash?"
He shrugged. "Why not?"

PACIFIC PLACE WAS A block up the street from the hotel,
across the street from Nordstrom's flagship store, in the
place where the Frederick & Nelson department store
used to be. Filled with high-end shops, the mall was
a paean to conspicuous consumption, proof that our
economy was built solely on the premise that all of us
should shop until we drop. All I saw, even in Tiffany's,
were yard sales waiting to happen. After all, how much
of all those things could any of us really expect to use?
And after a lifetime of accumulating all of it, it was
still just stuff.

Inside, the center atrium rose more than four stories
to a glass-paned roof that let in the sunlight. I willed
my feet forward, beating back panic that urged every
muscle in my body to flee. I felt foolish. It was broad
daylight. Lunchtime on a busy weekend. The mall was
filled with well-to-do matrons with nothing better to do
with their money than shop, kids from the suburbs, out-
of-towners with time to kill between their flights into
Seattle and their cruise ships up to Alaska. What could
happen?

Sets of escalators rose level by level on opposite
sides of the atrium. I rode up the nearest one, scanning
the large space. I imagined Thomas had posted agents
throughout the mall, but I didn't see any. The escalators
carried me slowly up to the fourth level. Shops filled
the first three. The top level housed several restaurants
and a multi-screen movie theater. Thomas suggested it
because plenty of people usually went in and out of the
restaurants. The only place to go from the top level was

down. He thought Takeshi would be easier to contain if he bolted for some reason.

I stepped off the moving stairs and strolled casually around the perimeter of the atrium as if deciding where to eat. The techies who put the wire on me stood in a tangle of video gear in front of the movie theater. To anyone else, they looked like a video production crew shooting an ad or some sort of film. There was no sign of Takeshi. I'd convinced Jian to stay at the cabin with the kids until this was over. But now I missed his company, his cheerful optimism.

A row of tables lined the railing overlooking the atrium in an alcove outside one of the restaurants. I took a seat at the end closest to the escalators. Across the open space, the video crew shuffled lights and equipment around, appearing to pay no attention to me. I spotted Mankiewicz seated at a table in front of a Mexican restaurant not far away, his sharp nose stuck in a menu. The mall swirled with color and constant motion. I kept an eye on the escalator near me and the one across the atrium. Each time I shifted focus, I scanned the crowds around the perimeter of the level nervously, afraid I might miss Takeshi.

I almost did. After one pass, I turned back to the escalator on my left. Takeshi had already gotten off and was walking purposefully past me. Built like a fireplug, he was shorter than I remembered, his stride short and choppy. The straight-sided black silk suit he wore made him look like a square-cut block of obsidian. A crew cut gave his head the same shape, his hard, flat features the result of someone chipping away chunks of black, revealing a lighter-shaded inner core. A black leather briefcase hung at his side, his fingers wrapped tightly around its handle.

"Takeshi," I said, rising out of the chair.

He stopped and turned, his expression unchanged. I stepped around the end of the table, gesturing toward my now-empty seat. He hesitated, then walked over and seated himself on the edge of the chair, his back ramrod straight. I eased into the chair across from him, my back to the atrium so he faced the camera. My hand started to shake. I pulled it off the table and let it drop into my lap, hoping he hadn't seen.

"You have the money?" I said, keeping my voice low.

His face twitched with annoyance. Wordlessly, he lifted the briefcase onto the table, released the catches and spun it so it faced me. I opened it just far enough to see inside. Never again would I be likely to see that much cash in one place.

"So, you have something for me?" he said.

I began to reach into my pocket, then paused and leaned over the table. "Why did you do it?" There was no flicker of recognition in those black eyes. "Why did you kill her?"

He glanced left and right. "You are mistaken," he said softly. "I am a Japanese businessman. I killed no one."

I held up the disc and waggled it. "Pretty strange business."

He sighed, letting me know he was making an effort to be patient. "Perhaps to your way of thinking. You will give it to me now, please." Maybe I'd been wrong. Reluctantly, I handed it to him.

He slipped it inside his suit coat. "So, this concludes our business." He got to his feet, stepped away from the chair and stood with his hands clasped in front of him, waiting politely.

I stood hesitantly. The video crew had taped the

transaction, if it was doing its job. He wasn't going to volunteer a confession, so I'd have to be satisfied the disc was enough to free me and put him away. I grasped the handle of the briefcase and lifted it. It had more heft than I expected. I came around the end of the table and skirted past Takeshi, heading for the escalator. I'd gone only a few steps when he caught up to me and spoke again in a low voice, stopping me.

"You will not contact me again." His eyes met mine. "It would not be wise." I backed away apprehensively. He stood motionless. I shrugged and turned toward the escalator. With astonishing speed, he dropped into a crouch, shifted his weight and swept his leg in an arc. His foot hooked one of my ankles and pulled me off balance. It happened in a blur. One minute my feet were firmly attached to the solid stone floor. The next instant, they were out from under me and I went windmilling soundlessly over the railing.

It always seems so much more dramatic in the movies. I had no time to scream, no time to see my life flash in front of my eyes, only a fraction of a second in which my primal brain took over. I would have thought the counterbalance of twenty-five pounds of currency would have made it more difficult for me to go over the edge, but instinct made me let go of the briefcase immediately. My arms flailed, hands searching for anything well-anchored to grasp.

My hand slapped the top railing and scrabbled to hang on to the polished wood. My fingers began to lose their grip as soon as the rest of me slammed into the wall below. I dangled for less than a second before slipping off the railing and dropping like a stone. Panic finally set in—I remembered the atrium floor was four stories below.

But I fell only ten or fifteen feet, stunned as I quickly crashed onto the escalator rising from the floor below, knocking down bodies as I landed. The toothy edge of one of the metal stairs dug into the side of my calf. An elbow, hip and shoulder banged hard into the cold unyielding metal.

I heard shouts around me now, some angry, some excited as people reacted, unsure of what happened. I tried to disentangle myself from the Pick-Up-Sticks pile of limbs on the moving escalator. By chance, I looked up and caught a quick glimpse of Takeshi riding down the adjacent escalator, briefcase in hand, face expressionless. When he saw I wasn't dead, his eyes turned hard. The corners of his mouth turned down in disappointment. He remained immobile as he rode out of sight.

"A little help here," I called out with more than a trace of anger and irritation. I worked harder to extricate myself.

A passenger above me scrambled down the moving steps, reached for my hand and pulled me up. Another man managed to right himself and together we helped a woman below us get to her feet before the escalator dumped us out on the next level. We staggered off and stood several feet away as the escalator disgorged a steady procession of people who looked at us curiously.

I apologized to those around me, saying over and over how sorry I was, even though I knew it hadn't been my fault. "Someone pushed me," I repeated. My voice sounded surprised. Indignation overtook my embarrassment.

The video crew rushed up and asked if we were all right. Two agents ran past us and bounded down the other escalator. The two techies crowded around with worried looks, Mankiewicz behind them looking oddly guilty.

I warded them off. "I'm fine." They backpedaled, startled.

"Okay, okay. Take it easy," one of them said.

"Check on the rest of these folks." They saw I meant business. One called for medical help while the other asked those around me where they'd been hurt. Pain pulled my gaze down at my leg. My trousers were torn and bloody, but the gash didn't look deep. More like a bad scrape. I gingerly tested arms and legs. Everything seemed to work, but I'd have some bad bruises later.

A crowd gathered now as the commotion roused more people's curiosity. Thomas bounded off the escalator then slowed when he saw me among the walking wounded. He pushed his way through the throng.

"Takeshi?" I said.

He shook his head slowly. "Took the sky bridge across to Nordstrom before we knew what happened." He looked quizzical. "How the hell did you let him get that close?"

"I didn't. It happened so fast…"

"Don't worry about it. We'll get him. We're already sealing up Nordstrom's and we'll search it floor by floor. Hang in here for a while, okay? Let the paramedics take a look at you." I nodded. Shock numbed me. I sat on the floor while the confusion revolved around me. Paramedics arrived ten minutes later, wheeling gurneys and gear off an elevator. They set to work on a woman who appeared to have a broken arm. A second team arrived. Before long they got around to me. As they cleaned and bandaged my leg, Thomas walked by, looking worried.

"No sign yet?" I said.

He detoured toward me and shook his head. "We'll find him." He paused. "Go get Ross. He'll help get that audio gear off you, and you can go home." Finished with me, the medics moved on. I went looking for the techie named Ross. He led me to a men's room where I stripped off my jacket and shirt and let him peel the wire and transmitter off my skin. He gathered up the gear, mumbled an awkward "Thanks," and left me there. I looked in the mirror and took an inventory of bruises, then slowly shrugged into my shirt and jacket. When I walked out, no one gave me a second glance, not even Mankiewicz.

HALFWAY ACROSS Lake Washington in the SUV, a sudden thought nearly froze me with fear. I called the cell number Thomas had given me.

"What is it?" he answered gruffly.

It took a moment before I could verbalize the horror in my head. "The kids. Takeshi can trace the phone number back to the cabin. He's—"

"He doesn't know it was a set-up," he replied. "He just saw an opportunity to get rid of you, that's all. He'll go back to Vegas. We'll get him there if we don't find him here."

"He's figured it out by now. You don't think he noticed the agents crawling all over that place?" My voice rose.

"I'll send a team up there to keep an eye on all of you," he conceded.

"It's too late." I nearly shouted now. "He's way ahead of us. I'm going to get them myself."

"You can't go back up there alone. I'm on it. We'll handle it. He won't hurt your kids, I promise."

"You can't promise that! You screwed up! Now I have to fix it!"

I DROVE THE NINETY MILES to the cabin in a little more than an hour, thoughts racing on the way as fast as the SUV ate up the miles. I'd been running too long. Away from danger. Away from life. Away from myself. I wasn't running away from this—not from my kids, not from Jian and Mei Lei, and certainly not from the woman I'd fallen in love with.

I went over and over the layout of the cabin in my head. Takeshi wanted us dead. But I felt sure he'd try to get Jian to give up the location of the lockbox containing the second disc. Only there was no lockbox. There hadn't even been a second disc until the techies had burned a copy that morning. I had two choices. I could go in on foot, try to circle around the cabin through the woods and sneak in the back. Or just barrel in the front and go for broke. Logic said a third option of waiting for the team Thomas sent was the smart one. But I didn't have time.

I roared up the narrow dirt road and saw two cars in the grassy clearing in front of the cabin. I recognized Amy's, nosed in off to one side. A large black Mercedes sedan faced me, its rear bumper only a few yards from the front steps. The driver's eyes widened as he saw the SUV headed straight for him. He held up a hand as if warding off a blow. *Air bags,* I thought, bearing down. I pressed the seatbelt release, pulled the door handle and hit the door hard with my shoulder, rolling out and away from the SUV. It crashed in an echoing clang of groaning metal and splintering glass. I tumbled in the dirt, a layer of pine needles barely softening my impact.

Before anyone inside could respond to the noise, I hauled myself to my feet and sprinted around the side of the cabin. I caught a glimpse of the driver in the Mercedes as I ran, head tipped back, blood dripping from his nose. The car's air bag had smacked his hand into his face.

At the rear of the cabin I forced myself to slow down and think. With any luck, they'd think whoever was driving the SUV was still inside. I glanced around quickly in search of a weapon. The small yard offered little to choose from—a charcoal grill under a tarp, two heavy metal wedges leaning against the step by the back door, a woodpile. I gripped a small log the length of my arm and hefted it like a club, then silently glided to the door. Cautiously, I peered through the pane of glass. It gave me a partial view of the living room beyond the kitchen.

A big man stood next to the front door leaning to one side for a look out the picture window. Takeshi stood near the couch, his back to me. The sight of his squared-off profile fueled the rage inside me, squeezing my fear aside. I counted four heads poking above the back of the couch, all female. I couldn't see Ty. Jian faced the big man, to his right. He turned to look at Takeshi, and his face flickered with sudden surprise and recognition. He looked away quickly, but I knew he'd seen me. If I didn't move quickly I'd lose the advantage of surprise. I tried the knob—unlocked. *Now or never.*

I went through the door fast, on the run. Jian surprised me yet again by taking a quick step and launching his body into a jumping front kick that snapped the big bodyguard's head back. Someone screamed. I focused on Takeshi. He hesitated, drawn by Jian's sudden movement, but turned at the sound of my approach. His hand swung up and I saw the gun. I wasn't fast enough. I heaved the makeshift club at him. He jerked sideways, but it hit him in the shoulder. He grunted, losing his grip, and the gun skittered across the wooden floor.

I should have gone for Takeshi. Instead, I dove for the gun.

As I went by, Takeshi whirled and chopped me hard between the shoulder blades with the edge of his hand, knocking me to the floor. My breath left me with a whoosh. Stunned, I slowly scrambled to my feet.

"*Tomare!* Stop!" Takeshi's guttural voice froze me where I stood.

Jian tensed over the unconscious bodyguard, unmoving. Amy and the girls cowered on the couch. Grace, Amy's little one, sat on her lap, face pressed into Amy's sweater. Takeshi had his back to the door, the recovered gun in one hand, his other arm around Ty's neck. Ty's eyes filled with fear, and in that moment, I thought my heart would break. I'd failed them all.

Takeshi eyed me, a cruel smile on his lips. "You will tell me where you keep the copy of the disc. Or you can choose who is the first to die." He waved the gun at Amy and the girls as if panning a camera. I glanced at them and immediately tried to shut the sight of their terrified faces out of my mind. I looked at Ty again and saw his eyes flick wildly at the gun Takeshi held, then focus on the arm around his neck. And suddenly I realized his fear wasn't for himself. He felt afraid for the rest of us. He glanced up at me, and I knew what he had in mind.

"How about her?" Takeshi said, his eyes on the couch.

Go! Go! I silently screamed at Ty. In that instant, he stomped down hard on Takeshi's instep and bit his forearm as hard as he could. Takeshi threw his head back and howled. I hurled myself at him. Ty snapped his head back, smashing the back of his skull into Takeshi's throat and Takeshi dropped him just as I leapt. Takeshi whirled toward me and fired. I hit him chest-high with the full force of my charge, smashing him into the door as the explosion rang in my ears. His head cracked into the door and he went down. I collapsed on top of him, feeling no pain, whirling pinpoints of light fading to black, the faint sound of sirens wailing in my head.

TWENTY-SIX

ON THE DRIVE across the floating bridge, I could see mountains stretching from Mt. Rainier to Mt. Baker. Boaters dotted the lake. The island spread out in front of me, vibrantly green. A song came on the radio, its bitter-sweet tune and poignant lyrics cutting through the jumble coursing through my head after one last debriefing session with Special Agent Thomas. For a moment, it also distracted me from the nagging pain where Takeshi's bullet had grazed my hard skull. In the space of a few short verses, the singer told the story of a lifetime of love and commitment. A picture of Amy's face popped into my mind.

Maybe it was relief, the letdown days later as the adrenaline faded from my system. Post-traumatic shock. Maybe it was because I'd never shed a tear for Mary. Or it could have been the fact that I knew now how good life could be when you loved and were loved in return. I was lucky to be alive. To have my kids. And to have found Amy. Whatever it was, the music triggered emotions that swelled my heart, filling me to bursting. My eyes started to tear, blurring the road in front of me. I pulled off the freeway onto the island's first exit ramp, rolled to a stop on the shoulder, and wept for a long time.

PHIL PRESTON CALLED ME at home a week later. "I imagine you'd like to know your status," he said.

"I figured no news was good news," I replied.

"You're a free man," he said. "The prosecutor's office has dropped all charges." For a moment I couldn't breathe. "I don't hear you celebrating."

"Sorry," I said. "That's great news. I was waiting for a 'but.'"

"No buts. It's over."

"I was sure they'd take it to trial no matter what."

"Special Agent Thomas was very convincing. Not only was your transaction with Takeshi recorded on tape, but his attempt to kill you as well."

"Glad to have been of help."

He ignored the sarcasm. "The FBI also uncovered another piece of evidence that assured your freedom."

I frowned. "What evidence?"

"They found a pair of leather gloves in Takeshi's possession."

"Matching what was found under Mary's fingernails?"

"Yes." He paused.

"Is there a problem?"

"No, no," he said hastily. "It's a perfect match." I waited for him to tell me the rest. "Jack, the gloves were made with human skin. Leather tanned from a human hide. The dye was actually a tattoo. Thomas surmises the gloves are a trophy from a traitor in the Yakuza organization that Takeshi had killed. Some of the members are reputed to have tattoos covering their entire bodies except their faces." I shivered at the thought, my stomach growing queasy.

"You were fortunate, Jack," he said quietly.

"What? That he only managed to kill Mary and not the rest of us?"

"No, that you prevented him from doing a lot more harm." It was small consolation to my children.

I HEARD THE CAR PULL INTO the drive, so by the time he reached the steps I stood on the porch waiting. He stopped and looked up at me, cupping a hand to his face to block the sun.

"Hey there," he said. I inclined my head in response. "Um, I just stopped by to tell you I hope there are no hard feelings."

"You were just doing your job."

"Yes, I was. But that doesn't mean I don't feel bad about not doing it a little better."

I shrugged. "I might have done the same thing in your shoes. Hard to say."

"Well, I'm glad it worked out for you. Really." Mankiewicz shifted his weight from one foot to the other and back again.

I nodded. There was nothing more to say. He started to turn. "You want to come in?" It came out of me without thinking.

His face brightened, but he shook his head. "Nah, that's okay. I have to get back to work." He took a few steps down the walk, then turned and squinted against the bright light. "Say, I heard some folks are organizing a fundraiser to help out with your legal bills." I nodded. Sue Thorvahl had told me her kids had given her the idea.

"I'd like to help out any way I can. If that's okay."

"I appreciate it, Detective." He walked back to his car with his shoulders a little straighter.

"*WHO SAID 'no man is an island'? Donne?*"

Sarah looked blank.

I waggled my hand, erasing the question. "Doesn't matter. Point is, it's bullshit. We're all islands. We're born alone. We'll die alone. The rest is all about luck. Vagaries of circumstance."

The vacant look turned to one of puzzlement. "What do you mean?"

I searched for the right words before answering. "Without wind to carry dust, without birds to drop seeds, without a current to wash ashore nutrients, without clouds to bring rain, or sun to bring warmth, nothing grows on an island. It's all a matter of how hospitable the conditions are that determines whether anything will propagate, flourish.

"It's the same with people. If we're isolated from all those things that nurture us, that give us mental and emotional sustenance, we wither and die inside. Or we become monsters." She looked at me curiously, but said nothing.

"I mean, how many of us are fortunate enough to find love?" I said. "Real love."

"Maybe more than you think," she murmured.

"Maybe more than I think," I agreed. "But not without a lot of luck." I fell silent, pondering my own good fortune and all the winds and currents and creatures that had carried it to me. Sarah watched me patiently.

"I'm not coming back," I said finally. "This is my last session."

She nodded. "I had a feeling you were ready. Do you know what you're going to do?"

I looked out the window at another gorgeously warm and bright spring day. "Yes," I said. "I'm going to lunch with the most beautiful woman in the world."

* * * * *

REQUEST YOUR FREE BOOKS!

2 FREE NOVELS
PLUS 2 FREE GIFTS!

MYSTERY **W⊕RLDWIDE LIBRARY**®
Your Partner in Crime

YES! Please send me 2 FREE novels from the Worldwide Library® series and my 2 FREE gifts (gifts are worth about $10). After receiving them, if I don't wish to receive any more books, I can return the shipping statement marked "cancel." If I don't cancel, I will receive 4 brand-new novels every month and be billed just $5.24 per book in the U.S. or $6.24 per book in Canada. That's a saving of at least 34% off the cover price. It's quite a bargain! Shipping and handling is just 50¢ per book in the U.S. and 75¢ per book in Canada.* I understand that accepting the 2 free books and gifts places me under no obligation to buy anything. I can always return a shipment and cancel at any time. Even if I never buy another book, the two free books and gifts are mine to keep forever.

414/424 WDN FEJ3

Name	(PLEASE PRINT)	
Address		Apt. #
City	State/Prov.	Zip/Postal Code

Signature (if under 18, a parent or guardian must sign)

Mail to the **Reader Service:**
IN U.S.A.: P.O. Box 1867, Buffalo, NY 14240-1867
IN CANADA: P.O. Box 609, Fort Erie, Ontario L2A 5X3

Not valid for current subscribers to the Worldwide Library series.

Want to try two free books from another line?
Call 1-800-873-8635 or visit www.ReaderService.com.

* Terms and prices subject to change without notice. Prices do not include applicable taxes. Sales tax applicable in N.Y. Canadian residents will be charged applicable taxes. Offer not valid in Quebec. This offer is limited to one order per household. All orders subject to credit approval. Credit or debit balances in a customer's account(s) may be offset by any other outstanding balance owed by or to the customer. Please allow 4 to 6 weeks for delivery. Offer available while quantities last.

Your Privacy—The Reader Service is committed to protecting your privacy. Our Privacy Policy is available online at www.ReaderService.com or upon request from the Reader Service.

We make a portion of our mailing list available to reputable third parties that offer products we believe may interest you. If you prefer that we not exchange your name with third parties, or if you wish to clarify or modify your communication preferences, please visit us at www.ReaderService.com/consumerschoice or write to us at Reader Service Preference Service, P.O. Box 9062, Buffalo, NY 14269. Include your complete name and address.

WWLI1B